MW00439854

REMEDY

A TULIP FARM ROMANCE

ALEX HALL

Published by Madison Place Press

madisonplacepress@gmail.com
Remedy
Copyright © 2021 by Alex Hall
Cover Art by Rebekah Slather Copyright © 2020

This is a work of fiction. Names, characters, places, and incidents are either the product of the author's imagination or are used fictitiously. Any resemblance to actual persons living or dead is entirely coincidental.

All rights reserved. No part of this publication may be reproduced in any material form without the written permission of the publisher.

First Edition

September, 2021

Print ISBN: 978-0-578-96424-9

Ebook ISBN: 978-0-578-96423-2

Warning: This book contains sexually explicit content, which may only be suitable for mature readers. This book also contains mention of homophobia, alcoholism, gun violence, and self-harm.

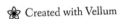 Created with Vellum

CHAPTER ONE

As far as Peter was concerned, the only thing of worth he could ever be was an Olympic show jumper.

He'd been born into it, after all. His mum was a McAuley. County Kildare stock, and for as far back as anyone bothered to keep track, the County Kildare McAuleys had been horse people. Peter's maternal grandfather and granduncle had made their fortunes breeding and racing thoroughbreds in Ireland. Peter's mum, Aine McAuley, was a track rat grown into Ireland's most decorated eventing star. And Peter's dad, though no County Kildare McAuley, had plenty of horse chops of his own. Gabe Griffin had ridden to team gold for Great Britain in Barcelona, the same Olympics Aine had tried—and failed by the slimmest margin—to bring home an individual medal for Ireland.

She always said she'd regretted the miss for exactly forty-five seconds, the time it had taken to dismount after her stadium round, toss her reins at her cousin and stand-in groom, Finley, and glance past her disappointed family at the young man with the salt-and-pepper hair watching from the shadows of the ingate.

That young man was Peter's da. He'd come over from the Olympic stables to get a glimpse of the McAuley winning machine at work and instead found himself captured by a pair of wide violet eyes over a petulant, spoiled mouth. Gabe had already heard more than a few things about Aine McAuley. Her easy way with horses, her exacting eye for breed lines. Her tendency to collect suitors like candy and toss them away again, half-consumed. And her—possibly obsessive—drive for excellence in all things.

"Bad luck," he'd famously dared say with typical British aplomb and specific Gabe Griffin bluntness as those furious violet eyes attempted to flay him from a distance for the sin of witnessing a McAuley nonperformance. "But not entirely your fault. He's off in the right hind, don't you know, just the barest whisper but enough to send him flat over the last three and cost you the time faults." Hands in his pockets, he shrugged when all three McAuleys glared at him in disbelief. "Like I said, just the barest whisper, easy for even the best of us to miss, but I saw it from up in the risers. If I were you, I'd have him looked at immediately."

"What the hell do you know about it?" Aine's father and coach, Shane, had blustered. Gabe was quite clearly wearing the track jacket of a British Olympian and a color-coded tag on a lanyard around his neck that meant he had unrestricted access to the Olympic barns, but that wasn't necessarily a point in his favor. Quite the opposite, in fact. "And why in God's name should we listen to the competition?"

Gabe shrugged again. He hadn't reached so far in life by backing down. "For the horse's sake, I imagine. He's a brave fellow, and bold. No matter the gruff show you put on for the papers, Shane McAuley, we each of us know the animal's welfare comes first, and a bit of healthy competition won't change that."

At last those remarkable violet eyes softened.

"The Olympics are hardly 'a bit of healthy competition,' Mr. Griffin," Aine said softly, her accent rolling pleasantly with the music of Ireland. "But you're not wrong. Oh, stop snarling, Da. I felt it when we landed fence six. A stinger, and after that he couldn't balance up. Poor Ross." She stroked the chestnut gelding's neck. The horse, still blowing hard, sniffed hopefully at her gloved hand in search of a sugar cube. "Let's hope it's not lasting." She tugged a sugar cube from her breeches pocket, smiled a challenge at Gabe. "Right hind, you say? Well. Why don't you come back with me to the warm-up ring and we'll look him over."

They were married less than a year later, and just like any sport horse carefully bred to succeed, Peter's fate—and that of his three older siblings—was sealed.

———

"BEAUTIFUL DAY FOR A RIDE," Kate Griffin told Peter cheerfully, smoothing long dark hair back from her forehead and securing it into a high ponytail with an elastic slipped from her wrist.

It was the same thing his older sister said before every first round, the same thing she'd said when they were children and he'd ridden his pony, Cricket, for the first time at Devon while she stood at the ingate, all pigtails and wide eyes and quiet confidence, and he'd won the class blue. It didn't matter whether they were indoors or out, whether he was showing first thing in the a.m. or after dark in the p.m., whether the sun was shining, or they were in the middle of a blizzard. Horse people were a superstitious sort and the Irish a superstitious people, which meant Kate and Peter Griffin were superstitious twice over and just fine with it.

"Remember," Kate continued as she stepped sideways to avoid being trampled by Annie's eager, dancing trot. "Six and Seven come up quick, balance her back. And Five will take some leg, what with the Liverpool, and we know how she feels about water in the indoor, poor Annie. She's not alone. Other people are having trouble."

"Fluorescents off the water muddle the ground line," Peter agreed mildly. He checked his weight in the stirrups, patted Annie's bay withers as the horse two ahead—a pretty little chestnut with lots of chrome on her face and feet—entered the ring.

"Lacy! On deck. Peter. One away," the gate steward called, smiling in Peter's direction. Thom Wait was one of his father's oldest friends, his chipper grin and handlebar mustache a fixed presence at the back gate during the East Coast Fall Circuit for as long as Peter could remember.

"Kate Griffin!" Thom added, glancing past Peter in surprise. "I haven't seen you in a bear's age. Last I heard you were too busy raising babies to leave Tulip Farm."

"This year's foals are dropped," Kate replied, returning Thom's grin. "And I've just found myself an excellent barn manager. I thought it was time to check on life outside of Connecticut."

She didn't say: *I've not spent more than fifteen minutes away from home since I divorced Mark. This is a massive step*, but Peter thought it for her.

In the arena the chestnut balked at the seventh fence. A brightly colored Swedish oxer at the end of a combination—airy enough to be deceptively large at 1.4 meters—came up fast. The refusal meant a four-point penalty and the chestnut, pretty but not bold, was already well over allotted time.

It would be a much happier horse on the hunter circuit, Peter thought, soothing Annie again as Lacy Kline and her gray gelding prepared to enter the arena. Lacy always liked to slap her rides once or twice on the rump before trotting through the gate—to get their head in the game, she explained. To Peter, it was a stupid and unnecessary show of dominance, a punishment when the horse deserved a reward for standing politely at the gate.

The chestnut balked again, this time at the Liverpool, running out to the left and almost unseating its rider. The buzzer sounded disqualification. Lacy and her gelding entered the ring as the other horse trotted out, blowing.

"Bad luck," Peter said to the exiting rider. The rider on board was red in the face, visibly suppressing fury. He started to spit a retort, then recognized Peter and forced a wide smile instead.

People did that now, ever since he was on the qualifying list for Paris. Smiled and clapped him on the back and offered to buy him a drink in celebration, some genuinely happy for his success, others thinking that he'd never have made the team if not for Tulip Farm's reputation.

Gabriel Senior's reputation.

"Thanks, Peter," said the man, whose name, Peter recalled, was Morris. He pitched his voice to carry. "Look out for the combination at Six and Seven. When I walked it, I thought it was set too short. Now I'm sure of it."

"As if. This is Old Salem's Halt Cancer charity event, not pony club," Kate murmured, returning to Peter's side. She slapped his boot companionably. "Mum just texted to say they're watching from the stands." In the arena, Lacy and her gray were making good time. The horse had a long, loose stride that ate up the ground. "Annie, darling, do your best and there's a lovely warm mash waiting for you."

"Ready, Peter?" asked Thom.

Peter nodded without taking his eyes from the arena. He could feel Annie's heart beating between his knees, steady. The hump of excitement he'd felt in her back before warm-up had melted away. Though comparatively young at only ten, she had a good brain and plenty of courage. Even more importantly, she loved her job. An Olympic horse, full of potential.

The gray approached the Six-Seven combination on stride, ears pricked forward, eager. Lacy was still as a stone in the saddle, competent, unafraid. They were five seconds under time, top of the leaderboard. They took Six without trouble. The horse, light in Lacy's hands, landed solidly, one stride, two strides—

The gelding hesitated just the briefest instant ahead of fence Seven. Peeking, not at the fence as was common, but sideways at the stands. The change in stride was so slight that possibly only Lacy and Peter—and probably Mum and Senior up in the stands—noticed. Then they were up and over and galloping toward Eight. A stellar course, in spite of the small hiccup.

Peter and Annie were in next. He ran a hand down Annie's mane as they entered the arena, another ritual, meant to reassure himself as much as his horse. Lacy passed them on the way out. She didn't look pleased.

"Some idiot up in the risers—" she began, but then she was past and Peter didn't hear the rest of what she said.

"And here comes Peter Griffin on Remedy," the announcer said over the loudspeaker as they entered the ring, using Annie's show name, "riding for Tulip Farm LLC."

A spattering of cheers went up. The risers were filled, people come out to see the best of the best in the show jumping world. Someone whistled, though that was very much against the rules. Probably Gabriel, Peter thought, amused. And probably Mum was giving his oldest brother a silent dressing down for the indiscretion. It wouldn't make a difference. Gabriel wasn't afraid to make a little noise or thumb his nose at stuffy tradition.

Peter circled Annie around to the center of the arena before giving her a final pat. The buzzer went off, signaling the beginning of his round. They crossed in front of the timer, signaling the beginning of their round, and immediately everything in the world except for Peter's pulse in his ears and the feel of Annie in his hands and between his thighs disappeared. They were as close to one mind as two creatures could ever be. Nothing else in the great wide world existed.

———

WHEN PETER WAS LITTLE, hardly out of his lead line days, Senior had sat him down at the dinner table and asked him why he wanted to ride horses for Tulip Farm.

It was a test, of sorts. One that Gabriel and Kate had passed, one that Mac had failed. Young Peter looked his father in the eye. Even at not quite six, he knew all the right answers: because it was the family business, because his mum and Senior wanted him to. Even: for the glory of the thing. But Peter had a different answer, one that made much more sense to his young heart.

Peter said, "Because when I'm on a horse, my brain stops making so much noise."

Senior blinked down at him, expression unreadable.

Peter wondered if he'd failed the test after all. Then he wondered if he could tuck into the lovely, warm stew Mum had put on the table before leaving the two of them alone in the dining room to talk. He wasn't worried. He knew that if Senior refused him access to the farm horses, he would still be able to ride his pony, Cricket, and that was all that mattered. At almost six he loved Cricket with all his heart, and at almost six he already knew that Mum would never forbid him anything that made him happy.

It didn't occur to him that if he failed Senior's test, someday he'd have to move away from the farm and make his own way with the "muggles"—as Kate liked to call everyone who knew nothing about horses—and, maybe, work in an office like Mac wanted to do once he was grown.

He didn't fail. After a moment Senior sighed and nodded.

"You're a McAuley," he conceded, before picking up his spoon and tucking into his own bowl of stew with quiet relish.

———

ANNIE'S HOOVES fell silently on the arena's prograde fiber and sand footing, but Peter could feel every step landing as if they were his own. Her ears were pricked toward the first fence, her upper lip twitching in excitement. The flex of her poll against the bit in her mouth ran up the reins to Peter's hands. Flecks of white spittle already dripped from her lips. She was relaxed and ready.

Bright thing, Peter thought, pride bringing a lump to his throat, *how you do love the game.*

They were up and over the first fence without trouble, stride so smooth it felt to Peter as if they were flying. Fence

Two, a rather overdone brush box festooned with bright spring flowers, came and went in a flash of color. Then it was a sharp left turn to Three and Four. Annie tried to grab the bit, wanting to run, but Peter held her steady to the bending line, balancing her up before Three to keep her from going over flat. She held her form and they landed as he'd hoped, still balanced, with a moment to take a breath and let Four roll up like they had all the time in the world.

A right-hand rollback next, and out of the corner of his eye he caught a glimpse of the large digital timer hanging over the stands: 45.2 ticking away on the clock. A respectable time and one that meant they had a chance at catching Lacy and her gray. But it was far too soon to celebrate. The Liverpool was up next, and Annie's ears were swiveling forward and back, at the fence and then at Peter, silently asking: *Are you sure?*

He couldn't blame her. Fence Five was a monster. A single oxer set at one end of the arena, black-and-orange striped poles crouched over a rectangular slice of water like a tiger over a pond. Arena lights reflected in the water, sparkling. Annie didn't think the tiger was a good idea at all. Peter could feel the muscles in her hind end bracing again she asked the question: *Are you sure?*

Peter clucked his tongue against the roof of his mouth, the eternal signal for *yes, go forward,* and tightened his legs just a smidge—*I'm here, I've got you*—and Annie, reassured, focused all of her attention on the jump ahead.

She took it like a champion, front and back feet lifting high to keep from clipping the poles, back round, mouth soft in Peter's hands. Her tail flicked in celebration when they landed clear—not a tiger's meal this day!—and Peter couldn't help a quiet whoop and a smile.

"Good girl," he murmured, knowing that up in the risers

his family was silently celebrating as well. "Good girl, Annie."

She was blowing hard, her nostrils pink, white foam decorating her chest and neck in flecks. But she wasn't tired. Like any high-performance athlete midsprint, she was just hitting her second wind. Her tail flicked side to side, eager, as Peter lined up to Six. Green and white poles over potted ferns, much less threatening than black and orange. Lithe as a dear, Annie rocked back and popped over. Crouched low in the saddle to stay out of her way, Peter gave the mare her head.

One stride, two strides. But just as they locked on to Seven, something changed. Something in the stands up and to the right, a flash of bright angry red light, not the reflection of arena fluorescents, something painful and blinding, in Peter's eyes and in Annie's.

Annie reacted before Peter. Horses were prey animals in a world made up of predators. Their instincts could be softened or redirected but never completely retrained. In the face of danger or pain, first and foremost a horse chose escape.

Annie swerved away from the stands, nearly out from under Peter. His own eyes equally dazzled, Peter couldn't see anything but agonizing red. Only a lifetime of experience kept him in the saddle. When he heard a gasp from the stands, he knew they were in trouble, too close to the jump to avoid it, and off-balance.

Shit, Peter thought, hoping against hope that Annie was not as blind as he, though from the panicked feel of her beneath him he feared she was.

Time slowed to a crawl. Blinking tears from his red-blurred eyes, he thrust his heels down in the stirrups, grabbed rein and mane together, and crouched down, trying to keep his center of gravity along Annie's spine. Someone in the crowd shouted. It sounded, impossibly, like Lacy Kline.

An image of Seven flashed through his head, the airy Swedish, more negative space than wood. Maybe they'd be okay. And thank God he wasn't an eventer like Katie's ex-husband, Mark, riding solid fences built not to fall apart on impact.

Peter felt the crash before he heard it, the impact reverberating through Annie and along his bones. A clatter of wooden poles falling, the louder crack of lumber breaking. Annie stumbled, started to go down, righted herself only to go up again, higher and higher, rearing in pain or terror.

He had a second to think *fuck* as screams rose from the crowd. He braced to launch sideways, out of the saddle, away from his 1,200-pound mount. But too late. They went over backward together and hit the ground as one. Peter suffered a shock of suffocating agony after the impact, and then the world went blessedly dark.

———

HE SURFACED BRIEFLY, muddled and confused. He blinked his eyes open, winced, and quickly shut them again. Everything was still blurry, and much too bright.

"Annie?" he managed. His tongue felt four sizes too big against the roof of his mouth. "Is Annie all right?"

"Peter. She's fine, she's good. Don't move, Peter. Don't move. We've got you. Christ Jesus, Kate, keep him still, don't let him move—" Thom, Peter identified, though the whooshing of blood against his eardrums made everything sound muffled.

"Where's the goddam ambulance?" And that was Kate,

very close, equal parts fear and spitting Irish temper. He wanted to reassure her that he was also fine, that the pain was gone, but the surge of adrenaline that had given him strength to speak was already fading.

Fuck, he thought, as he began to drift toward unconsciousness once more, *what a stupid way to go down. I know better. I should have bailed off in time.*

"They're waving it in now. I *told* the steward there was something fishy up in the stands. Here, hand me Annie, we need to get ice on that cannon bone right away—" Lacy Kline, gruff. Peter was distantly grateful someone had their priorities straight. Horse before rider, every time.

"Here comes Gabriel Sr., with the steward. Pale as milk, look at him. I guess I would be, too, if I'd just watched my dreams of Olympic family gold get flushed down the toilet." And *that* was Morris, sounding much more satisfied than he ought. Peter wanted to tell him to shut up and step off, but that would have to wait, because for the moment it was much simpler to just let go and slip away.

CHAPTER TWO

Reed Androku hated early mornings with the passion of a person forced regularly and by necessity to rise before dawn.

The passion, Reed thought glumly, standing at the kitchen counter in crisp boxers and a baggy SPBU sweat-shirt, palms pressed flat against granite, waiting for the water in the ancient coffee maker to boil, *of a thousand white-hot predawn suns.*

The coffee maker had come with the apartment and was far below Reed's standards—Reed's standards being simply "no appliances older than fifteen years"—but the apartment was otherwise so completely fantastic, the oppor-tunity so unbelievable, that Reed had supposed they could forgive Kate Griffin the bargain-basement Mr. Coffee until there was time to pop into New Haven and pick up some-thing better than just serviceable.

Reed had supposed wrong. Because working for Kate Griffin was turning out to be an every-hour-of-every-day sort of job, which left Reed with barely any time to spend on their own small herd, and zero time to pop into the city for even the most basic of supplies. And the ancient Mr. Coffee, after eight solid weeks of hard use, was sounding like what Reed supposed was the electronic equivalent of a death rattle.

At 6:00 a.m. on a Monday morning. And not just any Monday on Tulip Farm, either.

Today Peter Griffin was coming home.

"Come on, come on, come on," Reed begged the coffee maker in the Russian of their childhood, the language of their father, the one they used to encourage a flagging horse. They tapped their fingers on the granite countertop. "One cup, that's all I ask. One cup. You can do it."

The coffee maker gurgled, hissed, and in a final effort of goodwill dribbled ten ounces of steaming black coffee into Reed's favorite mug, an old Rumph Pottery classic in the shape of a Pegasus.

"Thank you, God." Reed patted the Mr. Coffee in heartfelt gratitude. Lifting the mug to their nose, Reed inhaled coffee-scented steam, waiting for the liquid to cool enough to sip. Outside the kitchen window, Tulip Farm was still mostly dark, the pastures and outbuildings sleeping. Safety lights illuminated the gravel walkways between Barns A, B, and C, as well as the curtain of rain falling steadily from the sky.

Spring was taking its own sweet time in coming. Though most of the bulbs and annuals planted around the farm were beginning to send up brave shoots, and the old magnolia tree in front of Barn A had begun to unfurl red-green leaves, the sky hadn't cleared for two weeks at least, and the pastures were more bog than field.

Reed took a cautious sip of coffee, groaning out loud and curling bare toes in pleasure as the caffeine hit their system. Yes, that would do for now. And maybe later they could convince one of the grooms to let them drive the farm pickup truck into New Haven on an appliance run, maybe bring everyone back lunch from Café Atticus, Reed's treat.

Christ knew they'd all need a boost by midday, once Senior finished making the rounds. The man was a strict taskmaster on a normal day. Three weeks off the farm, three weeks away from the business, there was no doubt in Reed's mind that Senior would come blazing through barn check ready to take names and kick some ass.

Gabriel Sr. was a perfectionist, and Tulip Farm flourished under his tutelage. Reed couldn't take issue with the way he put everything he had into the job. Senior's reliance on intimidation to keep his staff in line, on the other hand—

Well. Reed was just glad that Barn A was strictly Kate's province. Because Reed didn't tolerate bullies, and it was hard enough to keep their mouth shut when Senior started going at the rest of the staff within earshot.

You need this job. Tulip Farm is a dream come true. Don't muck it up over one sour apple. His son's just out of hospital, for Christ's sake. The whole family is under a tremendous amount of stress.

Out the kitchen window, past the dark pastures and sleeping barns, lights burned in the first-floor windows of the main house: the McAuley-Griffin clan already up and about, like Reed, preparing for a Monday that wasn't an average Monday, a morning that promised to be bittersweet.

Because today Peter was coming home.

The family's golden boy, the ex-Olympic hopeful, ranked fifth in the world of FEI show jumping. Come home in the back of an ambulance because none of the farm vehicles were wheelchair accessible, and the van the family had rented for the next few months hadn't yet arrived.

And Reed's teenage crush, of course. *Secret* teenage

crush. Because Reed was not a teenager anymore, and whatever they'd once felt watching Peter Griffin compete—lust, pure, mouth-watering lust—had long ago mellowed into something softer. Respect, admiration, professional curiosity.

"Just keep telling yourself that, Androku, until it sounds like you mean it."

They swallowed down the last dregs of still-hot coffee, rinsed the mug in the kitchen sink, and padded into the bedroom in search of rainproof clothes.

———

DRESSED WARMLY in an anorak and Wellies over jeans and a soft thermal, Reed bypassed the freight elevator—excruciatingly slow even on a good day—and thumped down the four flights of stairs from Barn A's upper apartment to the stable level. The perfume of farm life, always a muted presence upstairs, hit Reed like a solid wave. The earthy stink of horse manure, the sweeter smell of hay and bedding, leather and saddle soap, and the warm, wild musk of the animals themselves. Reed loved the smell of a barn the way some people enjoyed the scent of Chanel daubed on a delicate wrist or behind one ear. It was seductive, sexy, full of promise.

"Morning, boss!" John Dotty, Reed's assistant and groom in charge of morning feedings, was already tossing hay and checking water buckets. "Word from the main house is no turnout today. It's a pisser!"

Reed cracked a smile. "Isn't it just? Much more of this and I'll have to break out my pool floaties."

Rain pelted the barn on all sides as if in agreement, rattling plank siding. The horses, snug in their stalls, nosed contentedly at the hay John tossed their way. Most nickered a greeting when they heard Reed's voice. They appreciated John for the hay, but Reed was in charge of doling out morning grain, and that was the real treat. Down the aisle, Pritchard and Bob pawed their stall doors impatiently while Annie, taller at seventeen hands than any other horse in Barn A, stuck her dark, wedge-shaped head over the stall divider and whinnied.

John, ignoring the ruckus, threw Reed a wink. "Don't worry. Just as soon as you think we're all going to drown for sure, the sun will come out and bake everything dry. Midsummer you'll be praying for a piece of rain."

He'd know. John was a local who, like Reed, had grown up with horses and knew his way around a farm. Unlike Reed, he had dreams of a future in the big city and was working for Senior only until he'd saved enough money to pay his own way toward an accounting degree at the University of New Haven. A wiry kid in his early twenties, John wore Carhartt overalls over vintage band T-shirts no matter the weather, and never missed a shift.

He'd accepted Reed from day one, never giving Reed's dye-tipped hair, thick eyeliner or preference for flowery scarves and bright nail polish a second glance, or pretending not to understand Reed's heavy accent. Small things, but rare enough that Reed would be forever grateful and counted John a good friend though they'd worked together only a handful of weeks.

Now they moved through the barn in quiet companionship, John filling water buckets with a long hose while Reed pulled the feed cart down the aisle, measuring and dumping grain into individual buckets, adding supplements scooped from plastic containers and metal tins. Sport horses, even semiretired sport horses, were athletes and like their human counterparts needed a wide variety of nutritional support to keep their bodies operating at maximum efficiency. Reed dosed their small herd daily with organic supplements hand selected for each animal's individual need. And ever since Peter's Annie had been shuffled off to Barn A to recover from The Accident, Reed had switched the mare off her old big-box feed store regiment and onto organics.

"She's feisty this morning," John told Reed as they passed in front of the mare's stall, long hose and four-wheeled cart meeting but not tangling. "She's realized something's up. Horses are like that. Betcha she knows *he's* coming home today."

Reed studied the mare through the bars as she tucked eagerly into her grain, ears pinned, black tail swishing. Feisty was not unusual for a horse who'd been confined to stall rest for the past month, but Annie was taking it harder than most. Though Reed had managed to keep her coat shiny and her weight on, she was still losing muscle without regular work, and her friendly nature had taken on a grumpy edge.

She was bored, Reed knew, and lonely despite the genial presence of the other six horses. She'd been born to work, but she'd been put up on the shelf and forgotten while she healed.

"I emailed Senior last week." Reed grimaced. "About starting her back to work. No response yet."

John grunted unhappily. "Got other things on his mind, I guess. Could be he blames her some for the accident, which isn't fair. But Senior can be that way." Together, they watched Annie lip her grain bin and flick her tail. "Would be a waste not to bring her back, for her own sake. Mare like that needs something to do." He flicked a glance in Reed's direction. "Seems to me that would be right up your alley, wouldn't it?"

"Hmm." Reed had been thinking the same thing. Lying awake at night, in fact, imagining how they'd start her again, with chiropractic manipulation before slowly increasing exercise, massage and ice after. Suspensory injuries could be tricky, but luckily Annie's was only a bad pull and not a tear. With the proper care, she would recover. Which was why Reed had emailed Senior in the first place. Because it seemed criminal to let any horse, but especially a horse as talented as Annie, languish and fade.

"Seems to me," continued John, with the certainty of youth, "that maybe there was a reason Kate had that mare moved to this barn, your barn, your *rehab* barn. Doncha think?"

"Hmm," said Reed again, though they both knew John was right. Reed was learning it was just like Kate to dangle a challenge in front of a person's nose until they bit, and Annie was exactly the sort of case Reed liked to sink their teeth into.

Speaking of juicy treats, one by one along the barn aisle Reed's own special projects, having inhaled their grain, were peering through the stall bars, anticipating a morning tidbit. Fishing in the pocket of their anorak for the ever-present Ziploc of freshly sliced apple, Reed doled the wedges out one at a time, opening stall doors a crack to pat noses or stroke ears. They were all visibly pleased to see Reed. Pritchard, a bay gelding with ears like a mule's and a temper to match, tried—and failed—as usual to take off a few of Reed's fingers with his slice. Bob, a gentleman chestnut who had raced long enough to earn his previous owner a nice chunk of change and had the stress fractures to prove it, lipped his treat gingerly off Reed's palm. Angel kicked up bedding with her one hoof, more interested in ear scratches than apple. The big-boned black mare had spent more than a year alone and neglected in a backyard pasture before Reed had found her. She was a glutton for attention.

Ingrid and Charlie, the newest additions to Reed's little family, had both come off a farm near Saratoga and shared the same sire. They looked enough alike they might have been a matched set, with red bay coats and wide white blazes from forehead to nose. Ingrid had four white socks. Charlie had only three. Neither had seen the racetrack. Charlie panicked in tight spaces, which meant the large foaling stalls in Barn A suited him better than the usual ten by ten. Ingrid simply didn't have speed in her—if given the choice, she'd rather walk than run. She'd make someone a lovely show pony or trail horse once Reed had taught her not to bolt every time she saw a whip.

"Good morning, beautiful." Reed stroked her face while she ignored the apple they proffered and instead nosed at their pockets. Laughing, Reed relented, allowing her one of the sugar cubes they kept on hand for the babies.

"You spoil her," John teased, rolling up the hose. "My dad always says treats breed bad habits."

"She deserves a little spoiling," said Reed fondly. "They all do."

Although they suspected John's dad might be the primary reason the kid wanted to ditch the country for the city, Reed knew better than to outwardly criticize what he'd learned of Mr. Dotty's approach to horse care. Sometimes it was better to teach by example.

Giving Ingrid one last pat, Reed secured her stall door and zipped the front of the anorak firmly all the way up to their chin. If the continuing pelt of rain against Barn A was any indication at all, the shallow roof covering the breezeway between the building and the back wing where Reed's other charges lived would provide slim protection.

John said, "Good luck out there! See you at barn check."

"Even if I have to swim," Reed agreed. Taking a deep breath, they ducked through the heavy barn door and into the storm.

Rain and wind lashed Reed's shoulders as they ran across the breezeway, spattering their eyes and cheeks even under the hood. Water pooled on the gravel walkway. It splashed in angry gouts under Reed's Wellies, the water ink black in the predawn. The safety lights alongside the path flickered in and out as the wind gusts increased dramatically, and the clatter of rain against the breezeway roof sounded suspiciously like hail. Reed's breath hit the frigid air in puffs of smoke.

Christ Jesus. Reed shivered even beneath two warm layers. *Spring in Connecticut shouldn't be this cold. Goddamn climate change.*

The breezeway was only fifteen feet long, but it felt like twice that. Reed hit the door to the foaling barn at a run, punched the code into the security lock, and blew into the building on a blast of wet air. They groped for the light switch nearest the door before realizing—half a second late —that the overheads were already on.

That was wrong, because Barn B was Reed's responsibility. For the sake of precaution, Reed was the only member on staff who knew the unlock code to the building. Even John didn't have unsupervised access. Tulip Farm made most of its money in sales and stud service. The eight babies under Reed's care were quite literally worth their weight in gold. It was no small thing that Kate Griffin trusted Reed—who up until two months ago had been a perfect stranger—with their wellbeing.

A person stood partway down the aisle, half-turned Reed's way as if in surprise. Reed reached automatically for the hay knife they always kept sheathed on their belt. Bone-handled and a good five inches long, the knife was a necessary tool when it came to daily barn chores. It was also, Reed had cause to know, a nice security bonus when in the hand of someone trained, as Reed was, in self-defense.

"Whoa," the person in the aisle said, raising both hands in surrender as they turned the rest of the way toward Reed. "Hold up. There's no call for bladed weapons, Harry Potter, especially as I left mine at home."

"Wands." Reed relaxed a fraction but kept the knife in hand, a reassuring weight against their palm.

The person's brows went up. Now that Reed's eyes were adjusting to the change in light and they could see the intruder clearly, the panic eased. If the very faint lilt of Ireland—a generation removed—wasn't a giveaway, their features were: Aine McAuley's distinctive violet eyes and ink-black hair, worn long enough to brush the collar of the Burberry trench coat protecting a fancy suit. Neither the coat nor the expensive-looking suit did anything to hide the sturdy, long-legged Griffin build beneath. One of the McAuley-Griffin siblings. The brother who'd moved to the city, if Reed had to guess.

But that didn't necessarily mean he belonged in B Barn, alone and unannounced.

"Sorry?" the man said. Reed noted the way he kept his hands loose at his sides, visible so as not to provoke, deceptively inoffensive. In Reed's experience a man who knew enough to sham harmlessness in the face of a knife blade generally also knew how to hold his own in a fight.

"Harry Potter," Reed explained while at the same time taking a quick glance around their surroundings, "used a wand, not a knife." As far as they could tell, nothing had been disturbed. In fact, from the trail of wet leading from the door halfway along the aisle to where the fellow stood, pooling in drips and drops beneath the hem of that fancy coat, Reed guessed they'd entered the wing within minutes of each other.

"Whatever. Mind putting yours away?"

"Not quite yet." Reed showed their teeth in a dry smile. "I can see you're family, and because no horseman would be stupid enough to wear those city shoes out into the barn even if it wasn't raining buckets, that makes you the lawyer."

"McAuley Griffin," he agreed, violet eyes flicking from Reed's face to the knife in Reed's hand and back again. "Mac, if you like. And you must be the Russian. Katie mentioned you. Androku, right?"

"Thing is," continued Reed, still smiling, "Kate *didn't* mention you were coming into town, or that I'd find you standing in my barn at five a.m. on this ugly May morning."

"She doesn't know I'm here. Yet," Mac confessed. "I drove down last night because I wanted to be here to welcome my brother home. Only, I couldn't sleep a wink from the nerves. It's been a long time since I was on the farm. It makes me restless, coming back. So, I got up too early, as one does before a big day, which meant I'm here long before I'm needed." He shrugged. "I always used to come to Barn B, when I was a kid, when I was feeling low. To see the babies." His mouth turned up at the corners, a much more pleasant smile than the one Reed wore. "It just lowers my blood pressure, you know? The cuteness overload."

Reed got that. But still, there was the matter of security.

"Kate changes the door code every month. If she doesn't know you're here, how'd you get in?"

"Sure she does. But what you might not realize, as you've only been on the farm for a short time—and I must say you're exceeding expectations already, because you're still holding that knife, and it looks to me like you're just a little too willing to cut me if necessary. Senior would be so pleased—is that my sister has been using the same door code every May for the last ten years. Also, in consistent rotation: June, July, August, September . . . Well, you get the picture."

Reed sheathed the knife. "I did know that," they said. "And if you do, too, then you're probably who you say you are, and I won't have to cut you." Pushing back their hood, scattering more water, Reed flashed a genuine grin. "Wasted opportunity."

The man in the fancy suit and expensive coat relaxed for real this time, subtle lines of tension easing from his shoulders and face. He shoved his hands into the pockets of his trench. "Sorry. For startling you. And the early hour, and the ugly weather. It followed me all the way up from New York."

It was Reed's turn to shrug. For safety's sake they'd learned early on how to read people, and Mac Griffin didn't seem a bad sort. Sure, he dressed like a man with too much money and too little good sense, but he seemed genuinely pleased to make Reed's acquaintance, and although Reed hadn't missed the start of surprise Mac had tried and failed to hide when he'd glimpsed Reed's face beneath the hood, he'd passed quickly from bewilderment to comprehension and then blasé acceptance.

"*Katie,*" Reed imagined the younger brother would say to his sister over the breakfast table, "*you mentioned the new barn manager was Russian but forgot to mention he was so . . . progressive.*"

And Kate, always conscientious, would reply, *"They, Mac. Reed's nonbinary and prefers they/them pronouns."* And everyone at the breakfast table would nod, probably baffled and maybe disapproving, but willing for the sake of farm PR to play the part of enthusiastic allies.

But possibly that was unfair, because Mac offered a hand and when Reed took it, he shook in what seemed like honest welcome.

"I'll stay out of your way. I know how it is. Civilians just get under feet during feed time."

Reed unlocked the grain room. "Thought you grew up on the farm?"

"I did," Mac agreed, head tilted as he watched Reed measure out grain. "Moved away after high school."

"Then you know how to feed," Reed guessed, and from the flicker of resignation on Mac's face, they'd guessed correctly. "So, make yourself useful." They indicated the feed trolley. "You've already made me late, and barn check's at six."

Mac whistled softly. "Old man's still a tyrant, I see." But he gripped the trolley handle, tugging it out of the grain closet, Burberry coat flapping damply around his ankles. Reed had a completely unprofessional urge to laugh at the sight.

"Senior's dedicated to the farm," Reed replied, hoping they sounded less doubtful than they felt. "I'm told everything else comes second."

"Exactly." A muscle in Mac's jaw clenched. "And how well do you think that worked out for my baby brother?"

CHAPTER THREE

The ride home from Saint Luke's was Peter's idea of a nightmare. Kate, sitting in the back of the hired ambulance alongside the gurney, chattered aimlessly about their mother's recent and unexpected switch to organic cooking, the room they'd converted for him on the first floor behind the kitchen—*until he could do stairs again*—and, of all things, the weather. She squeezed his hand in hers while she babbled, which he supposed was meant to be comforting, but she also couldn't quite meet his eyes. That was almost understandable, considering he was strapped faceup like goddamn Frankenstein on what was basically a wheeled table, left leg made immobile by a cast from toes to thigh, ribs wrapped for transportation. Still, her distress felt like his shame, and although he tried his best, Peter couldn't help resenting the tears Kate tried to blink away before they fell.

You're not allowed to cry, he wanted to tell her, and had to bite his tongue to keep from speaking. *You're not the one with a future smashed to bits. You're not allowed to cry.*

But that wasn't fair, and he knew it. Kate had experienced her own share of trauma in the last year. The fact that she was there in the ambulance, trying to cheer him up and hide her tears, would have been remarkable if he'd found it in himself to care.

Senior sat up front with the driver, barking directions as the ambulance fumbled its way through back roads turned to bogs after the morning's storm. The driver, a middle-aged woman with tired eyes and endless patience, was doing a good job pretending she didn't want to pull over and kick Senior to the curb. Peter would have cheered her on if she'd tried.

"Almost there," Kate reported, pressing Peter's hand for the hundredth time. He knew he should be grateful he could feel the pressure at all, grateful he wasn't paralyzed from the neck down as everyone had at first feared, but mostly he wished she'd stop treating him like one bad fall had somehow turned him from two-time World Cup winner and Olympic hopeful to sloppy infant.

But when it came down to it, was she so wrong? He was wearing a diaper for the ride home, after all.

Three weeks in the hospital had passed slow as molasses. Peter had spent the entire time longing for home. The comfort of his own bed, a shower with consistent hot water, actual eggs and bacon for breakfast instead of processed mush, the smell of manure and horse sweat. He'd struggled through two surgeries with one goal in mind: Tulip Farm. He'd shed his own tears at night, into the threadbare hospital pillow, hoping the nurses were too busy to notice. And he'd spent even more nights awake, staring dry-eyed at nothing, wondering if he'd ever ride again.

"In a case like yours—even with multiple fractures of the femoral shaft and ankle—resumption of normal function is not entirely out of the question," the surgeon had told

Peter as his stint at the hospital rehab came to a close. "When there is damage to the soft tissue as well as the bone, recovery can be more limited. That's why we'll be recommending physical therapy, to help strengthen traumatized muscle. You'll want to start that as soon as possible, Mr. Griffin. Again, in cases like yours, the secret to success is actuation. And positivity, of course."

This particular surgeon had flown over from the Mayo Clinic on Senior's dime just to assess Peter's condition. She held his chart in one hand, a steaming cup of tea in her other. Although he knew she'd just spent almost an hour with his local doctors, he also knew from the way she hovered at the foot of the bed instead of sitting on the rolling stool near his head that she had nothing new to contribute.

She wore an encouraging smile like it was part of her daily uniform, an accessory to her black pantsuit and sensible shoes. Peter wondered how she expected him to believe in positivity when her smile didn't even reach her eyes.

"When can I ride again?" He'd been short with her, as he had been with everyone else who dared engage him in conversation, because he had no interest in niceties. He wanted answers, data, conclusions. Hard facts to help shore up the crumbling foundation of his life.

But none of the fancy doctors Senior had flown in dealt in certainties, and the placidly smiling surgeon was no different than the rest.

"Let's focus on walking first."

He let her see his contempt. "Horses are my life. I need to know if that's come to an end."

Disapproval pinched her mouth. "It's much too soon to tell, I'm afraid. I wish you luck on your journey, Mr. Griffin.

You're in good hands. Your father's put together an excellent team."

The rented ambulance bounced as it left a muddy side road, turning onto smooth pavement, signaling their arrival on Tulip Farm and shaking Peter back to the present. He wished he could see out the side windows. He could hear rain falling again, spattering against the windshield, and the squeak of rubber against glass when the driver turned on the wipers.

"Pissy weather," Kate said for what Peter thought must be the tenth time since they'd left the hospital. "Even for this time of year."

His sister had never been good at talking about anything other than horses, and now that she'd apparently decided— or maybe Senior had decided and issued a family decree— that horses were a taboo subject around Peter, she was obviously floundering. Peter knew he should say something flip to break the tension, crack a joke. It had always been his role as youngest child to be the peacemaker, the family clown, the calm waters when one of their father's storms was brewing. He'd never minded, at least not much. It was easy to rise above when everything was going your way, and he had a gift for making people laugh, especially his siblings.

But it seemed Peter had lost the give-a-shits along with the use of his left leg because Kate's discomfort only made the cold feeling that had taken up residence behind his cracked ribs the day he'd woken to find himself immobilized in a hospital bed grow icier. He desperately wanted her to stop talking, he desperately wanted her to let go of his hand, he desperately wanted out of the ambulance.

He desperately wanted to wake up and discover the last several weeks were nothing worse than a pre–Olympic anxiety-induced nightmare.

Up front Senior told the driver, "Main house is there, just past the far barn. Drive swings around under the portico, you'll see the ramp."

The ramp was a new wheelchair accessible addition to the main house, one of several. Although Peter hadn't yet had the honor, he'd seen plenty of photos sent from Gabriel's phone. His eldest brother did all the farm carpentry work, everything from throwing up a barn to repairing fences. He also ran a furniture refurbishing business on the side and tended to the family's two-hundred-year-old home like it was his child.

Gabriel had the emotional sensitivity of a hammer and didn't see why a flurry of "look what I've done so you can roll around the house" photos had only served to piss Peter off. He'd eventually put his eldest brother's texts on mute, something he'd never dared before, and that had resulted in a very unexpected hospital visit—Gabriel would rather face down a rabid bear than dress up for the city—and a muted sibling argument that satisfied neither participant at the end because Gabriel wouldn't raise his voice in a public place and Peter just didn't have the energy to engage.

But there was Gabriel now as the ambulance swayed to a halt and Kate flung the bay doors open, grinning in welcome as if Peter was just home from a turn on the circuit, as if everything was as per usual, as if Peter wasn't about to be wheeled flat on his back up the goddamned *ramp* because he couldn't come home under his own power.

"Bit soft out," Gabriel said in greeting. "Mac brought it all north with him."

"Why is it always my fault?" And there was Mac, not as tall as Gabriel, but still lanky, bending over Peter as Senior and the driver freed the gurney from the back of the ambulance, mouth turned up in a crooked grin. "Nice ride you've got there, golden boy. Bet the suspension sucks."

"Mac!" Kate scolded while Gabriel tried unsuccessfully to hide a wince.

"What?" Mac winked at Peter before backing out of the way of the gurney an instant before Senior barked at them all to *Move! Get out of the way! Mum's waiting on the porch!* and *The damp's not doing my arthritis any good at all!* Mac always knew better than any of them when Senior was in a mood, always had the sense to get out of the way before their da's temper blew.

Outside the van the air was perfumed with rain and roses and horse shit and cedar shavings. The scents of home. Peter breathed it in and out, chasing back encroaching claustrophobia, wishing he could see sky instead of the whitewashed portico ceiling as the gurney rattled across pavement and then up Gabriel's ramp.

Mum was waiting on the porch just as Senior had promised, sensibly attired in a chunky Fair Isle sweater and gray slacks, a general awaiting the return of her small battalion and, Peter had no doubt, ready to get down to business. She touched a hand to his forehead, gazed for a moment at his face. His heart squeezed hard in response when she nodded to herself as if he'd answered some question she hadn't asked.

"Welcome home, son," Aine McAuley said briskly. "You look like you've lost at least a stone. Luckily, I've got a lunch in the oven and cake in the pantry. Don't just stand there, children. Gabriel's made the parlor into a room for you, Peter, and I think you'll be pleased."

———

HE WASN'T PLEASED, obviously, but once he was settled in bed, the hired driver and her gurney dismissed, he found himself pretending for Gabriel's sake, and because his mum was still watching in that way she had, sideways so as not to spook a lad into running but candidly enough that he knew he'd better be on his best behavior. So Peter was thanking Gabriel for the hard work he'd put into turning what had been a stuffy room used mostly to display ribbons and trophies into a bright and cleanly furnished bedroom complete with a new hardwood floor, built-ins for storage, screens for windows that now opened, and a flat-screen television.

More importantly, the adjoining half bath was now wheelchair accessible, with a roll-in shower, bars along the walls, a sink at least a foot lower than Peter remembered, and a door several inches wider. He'd be impressed, if he allowed himself to think about it for longer than ten seconds.

Which he didn't.

"Bathroom floor's ceramic," Gabriel explained, animated even as he hunched his shoulders to better fit his large body into the small room. When it came to things like flooring and load-bearing beams, he was in his element. "Less wear under wheelchair tires, and less slippery once you're up on crutches. We all agreed, an accessible room like this might be handy when Mum and Da grow old, right?" Aine made a noise of amused agreement.

"The team sent welcome-home flowers," she said, indicating a massive arrangement on display by the television. "And Robert sent your favorite Brussels chocolates."

Peter winced. He owed his coach several missed phone calls, but the last thing he wanted to do was talk about his future with the USET. Unfortunately, Robert

Ridland wasn't easily ignored. Peter eyed the foil-wrapped box suspiciously, wondering if his coach had somehow managed to add a scathing note inside with the chocolates.

"Your chair arrives tomorrow morning," Senior told Peter without turning from where he stood looking out the windows.

Surveying his domain. Checking for any hitches in the system. An uncharitable thought, but also, Peter knew, the God's honest truth.

"And the accessible van will be here Friday," Kate added. "There was some holdup with the rental agreement."

"Your father wanted it wrapped with the farm logo," his mum said. She set a fork in Peter's hand and a plate of Irish beef and potatoes on an overbed table—brand new to match the bed, room, and bathroom—then turned the table across Peter's lap.

"Don't know what the problem is," Senior grumbled. "I said I'd pay to have it removed when we were finished with it, didn't I?"

Peter paused in forking up a potato, horrified.

"You wanted to wrap my handicap van in the farm logo?"

"Accessible van," Gabriel corrected. "You should learn the correct terminology, Peter."

"Fuck you very much," Peter snapped. "I've had the correct terminology repeated to me ad nauseum. And I don't want *my* van, my *very temporary rented handicap van,* wrapped up like some advertisement for tragedy!"

"Don't be dramatic." Senior turned from the windows at last, leveled Peter with a stare. "Every farm vehicle is wrapped with the farm logo, you know that. It's branding.

We're not changing now, just because you've gone and had a fall."

Gone and had a fall.

The room went so still and silent Peter could hear his mum's antique clock ticking three rooms away on the kitchen wall. Gabriel blanched, freckles standing out as the color drained from his face. Mac shoved his fists deeper into the pockets of his fancy coat, then whirled and left the room. Kate's eyes flashed indignation. She opened her mouth.

"Mum," Peter said before his sister could say something she'd regret later. "I'd love a slice of that cake you mentioned. Would you mind?" He held Senior's gaze as he spoke.

"Of course," Aine replied briskly. "We could all do with something sweet. Gabriel, Katie, come and help me."

Because she was a McAuley and brooked no disobedience, Kate and Gabriel followed her into the hallway without protest. Peter wondered if they'd find Mac in the kitchen, or if he'd had the good sense to escape the house before the shouting began.

Because *gone and had a fall* was what Senior said every time one of his children tumbled off a horse, had said since they were old enough to ride, which in Peter's case was before he'd learned to run. *Gone and had a fall* meant you'd had the bad manners to make an amateur mistake and was always quickly followed by: *Brush yourself off and get back in the saddle.*

Unspoken but always understood was: *Or prove yourself a coward.*

"Don't go upsetting your mum," Senior said now. He shoved his hands in the front pockets of his jeans, a tell Mac had picked up, and one Peter rarely witnessed. His father was a confident man with no time for uncomfortable emotions like embarrassment. "She's barely slept a night through since—"

"Since I fell." Peter realized he was still holding a fork clenched in one fist. He set it down on the flimsy hospital table. "An accident in which my ribs, my collarbone and, most importantly, my left leg and ankle, were badly fractured. Also, there's the small matter of a grade-three concussion."

"I know that." Senior scowled. He was not a large man, but a lifetime in the saddle had put muscle on his body that age had yet to strip away. He was solid and knew how to use that strength to his advantage, both when it came to people and to horses.

"Who d'you think's been talking to your doctors?" he continued, shaking his head. "At this point I know more about your body, son, than I ever cared to. And I'll be glad if I never have to look at another X-ray of your bones again."

"Then you also know I won't be brushing myself off and hopping back onboard. I may never ride again." It was the first time he'd said it out loud, and he had to work to get the words past the lump in his throat. He shouldn't *have* to say it out loud, not to the man who raised him. "I won't be attending any events for quite a while. And I sure as shit won't be attending them in an accessible van wrapped in the farm logo. Jesus, Da, that's just grim."

Senior's jaw clenched. He took his hands from his pockets and crossed his arms over his wide chest. Peter braced himself for the eruption but refused to look away from the flash of temper in his da's eyes. He'd never bowed his head to Senior. He didn't intend to start now.

But the shouting didn't come. Senior inhaled loudly, then blew out through his nose, sounding so much like a fresh horse remembering to breathe on course that Peter blinked. His da took a turn around the room, then another, while Peter watched in disbelief. It was obvious the man was trying to work himself down from a good cuss. Suppressed fury flushed his cheeks bright red.

As far back as Peter could remember, Gabe Griffin Sr. had never wasted any energy on trying to control his legendary temper.

After a third turn around the room, Senior stopped abruptly at the foot of the hospital bed. Though the rose of anger still bloomed on his cheeks, he spoke evenly, almost gently.

"You're right, of course. I wasn't thinking."

Peter caught himself gaping and quickly shut his mouth. It wasn't exactly an apology, but it was close. And just like Senior never wasted energy on controlling his temper, he never *ever* apologized.

"It'll take some getting used to, that's all," Senior added gruffly. "This change in our circumstances. You and I have dreamed of Olympic gold for a long time. This"—he indicated Peter and the hospital bed with a wave of both hands —"will take some getting used to."

Our circumstances. At last Peter looked away from Senior's face. The barely touched dinner on his plate was easier to stomach than the badly disguised pity in his dad's eyes.

"I'll go and get Gabriel. He'll help you take a piss and change your clothes for sleep. There's a bedpan around here somewhere."

"It's barely noon." Peter pointed out in disbelief. "I haven't had my cake."

Senior's smile was closer to a grimace. "Rest is the best

thing for you, son. And Gabriel knows he's expected to help with anything you need."

With that he was gone, striding from the room with a haste that suggested he had more important places to be. Peter, staring after, thought numbly that he would have much preferred the familiar screaming match to Senior's awkward new deference.

CHAPTER FOUR

On Wednesday, Annie decided to colic.

John found the mare pacing and sweating at evening feed. He immediately called Reed, who was in the middle of a reality TV marathon and almost halfway through a bottle of Stoli Lime. The trash TV marathon was a reward for a long day in the bag, and the Stoli was a Wednesday night ritual, because Reed's mother phoned every Wednesday when the sun rose over Saint Petersburg.

"She looks bad," John said. "I know it's your day off, but—"

"I'll be right down." Reed silenced the TV. Rolling off the couch, they capped the bottle of Stoli and took it with them back into the kitchen. "Get her out, start her walking. Keep her up while I grab the Banamine."

"Hell, Reed. If we lose her now, after everything . . . " His anxious swallow sounded loud even over the phone. "Senior will put us out on our ears."

"That's not going to happen. Stop panicking and start walking." Reed dialed Kate while digging a bottle of

Banamine and a sealed syringe out of the minifridge they kept in their bedroom strictly for horse meds.

Kate answered on the third ring. "What's wrong?" An after-hours call from your barn manager was almost never a good thing.

"Annie's colicking. John's got her moving. I'm on my way down. I'll let you know if I decide we need to call Doc Holliday."

There was a pause, followed by muffled conversation in the background. Reed stuck the Banamine in the pockets of their joggers and then had to go searching for their paddock boots forgotten behind the couch.

It had been that sort of day. Annie colicking was just the icing on top of an already exhausting twenty-four hours.

"Or I can call Holliday now. But I'd like to take a look myself first." Reed paused briefly to check their reflection in the blank TV screen. Hair more than a little tussled, spikes wilting, thanks to a restless afternoon nap. The Pink Jones concert shirt—washed soft, frayed along the neck, and emblazoned with one long-nailed come-hither finger across the chest—was probably not the most professional choice, but at least Reed hadn't spilled Stoli down the front. And anyway Annie didn't have time to waste.

"Senior and I will be right down," Kate said into Reed's ear as they took the steps down to the barn two at a time. "Don't call Holliday yet." She sounded about as pleased as Reed felt. "See you in five." The connection went dead.

Fantastic. A run-in with Senior over a colicking horse was the cherry on top of the icing on top of an increasingly shitty day.

Wednesdays, Reed thought with a sigh, *can just fuck off.*

———

JOHN WAS MARCHING Annie along the perimeter of Barn A's indoor arena. He glanced around when Reed slipped through the gate, expression grim. Reed thought with sympathetic amusement that John looked worse than the mare who, despite a layer of sweat and an angrily swishing tail, didn't appear to be in any danger of going down.

"She's breathing quick, biting her flanks. And in a generally pissy mood," John reported when Reed reached his side. "Passing gas."

"Poor thing. Good girl. Are we feeling rotten tonight?" Reed soothed a hand along Annie's withers. She pinned her ears in disapproval but otherwise didn't protest when Reed bent and pressed one ear against her warm belly.

Gut sounds didn't always indicate a colic. Visible changes in a horse's usual behavior was a more reliable indicator. But Reed's father had always sworn by the ping-and-pop test. Reed already knew Annie was colicking. The question was, why? Colic was the leading cause of medical death in horses, and causes ranged from something as serious as intestinal necrosis to the less severe and much more common gas colic—the buildup of painful gas in a horse's digestive tract.

"My father always said gas colic sounds like gunfire. More ping and pop, less gurgle." Much better than silence. Lack of gut sounds could be a very bad thing when it came to colic. Reed straightened, gave Annie a pat on the rump. "Sounds like she's got World War III going on in there. Kate's on her way down from the main house. Let's get the Banamine started."

John blew out a breath, making Annie start and flick her tail. "I checked her stall. No new poop piles since I picked it at four."

"Well," Reed said with forced cheer, taking Annie from John and leading the way out of the arena, "let's see if we can fix that, yes?"

Annie groaned as if in agreement. Reed was sympathetic. Horses couldn't vomit. Reed, a regular connoisseur of too much vodka and occasional consumer of cheap sushi in landlocked states, couldn't imagine suffering through a sick belly without the relief of a good puke.

"Fuck me sideways," John murmured. "You didn't say she was bringing Senior."

"You kiss your mother with that mouth?" But the sight of Senior standing near the barn crossties with Kate, his arms crossed and chin thrust pugnaciously in their direction, made Reed's shoulder blades want to climb protectively ear-ward. Reed forced them back down. Horses were sensitive to emotion. Reed needed to remain calm for Annie's sake.

"Reed!" Kate met them halfway down the aisle. She was dressed like she'd been out on the town, in pinstriped trousers and a cashmere sweater, hair pulled back into a French braid. Reed almost didn't recognize her as the same woman who spent every waking moment in Levi's and oxford shirts. "How is she?"

"Feeling poorly." Ignoring Senior, Reed led Annie into the nearest crosstie, clipping her into place. "John did the right thing in calling." Reed resisted tossing a wink the younger man's way. "As it is, I'm thinking gas colic, and hoping we've caught it early."

While Reed readied the Banamine—breaking the cap on the syringe and filling it to the 10cc line—Kate pried open Annie's mouth.

"Her gums look good. And her eye's still bright. Have you listened to her belly?"

"Yes," Reed began, belatedly realizing they'd come prepared with everything except the all-important alcohol wipe. *Fuck me sideways.* "John, would you please grab an alcohol wipe out of my trunk? Her gut sounds plenty gassy and I—"

"Old wives' tale. Are you sure you know what you're about? Is that vodka I smell? Katie, maybe let's wait for Doc. When's the last time the mare took a shit?" Senior interrupted. He raked Reed head to toe with an unfriendly stare, hitching pointedly on Reed's hair, again on Reed's Pink Jones T-shirt, the yellow paint on their nails, and stopping finally on the syringe between Reed's fingers. It felt exactly like being sized up by a bigoted grizzly with dinner in its sights. Or so Reed imagined.

But honestly, maybe that was selling the grizzly bear short.

"Not since four, sir." John returned with an alcohol wipe in hand. Reed tore the paper packet open and used the wipe to scrub a spot on Annie's neck. Annie, no dummy, snorted and then stomped her left fore nervously. Reed couldn't blame her. It really was turning into a shit evening.

"There's truth in old wives' tales," Reed told Senior calmly. "Where I come from, the old wives always know what's what."

"Oh, for God's sake, Da! Stop mucking around and let him do his job. It's Annie."

Reed recognized that the voice—dangerously rough, like gravel on a back-country road, with a dash of that sexy Irish lilt that Aine McCauley had passed to her children. It made immediate goose pimples spring up on Reed's arms. They were too busy injecting Annie to glance around, but from the way Senior, Kate, and John went still as mice caught all unaware by the household cat, Reed knew Peter Griffin had entered the barn.

"Not he, *they*. Jesus, Peter, don't you pay attention to anything said over dinner?"

That was Mac, muttering just a little too loudly, making Senior snort disdain. Reed finished soothing the spot on Annie's neck where the needle had bit, dug deep for patience, and turned around.

They'd not yet been blessed with the entire McAuley-Griffin clan in one place. Six pairs of eyes studied Reed with identical laser focus. The family had arranged themselves shoulder to shoulder in the barn aisle, a united front: Aine and Senior at the center, Kate in her fancy clothes, and Gabriel in Dockers and a flannel shirt, shin-high muck boots on his feet. Mac and Peter held up the battalion's tail end, Mac gripping the handlebars of Peter's wheelchair as though afraid to let go, while at the same time managing to look like he'd stepped out of the pages of *GQ*.

Peter, on the other hand, resembled the shit that hit the fan blades and then the wall after. He was not a tall man to begin with, but he sat hunched in the wheelchair like he wanted to disappear beneath the quilt tossed over his shoulders and his lap. His left leg in its cast was elevated, sticking out ahead of the chair and, as far as Reed was concerned, just asking to be accidentally jostled.

He was still beautiful: all muscle and sharp planes, arrogant jaw sporting golden stubble to match his messy haircut, a sullen mouth made for kissing. But Reed couldn't help noticing their ex-crush and USET's rising star had dark circles under his flashing blue eyes.

Probably he wasn't getting much sleep at night, what with the broken bones and the fractured Olympic dreams.

"Androku?" Kate prompted.

All of the McAuley-Griffins together, Reed thought absently, was definitely more than a Wednesday evening called for.

"The Banamine should have her feeling better quickly," Reed explained to six professional horse people, all of whom knew the routine as well as, if not better, than they did. "John, let's get her walking again, yes? I'll start mixing up some colic tea."

"Colic tea?" Six pairs of assessing eyes, and despite his irritation Peter's were still the softest blue Reed had ever seen. Like Lake Baikal in the summer, or the sky over Moscow after a passing snowstorm. "What the hell is colic tea?" Peter demanded.

Here we go, thought Reed, swallowing a sigh. It was too much to hope that holistic horse care was a USET staple. Yet. "Slippery elm bark, marshmallow root, fennel seed, and cinnamon," they rattled off. "Brewed up into a tea and poured over oats. Helps get the GI moving. Horses seem to like the taste of it, too."

There was a stunned silence, broken only by the clop of Annie's hooves on cement as John led her away toward the arena. Even as Reed braced for the inevitable disapproval, they noted with relief that the mare already seemed to be moving more comfortably.

Exactly as Reed expected, the family exploded en masse.

"What the ever-loving crap—Gabriel, get Doc on the line right *immediately*! I've—"

"Now, Da. I told you when I hired Reed they specialized in holistic management. Stop yelling! We agreed it was time to try something more up to date—"

"Katie, *m'inion*, please don't shout at your father. You

know he's had a rough time of it lately. Let's all just take a moment and—"

"Sir, Doc Holliday's on the line."

"—never heard of such nonsense! Colic tea! As if 'more up to date' means fancy herbs and green *eyeliner*—"

"Enough!" Peter said in that low rasp that still managed to be heard over the shouting. "Quiet! Everyone just be quiet!"

Interesting that he didn't need to raise his voice to shut down a room. Maybe it was because Peter had already become comfortable wearing the USET team captain's hat, used to telling people what to do without letting on he had the upper hand. Maybe it was because he knew his family well enough to take initiative.

Or maybe it was because Peter was sitting in a wheelchair and Reed was pretty damn sure they were the only one in the group not feeling uncomfortable about it.

"Gabriel," Peter continued, lifting his chin and looking Senior in the eye, "please tell Doc we won't be needing him tonight. We all know Annie's suffered a gas colic or ten on the road—"

"On the road," Senior pointed out gruffly. "Never at home."

"She's on stall rest," Kate said. "It was bound to happen."

"Banamine and walking usually knocks it out," Peter told Reed. "Or a trailer ride. Most often she shits before we've started the motor, she's that particular." And then he smiled and Reed, exhausted, on the defensive, and maybe the tiniest bit tipsy, felt their heart skip a beat behind their rib cage. If Peter Griffin's eyes were like the sky over Moscow in winter, his smile was warm enough to melt all the ice in Oymyakon.

Shit, thought Reed, *no wonder he managed to raise more money toward Paris than any other competitor in history. He's got charm in spades, and he knows how to put it on.*

Peter's smile grew, gathering tiny lines at the corners of his tired eyes, almost as if he guessed exactly what Reed was thinking. He held out a hand, leaning gingerly forward in the chair. "You must be Androku. We haven't met. I'm Peter, Peter Griffin."

"I know who you are." Reed could have smacked themself when Peter's smile froze. "Not because of the wheelchair," they rushed on, knowing they might be digging a deeper hole, but in for a penny, in for a ruble, and Reed wanted to make sure Peter understood. "Because all you McAuley children are beautiful like your mother, but you're the only blond, yes?" *And I've been following your career since I was fifteen. May have jacked off to your picture in* US Equestrian *more than once.* Reed felt themself flush.

"My fair-haired babe, my golden boy. We always said he was a changeling." Aine arched both dark brows in Reed's direction, then nodded to herself. "Peter, you'll stay and monitor our Annie. And keep that leg covered, we don't want dirt near the cast. Let Reed here tell you about their tea. The rest of you—it's late and we've already had a long evening. Back to the house with you."

Kate and Gabriel turned to go without protest. Senior let his wife pull him after, though the glare he threw Reed's way was sharp enough to cut wood. Mac, looming awkwardly behind Peter's chair like he didn't know quite how to stand without the New York skyline at his back, cleared his throat.

"Uhm. Bit difficult getting the chair over the gravel walkways. We need to fix that. But for now—could you?"

He waved a hand vaguely in Reed's direction.

"Thank you very much, Mac, but I can look after myself," his brother snapped, charm disappearing under a sudden grim storm cloud. "I know how to ask for help *if* I need it." Ignoring Mac's doubtful scowl, he began wheeling away down the aisle in the direction of the arena gate. Reed couldn't help but notice that the gloves Peter wore on his hands—to prevent blisters?—were Cavalleria Toscana riding gloves, and brand new from the looks of them. Reed owned a similar pair themself.

"He won't ask for help," Mac murmured. "He doesn't know how, and old dogs never learn new tricks. For God's sake, don't let him bump that leg on anything. One of Mum's cats jumped on him yesterday, and I thought he was going to pass out."

"No worries," Reed replied with much more confidence than they felt. "We'll be careful. I'll see him home once we know Annie's out of danger."

Mac touched two fingers to his brow. "Good luck to you. That one's been on stall rest much too long for anything good to come of it. And I don't mean the horse."

As soon as the barn door banged shut on the heels of Mac's pretty shoes, Reed stole a brief moment for a self-check and was relieved to discover they'd survived the whirlwind McAuley-Griffin clan with dignity intact.

"Right. Androku. Just promise me you're not planning on adding a dash of whatever you've been drinking to your magic colic tea. Because I'd have to say no."

Relatively intact, anyway, Reed thought, surreptitiously inhaling through their nose before explaining, "It's Wednesday. My night off. On Wednesdays I have vodka with dinner." If one counted a pint of Häagen-Dazs as dinner.

It was obvious to Reed that Peter hadn't quite grown

accustomed to the wheelchair. The cement barn aisle was probably easier to navigate than gravel, but it wasn't exactly hazard-free. In fact, it was littered with the usual detritus that came with horses: small piles of hay dropped over the top of stall doors, clumps of mud or manure or arena sand knocked out of shoes as horses were led through the barn, the occasional collection of twigs dropped by the sparrows nesting in the eves overhead.

Watching Peter work to maneuver his chair around a trail of manure crumbles without knocking his leg on any of the tack trunks lining the wall, Reed made a mental note to see the aisle was swept more often than the twice daily already on the schedule.

"Yesterday Mum pushed me into the back garden, and we brought half the soil back in on my wheels." Peter scowled as he deliberately avoided a trail of horse shit. Reed couldn't help noticing how the muscles in his forearms stood out as he worked the wheels. Cowboy muscles not yet gone soft. "Gabriel says he's ordered some special neoprene tire covers, but I plan to be up on crutches before they arrive. Do you always emit vodka fumes on your night off?"

It didn't sound like disapproval, more like mild curiosity. So instead of bristling, Reed shrugged.

"Wednesday evening my mother calls. When it's morning in Russia. She has a lot of opinions, my mother. About my late father, about the United States, about the check I send her every month," Reed added, carefully, so it didn't sound like a challenge. "I'm not drunk. Not even buzzed. It takes more than a few shots of Stoli to turn my head, and besides, I'm a professional."

"I get that, the thing with your mum." Parallel to the arena gate, Peter paused and glanced up, a wry smile on his lovely mouth. "Go and mix up your magic tea. I'll keep an eye on my mare while you do."

Reed almost didn't ask, but they just couldn't see how Peter would manage it on his own. "Can I open the gate for you? So you can see in?"

"Yes, please." The storm cloud returned and Peter's amusement faded. "Mac's wrong. I do know how to ask for help. Because lately I have no choice."

———

BY THE TIME Reed returned downstairs with a bowl of colic tea over ice—in their hurry they managed to slosh some of the cooling mixture onto their shirt and now they must stink of vodka *and* marshmallow root together. *Wonderful.*—Annie was back in the crossties and looking one thousand percent better.

"Took a nice big shit about five minutes ago," John reported. "Ripe as hell, but she's feeling better for it, aren't you, girl?"

She was, the sweat drying on her coat and the twitches along her belly subsiding. She pricked up her ears at the shiny stainless bowl in Reed's hands, trying to decide whether to beg or spook. Peter, too, looked much more relaxed, despite the hunch in his shoulders. This time the smile he tossed Reed was genuine, and Reed had to work not to bobble the bowl again.

Christ Jesus. It had been years since a man's smile had made Reed's stomach clench. Reed's body was suddenly remembering that it had been much too long since they'd had a good fuck and really, now was not the time to remember that Peter Griffin had always been open about his bisexuality and had a rumored list of hookups that would make most people blush.

"And we didn't even need to threaten her with the trailer to get things moving. She'll be right as rain in an hour. But don't let me stop you," Peter added, nodding at the bowl. "How do you plan to get it down her? Feeding syringe or mash?"

"Oh, well, I always try the mash on them first, don't you?" Recalling the matter at hand, Reed offered Peter the bowl. "Do you mind holding this for a second? Let me just grab some grain and a spoon, yes?"

They thought for a moment that Peter would refuse. Reed didn't miss the way his gloved hands flexed on the arms of his chair. Pain? Nerves? Or annoyance?

But then he shrugged, nodded, and accepted the bowl without a word. Peter didn't spill a single drop as he set it carefully on his lap. In fact, he managed the simple transfer over his splinted leg in a graceful movement that made Reed feel awkward just standing in place.

"I've watched you ride." The confession burst forth before Reed could stop it. "In London, back a few years. Not in competition, though I wish I had. In the schooling ring, on that spooky gray no one else wanted to sit."

Peter's brows rose. "I remember the horse. Fantastic jumper, terrified of Liverpools and wasn't going to change his mind no matter how many times his owners sent him 'round under a new rider."

"And you told them just that, though they didn't like to hear it. They'd paid good money for a strong horse in the jumper ring, and you told them it would never see the Olympics but might do quite well as an A-circuit hunter." The owners had been mad enough to spit nails. But they'd listened, because it was Peter Griffin telling them so. "You were right. You knew three minutes in that the horse would flourish in a different job."

Peter regarded Reed without expression. "Yes."

"Well." Reed squared their shoulders, reminding themself that they were much too old for hero worship, and when it came to horse care, Reed knew as much, if not more, than even the McAuley-Griffin family. "I'm telling you now what I've been telling Senior to no result since I started here. Your Annie's the sort of horse that needs a job to thrive. A different job, maybe, if she can't do the old. It's not just the standing in one place, it's the brainwork. She's listless, bored. She needs to go back to work or she'll colic again, or worse."

"I didn't realize you were a veterinarian as well as a *holistic consultant,*" Peter said coldly. Reed could swear they felt the temperature in the barn drop twenty degrees. There was that legendary disdain. *Cocky bastard,* people said in whispers, almost as often as *personable when he wants to be.* "Or maybe you have a degree in horse psychiatry I wasn't aware of? Maybe they give those out in Russia?"

"No." A lifetime of walking softly had taught Reed when to hold on to their temper. They supposed even the best masturbation fantasies could be assholes in person. "It's just common sense. Horse sense. And you'd see it, too, if you bothered to actually look. Instead of feeling sorry for yourself."

Shit. They hadn't meant to say that last bit out loud.

Now the tea colic did slosh as Peter angrily thrust the bowl back in Reed's direction. All over both their hands, onto Peter's elevated leg, and onto the barn aisle. Annie snorted her disapproval.

"John," Peter said sharply.

"Yes, sir, Mr. Griffin?"

"I'd like to go back up now. Would you help me, please?"

"Yes, sir." John hurried into place behind the wheelchair, tossing Reed a comically horrified look over Peter's head as he did so. "I'll keep you updated throughout the evening, if you like, sir?"

"Please do. And stop calling me sir. I am not my father. Androku?"

Reed met that glacier stare without flinching. "Yes?"

"I'd like a final report from you, tomorrow at the house, before barn check. So that'll be, what, five thirty a.m.? Don't be late. I have PT at six, and Gabriel says the woman's a real bear if I keep her waiting."

"I—" Technically, Reed worked for Kate and not Peter. But they couldn't see any way pointing that out would be a good idea.

"That's not too early for a *professional* such as yourself, Androku?" Each syllable snapped authority. Reed's mouth went dry, in desire or dismay. It was impossible to tell.

Shit.

"Of course not." Reed replied, smiling politely while cold colic tea dripped down their wrists. "I look forward to it."

Fucking Wednesdays.

CHAPTER FIVE

"It's not wrapped." Kate squinted out over her coffee cup at the front drive. "I can't believe he canceled the van wrap. I thought it was only Mum who can get him to change his mind."

"He's feeling guilty and doesn't know what to do about it," Peter hazarded. "Or maybe it's just old-fashioned pity."

"Nice. Next time I need his approval on my stud list, I'll let you and your leg do the talking."

They were sitting together on the front porch, watching Thursday's sunrise outline Tulip Farm in shades of white and gray. Kate was spread out across the porch swing, dirty boots on their mum's pretty white pillows, taking her first infusion of coffee in gulps. Peter preferred his coffee extra hot, savored one sip at a time. He cradled the warm mug in both hands as he slouched in his chair, studying the rented van parked in the drive.

His right shoulder ached beneath the figure-eight brace that held his healing collarbone in place, and his left leg throbbed angrily in time with the painful drumbeat in his head. He'd skipped his morning pain pills because he wanted to be clearheaded for the meeting with Androku, but now he was wondering if that had been a mistake.

"It's nice, for a rental," Kate said in approval. "Looks roomy. Can I take it to Walmart? Crap always blows around in the bed of my truck."

"Take Mac's car." As far as Peter was concerned, Mac's silver Mercedes, parked a few yards down from the van, was an affront to the eyes. At least the van—for all that he could barely stand the sight of it—was a Dodge. "I bet it's never seen a Walmart parking lot before."

Kate snorted. Peter took a slow sip of coffee and closed his eyes in pleasure. Hospital coffee was shit. Aine had a coffee addiction that she'd passed on to all four of her children, which meant the farm was always stocked with the highest quality beans. If Peter could figure out a way to inject the stuff directly into his veins, he would. Especially as he hadn't slept a wink the night before, and he suspected the new physical therapist Senior had hired wouldn't take "my horse colicked last night and I couldn't even get down to the barn to see her on my own" as an excuse to slack off.

"Oh, hey, what do you know?" Kate drawled, sounding much too pleased with herself. "Here comes your five thirty. I told you they'd show. And early, even."

Peter opened his eyes before grimacing. Truth was, he'd been pretty sure Androku would show as well, if only to make a point. Still, there was nothing wrong with hoping they'd been pissed off enough to give their dawn appointment a pass. Or, even better, pack their bags and beeline back to their last post in Kentucky.

Because Peter suspected he owed Androku an apology, especially as he'd spent most of his sleepless night reading the Russian's references, first in Kate's file and then on Google. Every review he could find was stellar. Apparently

Androku was both a miracle worker and a champion of lost causes.

Peter didn't do apologies. The few times in his life he'd tried, he'd only made things worse. He liked to think it was because Senior had never modeled the skill, but that was probably giving himself a pass he didn't deserve. The honest truth of it was apologizing felt too much like a defeat, and Peter had never in his life accepted defeat.

Peter doesn't ask for help.

"The times," he murmured sourly into his coffee, "they are a-changing."

"Dylan? You think?" Kate considered Androku as they skirted Aine's rain-choked flower beds and started up the drive. "Wouldn't have pegged them as a classics sort of person."

"Pink Jones," Peter said, remembering Androku's hoodie and joggers the night before. At least this morning they were dressed for business, in breeches and tall boots and a polo. Even the gauzy pink-and-yellow scarf wrapped casually around Androku's throat managed to look cheerful and charming against their olive skin.

"Good morning!" Kate called as Androku skirted around the van. "Look at you, all fresh and lovely. Peter and I are feeling a bit like something one of Mum's cats puked up. You'd think we'd be used to early mornings by now."

"Comes of being farm stock." Androku smiled at Kate with a real warmth that made Peter want to roll his eyes as he added "genuinely friendly" to the mental list he'd worked up overnight, right under "knows their stuff" and "probably not a con artist."

"Annie's doing well," Androku continued, shifting their smile from Kate to Peter. "Back on her feed and acting her usual self. But I suppose you know that. John says you were down to the barn again very early this morning. I would have sent word if there was more trouble."

That last sentence sounded vaguely accusatory, but Androku's cheerful expression didn't falter so Peter decided to let it go. He *had* been down to Barn A, three times in the past twelve hours. Brief, physically grueling trips to check in on the mare. He'd hoped his visits had gone unnoticed.

"Mac," he said when Kate tossed a quizzical look his direction. "You know he never sleeps. Besides, he owes me a favor or six." Which is why his brother had kept muttered complaints to a minimum as he pushed Peter to and from the barn at 10:00 p.m., midnight, and 3:00 a.m.

"Mac doesn't need sleep." Kate shook her head. "You, on the other hand, really, really do."

"She took to your tea mash," Peter told Androku, ignoring Kate's pointed sigh. "John gave her a second dose at midnight, and she wolfed it down."

"They usually do." Amusement blurred the edges of Androku's thick Slavic accent. They shoved their hands in the pockets of their breeches, rocked back and forth on the heels of their boots. "It's the pinch of brown sugar added at the end. Old family recipe, hasn't failed me yet."

"Come inside." Peter decided he wasn't going to cough up an apology under Kate's watchful eye. "Let's talk about those family recipes. I did some googling last night. Coffee?"

"Wouldn't say no to a cup. My machine is on its last legs. Can I get you a refill?"

Smooth as silk, Androku took up Peter's empty cup—and thank Christ for that because Peter hadn't yet worked out how to wheel about one-handed while carrying a hot beverage *and* keeping his leg out of harm's way.

At least the old house was blessed with wide doors and

spacious corridors, Peter thought as he sent his chair through the front door. Someone, probably Gabriel, had cleared the main hall of furniture and removed the antique runner Aine had brought all the way back from some secondhand shop in Belgium. Rugs, Peter was beginning to learn, were put on earth just to slip uselessly under wheels.

The kitchen was out of the question, the space between granite counters and the large country-style island too narrow for a wheelchair. But there was a coffee bar in Senior's office—a spacious room with no furniture other than a scuffed Stickley desk and three walls of built-ins. The floor was original oak, and on Kate's suggestion Senior had removed the old wool rug that had been there since before Gabriel was born. Senior hadn't uttered a single word of protest.

When Senior was in the house and working, the office door was kept closed. When he was away, which was most of the daylight hours, Peter had taken to using the space as a change of venue from his tiny parlor bedroom.

"Coffee machine's there, if you wouldn't mind?" Peter directed, the muscles in his arms burning as he edged himself into the room and behind the desk. He'd anticipated using this room for their meeting and prepared accordingly, asking Kate to roll Senior's ratty office chair temporarily out of the way and into the kitchen before he'd started brewing their first cup of coffee.

It was awkward parked sideways against the Stickley, but the desk was low enough and Peter's torso long enough that the proportions were almost right. He felt as close as he ever got to comfortable lately, with the desk between him and the world, and his own face staring back across the room from a number of newspaper clippings framed and displayed on the built-ins.

Reed Androku might have an impressive résumé, he reminded himself as Senior's state-of-the-art coffee machine hissed to a boil, but Peter Griffin's laurels rested on another level entirely.

"Definitely beats my Mr. Coffee," Androku murmured, gazing wistfully at the machine. "How do you take yours?"

"Black, thank you. Didn't realize they still made Mr. Coffees."

"Not sure they do. The one in my apartment's a real dinosaur." Androku set Peter's coffee in its delicate porcelain cup on the desk within easy reaching distance, shuffling aside a pile of Senior's papers to make room. They were doing it on purpose, Peter realized, anticipating his needs and meeting each without any of the fanfare or awkwardness that seemed to trip up his family.

Peter wondered if Androku realized they were doing it, or if they had learned the skill somewhere. Of course, Androku had a documented passion for rehabbing horses off the racecourse. Maybe they were just a natural caretaker.

Either way, Androku's ease around Peter's impairment —and, somehow, their cheerful scarf and matching pink-and-yellow eyeshadow—threatened to melt some of the ice around his heart.

Which just wouldn't do at all. He'd been working hard to feel nothing. He wasn't ready to let numbness go.

"Sit." Peter indicated the ladder-backed chair pushed up against the built-ins. "I'm afraid I've only got a few minutes before Gabriel comes to take me into town. So. Let's talk about Annie."

Androku shifted the chair in front of the desk and sat in it backward, cup of coffee—also black, Peter noted—held in one hand. They had pianist's fingers, long and elegant, slightly tapered at the tips. Peter found himself staring just a little too hard at those long fingers, admiring dark skin against white porcelain.

Androku gulped down what must have been a scalding mouthful of coffee before plunging right in. "She needs to work. She's worked her whole life. It's obvious to me she's one of those who doesn't know how to retire." They met Peter's stare. Androku's eyes were the color of the coffee in his cup. "I know your father doesn't agree. Which, I think, is very unlike him? Any other horse, maybe, and she'd already be back to rehab?"

"Yes. Under normal circumstances." What Peter thought but couldn't bring himself to say was, *I'd make sure of it.*

He hadn't dismissed Annie completely after the accident, of course he hadn't. But he hadn't exactly inquired too deeply into her well-being, either, other than to make sure that she was comfortable and being looked after. Kate had kept him in the general loop but hadn't bombarded him with details. Peter hadn't realized until last night she'd had the mare moved to Barn A. Probably it was a hint aimed at Androku. And the Russian had taken Kate's bait.

"Look, Androku—"

"Call me Reed."

"Reed." Peter braced himself. "I owe you an apology. You're right, of course. Annie's been my partner for a long time. I doubt she remembers life without steady work."

"Or without you. Sensitive creatures, horses." Reed bit their lower lip before plowing on. "I'll say it as I see it. She'll have noticed your absence. That, on top of the pain of her injury and the confinement . . . Well, in those neglectful circumstances, I'm only surprised she hasn't colicked earlier."

"You're not making this easy," Peter replied through gritted teeth. The Russian certainly didn't pull any punches. "But I won't say you're wrong. I'm realizing now I've failed her rather abominably. But you understand I've had other things on my mind." He indicated his elevated leg with a sarcastic flourish, then hissed when his ribs pulled in warning.

Senior would have bristled. Aine would have run for the baked goods. Kate would have teared up, Mac would have reached for a witty but inappropriate comment, and Gabriel probably would have offered to install a second ramp on the back of the house.

Reed just shrugged as if they hadn't noticed. "Now you're back home. Time to remedy the situation. I'll start her on the line tomorrow, just some walking and stretching to see how we do. And supervised turnout, in one of the round pens, I think. Meanwhile, get that very large brother of yours to push you down to the barn a few times a day. She'll find your voice and scent calming." They paused, then added: "You could start today, or tomorrow."

Peter didn't know whether to laugh or cry. *Down to the barn a few times a day.* Did the Russian really think it was as easy as that, the chair some sort of accoutrement, a less cheerful fashion statement than a colorful scarf but an accessory all the same?

"Fine. Maybe sometime this week." He cleared what felt like a brick from his throat, remembered to stay on point. "I wanted to apologize, also, for being rude. To you, last night. I was worried about Annie and forgot my manners, and I'm sorry for that."

"Oh." To Peter's surprise, Reed flushed. "Your coffee almost makes up for it." They tilted their empty cup in Peter's direction. "Offer me a second and we'll be even."

Peter didn't suppose it would be as easy as all that, but before he could pursue the matter, Mac strode into the office. His brother was dressed down in muted slacks, a gray cashmere sweater, and soft black loafers. He wore a pasted-on cheerful expression that meant Peter's time was up.

"You're welcome to a second cup," Peter told Reed before turning a resigned grimace Mac's way. "Drew the short straw, I see. I was expecting Gabriel."

"Don't be silly! There's nothing I enjoy more than a jaunt into town at"—Mac made a show of glancing at the gleaming watch on his wrist—"5:45 a.m." He followed Reed to the coffee machine. "Thank God for caffeine. Morning, Androku. How's the mare?"

"Recovering nicely." Reed nodded in Peter's direction. "Thanks for the refill. I'll just take it outside and join Kate on the porch."

The Russian left the room in a swirl of color and a clatter of bootheels. Peter paused over his own cup of coffee to watch Reed go, and then scowled when Mac flashed him a quizzical look. "What?"

"Nothing. Just"—Mac took a sip of coffee, swallowed, shook his head—"the last time I saw you staring at some-one's arse that way, it was Samantha Linell at Green's Bar during Dublin trials, and you had her—and also her groom, what was his name?—in your bed by the next morning."

"The groom's name was Rob." Indignation made him growl. "And you're wrong about Androku. It's not like that at all. We were just discussing Annie."

Mac shrugged. "Whatever you say, golden boy. Just don't get attached. What I hear, Senior's already looking for a way to run them off the farm."

"What, why?" Peter scowled. "Just because Androku's holistic approach doesn't fit into his worldview?"

"No. Because Androku won't be bullied. Did you know they carry a knife on their belt? Huge bone-handled sucker, definitely scary. And we both know Senior likes his employees feeling humble."

Not just his employees. They shared a glance of mutual understanding.

"Not my problem," Peter decided, and promised himself it would stay that way. "Making my appointment on time is." He wheeled away from Senior's old desk. It took him three tries to maneuver the chair around without bumping his leg, which Peter decided was two tries too many as Mac waved him through the door.

"Lead on, MacDuff."

———

THEY WERE fifteen minutes late thanks to a tractor on the road and a slow elevator in the medical building. Mac was muttering curses by the time the doors opened on the third floor. Peter was too exhausted by the drive to protest when Mac took the handlebars and propelled the chair along industrial carpet toward 302. He wasn't sure which was more tiring, sitting upright for twenty minutes in the new van or being out in public. New Milford wasn't exactly Hartford—what it made up for in small-town charm it lacked in privacy. He'd been terrified they would run into someone they knew in the parking lot, or in the building lobby. He'd found it impossible not to slump in his chair as the receptionist checked him in.

The door marked 302 opened not onto another receptionist as Peter expected but onto a cheerful, loftlike space with exposed brick walls, massive beams, and four large windows. Equipment in various shapes and sizes filled the room. Some of it—like the weight machines and massage benches—were familiar. The giant web on one wall made of pink pool noodles and the very large yellow plush bear in the center of the room were less routine.

"Good morning!" A compact woman with a big smile popped around from behind one of the weight machines, socket wrench in hand. Her skull was bald and covered all over in floral tattoos. She wore a black cotton T-shirt that read SÁNCHEZ PA, and black shorts that emphasized the size of her muscular thighs.

"I see you conquered our glacially slow elevator and emerged unscathed. Sorry about that. I've been telling the landlord for years that my clients need more reliable access. But new elevators in old buildings are expensive, and so long as it putt-putts between floors without stopping, my lawyer tells me there's nothing I can do."

She held out a hand. "You must be Peter. I'm Teodora Sánchez, but most people call me Teddy. Started when I was five and stuck. Welcome to Sánchez Physical Associates." Her fingers were small but strong. She squeezed Peter's before letting go.

"Teddy. Bear. My brother was having me on, I think. I take it you won't start growling if I'm a few minutes late." *Very funny, Gabriel.*

"Not with that elevator." Teddy aimed her smile up and over Peter's head. "Hi, McAuley. How's the big city treating you?"

"Better than I deserve." Mac cleared his throat. "So, do I stay or . . .?"

"Go. I like alone time with my clients. Better headspace. Be back in forty-five."

Mac left the room with the speed of someone who had just seen an actual bear. Teddy noticed Peter's baffled frown, and her smiled widened impossibly to show the sort of perfectly straight teeth people paid a lot of money for.

"You probably don't remember, but Mac and I dated for a couple of weeks in middle school. That was before I realized that penises aren't really my thing."

Peter didn't remember, probably because in middle school he'd been traveling the circuit with a tutor while Mac and Gabriel and Kate were struggling through New Milford High.

"So, Peter." Teddy's teasing smile disappeared. Suddenly she was all business. "You're slouching. Hell on the shoulders and the spine. Is that because your ribs are bothering you, or is it your confidence? Also, who measured you for that wheelchair? Never mind. Come over here by the computer and we'll do your intake. It's a shitload of boring questions, but after I'll reward you with a nice massage."

———

PHYSIO MASSAGES WERE NOT like spa massages: gentle, and often served up with a mimosa. Physio massages hurt like hell.

Face up on the table, broken leg elevated on a wedge, fists clenched, and eyes squeezed shut, Peter bit the inside of his cheek to keep from yelling as Teddy's diabolically clever fingers bit into his good thigh. She'd found a tight spot and seemed to take the angry muscle personally.

Thank Christ he'd given in and taken his pain pills before leaving the farm. Otherwise he'd be reduced to a sobbing mess at his first appointment, and he hated making bad first impressions.

"Hurts, does it? Good. Man up, Griffin. You should

know by now PT's no walk in the park." She pressed down hard. Peter groaned through a flexed jaw. "Trauma effects the whole body. It's thrown completely off balance, in more ways than one. Especially the muscles, the fascia."

Peter groaned again and then gasped when the knot let go. Relief was instantaneous, making his heart pound and his tender head swim.

"They're overcompensating. Or being used in new ways. You need to be careful not to overdo it in the beginning."

"I know that." Peter growled at the ceiling as Teddy moved on to his calf muscle. "I'm an athlete. This isn't my first go-round with rehab and recovery." He'd broken more bones than he liked to count. It was just part of the job.

"Recovery. Here. Up we go." She helped him roll and sit upright, swinging his bad leg slowly over the edge of the table with an efficiency he might have found impressive if he was watching her do it to someone else. As it was, the distant, angry ache made his stomach hurt. "*Recovery* is a nice, optimistic word. It also suggests an endgame. Which is why we don't use it here. Because my clients need to know there is no endgame, only forward progress up a fucking steep hill."

"That's cheerful."

"You're not paying me to be cheerful."

When Peter sat propped up on the table, weight resting on the aching palms of his gloved hands, they were almost eye to eye. He squared his shoulders. "I'm paying you to get me back on my horse."

"I'm not a doctor." Her easy grin didn't falter. "So I don't pretend to have all the answers. But femur breaks, especially ones like yours where the bone and muscle were damaged in multiple places, are hard things. And then there's the high ankle fracture. Will I get you back in the saddle? Possibly. Will your body be as strong as it was before the fall? Too early to tell." She tapped her chin. "I'm more concerned with the concussive incident I saw mentioned on your intake papers."

"Head injuries are not uncommon in my line of work. I've had my fair share. It's why we wear helmets." Sure, he'd never been knocked unconscious for longer than a few seconds before, or knocked so hard he was still feeling the aftereffects weeks later—double vision when he was tired, or the throb in his temples that just wouldn't quit.

The fall hadn't actually fractured his skull. As far as Peter was concerned, that was the important thing.

"Sure." Teddy squeezed his shoulder. "Just like most of the NFL. Look, all I'm saying is, your new normal has changed. I'm here to help you adjust. Physically. I don't do the mental crap, I'm in no position to give out advice. But I do recommend a therapist. Got one? Psychiatrist, psychologist?"

"No." The McAuley-Griffin clan as a whole would rather face a firing squad than a therapist. Peter didn't expect he'd break with tradition. Just the thought made him shudder.

"Get one. Also a nutritionist. Your body will thank you for it."

Peter said coldly, "I don't think I like you very much, Teddy."

"I don't blame you, champ. Give it a month and you won't know how you got on without me." She reached under the table, pulled out a larger version of the T-shirt she wore. "New clients get swag. Good for advertising. Now go home and take a nice hot sit-down shower. You'll be sore tonight."

———

"WE CAN FIND SOMEBODY DIFFERENT," Mac suggested when Peter's silence grew too long and even NPR on the van's radio couldn't fill the uncomfortable space. "Someone who's paid to be cheerful and won't suggest a shrink." He shivered dramatically.

"What?" Peter frowned. "Were you listening at the door?"

"Well, I wasn't going to leave you alone with her, undefended. Teddy's badass, she scared the shit out of me even in middle school. I figured you might make a dash for it."

"Me? You're the one who runs at the first sign of conflict."

"Good for both of us you didn't need rescuing," Mac said lightly before his expression turned subdued. "Peter, seriously. If she's not the right match—"

"No." Peter stared out the window. Gray clouds were gathering in the morning sky, threatening more rain. They suited his mood nicely. "It's fine. It's all fine."

CHAPTER SIX

Reed was busy reminding Pritchard that the lunge line meant work and was definitely not an excuse to play bucking bronco when Gabriel stuck his head into the arena and startled them both.

"Fuck, sorry! I was whistling. I thought he heard me coming," the big man said as Pritchard did his best imitation of speedboat, Reed on the towline, bootheels dragging across the arena. Waterskiing, they'd called it back home. Although Reed was pretty sure when you crashed face-down behind a boat, you didn't end up with a mouthful of arena dirt.

Reed didn't intend to make a fool of themself in front of Peter's brother. Also, they knew all of Pritchard's tricks. So instead of risking a mouthful of dirt, Reed let go of the line. Not usually something they would recommend: a loose line could become dangerously tangled around a horse's legs. But Pritchard was different. Pritchard immediately slid to stop, all four hooves planted neatly on the ground, lunge line settling harmlessly behind.

"Not your fault. He probably did hear you coming.

Pritchard uses any excuse to act like a jerk. It's why he's still in my care and not adopted out as some nice family's lawn ornament."

Together Gabriel and Reed regarded Pritchard. Pritchard pinned his mule ears. Reed sighed.

"Honestly, he's come a long way. Used to be he'd bite first, ask questions later. Now I only have to worry about his teeth at feeding time. And he's really got a very lovely gait. When he uses it."

Gabriel quirked an eyebrow. Reed had seen the same dubious expression on Kate's face a number of times. The siblings were obviously a skeptical lot.

"Show you, if you like," Reed offered. "After a few more turns on the line."

"No time. Came down to say you're wanted up at the house."

Peter's oldest brother looked less like his McAuley-stamped siblings and more like Senior stretched an extra eighteen inches. He had his father's wide shoulders and chiseled jaw, his father's wavy hair, his father's cowboy stance.

But Gabriel didn't appear to share Senior's tyrannical inclinations.

Like Kate, he smiled easily and seemed confident that the world wouldn't throw him anything he couldn't handle, and if it did, maybe he'd learn something along the way. Like Kate, he seemed content with his place on the farm, happy to spend his time as manager and handyman.

"Need help catching him?" Gabriel suggested. Reed realized they'd been staring at the man's smile just a little too long, idly remembering how the McAuley grin had softened Peter's sharper features.

"No need. He won't move again until I ask."

"That's handy."

"Pritchard's last home was a ranch in Montana. Owner used whistle cues from the ground, hot mash as an award. Pritchard was a star student. He likes hot mash." Reed slipped a sugar cube from the pocket of their breeches, crossed the arena. He gathered up the line, then fed the gelding sugar. "Happily for me, Pritchard also likes sugar cubes and has a long memory."

Gabriel stood in the barn aisle talking to John while Reed tossed a cooler over Pritchard's back and clipped him into the barn crossties. Gabriel jerked a thumb in the direction of the main house.

"John'll finish cooling him out," he told Reed. "Let's not keep Senior waiting."

Reed's heart sank. It had been a least two weeks since Senior had called them onto the carpet for misdeeds imagined or real, and Reed had been hoping the streak would hold. It couldn't be about billing. It was the wrong time of month and besides which, Reed had made sure to put the new ionic standing wraps they'd ordered for Annie on Kate's private credit card.

Outside Barn A spring was looking up. Midday sun warmed the flower beds. The old magnolia's pink blossoms were beginning to bud. And the sky was, for once, a clear blue. Not a cloud in sight. Reed inhaled gratefully, enjoying the warmer air.

Gabriel wasn't much of a talker, but Reed didn't mind. They walked the path up toward the house in silence, each lost in their own thoughts, gravel crunching under their bootheels.

Gravel.

Reed stopped.

Despite making a note in their management binder

under the Accessibility checklist, Reed had almost forgotten. They'd meant to chase down Gabriel over the gravel problem days earlier, but as usual barn life had caused havoc with any normal schedule. And by the time things had calmed down enough to go over that daily checklist, it was often after four in the morning. Not a time for quick phone calls, unless one of Reed's herd was in danger.

"What is it?" Gabriel crunched to a stop.

"I've been thinking . . ." Reed hesitated, then shrugged. In for a penny, in for a ruble. "These gravel walkways, they're old, I think? Uneven, pitted with holes. Not great for the horses and very difficult for your brother to make his way from the house to the barn even with someone to push his chair. Wheeling himself is almost impossible."

"Surgeon says he'll be out of the chair soon. Maybe another three weeks and then crutches."

"Three weeks is a long time to be away from his horse. And I don't think old gravel will be much easier with crutches, do you?"

Gabriel blinked thoughtfully at Reed. Reed tried not to fidget beneath his stare. Those Irish McAuley eyes seemed to see everything.

"It would be an improvement," Reed added. "Why your parents chose gravel in the first place I don't know. A recipe for hoof disaster all around, you ask me."

"Drainage," Gabriel said slowly. "And also, it was a long time ago, not so many options. Been meaning to change it out for years, honestly, but then the roof needs replacing or the well's gone bad. You know how it is. And the walkways get moved to the back of the list."

Fucking lists, Reed thought, sympathetic. They said, "I understand. But it's been ten days and Peter hasn't come down to visit Annie as he promised. And I got to thinking. It must be so difficult, with the slope, and the wheelchair."

"Promised?" Gabriel rubbed the back of a work-calloused hand across his forehead. "Peter? I don't know what you thought you heard, Androku, but there's no way Peter told you he'd come down to the barn, not unless Annie's poorly again, and maybe not even then. Lately he only leaves the house for medical appointments. The rest of the time we can barely coax him out of his room. Even Mac's thrown up his hands and gone back to the city."

"Well," Reed said, kicking pointedly at the pathway. *Crunch.* "Peter seems the sort of person who keeps his promises. So. Maybe he would come down if the way were at all accessible. As it stands, his choices are gravel or swamp grass. Apologies to Ms. Aine, but the rain *has* done a job on the lawns."

"Don't I know it." Gabriel replied, frowning at the spiderweb of gray gravel and the sloping expanse of grass that was more marsh than lawn. "Look," he said. "It would be a lot of time and money. But of course I'd get it done, if I thought it would help. Only, since the doctors refuse to clear him to even walk, never mind ride, he doesn't ask to come down, and I think maybe the horses make everything worse. He says he just wants to stay in and"—he glanced sideways as if betraying the darkest of secrets—"watch *Doctor Who* reruns."

"Jesus." Reed widened their eyes in mock horror. "*Doctor Who?* Say it isn't so." They exhaled hard. "Well. He's coming off a big disappointment. His body will catch up before his mind does. He's probably still in shock. Give him time. But," Reed added quickly as Gabriel started to turn away, "give him the opportunity, too. Of course he's not going to ask, when it's obvious the rest of you are up to your earlobes in to-do lists."

"Eyeballs. I think it's 'up to your eyeballs.'"

"Not where I come from." Reed pressed on. "New paths would be a lot of work and a lot of money, but they'd also be a farm upgrade benefitting both your brother and, long term, the horses. I think they'd thank you for it."

"You don't know Peter very well."

I'd like to know him better. Reed sternly quashed the thought. *Now is not the time, Androku.*

"He's more likely to get angry at the interference and not talk to me for six months," Gabriel added, shaking his head. "But you're right. He's like a badger in a hole up there. I redid his room for sleeping, rented a fancy van for going to town, but didn't really think hard on the time in between. Peter's always kept himself busy." Gabriel acknowledged quietly, "He's never liked the big house much. He'd always be down here at the barns, when he wasn't away. You're right. I'll do some research after dinner, see if I can find an accessibility-rated composite."

Reed hoped the heat they felt rising up their neck didn't show. "Actually, I did a little research." Late-night insomnia always led to out-of-control googling. "And sent some emails. Turns out there are several suitable products that meet ADA standards. I'd, uh, I'd be happy to forward what I found."

Peter and Gabriel might not look much alike, but they shared the same slightly baffled frown that Reed hoped meant *I'm listening even though I suspect you're wasting my time* but possibly just meant *You're wasting my time.*

"Thank you, Androku," Gabriel said. His brow wrinkled. "That would be very helpful."

———

SENIOR WAS WAITING in his office, which was impossibly more cluttered with paperwork than the last time Reed had been there. Reed side-eyed the gleaming coffee maker but figured the chances of getting a cup were low. They were pleased to see that—even though Senior's large personality made the space seem smaller—the changes they'd noticed during that early morning with Peter were still in place. There was a bright rectangle on the wood floor where a rug, now gone, had probably lived for decades. All extraneous furniture had been cleared out of the room, leaving behind only Senior's low desk and the built-ins, filled with books and trophies, lining the walls. If Senior ever used an office chair, it wasn't in the room.

He stood behind the old desk, arms crossed, staring down his nose at a small package on the blotter. The package was rectangular, the size of a shoebox, and wrapped neatly in brown parcel paper. Senior was looking at the box the way Reed looked the June bugs that had come creeping into Barn A with the warming weather. And Reed thought June bugs were one of God's ugliest mistakes.

"Androku," Senior huffed, stabbing a finger at the parcel on his desk. "This came for *you*. To *my* house."

Reed didn't recognize the spidery writing on the brown paper, but the international stamps were unmistakable. A spike of unease clenched behind their ribs.

"I'm sorry, Mr. Griffin. I don't know how—My mail comes to a P.O. box in town. I'd never give out your private address as my own."

"It's from overseas. *Russia.*"

The last word was said with a distaste that woke Reed's temper. Good. Anger felt so much better than regret.

Anything was better than the guilt the sight of those international stamps woke in Reed's gut.

"So am I, Mr. Griffin." Reed pointed out with some emphasis. "From Russia, I mean. And proud to be so."

"Until I saw the stamps, I thought it might be a threat. Come to my house!" His voice cracked on the last syllable. If Reed hadn't already known Senior was an angry bastard, they might have thought the man was honestly afraid. Of a package?

But of course he wasn't afraid. Senior probably didn't even know what fear was.

I need this job, Reed reminded themself. *This is a good place. My herd is happy here. I need this job.*

"No, Mr. Griffin. I'm sure it's very safe. May I have my package, please?"

They regarded each other across piles of paper stacked haphazardly on the old desk. For a second Reed thought Senior would actually refuse. But then he shrugged.

"All right, take it. But I don't want to find any more of your mail on my front porch, understand?"

"Yes, Mr. Griffin, I understand. Thank you."

Reed grabbed up the parcel and exited the office as quickly as manners allowed. It was lighter than Reed expected, the paper rough in their hands. And, yes, underneath the paper was surely a shoebox. But even up close, the handwriting was not one they recognized.

Anxiety squeezed again, like a fist on a sponge. They lengthened their stride down the hall, eager to escape. But the muted sound of the Eleventh Doctor's voice coming from within the front parlor made Reed pause.

He says he just wants to stay in and watch Doctor Who *reruns.*

The front parlor had a new door, recently hung from

the look of it, generic and out of place in the two-hundred-year-old home. The door was firmly shut against the rest of the house and probably, Reed hazarded a guess, against the rest of the world.

The parcel under Reed's arm demanded immediate attention, and the closed door was a statement so pointed as to be too on the nose, but somehow instead of doing the smart thing and running home, Reed knocked.

It was a solid thump against a flimsy composite door. The door rattled gently in its generic frame. Reed waited. There was no sound from within other than Matt Smith's proper English vowels. But Reed thought they caught a glimpse of shifting light underneath the door's bottom, a shadow approaching and then receding again.

Reed knocked a second time. It was the kind of knock that was meant to say: *I know you're hiding in there!* and *Your mare still looks for you every day!* and *Though we all wish it otherwise,* Doctor Who *can't solve everything, and you know it.*

"Androku?" Senior growled, making Reed jump and bite back a curse. How was it possible the man had snuck up from behind—in paddock boots, for God's sake—without making a sound? "You still here? Why are you still here?"

On the other side of the closed door, the television suddenly went quiet.

"Just leaving," Reed said, and made a hasty exit.

———

ONCE INSIDE THEIR apartment above Barn A, Reed set the parcel on the kitchen counter and regarded it suspiciously. The brown parcel paper was a strange, outdated aesthetic. The international stamps suggested it had been sent Russian Post, which explained the date.

"October? You've been traveling for quite a while." They squinted at the writing. Reed's mother had a school-teacher's perfect hand. Besides, she'd never waste her money on something so frivolous as international mail. But she was the only one who knew Tulip Farm's address. She'd demanded it when Reed had decided to relocate. For safety's sake, she said, and in case of a family emergency.

But she'd never give it out without asking Reed first. Would she? No. She wouldn't risk her only child that way.

Still, someone had tracked Reed down. The proof was sitting right there on the kitchen counter.

There was a bottle of Stoli in the freezer. The vodka would help with the embarrassing shake in their fingers. But it wasn't Wednesday. Reed had responsibilities waiting for them downstairs.

They grabbed the knife from their belt. The handle was familiar, reassuring. Gradually the shakes eased up. When their hands were steady again, Reed used the knife to trim away brown paper.

Beneath the wrapping Reed found a shoebox, just as they'd expected. Battered cardboard was adorned with an orange Nike swoosh. Sturdy packing tape kept the lid in place. Rough travel had crumpled the box's corners and left several small divots, but otherwise it seemed to have survived the journey intact.

A lucky thing that it had made it at all. Russian Post was notoriously undependable. What wasn't lost was often stolen.

Reed cut the tape with a few flicks of their blade. Then they sheathed the knife back on their belt and took a deep breath. It really wasn't fair that after so much time, Moscow still felt dangerous. It took all of their courage to lift the lid.

The first thing Reed saw was a crisp white envelope, their name written in a messy black Sharpie scrawl across the front: R. Androku. Reed picked it up, set it carefully aside. Beneath the envelope was a large Ziploc bag containing a small stack of what looked like old Polaroids.

The mouth of the bag was folded over twice and taped shut. Someone had taken care to make sure the photos were safe. Reed swallowed hard. They placed the bag on the counter next to the envelope and reached for the last item in the shoebox.

It was a T-shirt, soft with age and use, neatly folded. Reed recognized it at once, even before they held it up and the folds relaxed to reveal the Pink Jones logo printed across the front, the old tour dates listed across the back. Except for the frankly ugly color—a blue so bright it made Reed's eyes water—it was twin to their own.

Fuck, who were they kidding? It wasn't the frankly horrendous color spoiling Reed's mascara, making helpless tears run in tracks down their cheeks. It was grief, still as painfully fresh as if it were brand new, not a decade old, and it was tenderness, and it was regret.

Reed pressed the shirt to their face and inhaled. Their lungs hitched. It hurt to breathe.

The shirt still smelled like Michael, of Old Spice and cigarettes and, faintly, of the oranges he'd carried in the pockets of his coat and eaten like candy.

"Michael," Reed said, muffled, into the shirt. "I can't take any more of your surprises, *lyubimiy*."

Michael didn't answer. Of course he didn't, because Michael was five long years dead and Reed didn't believe in ghosts.

Inside the envelope was a card with a picture of Van Gogh's sunflowers on the front. Michael had adored Van Gogh. His favorite had been *Laboureur dans un champ*, the view from Van Gogh's hospital window. Reed had never understood why that one until it was too late.

The note scrawled on the card was in English.

Reed— Your mother says that America is treating you very well. I'm glad. Now that Papa is gone, Mama is selling our house in the country and moving to a small apartment in the city. I found these in the attic when we were cleaning; Mama won't know to miss them, and I think Michael would want you to have them. —Isabella

Isabella was Michael's youngest sister. Reed had never paid her much attention. She'd been sixteen to Reed and Michael's twenty. Back then, four years had seemed like an unbridgeable gap. That she cared to do Reed any kindness after what had happened was a small miracle.

They took the T-shirt and the Ziploc bag to the couch. When Reed pulled at the tape, the plastic bag tore down the middle. The Polaroids scattered across Reed's lap. Reed gathered them up one by one, careful to touch the corners and not the film. Reed had given Michael a Polaroid camera for Christmas their last year in Saint Petersburg, and after that it had been all about documenting their final semester together in university.

Documenting their time alone together, too, but Reed had made Michael destroy those photos before they left SPBU. Michael had been a fool to take them in the first place.

"I want something for my cock to remember you by," he'd teased. "Three months in America is a long time."

"Six years in prison for distribution of pornography is much longer." Ignoring his loud protests, Reed had snatched the photos from Michael's hand, tossed them into the small grate that warmed Michael's room in the winter, lit a match. The photos went up in a rush of blue flame.

The Polaroids Isabella had saved from her father's attic were completely harmless. Group shots, for the most part, taken during those last few months when Michael had carried the camera with him everywhere.

Their rugby team posed in front of the Twelve Colleges, blue-and-white uniforms bright against red brick, Michael's arm slung around Reed's narrow shoulders. A handful of Michael's drinking buddies, Reed among them, leaning on the bar at Tower Pub, huge smiles on their faces. The club crowd inside Blue Oyster, all the colors of the rainbow, Reed dancing center frame, eyes closed, head thrown back, a white feather boa wrapped around their neck and shoulders.

Reed remembered that night. Reed remembered every minute they'd spent with Michael, in a group or otherwise.

Tucked behind the group photos were several snapshots of quiet moments spent alone. One Reed had taken of Michael reading a book beneath a birch tree in Sosnovka Park, late evening turning his short white-blond hair into a cap of shadows. One of Reed laughing in the snow in front of the Winter Palace—he'd just thrown a snowball Michael's way and missed terribly. Reed balanced on horse-back over a jump at the Bitsa Equestrian Club. Reed spread-eagled and on the mattress in Michael's back-alley apartment, blissfully asleep, threadbare jeans twisted and riding down almost beneath their hips.

That last was close enough to porn that Reed would have burned it with the others had they known it existed. It shocked them that Isabella had included the photo with the rest. Maybe she was more like her brother than Reed remembered.

"Proud," Reed whispered, running one thumb gently around the snapshot of Michael in front of the palace. "Sentimental. And careless, to leave me behind with your messes, yes, *lyubimiy*?"

They hated that their breath caught on the last syllable. It had been a long time since Reed had cried for Michael, and they didn't plan to start again now. Knuckling back traitorous tears, they gathered up the Polaroids and returned them to the shoebox.

The shoebox went into the bottom drawer of the bedroom armoire where—beneath a pile of neatly folded jeans—Reed kept important things like their passport, a bundle of emergency cash rolled in an old sock, and a picture of their father.

Then Reed took Michael's T-shirt with them to the refrigerator and the comfort of vodka.

CHAPTER SEVEN

Peter was working on the Sunday morning crossword when Kate stuck her head into his room without knocking first.

"Androku's here and asking for you."

"Is there an emergency?" Peter made a point of not looking up. He was stuck on three down, QUICK BOARD MEETING? (10 LETTERS), and feeling sour about it. He'd slept only in fits and starts the night before, which was nothing new, but the dark hours had seemed even longer than usual, the dark thoughts louder. At dawn he'd made the switch from bed to chair, but that change in position hadn't eased the ache in his bones or the pounding behind his eyes.

"I'd say so. It stinks like sweaty, unwashed man in here. You ask me, it's time to call 911 on your hygiene, baby brother."

She wasn't wrong. Peter could smell himself. But since Mac had fled back to New York, Peter's shower schedule had become unreliable. He either had to wait on Gabriel's free time for help or manage the task himself, and lately energy was very hard to come by. What reserves he had left after a night of tossing and turning were spent on rehab and Teddy's masochistic tendencies.

"Mum's making Reed a sandwich and then I'm sending them in," Kate warned. "You've got five minutes. Maybe do something with your hair or, I don't know, shave that half-arsed beard."

He did look up then, thinking he preferred her tears to her recent bout of nagging. That, too, was Teddy's fault, for pointing out that he wasn't in fact a toddler and should be expected to handle the majority of his self-care. And Mac's fault, too, for running off, because now Kate drove him to rehab, and over the past few weeks, she and Teddy had become thick as thieves.

"Fuck you, Katie," he said in his best glacier tone.

"Right back at you," she called in reply, leaving his door open as she disappeared down the hall. "At least brush your teeth."

Peter didn't brush his teeth or shave the scruff from his face. The bathroom just seemed too far away. But he did scrub a hand through his hair, which had gotten longer than he liked and tended to stick up in tufts. And he adjusted the blanket on his lap to hide the coffee stains on his pajamas from when he'd bobbled his mug at breakfast. Then he stared warily at the open door.

He preferred that door closed, the way it had been when Androku—Reed—had knocked a week ago.

He just wanted to be left alone. But the rest of the world seemed dead set against cooperating. His family had an excuse. Family was meant to stick together, even to the point of intolerability. But Reed was a stranger and an employee. Peter didn't need their interference on top of everything else.

Cheerful whistling preceded his unwelcome guest

down the hall. Peter thought he recognized the tune. "Patience" by Guns N' Roses?

"I'm beginning to sense a theme," he greeted Reed with a scowl. "Which is surprising. You really don't look like the hair metal type."

"Don't be rude. The term is glam metal," Reed corrected archly. They were carrying a lunch plate in each hand. Peter recognized his mum's famous egg salad sandwich. His stomach, neglected since breakfast, immediately let out an angry rumble.

"Ms. Aine said you'd be hungry." Reed unloaded a plate and fork on the hospital table next to Peter's crossword before propping themself up against the wall and digging into their own portion. "And I like all sorts of music, but a good rock ballad gets me every time."

If only to quiet his stomach, Peter tucked into lunch. "'Good' would be the sticking point," he said around a mouthful of egg salad and toasted bread.

"There's no accounting for tastes. Holy Jesus, this is fantastic." Reed closed their eyes in appreciation. "Death by carbohydrates but so worth it. Your mother knows how to do comfort food."

Peter paused in chewing to study the Russian, wondering if Reed was in need of comfort food. Aine had a particular knack when it came to feeding the barn staff, producing birthday treats on the regular, pitchers of lemonade on the hottest summer days, and pots of warm stew in the worst winter weather, all seemingly without any foreknowledge. She called it culinary second sight, and blushed when Senior teased her about it.

She'd been tempting Peter's reluctant appetite with a variety of his favorite meals since he'd returned home. And egg salad sandwiches had been at the top of his list since before he could ride.

But now that he took a look at his unwelcome guest, Peter couldn't help but wonder. Reed seemed somehow subdued, despite the periwinkle-blue breeches and matching silk scarf knotted around their throat. Maybe it was the shadows like bruises under Reed's eyes, made no less visible by a heavy application of silver mascara. Maybe it was their faintly flattened smile, or the way they slumped against the wall as if in need of support.

Peter felt a pang of sympathetic curiosity and chased it away with a mouthful of deviled egg. They ate together in a silence that should have been awkward but instead bordered on companionable until Peter scraped the last crumb from his plate and was forced to face the fact that ignoring Reed hadn't made them disappear.

"What do you want?"

Reed licked a daub of dill and mayo from their lower lip. The tip of their tongue was very pink, their lips tinted red, fuller than Peter remembered. Warmth flared low in Peter's belly, surprising him.

Desire. The body-wide twist of lust that coiled just below his belly button. His cock, having spent the weeks since the accident mostly dormant, twitched.

"I'm busy," Peter gritted out, adjusting the blanket on his lap. The very last thing he wanted to think about was sex.

"I can see that," Reed replied easily. "Three down is 'speed chess,' by the way. Fun puzzle. I finished it this morning." They tossed Peter a wink, then turned somber. "Look, I won't take up much of your time. But I wanted to show you something. Now that you've eaten." They reached into the back pocket of their breeches and pulled out their phone. "I thought, if you won't come down to the barn, I'll bring the barn to you."

They opened a video on the screen, held the phone out. "Just press play."

Peter wanted to swat the phone away. But Reed's expression was so hopeful. And the lines of sleeplessness around the Russian's eyes felt like a personal rebuke. Peter knew what it felt like to lie awake at night waiting for the dawn.

So he took the phone and pressed play. Then he inhaled sharply.

It was Annie. He'd expected that, guessed the game Reed was playing. He hadn't expected to see his mare fully tacked up, Reed in the saddle, the supple, long-limbed trot that had made Peter fall in love with Annie as a filly on full display.

"Beautiful." John's voice. He must have been filming. He was obviously impressed. Peter couldn't blame him. "Sound and strong. She's already putting some muscle back on."

"She likes to work," agreed Reed from the saddle, face hidden by the shadow of their helmet. They had a very good seat and light hands. Annie moved forward, relaxed and happy. "Also the organic beet pulp. She really likes the beet pulp."

"Dressage," said Peter, eyes fixed on the screen.

"What?"

"Your background is dressage?" It hadn't occurred to Peter until then to wonder. Rehabbing a horse was one thing, riding another. But Reed was a beautiful rider, displaying a grace and confidence that spoke of a lifetime in the saddle. "I didn't realize you were competition level. Classically trained?"

Reed laughed. The unselfconscious, happy sound made Peter look up. Amusement chased some of the weariness from Reed's eyes, straightened their shoulders.

"If you say so. Dressage at Bitsa, yes. Also, sometimes the steeple chase. But before that it was herding and roping on the family farm. When American beef came to our city, my father was first in line. He loved his cattle, and his horses."

The Equestrian Centre Bitsa had been built in Moscow for the 1980 Olympics. A huge complex boasting both indoor and outdoor arenas, and dormitories for live-in students, it still housed several very selective riding schools. Peter had competed against more than one Bitsa graduate and come away from each experience a better rider for the competition.

"Kate didn't tell me you were at Bitsa."

Reed only shrugged. "I left that behind when I came to America." The corners of their mouth quirked in a real smile. "But if Bitsa means you're impressed enough to see what I can do on your mare, who am I to argue?" They tilted their head, brows raised coquettishly. The silver mascara on their lashes sparkled. "Come down to the barn. I'll have John tack her up. You won't regret it."

Peter looked from the phone still in his hand to the crossword on the table.

"All right," he relented, suppressing a shiver. Fear, or anticipation? "Let's go. But don't touch my handlebars unless I ask for help, understood? I need to do this myself."

"Wouldn't dream of it," the Russian replied easily. "I like to watch your hands on the wheels."

———

I LIKE to watch your hands on the wheels.

All the way down to Barn A, the words echoed in Peter's head. He couldn't stop thinking about the way Reed had looked when they'd dropped that little bomb. Grin deepened to a smirk—they had a dimple like a thumbprint that only showed itself when Reed really smiled—the dart of their tongue again across their lower lip. Which undoubtedly meant Peter hadn't hid his interest very well at all. Reed must have noticed. And was the Russian actually flirting?

It sure felt like flirting, Peter decided as he wheeled out of the house, down Gabriel's ramp. It used to be he could spot potential hookup material from a mile away. Maybe because he'd had plenty of "fuck me yes please" invitations, and none of them had been subtle. He was an athlete, after all, with an athlete's well-cared-for body. Fame had been an incidental added attraction. For a while it had seemed like everyone wanted a piece of whatever the US Equestrian Team's youngest World Cup winner had to offer, and Peter hadn't said no very often. He liked sex, had a healthy appetite for pleasure.

But things were different now. His world had been turned upside down and been torn apart. He could barely stand on his own, let alone walk. His battered brain wouldn't let him rest, and after googling "NFL" and "CTE," he seemed to have forgotten how to sleep. Sex was out of the question. Even if his cock was willing, the rest of his body was dragging far behind.

"Loch Ness at twelve o'clock," Reed announced casually, startling Peter out of his thoughts.

He'd chosen the grass slope down to the barns because the gravel pathways were impossible to navigate on his own even with the new, thicker outdoor tires on his chair. And in

midsummer the lawn probably wouldn't have been a problem. But the heavy spring rains had saturated the ground
and collected in large puddles wherever the slope leveled
out. The water didn't look like it was going to dry up
anytime soon. Gabriel had said something about ground
water and climate change turning the lawn into a Florida
swamp, but Peter hadn't paid his brother any attention.

"Swear I saw Nessie stick her head out just this morning. Looked hungry and pissed about it. Wouldn't get close
to the bigger puddles if I were you."

Reed's gentle teasing softened a depressing truth. There
was little to no chance he'd make it the rest of the way down
the sodden lawn without getting his tires stuck in mud,
rolling into an uncontrolled slide, or—Peter grimaced—overturning, possibly into one of the several lake-size puddles
spread over the lawn. The thought made him feel cold. The
very last thing he wanted to do was make contact again with
unforgiving ground.

Reed offered, "Gabriel said something about hoses and
a vacuum truck, but there's more rain in the forecast next
week so I'm thinking it's a build a boat and load the animals
two by two proposition."

"Senior must be pissed." Peter flexed his fingers on his
rims. The riding gloves he'd chosen to protect his hands
from blisters were a familiar comfort. "He's always been
obsessive about that lawn."

Reed didn't reply. The afternoon sun beat down on the
top of Peter's head, on his shoulders, on the blanket he still
wore on his lap and over his elevated leg. The grass
steamed. Down at Barn A, a horse whinnied annoyance. It
sounded like Annie. He knew her frustration as well as his
own, maybe better.

"That difficult to ask, is it?" Reed wondered quietly.

Peter stared up at the clear blue sky until his eyes stung. "Easier with family. At least I know what to expect." Pity from Kate, tasteless jokes from Mac, distracted resignation from Gabriel.

"I used to be afraid of the diving platform off Lake Baikal, where my mother would take me to swim during summer vacation. None of my friends were frightened by the height, only me. And I couldn't be the only jellyfish in our group, you know?"

"I think you mean chicken."

"Jellyfish, chicken, whatever. Coward. I couldn't be the only coward among my friends, so one day when I'd just turned ten and felt like it was time to be brave. I climbed the ladder all the way to the top of the platform. Two meters up, my body shaking the entire way. And when I finally looked out over the edge at the water below, I knew I couldn't do it. I just didn't have the guts, the courage."

Peter's heart was beating quickly in sympathy, echoing in his skull. He'd never been overly fond of heights himself. "What did you do?"

"I closed my eyes," Reed told him. "And jumped. And it wasn't so bad as I thought. Maybe not fun, a little painful when I hit the water, but not intolerable. I climbed the platform many more times that summer, and none of my friends ever called me a jellyfish again."

Painful, but not intolerable. Peter nodded once and closed his eyes. He took a deep breath, exhaled through his nose. The question came out as rough as the ground beneath his wheels.

"Would you mind pushing my fucking chair down the fucking gravel to my fucking barn?"

Asking for help still felt an awful lot like jumping out

over empty space, and his ego suffered, but Reed wasn't wrong. It was easier to do blind.

"My pleasure," replied Reed. They sounded like they meant it.

———

JUST AS REED HAD PROMISED, John had Annie tacked up and waiting in the crossties, ready to go. She turned her head when Reed pushed Peter through the barn door, ears pricked forward. When she saw Peter she nickered low in her throat, the same enthusiastic greeting he'd become accustomed to hearing at least twice a day for the last six years of his life.

Unwanted tears stung his eyes. He wiped them away angrily with the edge of his sleeve, glad he and Reed were the only people in the aisle. He could hear John whistling in the arena. Somehow it didn't matter that Reed saw his regret, but John was another story.

Annie nickered again. She pawed the ground, eyes and ears directed Peter's way.

"She's looking for a sugar cube," Peter told Reed gruffly. "Treats before work, I know it's a bad habit, but I never could resist her begging. Would you mind? There should be plenty in that trunk there." Annie's competition trunk. The last time Peter had seen it was in Old Salem. Now it sat against the wall in Barn A, gleaming a cheerful cobalt, recently wiped down.

But obviously Reed knew where the sugar cubes were kept, Peter realized as the Russian popped the tack trunk lid, reached inside, and came back with the container used to hold Annie's treats. Reed offered it to Peter, a question in their dark eyes.

"I'm also a firm believer of treats before work," Reed said. "But I call them bribes."

Peter smiled despite himself. He held out his hand. Reed shook two cubes onto the palm of his glove.

Peter looked at Annie. Annie scraped a hoof on the ground. Bad manners, but Peter had always indulged.

"She didn't spook at the chair last time you were here," Reed volunteered. "Just watch your leg."

"Is part of your holistic approach mind reading?" Honestly, the Russian always seemed to be one step ahead. It was equally disconcerting and impressive.

"No. It's just the first thing I'd worry about, in your place." Reed shrugged, stuck their hands in the back pockets of their breeches. The fluorescent barn light highlighted the lines of exhaustion on Reed's face, and again Peter felt a stab of empathy that he quickly buried.

He hardly knew Reed. The Russian wasn't family, or a teammate. And Peter was no longer team captain, expected to ease his colleagues over any emotional bumps in the road. Whatever was wearing at Reed, it wasn't Peter's problem.

"She's not worried." A glance across Annie's topline and he could see how relaxed she was. His new wheels, his awkwardly protruding leg, meant nothing to the mare. The sugar in his hand was another matter.

Carefully, just in case she changed her mind at the last second, Peter wheeled forward until he was perpendicular to her front. He still didn't have the skills to maneuver the chair one-handed, so the sugar cubes got crushed some against his rims, but that didn't matter. Annie lowered her head as he approached, licking her lips eagerly.

Submission, Senior would say. But Peter knew it was simple greed. His star F.E.I. mare was a stomach on four legs.

She gobbled up the crumbles of sugar in his hand, then licked the palm of his glove clean.

"She looks good," Peter admitted grudgingly. Not that he wished otherwise, or even resented Reed for being right. But it was hard accepting that Annie, just like everyone else in his life, might go on unchanged while he was still stuck in limbo.

And wasn't that a shitty attitude, he thought, *and aren't you a sick fuck to have it?*

Annie lowered her big head toward his lap. Automatically, he reached up to scratch her ears. The brace around his shoulder pulled in warning, but the pain in his collarbone was tolerable, the bone slowly healing.

"Better even than last I saw her," he added. "Put on some muscle. Radiographs on the leg?"

"Scheduled for next week, just to be sure, though she's completely sound. And it's mostly fat she's put on. But that's okay. Weight's good. The rest will come back. Shall I hop on?"

Peter nodded. He backed off, allowing Reed room to work, and found himself looking directly at the Russian's arse. It was a nice arse, firm from years spent in the saddle, and it definitely fell under the category of unwanted distractions.

Fuck.

He blamed Mac for putting the idea in his head in the first place.

"The last time I saw you staring at someone's arse that way, it was Samantha Linell at Green's Bar during Dublin trials, and you had her—and also her groom, what was his name?—in your bed by the next morning."

"Flash is too tight, loosen it one hole," Peter said gruffly, willing his body to stand down. "She likes some movement.

And check her girth, she'll fool you by blowing out if she can."

That last thing was the sort of horse trick that would fool an amateur, not a graduate of Bitsa. Reed, to their credit, didn't bristle. They loosened the flash around Annie's mouth and adjusted the girth up two holes.

"Good," Peter conceded when Reed arched an eyebrow his direction. "But don't let her bully you down the aisle. She'll try. She always tries."

Reed made a noise that sounded suspiciously like a smothered laugh before putting on their helmet, unhooking the mare from the crossties, and leading her down the aisle. Peter tried not to resent the muffled amusement. He was grateful for the care Reed took in walking Annie through the barn. She did indeed try to bully the Russian, turning her head sharply toward Reed's shoulder, teeth bared—but only once. Reed stopped her with a sharp "No!" and a light slap of the reins against her chest. Annie immediately recalled her ground manners. Peter realized it wasn't the first time she'd tested Reed's limits and lost.

John met them at the arena gate, rake in hand. He brightened when he saw Peter, then panicked visibly when he realized there was no way Peter's chair would make it across the deep arena footing to the risers opposite.

"Hook that gate open," Peter suggested as Reed walked Annie into the arena. "I'll watch from here. I'm sure Androku won't let her dive for home. Right, Androku?"

"Certainly not." Reed checked Annie's girth a second time before making use of the mounting block Gabriel had hammered together out of reclaimed Connecticut barn wood when they were still children.

The Russian had Annie in a dressage saddle, with a deeper seat and longer leg flap than Peter's close-contact jumping saddle. Annie had been schooled in basic dressage —Aine subscribed to the European theory that dressage work increased a horse's balance and flexibility, so every working horse on the Tulip Farm string knew a twenty-meter circle long before they ever stepped over a jump.

Peter, while acknowledging that the practice was sound, secretly thought riding dressage was more boring than watching flies on manure. He hadn't given up the work, that would have been both stupid and lazy. But he had given up the tack, riding Annie in his comfortable Voltaire jumping saddle even when schooling dressage. Aine, knowing her youngest child's limits, had pretended not to notice.

But Annie didn't seem to mind Reed's saddle, or the dressage pad blinged-out all along the edge with tiny crystals, or Reed's seat, or Reed's hands. She looked completely at ease as Reed urged her away from the mounting block, already relaxing long and low into a swinging walk.

She looked happy.

"I prefer to warm her up from the saddle, when I can," Reed explained. "I get a better feel of a horse when I'm on their back. The lunge line is for strengthening work, in my opinion, and the legs are for warm-up."

Peter looked down and away, acutely conscious of his own leg in its fiberglass cast.

Reed, possibly realizing their gaffe, hurried on. "But I asked John to warm her up on the line for me this afternoon. I wasn't sure how much of your time you'd be willing to give, but I figured I could lure you down here for at least a few minutes, once you saw the video."

Lure? Peter wasn't sure whether to be annoyed or intrigued. But the wink Reed sent him as Annie circled past tipped him over to reluctantly amused. Reed definitely didn't suffer from low self-esteem.

"Right. Your cunning trap worked." It was difficult to sound annoyed when Annie was going around the arena at an absolutely gorgeous trot, not a single bad step in the bunch. A flicker of satisfaction threatened to melt some of the ice he'd worked so hard to build around his heart. "She looks sound. How does she feel?"

"Fantastic." Reed sent Annie into a leg yield across the diagonal. She responded to the pressure without hesitation, straight and supple. "But I think that's obvious."

Peter folded his arms. "We'll see. Look, you've got a beautiful seat for dressage, but this mare's a jumper. She's used to more room. Come off her back just a little bit, that's right, and this time when you take her across use more calf and less thigh. She'll like you better for it."

Reed did as Peter suggested. Annie, allowed to move forward, began to swing her shoulders. Peter watched her minutely for any sign of pain or stress but saw only a solid forward trot and a soft eye.

"You're grinning," Reed pointed out as the pair passed again. "I don't think I've ever seen you smile like that. It's my beautiful seat, isn't it?"

"You know it's not." He *was* grinning. He thought he'd forgotten how. "Although I do like to watch your hands on the reins." Hadn't he just promised himself no distractions? But the line was ripe for the taking, and wasn't it worth it when Reed almost bobbled those same reins in response?

"Was that—are you flirting with me, Peter Griffin? Because as your employee, I should warn you that's sexual harassment."

"I wasn't. Besides which, you work for my sister, not me," Peter decided. He tapped the gloved fingers of one hand on his wheelchair. "Pay attention to what you're doing," he coached. "Good. Very good. You're the rehab guru—"

"Holistic consultant."

"—so I'm relying on you to tell me when she's had enough, but if you think she's got it in her, I'd like to see the canter."

CHAPTER EIGHT

"Listen, young man, I've been branding Tulip Farm's weanlings for twenty-five years, and Senior will tell you there's none better at doing it quickly and painlessly."

Reed didn't budge from where they leaned casually against the weanling turnout gate, effectively blocking the vet from his quarry beyond. Doc Holliday, a grizzled mountain of muscle dressed exactly like Reed imagined James Herriot must have on the Yorkshire Dales, in a waxed-canvas coat and thigh-high Wellies, did look as though he had been branding babies for several decades and relished the job.

For the most part, Reed had managed to stay out of Holliday's way since starting work on the farm. The staff knew that Senior and the old veterinarian were bosom buddies, that Holliday had cared for Senior's horses before Tulip Farm was even a twinkle in Aine's eye. Holliday wasn't a bad man, but he was set in his ways, and as far as Reed was concerned, some of those ways—like applying molten iron to an unsuspecting weanling's rump just for purposes of identification—definitely deserved to be thrown out with the trash.

"Senior made the branding appointment months ago. Ten o'clock on Wednesday the twelfth, eight weanlings," Holliday continued, glaring down his nose at Reed. "It's Wednesday the twelfth, ten o'clock sharp. The eight weanlings are right there as expected." He pointed a bony finger past Reed's shoulder at the pasture beyond. "I expect Senior to show at any moment, and I'd like to get on with the job before he does."

Reed happened to know that Gabriel Sr. was busy dealing with the construction crew plus backhoe that had arrived after breakfast, a full three days earlier than expected. Two days too early for the McAuley-Griffin clan, none of whom had yet ginned up the courage to tell Peter the farm landscaping was about to be expensively read-justed for his benefit.

"Ms. Griffin's on her way down," Reed explained for the second time. "Senior's been held up." The weanlings were Kate's responsibility, after all, and thank Jesus for that because Kate was an open-minded person who understood that change was usually for the better.

Unlike inflexible old geezers who insisted on blinking like a sunstruck owl when Reed explained they were nonbi-nary. But Reed would put up with being misgendered on a (*fucking*) Wednesday morning so long as they could save the eight foals from a branding.

Besides, Reed suspected blocking snarly old Doc Holl-iday from the pasture was a cakewalk compared to the family fiasco up at the main house.

"Oh, listen!" Reed cheerfully interrupted Holliday's grumbling. "Here she comes. Just as I promised, yes?"

The shrill snarl of Kate's Honda dirt bike reached them

a full thirty seconds before she came into view, speeding along the fence line as if all the hounds of hell were behind her. The weanlings and the two old geldings that served as full-time babysitters scattered across the grass, snorting and squealing in delight. They weren't afraid of the little machine. Like most of the farm equipment, they'd been exposed to it every day of their lives.

Reed had told Kate several times that if she insisted on riding like an idiot, she should at least wear a helmet, but she always retorted helmets were for riding horses and that she never took the little motorcycle on pavement anyway.

"Sorry, Doc!" Pulling up alongside the gate, Kate quieted the bike and hopped off, brushing flyaway strands of dark hair from her eyes. "Bit of a to-do up at the house this morning. Da sends his regards." She took in Reed spread casually but firmly across the gate, the weanling halter in Doc's hand, and the branding bucket already set out on the grass. "No time to waste. You've got the microchips in the truck, I assume?"

Doc scowled at Reed. "Figured I'd brand 'em first, Ms. Kate."

"Oh, we're not doing that anymore." Smiling sweetly, she took the small halter from Holliday's hand and passed it to Reed. "It's just not cost effective to do both. And the microchip's required for competition everywhere now. I know Da must have spoken to you about the change when he made the appointment. He's very excited about the new technology."

None of the three of them believed that for an instant, but Holliday wouldn't dare contradict Kate. The babies were her business. Plus, she'd turned up the McAuley charm past eleven, all soft Irish lilt and wide violet eyes over a stubborn jaw. Doc Holliday knew better than to tangle with Aine's children. Probably he'd complain about Kate to his wife over dinner, but it certainly didn't stop him from admiring her breasts when she bent to grab the branding bucket and her button-down shirt pulled tight.

Lecherous old man, Reed thought in disgust.

Kate shot Reed a narrow look over her shoulder as she herded Holliday toward his truck.

"Androku. We'll start with Jasmine's filly. Thank you."

"Yes, ma'am." Reed slipped through the gate and obediently marched in the direction of Jasmine's chestnut foal, a pretty little thing with lots of chrome who happened to be standing all the way on the other side of the turnout. Which meant Reed had plenty of time to cool off before they had to smile at Doc Holliday again.

———

"CALL ME MA'AM EVER AGAIN and I'll revoke your coffee privileges," Kate told Reed as they watched the vet's truck bounce away at last toward the main road.

It had taken a good two hours, but all eight babies were chipped, their personal ID numbers entered into the handheld scanner Holliday had needed help turning on. The miniscule computer chips, about the size of a grain of rice, were inserted under the skin in a horse's neck by way of a syringe. None of the weanlings had managed to stand still for that unhappy poke, but an injection was much less painful than hot iron, and much less invasive. The small herd had already forgotten the passing trauma and were grazing happily under a copse of shade trees.

"Sorry." The morning was finally turning from mild to warm. Reed closed their eyes briefly and lifted their face skyward, grateful for the sun. "Don't know what I was thinking. That man makes me feel twelve again, all elbows and knees and spots on my face."

"He makes everyone feel twelve. That's why he's still working the farm. No one has the balls to fire him. Most of us don't have the balls needed just to say no to him, but you did. Wait until I tell Peter. He's always been secretly terrified of Doc, ever since he was five and Doc asked him to sit on Cricket's head to keep her down in case she woke up in the middle of sewing her tongue back together. That pony was always eating the wildest things. We never did figure how she'd split it open."

"And did she wake up?" Reed could imagine Peter as a small child, all tussled blond hair and elfin face, scowling fiercely as he did his best to assist the vet.

"No." Kate snorted. "But there was a lot of blood. Mac and I laid odds on whether Peter would faint, and Doc would have both the boy and the pony laid out in the field. Didn't, though. Peter can be stubborn as all fuck, but I guess you've figured out a way around all that."

"Have I?"

She only laughed at Reed's carefully mild expression. "John took great pleasure in telling me my little brother's been down to Barn A twice this week."

"He likes to watch Annie go." Embarrassment heated Reed's cheeks.

"Likes to watch you go, more likely." But Kate held up her hands in surrender. "Your business, Androku. I'm only saying, his good mood was a nice change, while it lasted."

Reed snuck a glance back up the hill at the main house where dump trucks and the backhoe grumbled. "That bad?"

"Gabriel told me he warned you. Peter doesn't like to be managed. Rehabbing Annie is one thing, sticking your nose in family business is another." She sighed. "Doesn't help his temper any that his neurologist wants another CT of his brain before she'll sign off on surgery to remove the pins in his ankle."

Reed resisted a nervous urge to play with the ends of their secondhand Burberry scarf. "I didn't think it would be such a large project. But," they added stubbornly, "anyone could see he was going stir-crazy stuck up at the house. Nobody else was doing anything."

"Yeah." Kate shook her head as she climbed back onto her motorcycle. "That's the thing about my family. Everything seems to go more smoothly when we ignore the elephant in the room, and by now we've got a whole bloody circus."

———

THE BACKHOE SCRAPED and the dump trucks growled for three long days, rising with the sun and stopping only as the last light faded. Strangers in hard hats and orange safety vests wandered the property, sketching out underground utilities with spray paint. One wandered down behind Barn B where they definitely didn't belong and made kissing noises at the babies until Reed gave them an earful.

"Sorry, sorry." They rolled their eyes, waving Reed off. "They're just so cute, you know. Used to have a pony when I was a kid, but it was nothing fancy like these. People who live here must be super rich, huh?" Their black hair was loose under their hard hat, falling down past their shoulders in long, silken curls. Reed wondered if they knew how easily long hair could snag in heavy equipment.

Instead of asking, they bristled and showed Hard Hat the knife on their belt. The construction worker took the hint and hustled back to work. The backhoe and the dump trucks continued to growl.

The horses hated the noise and the smell. The barn staff hated the noise and the inconvenience. Reed hated the noise, and the smell, and the inconvenience, but most of all Reed hated second-guessing decisions.

Instead of spending sleepless witching hours working on barn management, they found themself staring worriedly out the kitchen window at the main house, watching the lights in Peter's front bedroom go on and off and on again throughout the night.

On the day the construction crew began laying down huge quantities of a stabilizing crushed granite mixture—which Reed knew from their research was massively expensive—they phoned Russia in a midafternoon panic, frightening their mother who was preparing for bed.

"You've always been a bit of a busybody, my love," she said gently once she understood it was a crisis of conscious and not a medical emergency prompting the unscheduled call. "It's in the blood, your father was the same way. Remember when he drove Uncle Dima all the way into Saint Petersburg for hearing aids when Dima was just pretending to be deaf because he was bored of talking to your auntie?"

Reed remembered Uncle Dima and Auntie Lada only vaguely. But Lada was a family legend for her inability to hold her tongue, infamous for interrupting Easter service not once in her life but *four times*, so Reed felt some sympathy for Dima.

"Peter's not pretending he can't walk, Ma."

"No, of course not." Reed could hear his mother's mattress squeaking and knew she was settling against her bolster pillows with whatever book she planned to doze over before turning out the light. "Poor man."

"And when I suggested Gabriel redo the paths, I didn't realize the project would be quite so . . ."

"Gigantic?" she suggested.

"Well, yes. And disrupting. And costly. I didn't realize how much footing it would take. And with any luck he'll be out of the chair and using a walker before the month is out. No wonder he's furious. What if Gabriel's bankrupting the farm because I wanted Peter to spend more time in the barns? I shouldn't have said anything."

"Always trying to manage everyone into happiness. All because you couldn't save your papa." His mother sighed. "This is like the time you tried to convince Michael to lease a Bitsa horse when you knew his family wouldn't allow it, all so he'd spend his off hours with you at the barn. Have you got a crush on this young man?"

Reed winced. Five thousand miles away, and she still managed to hit her mark.

"I'm not a teenager, Ma." *Although lately that's been easy to forget.* "Speaking of Michael. I got a package from Isabella. I thought we were going to keep my address just between the two of us." Reed's heart beat a little faster, anxiety they thought they'd buried stirring behind their ribs.

Her sigh sounded hollow over the line. "Isabella Turgenev is a good girl. Just like her mother, Sophia. She'll keep it to herself. Besides, now that Sacha is no longer running things, I think you have nothing to worry about."

Reed rubbed a hand over the back of their neck, kneading away tension. "Maybe. But nothing is for sure. Sacha has connections. Here and there. Remember Seattle? I'd like to stay in one place for longer than a year, Ma. Please promise me you'll be careful."

Another hollow sigh. "You know I am. Always. Don't worry so much. Now," deftly she changed the subject, "you're not fooling anybody. It's obvious you like this man, this Peter. And you're very kind. Very thoughtful. It makes me proud. But sometimes the kindnesses you do are as much about yourself as anyone else. Yes?"

"Yes." The truth hurt, Reed thought, whether you were eighteen years old and apologizing to your boyfriend's angry father or twenty-five and wondering if you'd just busy-bodied yourself out of a job. "Should I apologize?"

"Depends. Would that be about making him feel better, or you?"

"Ma!"

"Maybe let the dust settle first," she suggested. Her yawn was loud in Reed's ear. "Back to work with you now, darling. It's late here and I have a new James Patterson I want to start. I'll talk to you Wednesday."

———

BY THE TIME the dust settled—*Very funny, Ma.*—and the stabilizing mixture had cured enough for even the horses to walk the new paths, Reed began to cautiously hope they weren't out of a job after all. Spring began to look more like summer. It was difficult not to be optimistic when the days were heating up. Birds were singing in the old magnolia tree outside Barn A, the grass in the turnouts, pastures, and front lawns was drying out, and it was finally warm enough to properly bathe a horse. Granite flecks made the new walkways sparkle under a clear blue sky.

Annie's radiographs came back clear, a reason for cele-bration. But Peter didn't come down to the barn. Reed firmly reminded themselves that it was Barn A they were supposed to be managing, not Peter Griffin.

Reed's small herd were experienced bathers. Only Charlie was afraid of the enclosed wash stall. None of them minded the hose, which Reed knew looked just a little too much like a snake for peace of mind. Angel liked to splash in the puddle around the slow drain. Pritchard, the silly gelding, enjoyed a blast of the hose straight between the eyes, and Ingrid tried to drink the apple cider vinegar and ylang-ylang rinse mixture Reed preferred straight from the wash bucket.

Bob and Annie stood like lambs under the hose, apparently content to enjoy the warm water as Reed massaged the sweet-smelling rinse into their coats. They were so well behaved, and the day moving along so smoothly, that Reed decided it wouldn't hurt to start one or two of the babies in the wash stall. Their shirt and breeches were already soaked through, and the afternoon was still hot enough that there was no risk the weanlings would catch a chill.

It seemed like an opportunity too good to pass up.

"Your funeral," John said cheerfully. "I'm needed at the east fence line, so you're on your own. Scream if you get trampled. Maybe they'll hear you up at the house."

Reed wasn't particularly worried. At around five hundred pounds, the weanlings were barely half their full-grown relatives, and Reed was quick enough and experienced enough to stay out of their way even when they were panicking. Handling skittish horses was what Reed *did*. Besides which, if something went wrong, there were plenty of staff around to hear Reed shout—they wouldn't need to rely on the main house for rescue.

And it wasn't as if Reed was going to give them a full bath. It would be enough to coax a baby into the narrow stall, maybe run a little water across their back. Hell, if they stood still without immediately doing a run-out, Reed would count it a win.

Reed loaded the pockets of their soaked-to-the-skin breeches with sugar cubes and set to it with a smile. The first foal, a brave little warmblood colt Reed had secretly dubbed Gagarin for his adventurous nature, went into the three-sided wash stall on the first try. Seeing the hose coiled along the wall, Gagarin went out just as quickly, this time at a jog, the lead line jerking in Reed's hand.

After that it was forty minutes of in and out, one step forward and many back, and plenty of sugar cubes and patience before the colt forgot about the hose long enough to stand in the stall while Reed petted his withers and murmured encouragement.

"Good boy," they crooned while Gagarin blew suspiciously through his nostrils, tail raised high. Adrenaline made the colt's legs tremble, but he didn't bolt. The sugar cubes Reed kept stuffing into his mouth were too tasty. "That's right. Now walk out with good manners and we'll call it good."

But a yearling, even one so brave as Gagarin, never walked anywhere with good manners, which meant Reed had to spend another twenty minutes in the barn aisle, gently but firmly reminding the colt that people were not for biting, all four hooves were meant to stay on the ground, and his proper spot was at Reed's shoulder, not behind by five feet or ahead by ten.

By the time the day's lesson was over and Gagarin back in his pasture, more than three hours had passed. Reed, though pleased with the afternoon's progress, was nursing a bloodied lip and a new bruise below their eye because once inside the gate, Gagarin's patience had run out. He'd wheeled, clocking Reed in the face with his head as he'd bolted for the safety of his herd mates.

"Please don't say 'I told you so,'" Reed said as they trudged into Barn A. "We'll work on turnout etiquette next week."

"That's Kate's responsibility, not yours. What the hell happened? You're bleeding."

Distracted by a rapidly swelling cheek, Reed had assumed it was John lurking near the crossties. It wasn't. It was Peter, growling like a thunderstorm about to break, dressed all in comfy black cotton, leaning heavily on shiny new crutches, banked lighting behind blue eyes.

Still pissed, then. But down in Barn A, from all appearances on his own power, and carrying a bottle of Grey Goose in a net shopping bag around his neck.

"You're here," Reed said stupidly. *And absolutely delectable in all black,* their brain supplied helpfully. "With vodka?"

"Mum always says a favor done deserves a thank-you gift. I understand you're the one responsible for the new landscaping."

Reed used the edge of their sleeve to dab at their bleeding lip. "No, that was your brother. I just made a small, possibly out of line, suggestion."

Peter looked Reed up and down. It felt to Reed like Peter was—maybe for the first time—actually paying attention. His blue gaze swept across Reed's face, lingering on Reed's split lip before sweeping across their still-damp polo, grubby breeches, and muddy boots.

"Rough day?" he suggested just when the silence was moving out of uncomfortable and toward terminally fierce.

"Very productive." Reed's every nerve was standing at attention. They recognized a thorough once-over when one scraped across their body. But was the heat in Peter's stare desire? Or anger?

Because anger was something Reed had no interest in inviting upstairs. Desire, on the other hand . . .

Then Peter smiled that honest, warm McAuley-Griffin smile that somehow made everything right in the world, and Reed felt like they'd won the American lotto.

"Better get some ice on that eye." Peter offered up the bag with the bottle of vodka. "Sorry about the brand. Target doesn't carry Stoli. I asked the clerk."

"Grey Goose is fine. Grey Goose is wonderful." *He went out and got it himself, specifically for me. For us?* "Come up and join me for a predinner drink?" *Say yes.* "Good vodka is meant to be shared."

Surprise chased the warmth from Peter's face. His mouth flattened, his gloved fingers flexed and unflexed on the crutches. Reed knew he was going to refuse. Of course he would. This was Peter Griffin, who could have anyone he wanted in his bed. He hardly knew Reed as anything other than a busybody with a nice seat and a recipe for colic tea.

But no. Peter cleared his throat, nodded once. "I'd like that. How's the freight elevator? Still shiftier than the San Andreas Fault?"

Reed laughed in startled delight. A wave of relief and anticipation made them giddy. "It's not that bad. Anyway, what's life without a little adventure. I'm willing to risk it if you are?"

The corners of Peter's mouth curled upward.

"Yes," he said. "I think I am."

CHAPTER NINE

At first, Peter had been furious. Furious enough to fling the latest issue of *The Chronicle of the Horse* onto the bed and drag himself down the hall to the office—crutches, it turned out, even the fancy ergonomic kind, were far more exhausting than a wheelchair—where he caught his father and oldest brother in a conspiratorial huddle behind Senior's desk.

They both looked up when Peter entered. Gabriel, being Gabriel, couldn't hide the guilty expression that flitted across his face.

"What now?" Senior demanded. Radiating irritation, he neatened the file of papers he and Gabriel had been examining then slapped it down on his desk. "You look like you just found mouse shit in your Cheerios."

Gabriel winced. "Don't let Mum hear you say that, even as a joke. You know she'll start bleaching down the kitchen. Remember last year's sugar ant debacle?" He laughed, looking everywhere but at Peter's face.

Knew I'd be pissed, didn't you, big brother?

Coldly, Peter said, "There's a construction crew in our

front yard. Digging up the lawn. You must have noticed; the whole house is shaking. When I texted Kate about it, she said they were here to, and I quote, 'Make it easier for our fair-haired boy to haul his arse around the farm.'" The last was directed at Gabriel, who winced visibly.

"Your sister has funny ideas." Senior dropped into his chair. "We've needed new landscaping for a while now. You know the lawn turns into a swamp every spring. I'm tired of walking through mud and then paying to have it reseeded. Your mother's bulbs won't grow properly in the beds. And Gabriel here says he's sick of ordering in truckloads of gravel to redo the paths."

"Gravel is expensive," Gabriel confirmed, jaw set. Now he did meet Peter's accusatory stare, chin thrust just a little bit forward. It was his "We all hate barn chores but someone has to shovel manure so let's just get through it!" expression, vintage age ten. Peter knew it well. "And messy. The composite Androku found is one quarter the cost, long run, and yes, it's also accessibility rated. You've been spending time down at the barn lately. That's good. Really good." He spread his hands. "While you're healing you should be able to go wherever on the farm you want, whenever you want, without having to rely on one of us. And," he added, "it's about time we bring the place up to ADA standards. We're a business, after all."

But Peter had stopped listening. His heart was pounding in his ears, an angry thump that muffled even the backhoes snarling on the lawn.

"Androku? This was *Androku's* idea?"

"Listen, son." Senior scrubbed a hand through his hair. "Personally, I think he's—"

"They," Gabriel corrected.

"—*they's* full of shit and selling a bunch of snake oil, but

Katie's buying and we all want to keep her happy. Plus this time he . . . *they* are making some sense. The drainage needs updating, you need to be able to get around the farm under your own power because God knows you'll never leave the house otherwise, and your mum's already picked out new plants."

"You might have asked me first, before you blew what must be half a year's budget on *landscaping*," Peter replied sharply. It was the van wrap all over again. He wasn't sure why he'd believed Senior would change. Could change. "What makes you think I want to stay on the farm, anyway? I'm tired of being managed. And maybe I'm finished with the family business. Maybe I'd like to start over somewhere new, somewhere the air doesn't stink of horse shit, somewhere I can make my own decisions and my whole family's not hovering around waiting to catch me when I fall. Hawaii, maybe. Or Jersey. Ridland's suggested I go down and do a little team PR, shake a few hands, while my ankle heals."

Gabriel and Senior both gaped at Peter as if he'd grown another head. After a moment of stunned silence, Senior sighed.

"Don't be so dramatic," he said gruffly. "You're a McAuley-Griffin. The farm is in your blood. You'd miss it were you gone. Take a vacation, if that's what you need. No one would blame you. But we'll still fix up the goddamn paths, because it's the right thing to do."

———

"HAWAII?" Kate covered her laugh with one hand. "You can barely stand the summer humidity here. Plus, the cost of living on the Big Island is a nightmare."

"It was the first place that popped into my head. Anyway, Ridland was just being kind. Everyone knows I don't have the patience for a PR gig. But Senior doesn't have to know that, does he?" Peter grunted. He was on his back on a mat in Teddy's studio, struggling through one-legged knee-to-chest leg lifts. The elastic resistance band was slippery in his sweaty hands. His leg seemed to grow heavier after each repetition, and throbbing that lately seemed a constant in his skull had increased to a drumbeat.

"I wasn't exactly thinking straight," he muttered. "I was too fucking angry. And don't think you're immune, Katie. I'm just being polite because you drew babysitter duty."

"What's the big deal?" Kate demanded from where she sat perched on the edge of Teddy's massage table. "Gabriel's right. The farm needed the upgrade. Sometimes, *golden boy*, your ego's a real pain in the arse."

"It's called ableism," Teddy interjected. She sat cross-legged on the floor by Peter's side, watching carefully as he worked through the lifts, occasionally adjusting his grip— one hand on the resistance band, the other on his knee. She wore a pink SÁNCHEZ PA tank and a matching baseball cap. "Just because you all had good intentions doesn't mean it's okay."

Kate stiffened, scowling. "Putting in composite walkways so Peter can more easily get around his own home is not discrimination."

"It is if you don't bother asking for his input first." Teddy met Kate's unfriendly glare with an easy smile of her own, but her tone was cool. "Or did you think a debilitating accident means now you need to treat him like a five-year-old?" As Kate sputtered, Teddy cut her eyes Peter's way. "Sorry, I'm not doing any better. You can defend yourself. Except I'd bet my lunch—and it's fuckin' vegan Thai from

Ricky's—that you wouldn't recognize ableism, either, even if it bit you on your luscious ass."

"I'll google it." Leg again on the mat, Peter lay flat with a groan. His brain felt like it was knocking against his skull. Lights flashed on the edge of his vision. At least his ribs and collarbone felt almost back to normal. "Just as soon as I can move my arms again."

"Passive range of motion is important," Teddy lectured. "For both your upper and lower body. When you finally get those pins out of your ankle, you'll be glad the rest of your body is up to par. The elastic goes home with you today, bud. Get yourself a mat. Make sure you do all your lifts— side, knees to chest, extensions, and knee pulls—on a hard surface. No cheating and exercising in bed."

"Gross." Kate was already thawing. Of all Peter's siblings, she was the least likely to hold a grudge. "Look, I guess we owe you an apology." Peter couldn't help noticing she looked at Teddy and not down at him. "And I guess maybe we're not doing too great, as a family, trying to figure this thing out. As a whole, we're better with animals than people. None of us mean to treat you like a child, Peter. Even if sometimes you act like one."

Teddy snorted. "Look, it's a learning process, for everyone involved. I'm a physical therapist, not a shrink. But if you want some pointers . . ."

"Ricky's Thai is my absolute fave!" Kate said quickly while Peter put his arm over his face. "How about lunch next week, you and me? I can pass your advice on to the fam, right, Peter?"

"Right." Peter said into his armpit. He didn't know if it was a good idea, but Kate hadn't exactly been a social butterfly since her divorce. A girls' lunch might do her some good. "Bit like closing the paddock gate after the yearlings have got out, but . . . sure." He took a breath, braced himself. "Hey, sis?"

"Yeah?"

"Why don't you go get the van ready? I'll be out in a few. I want to talk to Teddy about a couple of things before we go."

"I can wait." Kate shrugged, oblivious, as she grinned at Teddy. "Doesn't take long to get the van ready."

Siblings, Peter thought, *are the absolute worst. Maybe Hawaii isn't such a horrible idea after all.*

"Katie May," he said, using her middle name in warning as he propped himself up on his elbows. He could already feel the blush rising on his cheeks. "The couple of things I want to ask Teddy about involve safe sexual positions when one is recovering from multiple fractures."

"Oh!" Kate squeaked while Teddy let loose a delighted laugh. "Oh. Good for you." She hopped off the table. "Great. I'll just—"

"Get the van ready," Peter suggested.

"Get the van ready," his sister agreed, and fled.

When she was gone, Teddy turned a narrow stare Peter's way. "Sex is a lovely idea. I know you have a reputation to maintain and kudos for optimism, but I'd take it slow. I'm concerned about your head as much as your leg. I know a concussive migraine when I see one. So. Let's discuss. Between one and ten, what's your pain level?"

———

THE GREY GOOSE was an impulse purchase. He asked Kate to swing by Target and put up with her affectionate needling—"First sex questions and now date booze? Good for you, little brother!"—as they searched the aisle for a passable vodka. He wasn't sure he deserved her applause.

Because, honestly, Peter hadn't decided whether he wanted to thank Reed for trying to help or throw the bottle at their head and order them off the property. It would be easier if Peter didn't know Reed meant well even after Teddy's accusation of ableism. After some research Peter was pretty damn sure he'd accidentally made more than a few ableist assumptions himself in the past, and probably would again. Landing in a temporary wheelchair didn't mean he suddenly knew any better.

The Grey Goose sat on Peter's bedside table while construction crews tore up the lawn and early summer turned hot. Kate rolled her eyes at it when she dropped off his mail, but mercifully she kept her opinions to herself. Aine asked gently if maybe Peter wouldn't prefer a good Irish whiskey with dinner instead, and then scolded him without heat when he said really what he wanted was a mum who minded her own business.

Six days after the first backhoe first rumbled onto Tulip Farm, Peter made up his mind. The construction crew had returned to whatever noisy hell they called home. The evening air was clear of diesel fumes and dust. The birds, no longer terrified, were singing again in the branches of Aine's beloved magnolia trees. And the new composite pathways sparkled gently in the late sun.

Trying not to think too hard about what he intended to do, Peter showered slowly and dressed even more slowly in a clean pair of sweats, his favorite black Henley, and a pair of Crocs Teddy had given him on his one-month therapyversary. Previously Peter wouldn't have been caught dead in foam sandals, but he had to admit they were surprisingly comfortable in the humid weather.

He packed the vodka in a shopping bag and hung it around his neck for ease of carrying, then he grabbed his crutches and left the main house without fanfare. On the porch, summer humidity hit him like a slap in the face. He'd grown too used to air conditioning, something he'd rarely had on the circuit. By the time he'd maneuvered down Gabriel's ramp, he was sweating through his shirt, in need of a second shower.

If it had been a riding day, he would have wet a kerchief and worn it around his throat, a stylish and practical antidote to the heat. But while a kerchief under the collar of a polo, color matched to a pair of summer-weight breeches, was definitely de rigueur in the equestrian world . . .

Well. It was a uniform Peter didn't expect to wear again any time soon. The riding gloves he still wore on his hands—to prevent blisters, he continued to tell himself—felt like the last trace of the man he had been.

Buck up, golden boy, Peter told himself sourly. *At least you're on your feet again.*

A new, shorter leg cast and ergonomic crutches allowed more freedom than the wheelchair. But he'd discovered that even elbow crutches were incredibly draining. Just trying to limp a few feet tested a whole new set of previously unused muscles. His wrists hurt. His joints complained. And he'd developed painful chafing on his elbows, which Teddy was trying to cure with added padding.

If he sometimes secretly missed the wheelchair, he refused to admit it. When Teddy pointed out that there was no logical reason to rotate the chair out of his daily routine, he snarled.

"Back in the saddle," Senior whispered in Peter's head, a near constant reproof. *"Or prove yourself a coward."*

Sighing, Peter squinted at Tulip Farm's new hardscape.

Now that he was faced with the finished project, he had to admit the landscapers had done a fabulous job. The old sloping lawn was now subtly terraced, bright green in places where lawn seed had been spread. He assumed an updated drainage system lurked beneath the new lawn, and the large, neatly mulched flower beds waited for Aine's green thumb. His mum's many magnolia trees had been spared the reorganization. The landscapers had installed unobtrusive lights against their trunks and along the new path from the house to the barns.

It looked like money well spent. Gabriel would be satisfied. Aine would be pleased, and that meant Senior would be content.

But it wasn't Gabriel or Aine or Senior who had to hobble their way down the slope on crutches and in Crocs, risking another tumble.

At least the composite looked a thousand times more stable than loose gravel. The path down was twice as wide as the old. And it had been cut across the slope between flower beds and lawn with a gentleness that was just short of meandering, stamping out any real danger of a terrifying, headlong trip into chaos.

"So what are you afraid of, Griffin?" he muttered. Although the answer was easy: *falling*.

The sparrows in the nearest tree squeaked encouragement. Peter wiped swept from his brow with his sleeve. He glanced over his shoulder at the house, but the windows were shuttered against the afternoon glare. No one paying him any attention.

He was used to an audience. He'd been judged by enthusiastic crowds most of his life. But this was different. Before, he'd been healthy, confident, naively certain he was in control of his destiny. Now he knew better.

Back in the saddle . . .

Once he got started, the fear eased. The composite was smooth under his crutches, the path wide enough he didn't worry he might stumble on an edge every time he overcorrected around a curve. He had to stop every few feet to rest. But it didn't matter. No one was watching his imperfect performance, not even the babies in their turnout at the bottom of the hill. They were too busy kicking up their heels and racing in circles, spooked by something only they could see.

By the time he was three-quarters to the bottom, Peter began to relax. He paused to scrub more sweat from his face and enjoy the view. Tulip Farm with its cheerful red outbuildings and rolling pastures was a beautiful place in any season. He'd forgotten its charm when he was on the road, too focused on Paris to think about anything but the next challenge ahead.

And Senior wasn't wrong. Tulip Farm was in his blood. In that, Peter was no different than his siblings—even Mac, who made a big deal about city living but still found his way back to Connecticut for a visit every quarter. They'd been born to it, raised among the magnolias and boxwood hedges, the rhythms of farm management, the joys and sorrows that came with raising sport horses.

He'd seen Tokyo, and Milan, and London, and Beijing, and many other places equally exotic. But Tulip Farm would always be home, no matter how hard he tried to pretend otherwise.

The question was, now that everything had changed, what did home mean to Peter Griffin, ex-Olympic hopeful?

———

TURNED OUT, the weanlings had good reason to kick up their heels.

"First baths are a two-person job," Peter lectured Reed as the freight elevator winched its way to the top of Barn A. "Half a ton of spooky horse is nothing to take lightly."

"I wasn't." When Reed smiled—and they hadn't stopped smiling since before the elevator doors had shut—their lip oozed blood. The bruise beneath their eye was developing into an ugly shiner, and Peter was pretty sure they'd never get the mud stains out of their breeches. But they clutched the bottle of Grey Goose to their chest and grinned like they'd just won the lottery.

"Really, it was no big deal." When Peter snorted in disbelief, Reed relented. "Okay, fine. Maybe I should have waited for John. But I'm used to doing things on my own. Back at home there weren't always enough of us to double up on farm chores."

"You'll tell me about that?" Peter asked as the elevator door squeaked open. Suddenly it seemed very important he know everything about Reed's life before Tulip Farm. "What it was like growing up in Russia?"

Reed grimaced. "Only if you get me very drunk first." They opened the door to their apartment, performed an elegant little half bow, and gestured Peter through. "Welcome to *chez Androku.*"

Peter had forgotten what an excellent space the barn apartment was, with the vaulted ceilings, large southern-facing windows, and reclaimed wood floor. Even the outdated kitchen wasn't much of a minus. The Formica countertops appeared to have weathered the years intact, and the appliances looked as if they'd been replaced in the last decade.

"Let's give it a moment to chill, yes? Make yourself

comfortable," Reed said, opening the freezer, wedging the bottle into the drawer, and pulling out a Ziploc baggie filled with ice: an equestrian's first line of defense against bruising.

"In Moscow, for a special occasion, we'd have caviar with our drink." They tossed Peter a wink before holding the baggie to their face. "No caviar here, but I think I have some herring and sliced sweet pepper in the fridge. Maybe also some pickles."

Peter didn't know herring from cod, but pickles sounded okay, if a bit strange. "Sure. I like what you've done with the place."

Reed laughed, but Peter hadn't been joking. Although the apartment was sparsely furnished, it was comfortably and cheerfully done. An overstuffed sofa sat across from a television perched on a stack of battered apple crates. A second, double-wide stack served as a coffee table in front of the sofa. A small dining room table was pushed into one corner, a laptop computer and a neat pile of what looked like junk mail taking up surface space next to a pair of spurs and a coupon for the local feed store. Plump, colorful pillows and a crocheted blanket the exact hue of sunset brightened an already open and airy space.

"I've moved around a lot," Reed said as they arranged pickles one-handed around cheese and herring on a melamine platter. "It seemed silly to own many things. Rugs, art. Besides, you know how it is. My paycheck goes straight into maintaining my herd."

Six horses, Peter remembered. All of them broken, none of them earning a dime.

"I'm surprised you can afford herring and pickles," he admitted. Then, because Reed's damp polo was sticking to the flat plains of their abdomen, dangerously close to riding up and revealing bare skin, and despite his previous resolve Peter really, really wanted to help it along with his hands and his mouth: "Maybe you should put on . . . cleaner . . . clothes."

Reed froze, regarded Peter owlishly from behind their bag of ice, then laughed out loud. "Oh, God, I'm sorry. You're right. I must look a mess, dripping blood and mud onto our crudités. I completely forgot. I'm just—" They took a deep breath and set the ice on the kitchen counter so Peter could see all of their smile. "I'm so glad you're not angry."

"Still angry, you mean," Peter corrected, but then he relented. "Go and change."

"Back in a flash." Reed turned on a bootheel and made for one of the two closed doors at the other end of the apartment. "There's garlic dip in the fridge. Top shelf, in the back. We'll eat it out of the tin. If you wouldn't mind grabbing it while I change."

Then they were gone, the bedroom door closing firmly at their back.

Peter's mouth was watering, and not because he was hungry for garlic dip and crudités. Sternly he reminded himself that he was in no way ready for anything more than drinks and small talk. And although from the signals they were sending Reed was definitely interested, the question was: interested in what?

Teddy would say—had said—desire was a healthy sign. And Teddy would also say Reed was a caretaker with ableist tendencies, and maybe she would be right. But Teddy hadn't met Reed, let alone seen their abs under a wet polo shirt.

"Just don't overdo it," she'd said, laughing at his scowl. "Go slow. Keep the weight off your leg, your ribs, your shoulder. I know your rep, Griffin. I'm sure you've got plenty of inventive tricks up your sleeve."

The vodka has got to be chilled by now. And if not, fuck it, we'll drink it warm.

He maneuvered into the kitchen and was promptly stonewalled by the refrigerator. He could tug the door open without much difficulty, but balancing on one leg while reaching into the depths of the appliance was surprisingly difficult. The muscles in his good thigh, already strained by the walk down the hill, threatened to cramp. His balance wavered, and in his panic he forgot his crutches. He grabbed the refrigerator to keep from tipping, making milk bottles in the door clatter.

His head pounded warning. He clung to stainless steel as spots bloomed behind his eyes for a good fifteen seconds before he realized two things.

One, he'd overdone it just by reaching for a tin of dip, and two, digging the vodka out of the freezer pullout required more strength than he currently had.

Such a simple goal, and it seemed a bigger reach than Olympic gold.

CHAPTER TEN

"I hope you're not in a hurry," Peter said tightly when Reed rushed back into the living room. "It might be tomorrow morning before I manage to open the refrigerator." He was leaning heavily against the kitchen counter, breathing shallowly and looking decidedly pale.

"I'd count myself lucky to have you still with me here tomorrow morning," Reed replied, honestly, and hurried to insert themselves under Peter's arm. "Shit, I'm sorry, I should have realized . . . I'm a terrible host . . ."

Once Reed had helped him across the room, Peter slumped gratefully into the sofa. He closed his eyes and exhaled through his nose. Reed took his crutches and gently propped his leg on the coffee table. "Let me get you some water." They dashed back into the kitchen.

"I'd prefer the vodka. Please. And it's not your fault. Before today, I haven't walked more than fifty feet since the accident. I should have used the chair, but I wanted—"

"To prove that you could do it." Reed sloshed Grey Goose into two shot glasses, carried the glasses and the bottle back to the sofa. Returned to the kitchen and was back with the platter of vegetables and two small plates. "I understand that. The diving board at Lake Baikal, remember?"

Peter glanced up, really looking at Reed for the first time, and there it was: slowly dawning appreciation. Well, Reed *had* dressed for the moment, deciding on sexy-snuggly to match Peter's casual lounge set. From the look on Peter's face, the flush that spread across his cheeks and the bob of his Adam's apple when he swallowed, the oversized, off-one-shoulder DRESSAGE QUEEN T-shirt and tattered denim shorts were just the thing.

"You're wearing fuzzy socks," Peter murmured. Then he licked his lips.

Reed's mouth went dry. Their eyes met and held. Was it restrained lust that darkened Peter's eyes almost to black, made the muscles in his jaw bunch?

If so, Reed wouldn't mind seeing what happened when that restraint collapsed.

"The floorboards are cold." They wiggled their toes, hid a smile when Peter quickly returned his attention to Reed's feet. "Even in warm weather. Here," they added, handing Peter a shot glass. "Drink up. Straight down the slide."

"Shoot," Peter corrected, sounding steadier. "Straight down the shoot. *Slainte*."

"*Na Zdorovie*," Reed replied. "To your health."

Reed tossed down their shot, grinned as Peter did the same. The vodka burned all the way down. It wasn't Stoli, but it was still very good. They refilled both glasses.

"So, what can I get you? Some herring? And try the pickles in the dip, but not too much, just the slightest . . . " Reed demonstrated, delicately baptizing one end of a tiny gherkin in creamed garlic. "So as not to overwhelm either the pickle or the vodka, you see."

"Looks . . . delicious. No, really. A little bit of each, please, if you wouldn't mind." Peter was laughing now, and how beautiful he looked as he watched Reed load up a plate, relaxed again, his expression soft and open. A far cry from the careworn man who had snarled at Reed over Annie's colic.

"I'm glad you've decided to forgive me," Reed said before they could think too hard about the confession. "Annie's missed you in the afternoons. And so have I."

A small frown creased Peter's forehead. He took a minute to taste each of the crudités on his plate, long enough that Reed began to worry they'd made a mistake. Then Peter sighed.

"I'm going in for a scan next week. They need to take the pins out of my ankle, and recast it, but not until my neurologist takes a closer look at my head. I'm still having migraines. Missing sleep. Seeing double sometimes." He paused to knock back a second shot of vodka. "And it wasn't my first concussion, or even my fifth. CTE—chronic traumatic encephalopathy—is a concern. Apparently, it's not just for NFL players anymore."

Reed winced. Swallowed vodka down. Refilled their glasses. Collapsed onto the couch next to Peter, so close they could feel the warmth of his hip against their own. "I know a fellow in Del Mar. Had one too many falls. He only coaches from the ground now, on doctor's orders. Most people don't have that luxury. It's back in the saddle or no paycheck."

"I'll always have a place on the farm no matter what I decide to do." Peter dipped a pickle, took a bite, made a sound of pleasure that had Reed's toes curling in their fuzzy socks. "But I've been the "golden boy" of show jumping for as long as I can remember. If I don't get back in the saddle, I'll just be another cautionary tale. Or worse, I'll get back on and there's no guarantee my leg will ever be as strong as it was, my seat as solid." He tossed back vodka, turned the empty shot glass in his hand, looked at Reed. "All I've ever wanted since I was a kid was to ride in the Olympics. Now that's gone. And maybe I'm taking it out on everyone around me. When I'm letting myself feel anything at all."

"I won't tell you everything's going to be okay." More than anything, Reed wished they could. "But the truth is, it will probably be better than you're imagining. It usually is, I've discovered."

"Fear of the unknown," Peter agreed. He was very close now, slumped a little sideways into Reed, his breath tickling their cheek. "And maybe not so easy, this time, as closing eyes and jumping in. I'm not sure I know how to be anyone other than Peter Griffin, equestrian star. It's scary to think about."

"Yes." Reed turned their head. Peter's eyes were large and dark, the depths of Lake Baikal in summertime. "Fear is an ugly thing. Growing up in Russia, out and queer, can be difficult. Scary, even."

"I bet." When Peter frowned, tiny wrinkles gathered over his nose. "You weren't afraid to be out?"

Reed thought the little lines were adorable. And sexy. They wanted to kiss them away. They licked their lips. Peter's dark gaze dropped to Reed's mouth and clung.

"Terrified," Reed admitted softly. "Almost all the time. But I'm the sort of person who rises to a challenge. Speaking of, I'm going to kiss you now, if that's okay?" From the expression on Peter's face, they thought it was more than okay.

"Please." Rough, low, and definitely needy. The single

syllable went straight to Reed's head, more potent than the three shots of vodka.

Peter leaned down and sideways the same instant Reed stretched up. Briefly Reed was afraid they were going to knock noses. But at the last moment, Peter adjusted his aim —of course he did, he was good at seduction, Reed had heard the gossip. Peter Griffin knew all the moves on the course and in bed—and then their lips met and Reed stopped thinking.

Everything narrowed to that one point of contact, Peter's lips chapped and just perfect as they brushed gently across Reed's mouth, asking a question. Reed groaned and opened their mouth in answer. Their hands shifted to Peter's shoulders, kneading hard muscle in encouragement. Peter made a noise in the back of his throat, and then he was kissing Reed in earnest and not gently, making the cut on Reed's lip throb. Peter's tongue swiped across it, then against Reed's teeth, then plunged deeper. Retreated to set fire to Reed's lower lip once more.

A shock of longing surged through Reed's body, so acute it was almost painful. They inhaled sharply.

Peter drew back. "All right?" he asked hoarsely. "Too much?"

"No. I . . ." Reed paused. Michael had understood, but there was no guarantee Peter would. "Sometimes my body takes me by surprise, that's all." They searched for the right words. "Sometimes when I'm turned on, I want to be touched. Everywhere. And sometimes I want to pretend my body doesn't exist." They hated that, after so many years, they still had difficulty explaining. "And then kissing is about all I can handle. You're like fireworks in my blood, Peter Griffin. Beautiful but shocking." They touched their fingers to Peter's cheek. "So much at once."

"Okay." The wrinkles were back over Peter's nose. He looked quizzical, but not at all put off. "And what do you want tonight?" He cleared his throat, turned his face into Reed's palm, golden stubble scratching sensitive skin. "I'm up for anything you like. Literally."

Reed's heart went pitter-patter, dancing a rhythm of joy and relief. They tsked. "Aren't you confident! In Russia, first dates are for kissing only. And maybe, if you're up to it," they purred, pulling their legs up and setting one socked foot at a time into Peter's lap, "a foot massage."

———

"THAT ISN'T TRUE, IS IT?" Peter asked much later, as they lay together in Reed's bed and listened to the sounds of twilight outside through the open window: the cicadas playing a symphony broken by familiar noises of one of the hands graining the horses below, and in the distance the muffled sound of a tractor at work in the fields. "That in Russia you don't hook up on the first date?"

They'd moved from the couch to the bed when kissing across Peter's splinted leg became too awkward, leaving a mostly empty bottle of Grey Goose and a very empty platter of crudités behind. Reed was pleasantly buzzed. On vodka, on kissing, on the way Peter smiled when he thought Reed couldn't see him past the fresh baggie of ice pressed against their face.

Peter was more than buzzed, which was why Reed had cajoled him into a lie down instead of a walk home. It was obvious he didn't have Reed's tolerance for strong alcohol, and the last thing he needed was more broken bones.

"Of course it's not true." Reed snorted. "In Russia, we fuck like everyone else, only stronger and better." When

Peter giggled, a sound that made the twilight seem suddenly brighter, Reed added: "In Ma Androku's home, however, there was no fucking until after you were married in the Orthodox Church. Ma prefers to pretend I'm still a virgin, although Jesus knows Michael used to tease her about it mercilessly."

"Michael?" Peter's arm flexed around Reed's shoulders. He was propped up at both ends, his shoulders against Reed's headboard, his leg on a bolster. Reed, snuggled against his side, mouth throbbing, and feet still tingling after more than an hour of thorough attention, soothed a hand down Peter's chest, rumpling the cotton of his shirt. He'd lost weight since the accident, and probably some muscle. Aine was right. He needed feeding up.

"I'm not one of your rehab projects," Peter cautioned, squeezing again. "So stop frowning over my topline. You said you'd tell me about growing up in Russia, if I got you very drunk."

Reed wasn't *very* drunk but Peter was, which possibly meant he wouldn't remember much in the morning, so Reed gathered their courage and began.

"I loved growing up in Russia. Russia is very beautiful, very fierce. Some parts are mountains, some parts are flat. The sky is bluer there, the grass greener. The vodka is better there." Reed skimmed their fingers back up Peter's chest, making him shiver. "The food, not so much. The cities seem very old, compared to where I have lived in America, even Saint Petersburg, which rivals New York for diversity of people and entertainment." Their fingers stilled. They confessed, "I was very sad to leave."

"Why did you?"

This was the hard part. Even several shots of Grey Goose couldn't make it easier.

"I didn't mean to, not really. It was supposed to be for three months. A summer internship at a breeding farm in Seattle. A friend in Bitsa arranged it. She knew the farm owner from way back, and what horse farm doesn't appreciate free labor?" The plane tickets had been expensive, and the bribes for the visa. "My father had left me some money in his will. Just enough to make it come together." Reed missed their father desperately, hated the cancer that had snatched him away when Reed was barely fifteen, hated the relief they sometimes felt that he was no longer in pain, no longer withering away in a hospital bed and Reed unable to help.

"What happened in Seattle?" Peter was listening, rapt. His cheeks were pink with drink, his lips slightly parted. Reed wouldn't mind kissing him again, kissing him until the sun set and the stars came out.

Instead, they said: "Seattle was very good for me. I learned so many new things. Made connections of my own. People were very friendly. I worked constantly, and that was wonderful. Even better, on my off time, I was allowed to ride. Every day seemed to pass in a blink of an eye; I barely had time to eat or sleep." Reed swallowed. "It wasn't so good for Michael, the boyfriend I left behind. He was closeted, very much so, and it turned out he didn't do well with separation, or loneliness. He started visiting the gay clubs in Saint Petersburg, and he wasn't careful about it. Maybe he was just trying to make time go faster with booze and sex. Or maybe he thought if he got into trouble, I'd come hurrying home. Rescue him. I have a habit of doing that. Rescuing. Maybe you've noticed."

Peter grunted. "I take it he got into trouble. And you didn't hurry home?"

"By the time I knew, it was too late."

Peter didn't need to know that Michael's family was *Bratva*, OPG . . . mafia. Or that when word got around he was visiting the clubs in Saint Petersburg, one of the rival OPG decided to take advantage, make a point. Michael was his father's weakness, his Achilles heel. And Michael suddenly outed as gay was just the excuse they needed.

Peter didn't need to know exactly how Michael had ruined Reed's life. And maybe it was the other way around. All these years later, guilt was still a heavy weight on their shoulders.

"Are you crying?" Peter reached down, nudged away the baggie. "Oh, Christ. You're crying. This was a bad idea."

"Am I?" Surprised, Reed dabbed a finger at the wetness on their cheeks. "No, that's just the ice." Maybe they were drunker than they thought.

"We can stop. Let's stop. We can talk about something else. Go back to assessing my soundness. I don't like tears."

It would be easier to stop. Some old wounds were better left to scab over. But Michael's loss and what had come after was like a pocket of infection that refused to completely heal. Reed wished they could lance it completely. And he wanted to give Peter at least part of the truth. Michael deserved that much.

"No," Reed said, "I want to. You asked, and I think you should know. Will you hear the rest?" They caught themselves rubbing at their swelling eye, forced nervous fingers to still.

"Of course." Peter caught their restless hand, folded it in his, pressed it to his mouth in such a tender gesture that Reed almost forgot how to breathe. "But only if you're comfortable," he added earnestly.

Reed summoned a shaky smile. "You're very gallant, I

think. I always knew the gossip about you couldn't be *all* true. Charmer in the stands, arrogant bastard in the ring."

Peter kissed Reed's fingers again. Then, "It's true. Most of it. I can be a bit of an arrogant bastard, but that's because I'm in it to win it. And I'm good at what I do. What I did." He looked away briefly, and then back. "I don't suffer fools, and I don't like drama. There are a lot of both in the horse world. But you are *not* a fool," he pronounced each syllable carefully, as though trying to make sure Reed heard him past the vodka, "and this is not *drama*."

"Right. Yes. You're right." Peter's reassurance dried Reed's tears. Still clinging to his calloused hand, Reed straightened and continued more steadily.

"The papers said it was a robbery gone bad, but everyone knew it was murder. He was beaten almost unrecognizable outside the Cabaret Club and left behind a trash bin to die."

Peter squeezed Reed's hand. "I'm so sorry. So terribly sorry. Hate crime?"

When the club owner had called in the police the next morning, everyone knew what it meant. Sacha Turgenev's youngest son was *blue*—gay. Sacha's rivals were very quick to put the news about, to shame the family, to undermine his influence in the Bratva.

"In Russia, even now, we are not so enlightened as some other countries," Reed hedged. "And even just five years ago, it was much worse."

Peter was white around the mouth, his hand a vice on Reed's fingers. Gently Reed pulled away.

"What did you do?" Peter asked. His voice turned to gravel again, which made Reed wonder if strong emotion turned it rough.

Something, Reed thought distantly, *to remember for later*.

But for now: "I wanted to go home at once. But I couldn't. Ma warned me against it. And many other friends. America is safer, they said. Stay away. And it's true. America is safer. For the most part."

Sacha had blamed Reed for Michael's death. Even as the old man's influence in the mafia dwindled, he still had plenty of thugs who were willing to do a little wet work for the right price.

Because I had never hidden who I am, and he thought I dragged Michael down.

"You carry a knife."

"When I'm out and about." It was safely in Reed's bedside drawer at the moment, within easy reach if something woke them in the night. "It's true. Michael's death shook me." Reed had been terrified, sick with grief, and so, so angry. And certainly Sacha would find a way to punish them even in America. The Bratva's connections were far-reaching, and not limited to Russia. Sacha was like a spider with a few lines of silk left in his web.

"I found a man in Portland," explained Reed. "He taught me how to protect myself with a blade. And it turns out I have a knack, I'm very good."

"Fuck," said Peter, somewhat breathlessly.

Reed hid a small smile behind the ice baggie. "I reupped my work visa and stayed. And worked and learned. Eventually I started my own business. Holistic consultant. I reup my EAD when it's needed, go where there is work. Lately there has been plenty of work, so I can choose where I want to go, where my talents and my little herd will be welcome. For a while, I was still afraid. Maybe I expected what happened to Michael to happen to me. Why did I deserve to be happy when he was dead?" The Bratva obviously felt the same way. They tried first in Seattle, the room Reed was renting tossed while Reed was out, everything broken and smashed. Reed couldn't prove it was Sacha's doing. But they knew.

Reed shrugged as they continued, pretending casualness. "Then, one time in Kentucky, a man jumped me in a grocery store parking lot. He was very big, very strong. When I kneed him in the balls and cut him with my knife, he ran away." Cursing and shouting threats in Russian as he left a trail of blood on the pavement, but Peter didn't need to know that part. "After that, I felt better. I had proved I could protect myself. I felt more in control."

And since Kentucky, nothing. More than a year had passed. Reed had begun to hope Sacha had given up. But they didn't plan to give up their knife any time soon.

"Fuck. You fought the guy off," Peter said. "That shouldn't be a turn-on, but it is."

"Is it?" Amused, Reed abandoned the ice and rolled until they sat with one knee on either side of Peter's chest, careful not to bump his leg. "Like my hands on the reins, my fuzzy socks, and my beautiful seat?"

"Yes." The word was a low rasp in Peter's throat. His hands lowered to frame Reed's hips. "All of that. All of you. You're amazing."

That was surely the drink speaking, but Reed didn't mind. They'd take the compliment as due.

"You're not wrong," they purred, leaning down, smiling when Peter's eyes widened. "Now kiss me some more."

CHAPTER ELEVEN

Peter woke all at once in Reed's bed with a pounding headache, a pulsing left leg, aching ribs, and a dangerously full bladder. It was not the first time he'd opened his eyes to sore bones and an angry hangover in someone else's bed. It was, however, the first time he'd woken alone, abandoned by his lover.

Oh, how the mighty have fallen.

Groaning, he hitched himself up on his elbows and took stock. He hadn't paid much attention to Reed's bedroom the night before. He'd been far more interested in the feel of Reed's mouth on his own. But now he saw the tiny room was just as eclectically homey as the living space: rumpled linen sheets the color of a ripe banana, another knitted blanket in shades of lavender, and a healthy supply of plump pillows.

The walls were bare, the shades over the two east-facing windows pulled down, making it hard to tell what time it was. A single lamp, switched to low, softly illuminated an orange crate side table.

A glass of water and a bottle of acetaminophen waited

in the circle of light, next to a folded piece of paper with Peter's name on it. Peter's phone, and Peter's crutches, were balanced just within reach.

Reed's handwriting was bold and precise. **Had work. Three pills, all the water, and come give me a kiss before you do the walk of shame. — R**

Peter snatched up his phone and checked the time: 10:03 a.m. He hadn't slept so late since before the accident, and *fuck* they were probably panicking up at the big house. Hissing at the pain behind his eyes, the pain in his leg, the pain of embarrassment, he unlocked the phone screen.

Three phone calls between the hours of 8:00 and 11:00 p.m. Two from Kate and one from Gabriel. Only three? Knowing his family, he'd expected no less than twenty. He thumbed open the messages, frowning.

(Katie 11:15 p.m.): Nice going, golden boy. Just don't break my barn manager. I'll cover for you with mum.

(Gabriel 6:00 a.m.): Seriously? You've lost me a tenner to Mac. Better get your arse back to the main house in time for your neurological appointment at 1.

(Reed 9:30 a.m.): You were sleeping so peacefully last night I texted Kate and let her know where you were. Hope that's okay. Drink ALL the water. Then come and find me in the arena. xxx

His siblings' good-natured badgering and Reed's three *x*'s made Peter smile past the hangover claws in his head. Obediently he swallowed down three acetaminophen, gulping water, which immediately made his bladder situation intolerable. Using Aine's favorite Irish curses with pained relish, he inched sideways until he could lower his leg in its unwieldy cast over the edge of the mattress, grabbed his crutches, and—still swearing—hobbled his way across the tiny room into Reed's even tinier bathroom.

Blinking stupidly at the caravan of rainbow ponies galloping across Reed's shower curtain, Peter balanced over the toilet, yanked down his joggers, and released a stream that would have done any stallion proud.

———

HE FOUND REED downstairs in the arena, just as they'd promised. Peter had expected Reed would be in the saddle, working one of his herd before the day warmed up. Instead they were standing in the center of the arena, calling out friendly instructions to a young girl on a chestnut pony that Peter knew didn't belong on the property.

He may have banged his head and broken a few bones, might have briefly checked out of life and in with Doctor Who, but he sure as hell still knew the farm stock like the back of his hand.

Not that she wasn't an adorable specimen, Peter conceded, leaning against the arena gate to take some of the weight off his crutches. Close to fourteen hands—which in the entry books meant pony, large—with four white socks and a stripe on her nose. Her head and eye made him think Arabian cross, because the rest of her screamed Quarter Horse.

She would have been a pretty mover if the girl on her back wasn't taking too much of her mouth. The kid clutched hard at the reins, making the mare swish her tail in annoyance.

"Deep breaths, Jolene," Reed said from the center of the

arena, turning to watch the girl and the mare as the pair trotted in a large circle. "She's not going to run away with you, I promise. Deep breaths and relax."

"Jolene had a couple of scary moments lately," John explained, popping his head out of the grain room, making Peter start in surprise. "Her dad's moved buffalo onto the property and the pony's having trouble adjusting. Pepper's got a pretty good brain, but, well, you know how it goes. She's started spooking and running every time the buffalo graze near their outdoor." He tossed Peter a wink. "I'm not supposed to be watching the lesson. Jolene says it throws off her concentration. But I can listen just fine from in here."

"Lesson?" Peter let the disbelief he felt show plainly on his face. "You know those two?"

The grin faded from John's face. "That's my littlest cousin, Jolene, sir. Reed's been coaching her since April, just once or twice a month. Honest, the two of them don't need much, but with the buffalo, well, Reed thought a tune-up might be in order."

"Tulip Farm," Peter enunciated clearly just in case he wasn't the only one who'd bumped his head lately, "is not and never has been a lesson barn. We have very strict haul-in procedures, John, surely you haven't forgotten."

"Mr. Griffin," Reed called from the center of the arena, saving John, who looked like he wanted to retreat back into the grain room, "why don't you come on in? If you have a minute, I know Jolene would dearly love to make your acquaintance."

Who the hell names their child after a Dolly Parton song in this day and age? But when Peter glanced back over the arena gate, child and pony were both stopped next to Reed, and all three were looking his way.

"Here, sir," John said quickly. "Let me just get the gate for you. It's heavy."

"I thought I told you not to call me 'sir.' Do I look like my father?" But he appreciated the young man's help with the gate. It *was* heavy, something he'd never noticed before he was hampered by crutches and a sore leg.

"No, Mr. Griffin. Everyone agrees you're your mother's child, except for the hair. The other Mr. Griffin likes to laugh about how you were the cuckoo in the nest."

Mac, Peter deduced with a sigh. Only Mac would make a comment like that within the staff's hearing.

"Better go back to not watching the lesson, John," he suggested. "Jolene's looking rather put out."

The kid's lower lip was protruding like a landing strip, but at least her pony—What had John called the mare, Pepper?—had finally relaxed, resting a back foot while they all watched Peter inch his way across New Haven's most expensive indoor footing. Good for the horses, not great for a leg in traction. But not as frightening as loose gravel on a muddy slope. As he made his way slowly to Reed's side, Peter couldn't help but think again of the brand-new composite pathways ringing the farm, and he felt humbled.

Which meant he was able to meet Reed's smile with one of his own. And it was genuine, despite the bloody hangover and the bloody strange pony in his ring.

"Good morning, Mr. Griffin." Reed was sporting a full shiner, black and red and very swollen, but otherwise looked their usual chipper self. Dressed in clean, baby-blue breeches and a spotless white polo, light blue scarf knotted around their throat and color in their spiked hair, they looked unfairly as if they'd never even heard the word *hangover.*

"Let me introduce you to Jolene Dotty and her Super

Pony, Pepper," Reed continued, executing one of their funny little half bows, and Peter couldn't help but glance at the long knife on Reed's belt and remember: *He taught me how to protect myself with a blade. And it turns out I have a knack, I'm very good.*

Swallowing, Peter shifted minutely on his crutches. Now was definitely not the time to get hard. He made himself listen to what Reed was saying.

"Jolene and Pepper are something of a star team around town—"

"In the state," Jolene Dotty interrupted. She was young enough that if she'd been in the hunter ring, she'd still be in pigtails, hair bows, and jodhpurs. Old enough to dress down for her lesson in jeans and a tight T-shirt, which was too casual for Peter's taste, but at least she'd put her hair up in a net under her helmet. "Last year, we almost qualified for a Children's National Championship."

"This year you will," Reed said. He slapped Pepper lightly on the withers. "Kate was kind enough to offer up my services for a little extra help. Usually Jolene's mother coaches her, but—"

"Mom's having a baby in September and has to stay in bed. It totally sucks." Jolene scowled. "If she'd been with us last weekend, probably Pepper wouldn't have spooked at the buffalo. Pepper's calmer around Mom."

"I hope you don't interrupt your mother the way you interrupt Reed." Peter raised his brows. "My youth coach would have set me ten minutes no stirrups and thirty cleaning tack for bad manners like that."

Jolene's blue eyes widened beneath the brim of her helmet. She opened her mouth, shut it, tried again: "Sorry, Mr. Griffin."

"It's not me you should be apologizing to."

"Sorry, Reed." She ducked her head, played with her pony's mane.

"Jolene's generally more focused," Reed explained gently, nudging the rubber foot of Peter's left crutch with the toe of their boot. A warning? "But the baby and the buffalo are a bit of a distraction. And she's got a qualifier coming up soon."

"Okay." Peter started to ask if Senior knew Katie had a charity case going in Barn A, then decided he didn't care. As there was no way his sister would risk her babies' health, he had to assume the pony was up to date on vaccinations. "I get that."

The pony was cute. The kid just arrogant enough to remind him of himself. And he had a few minutes before he was needed back up at the house. "Tell me, Jolene, how long have you and Pepper been a team?"

She peeked up at him, lower lip quivering. "Six years, Mr. Griffin. Since I was seven. We got her off a rescue. I'm fourteen now."

"That's a good long while." Pretending contemplation, he hobbled a slow circle around Jolene and her pony, taking time to run a hand along Pepper's spine, check the girth, adjust Jolene's foot in her stirrup. "Nationals, huh? That's nothing to sneeze about. And you both look like you know what you're doing. She ever run away with you before?"

"No, Mr. Griffin." Now the kid looked less like she wanted to cry and more like she thought he walked on water. He was used to hero worship. He wondered how Jolene still thought he deserved it. "Never before. Pepper's a good mare. But the buffalo scare her. They're big, and really stinky, and kind of loud." She made a face. "I wish Dad had stuck with beef, but he says bison have a lower environmental impact."

"Well. I don't know much about buffalo, but I do know plenty about horses. And you've got yourself a good one." If Pepper had come off a rescue, then someone, probably the mother, knew what they were doing because the mare had a kind eye and good manners to go with her pretty movement. "I really don't think you have anything to worry about. So long as you remember this one very important thing I am going to tell you." He lowered his voice to a whisper, leaning close so the mare's ear turned, and the girl bent forward to hear.

"What's that, Mr. Griffin?"

"I can one hundred percent guarantee there will be zero buffalo at every show you attend this season. No buffalo? Nothing to worry about. See what I mean?"

The kid's expression was so surprised it was almost comical. Obviously Jolene, like her mare, hadn't been able to work past the distraction of big stinky buffalo to more logical thinking.

"You're right!" The kid exhaled, and her fingers relaxed on the reins. Pepper immediately sneezed in relief. "I didn't think of that! Why didn't I think of that? Thank you, Mr. Griffin."

"There's the smile I've been missing." Reed thumped Jolene on the ankle. "I guess there's a good reason Mr. Griffin was voted the *youngest team captain in USET history*." They winked at Peter. "Take her back out, Jolene, and let me see the canter."

Reed and Peter stood shoulder to shoulder, watching as Jolene took her mare large.

"Her mom and I've been giving her a list of things to do at home to help the mare get used to the buffalo, but no go. The pony was getting better, but Jolene not so much."

"That's because the kid's more worried about her scores

than the actual buffalo. Probably if Mom and Dad weren't preoccupied with the baby thing, they would have worked it out."

"Beautiful, Jolene! That's gorgeous! Keep her balanced in the corners, that's right! More right leg! Maybe they would have." But Reed shook their head. "Or maybe you're just good at what you do. How are you feeling? Beautiful, Jolene! One more time around and then let her walk and rest!"

"Like someone's hammering nails in my head. Though that's not unusual, lately." But Peter smiled. "How's the eye?" It really did look painful. And one corner of Reed's mouth was cherry red, whether from tangling with the yearlings or from Peter's kisses.

He wanted to run his thumb along Reed's lower lip, soothe away the scrape.

"It could do with some more ice, I think." Reed was watching him sideways out of their good eye, up through blue-tinted lashes. "I was just about to go up and grab some. Care to join me?"

Yes. Christ, yes.

"I can't." Peter adjusted the front of his joggers, glad the kid and her pony were too busy to notice, hoping against hope John wasn't stealing glances over the arena gate. "Neurologist appointment this afternoon. But I wanted to thank you."

"Thank me?"

"Sure. For sharing . . ." He paused, cleared his throat, searched for a perfect declaration of sentiment that didn't come. "About Michael. I know it was hard."

"Oh. You remember."

"Of course. I'm not that much of a lightweight." Peter frowned. "Is that a problem?"

"No." Reed stuck their hands in their pockets, turned toward Peter, tilted their face expectantly. "But it will be if you don't kiss me goodbye."

"In front of the kid? During a lesson?" Like jeans and a T-shirt instead of a polo and breeches, PDA in front of a client definitely went in the "unprofessional" column.

"Lesson's over." Mischief creased the corner of Reed's mouth, and fuck but Peter couldn't resist.

"Fine." He complied. It was meant to be gentle, a light brush of mouth against mouth, an appropriate goodbye. But Reed stood on their toes and chased Peter's tongue back into his mouth, and Peter forgot all about goodbyes. Reed tasted like coffee and apples. They squeaked a little when Peter licked at the bruised corner of their mouth, and that small sound quickly turned breathy.

"Reed. Mr. Griffin."

All the blood in Peter's body had rushed south, leaving him light-headed and painfully aroused. And just his luck, when he opened his eyes the kid was waving at them from across the arena.

"You'd better stop that before John sees," Jolene called cheerfully. "I'm not supposed to know about kissing until I'm sixteen."

———

"THE BEST AVAILABLE evidence suggests that chronic traumatic encephalopathy is caused by repetitive hits to the head sustained over a long period of time." Dr. Sturgess, sitting across the table from Peter and Aine, looked much too young to be out of med school. Definitely too young to be making dire pronouncements. And yet here they were.

"The media likes to talk about CTE in relation to football, to the NFL. But it's prevalent in other sports as well. We've seen and studied it in boxing. Soccer. Hockey. Professional motocross. And, of course, many of our veterans are diagnosed with CTE as well."

MRIs of Peter's brain were displayed on a large monitor next to Sturgess's head. Peter could read a scan of any part of a horse's body as well as, if not better than, old Doc Holliday. But his own brain on a computer screen just looked like a giant cauliflower.

"Equestrian sport is probably most similar to motocross when it comes to concussive and subconcussive incidents," continued Sturgess. "You're not suffering the constant impact of, say, a cornerback in the NFL. But serious equestrian sport starts at a much earlier age and hard, concussive falls are to be expected over the long term."

"Listen, Doc—"

"Peter," his mum cautioned. She was dressed for gardening instead of a trip into the city. She carried off her Carhartt dungarees and Dansko clogs with an innate elegance that made Peter feel downright sloppy in his lounge clothes.

"Sorry. Dr. Sturgess. The USET doctors go over this with us every time we have a bad fall, which is not very often at my level. Last time I hit my head, they made me go in for scans." Peter shifted restlessly in his chair. "It's part of the routine, like getting a new helmet after a head hit. I'm just here so you can tell me I can tell my orthopedic surgeon I'm cleared to have the screws in my ankle removed."

"I see no reason, at this juncture, to avoid further orthopedic surgery." Sturgess played absently with the hospital lanyard around his neck. The man was nervous. Peter could see the sweat beading on his skin as he prepared to deliver bad news. "However."

Here it comes.

"That's all I need to know." Peter levered up out of the chair, reached for his crutches.

"Peter." This time Aine put her hand on his arm while Sturgess sweated behind his desk. "Let the doctor finish, please."

Fifteen seconds passed as Peter stood half upright. Fifteen seconds separating a world in which he could still pretend competition was in his future, and a world in which he had to face a few more hard truths.

But he already knew, didn't he? He'd suspected when the headaches and double vision hadn't gone away like they usually did. It was never his leg that was the deal breaker. It was the gray matter between his ears.

"Fine." He sank back into the chair, reminding himself he'd never been the sort to refuse a hurdle. "I'm listening."

"There are some changes that suggest postconcussive syndrome, which is concerning. Your orthopedic surgeon mentioned migraines, blurry vision? Trouble sleeping?"

"Yeah. Like I said, I've hit my head before. This is nothing unusual, except maybe it's gone on a little longer than I expected."

Sturgess made a note on the chart in front of him. His expression was anything but reassuring. "Right. You said you've had scans. The last time you hit your head. Tell me about that."

CHAPTER TWELVE

The very last thing Reed expected was an invitation to dinner at the main house. More than three months living on Tulip Farm and they'd never been invited up except for business. Senior liked staff to stay in their place: out of sight except when needed.

"Nonsense," Aine McAuley said when Reed, woken by her call a good fifteen minutes before their alarm was set to go off, sleepily protested that they'd promised Kate an afternoon holding weanlings for farrier practice. "It's Peter's birthday! Katie will understand. She can pretend to be a farrier another time. Today we're having barbecue. It's a family tradition."

The alarm clock next to Reed's bed said 5:15 a.m. They certainly didn't have the courage to say no to Aine at midday, let alone barely after sunup.

"I'd be delighted." Reed stared up through milky light at the ceiling. "What can I bring?"

"Nothing but yourself, dear. Peter hates pressies. He feels awkward opening them in front of people, poor thing.

Senior will be manning the grill, Gabriel's already got the pig in the ground, and Mac's brought some sort of fancy dessert with him from the city. We'll be doing it up right, and I'd hate for you to miss out."

"That's very kind of you, ma'am. I wouldn't miss it for the world."

"Excellent. Peter will be so glad. Dress is barbecue casual. We'll see you around noon."

Reed dropped the phone onto their pillow and scrubbed their fingers through their hair. Would Peter be glad? He'd been pointedly uncommunicative in the two days since Reed had wheedled a kiss in front of Jolene, replying to Reed's flirtatious texts without visible warmth, pleading a headache when Reed had dared suggest lunch out in New Haven. He certainly hadn't mentioned his birthday.

Reed had taken the hint. Tried, and failed, not to over-think things. They hadn't outed the man, for heaven's sake. As far as Reed knew, Peter had never tried to hide his bisexuality, not from the media, not from his friends and family. And he certainly hadn't rejected Reed's advances. In fact, remembering his enthusiasm made Reed blush.

Shyness, then, because of the audience? Reed was an innate extrovert. They'd assumed Peter was, too. A logical assumption, seeing as how Golden Boy Griffin had seemed to very much enjoy his place in the spotlight.

Assuming makes an ass out of you and me. It was one of Michael's favorite retorts, probably because he'd found English such a funny language, and one that Reed often forgot. Usually on purpose. Reed had a knack for reading people, just like Reed had a knack for reading horses, and 95 percent of the time their assumptions were dead-on.

From downstairs in the barn came the distinctive thumping of a horse pawing against stall boards, then a whinny. They were inpatient this morning—6:00 a.m. was still more than half an hour away. Even with the sun rising earlier every day, the horses usually knew better than to sound off until they heard Reed's boots on the stairs.

"I'm coming! Coming!"

But maybe coffee first. Reed threw off the covers and dressed hastily, taking a moment in the bathroom to brush their teeth and scowl at their reflection in the mirror over the sink. The skin around their eye was an impressive rainbow of blue and green, but at least the swelling had gone down.

There was more noise from downstairs. Reed recognized Charlie's shrill neighing. He didn't call like that unless he was anxious, and that didn't make any sense. Something was off. Coffee forgotten, Reed took the stairs down from the apartment two at a time.

They smelled the smoke immediately. Cigarettes, more than one by the way the stink lingered in the barn aisle. And on the floor close to the crossties, the unmistakable yellow-orange gleam of a butt not quite snuffed.

What the hell?

Reed grabbed the nearest fire extinguisher off the wall. Thanks to the care Senior's staff took to sweep the aisle free of debris morning and evening, it looked as though the smoldering cigarette was on its way to putting itself out without igniting anything flammable. But Reed felt better with the extinguisher in hand. Because nearly everything in a barn was flammable, and there was no greater risk to stalled horses than a careless fire.

Tulip Farm's run like a machine. Carelessness just doesn't happen. No one would dare bring cigarettes onto the property, let alone light one.

Or several, from the small pile of blackened butts near

the crossties. Reed doused the collection with a bucket of water snatched from the nearest stall. Talking gently to the unhappy horses, they threw open the barn doors in the hopes that some of the stink would escape.

And what about the fucking smoke detectors? Shouldn't they be screaming to high heaven?

Reed craned their neck, squinting at the detectors in the barn ceiling, but the haze of smoke and rising sun through the barn doors made it difficult to tell if the red indicator lights were blinking.

"Jesus, Mary, and Joseph. Are those *cigarettes*? Christ on a stick, it stinks like a bloody casino in here!"

Wonderful. Reed blinked once in slow frustration before pasting on a pleasant smile and looking around. They clutched the fire extinguisher to their chest to hide their trembling. Just the thought of what might have happened made them feel sick. "Mac. Your lovely mother said you were back home. This isn't . . . quite . . . what it looks like." But what was it?

"It looks like someone's been smoking like a bloody chimney, *in* the barn." Two long strides and Mac was at Reed's side, squatting to examine the soggy evidence. He was dressed in gray slacks and a light V-neck sweater. Foolishly, Reed wondered if the crisp outfit was what passed for barbecue casual in Mac's world. "Turkish Royals." His scowl deepened. "Imagine that."

"Well, yes, I—" Reed, too, had recognized the brand from their days at university. Relatively cheap and easy to find, even in Russia. Then sudden horror clenched like a fist behind Reed's ribs. "The babies, I need to check—"

Mac stopped Reed with a quick shake of his head. "They're fine. I just came from Barn B. Heard the noise and

. . . " He straightened and squinted at the ceiling. "Speaking of noise, alarm didn't go off. Why's that, I wonder?"

Reed tried not to bristle. "The company's out every two months to check them. Like clockwork. Senior insists upon it, and I keep my own records. The alarms were tested in May. They *should* have gone off."

"Calm down. That wasn't an accusation. Seems to me you've got the most to lose if this place went up." He waved at the horses in their stalls. "Why don't you see if you can calm them down. I'd like to take a look around before anyone else realizes something's up. Leave those there." He meant the damp cigarettes. "And keep this little incident to yourself for the moment, if you wouldn't mind."

"None of the staff would risk smoking on the farm." Reed would stake their life on it.

"I agree." Mac's violet stare flicked across Reed's bruised face and then down to the knife on their belt. "I'd keep your weapon close at hand, Harry Potter. Something stinks, and I don't just mean the Royals."

———

BY NOON REED was half convinced it must be the Bratva. It was too soon on the heels of Isabella Turgenev's package to be a coincidence. Maybe Sacha had gotten wind of Reed's newest address at last and sent someone up from New York as a reminder.

The old man will never forgive me, Michael.

Reed didn't back away from trouble. They hadn't run when the Bratva had found them in Seattle. They hadn't backed down in that Kentucky parking lot. But a potential barn fire was a different level of threat. Lives—horses, maybe even human—were on the line, and Reed couldn't have that.

They spent the hours between breakfast and noon soothing their little herd with groundwork, and later holding the ladder Mac hauled in to examine each smoke detector in the barn one by one, all the while chasing worst-case scenarios around in their head. When they finally found themselves at the main house, a bundle of late-season tulips in hand, they were a knot of nerves and fury and in no mood for celebration. They'd dressed in their most expensive pair of jeans and a secondhand Tom Ford floral shirt, then winged on purple eyeliner with a surprisingly steady hand.

Fashion was armor, and some days Reed wore color like a shield.

The person who opened the door to Reed's knock was a stranger. Muscular and bald, they were covered with some of the most beautiful floral tattoos Reed had ever seen.

"Welcome! Oh, Aine will love these!" they said, exchanging the bouquet in Reed's hand for a silver tumbler. "Blackberry mint julep. Kate's specialty. I was told to make sure you got one immediately upon arrival. Don't drink it. I'm Teddy: she/her. Peter's physical therapist. And you're Androku. I heard all about your poor eye. Come on in, everyone else is in back."

Teddy had the kind of smile that suggested mischief. The lacy white caftan she wore billowed around her ankles as she led Reed through the house, turning often to make sure she was being followed, grinning all the while. Reed decided immediately that she was worth knowing better. They wondered if she'd be willing to share the story of the tattoos that covered her shaved skull and shoulder blades.

Teddy paused in the modern kitchen where Aine and

Kate were putting together a complicated-looking potato salad. She presented Reed with fanfare as she heaped the bundle of tulips into Aine's arms.

"Your last guest has arrived, Ms. Aine, and they brought you Monsellas, a much more thoughtful gift than my baked beans."

"Baked beans are an essential part of every birthday barbecue." Aine winked at Reed, seeing their confusion. "Monsellas are the type of tulip, hard to find this time of year. See the yellow and red, the curled edges to the blossoms? Very distinctive, thank you."

"Monsellas?" Reed tried the word, decided they liked its flavor. They had chosen the flowers for the dramatic coloring and was pleased they were appreciated. "Monsellas. I'll remember that. They were lovely and unusual, much like yourself, so I thought they might suit."

Aine, to Reed's surprise and secret amusement, blushed just as easily as her youngest son. "Isn't that a nice thing to say."

"Racking up the points, Androku." Kate paused in chopping green onions, pointed the tip of her knife in mock threat. "Teddy, take my barn manager outside before Mum decides to adopt them. Drink up, Androku. I don't make my blackberry julep for just anyone."

Aine squeezed Reed's shoulder as they passed. "Peter's out back helping Gabriel with the pig. He'll be so glad to see you. He's always hated birthdays."

Reed wasn't sure what to say to that, so instead they took a large swallow of blackberry julep and immediately regretted it. Bourbon scorched their throat and made their eyes water. Teddy, smirking, took Reed's elbow and helpfully steered them away from the kitchen and through a bright sunroom full of houseplants.

"I warned you, didn't I? Katie doesn't drink, so she has no idea that her blackberry julep is a deadly weapon," she explained in a stage whisper. "It's a family joke, I think, and now we're in on it. I dumped mine there." She indicated a healthy-looking potted palm in the corner of the sunroom. "After I saw Mac and Gabriel water it first."

Reed, blinking tears from their eyes, clutched the silver tumbler. "Seems wasteful. It tastes expensive."

"Your choice, but don't say I didn't warn you. Twice." She had Reed's hand now, her fingers linked with theirs in a casual affection that seemed natural instead of awkward. "This way, around the hydrangea. If we go straight across the lawn, Senior will want to tell us all about his new grill and I've heard it already."

Reed had never seen the garden behind the main house, but they'd heard stories from other staff members who had. Of the flat, manicured lawn—the McAuley-Griffin siblings had learned lawn bowling at their mother's knee—of the gazebo overhung with wisteria, and the white roses planted in regimented rows behind. Purple and blue hydrangea grew in enormous mounds along the edge of the lawn. Broad-leafed hostas sprouted in large clay pots. At the back of the lawn an enormous magnolia provided some shade in the sticky afternoon.

The scent of roasting meat filled the air.

It was, Reed thought, exactly like they'd just stepped into a summer issue of *Southern Comfort* magazine.

"This way." Teddy tugged Reed around a flowering shrub and onto a private path made of flagstone and moss.

The path skirted the garden, tucked between hydrangeas and the white fence that backed up the west pasture. Here and there it widened to allow for a bench or a birdbath. Reed could easily imagine Aine sitting on one of those benches, watching the sun set on the horses below. Variegated hostas and more white roses brightened the shade beneath the hydrangea shrubs.

The scent of roast pig grew thick. The flagstones curved away from the fence line toward the old magnolia, then popped out through an arched trellis onto a square of grass bordered by ferns and commandeered by the McAuley-Griffin brothers. Gabriel, out of barn clothes for once, wore rumpled linen and boat shoes. Mac held a longneck in his hand, his mouth set in somber lines. And there was Peter, leaning casually on his crutches while sipping a Diet Coke.

All three shifted their attention away from the pit at their feet. Gabriel lifted a hand.

"You're just in time," he said. "We're about to pull it out. Good to see you, Androku. Glad you could make it."

"Wouldn't miss it." Reed almost meant it. A second, cautious sip of blackberry julep warmed their belly and muted their jangling nerves. "Happy birthday, Peter."

"Good Christ, are you actually drinking that?" Mac's brows rose. "Nobody actually drinks Katie's julep, Androku. The last person who did"—he cast a pointed glance Peter's way—"spent twelve hours on his knees in front of the porcelain throne, if you know what I mean."

"I was eighteen, and you all didn't warn me," Peter retorted mildly as Teddy laughed. He snagged a beer from the blue cooler near the edge of the cinder block pit, popped the cap, then hobbled his way to Reed's side. He deftly traded longneck for silver tumbler, pouring the rest of the julep out onto the grass.

"She won't say what she puts in it," he confessed with a lopsided grin. "But we're pretty sure her 'secret ingredient' is lots of bourbon." He took a swig of Coke, watching Reed out of the corner of his eye. "Good you could make it." He sounded like he meant it, low and gravelly, while the corners of his mouth twitched upward, which had Reed unexpectedly blushing.

They hoped Peter would blame Kate's gin and bourbon for the color in their cheeks.

"I've never been to a proper Southern pig roast before. Or any pig roast. It smells delicious. But I'm not sure about watching the pig come out."

"Didn't take you for the sensitive stomach sort."

"Not the stomach." Reed watched as Teddy and Gabriel bent together to peer under the piece of galvanized steel covering the pit. "The heart. I know where the meat on my plate comes from, obviously. But that doesn't mean I want to look it in the eye as it's served."

"I get that, but I can't say I've ever turned down roast pig." Peter shook his head mournfully. "Because it's fucking delicious." He pointed with his drink back through the trellis. "Listen, now that Teddy's here, the three of them will have it under control. Walk with me? Mac told us about the incident in Barn A."

He led the way through the shrubs to the closest bench where he sat. Arranging his crutches to one side and his leg stiffly to the front, he looked up at Reed. Filtered sunlight danced on his fair hair. His Lake Baikal eyes were one shade darker than the hydrangea blooming on the hedge at his back, his plain white polo matched the buds on the nearest rose. When he stretched his arms along the back of the bench—Coke dangling from the fingers of one hand—the corded muscle in his arms flexed gently.

It was as if he'd been styled and posed for Reed's private appreciation. And Reed sure as hell wasn't going to complain.

"Can't wait until I get this thing off. Feels like it's been half a lifetime." Peter sighed. "Fuck, I'd like to burn the crutches, but the doctor says not yet. Come sit?" He patted the bench next to his denim-clad thigh.

Not likely, you horrible, beautiful man.

Reed took a casual swallow of beer. It wasn't half as strong as Kate's julep, but that was probably a good thing. "Did you bring me back here for more necking, Peter? After crudités and kisses at my place and then two days of the cold shoulder? I don't think so." As if they hadn't been swooning in bed remembering Peter's kisses only hours earlier.

A tiny wrinkle formed over the bridge of Peter's nose. He looked genuinely baffled. "I didn't mean to be cold. Did I come off as cold?"

"I asked you to lunch three times. You said you had a headache. Three times."

"That wasn't an out!" Peter protested, frowning. "I did have a headache. I was flat on my back for twenty-four hours because nothing would kill it. It only just eased up this morning, and thank Christ for that because I could do with a little enjoyment. Even if it is a birthday celebration."

"Oh." Reed blew out a breath. "I thought . . . well, never mind what I thought."

"Nothing good, I can tell. That's okay. I'm used to it." He held out a hand in invitation. "Sit. I want your take on the fire. Mac says the power to the panel in A was cut outside the barn, the battery backup disengaged. Someone didn't want the alarms to go off, someone who knew what they were doing."

"Yes." Reed shook their head at Peter's hand. The nerves they'd thought were under control got the best of them at last, sent them pacing in front of the bench. *Delib-*

erate sabotage, Mac had said, the words sharp as nails. *Someone trying to make a point.*

A warning directed at Reed, just when they'd begun to hope they'd left their past behind?

"He should have the police out." Not that it would do much good. Reed expected the Bratva knew how to cover their tracks. "Did he file a report? Someone dismantling the alarms, setting a fire, that's not a thing you should ignore."

"Mac's handling it. That's his job, as the family lawyer. Da's helping. But, listen. I wanted to tell you, while I had a chance. I know you must be worried. Don't be. We'll take care of it. I won't let anything happen to you, or to the horses in that barn." His jaw was set, his blue eyes fierce.

Reed appreciated the sentiment but doubted Peter could keep his promise. They touched the knife on their belt. "I'm not worried. I'm angry. And now I know to keep an eye out it won't happen again." *If I have to sleep in the crossties to be sure.*

"It won't," Peter agreed calmly. "We've been dealing with my sister's ex for much too long. We know most of his tricks, although I admit pyromania is a new twist. We'll be adding extra security. A couple of guys to walk the property at night. More cameras. And the gate across the drive that we never use, we're going to start keeping it closed. Mac'll give you the new code, once he gets it set up. But that's the thing. Reed. I can see you're upset. Stop walking in circles for a minute and look at me. Please?"

Anxiety always made Reed want to move. Run, fight. Talk too fast, drink too much. When it came to flight or fight, Reed was blessed with a double handful of both.

But Peter's take-charge tone was irresistible in the best and worst way. Reed's feet slowed their distressed march. "Your sister's ex? Are you sure?"

"Yes. We're certain of it. I know you're worried," Peter repeated. "And, of course, I understand why you would be, after last night and . . . Michael. I know how important it must be for you to feel safe. But, let me just explain. There's been trouble on the farm for a couple of years now. The fire was just more of the same. A family problem. It has nothing to do with you."

CHAPTER THIRTEEN

Peter wasn't sure exactly which of his repeated reassurances worked, but he could see the moment Reed stopped being afraid. The Russian's shoulders relaxed, their chin came up, they exhaled in quiet relief. It hadn't escaped Peter that Reed was close to some sort of edge. He'd seen a similar straw-that-broke-the-camel's-back expression reflected back at him from his own bathroom mirror too often in the last few weeks. The extravagantly cheerful floral shirt, the upbeat purple applied to eye and hair and lip, even the extra-tight jeans—and Christ they fit Reed like a second skin, leaving almost nothing to the imagination—might have fooled most people. But Peter wasn't most people. He paid attention.

Awfully aware, for an arrogant bastard, a coach had told him once. *But I imagine you prefer to keep that to yourself. Don't worry, it's our little secret.*

Because he wanted to make sure Reed was hearing him now, Peter repeated, "This sort of thing has happened a few times before. Harassing phone calls. Threatening mail. Truck tires slashed a couple of times. Last night was different. Fire in the barn is a definite escalation." He could tell from Reed's tightly crossed arms that they were still doubtful. Not that he blamed the Russian. A fire in the barn was every horseperson's worst nightmare. Reed must be terrified. And Peter hated to see the way fear turned Reed distant, muting their usual exuberance. He relented. "Okay, look, it's not really my story to tell—"

"No, it isn't. But probably you should have said something to *me*, Peter Joseph. Jesus bloody Christ! He's setting fires now?"

Shit.

He'd been so intent on Reed's distress that he hadn't noticed Kate come up around the shrubs from the house, beautifully plated hors d'oeuvres in hand.

"Katie." A flood of guilt made him wince. "We were going to tell you, but what with the barbecue . . . Well. Mum thought we should wait." *We're in it now,* he thought, and wondered if he could plead a birthday pass and let Mac and Gabriel deal with his sister's temper.

The hors d'oeuvres quivered as the color rose in Kate's cheeks. Reed grabbed the tray before it hit the ground, which unfortunately meant her hands were now free. Peter shrunk back against the bench. His elder sister hadn't walloped him since the McAuley-Griffin siblings were young and fighting regularly like feral cats, but from the way her fingers curled into fists as she leaned into his space, he wasn't 100 percent sure she wouldn't box his ears.

He supposed he deserved it. He held up his own hands in supplication. "I'm sorry, Katie. We didn't want to upset you when you were having such a lovely time with the preparation and . . . things." He knew better than to say out loud that the family had noticed how Kate had blossomed since a certain physical therapist had come into their lives.

"What happened?" The airy sundress emphasized her petite stature and made her look delicate. Peter knew she was anything but, so he braced himself and gave it to her straight.

"Someone cut the lines to Barn A's alarm. Early this morning. Set a little fire using half-smoked cigarettes and a rag soaked in linseed oil. Luckily Androku realized something was up and interrupted before the fire was lighted. Katie, the cigarettes were Royals."

"Royals!" Kate echoed at the same time Reed demanded, "Linseed oil?"

"Rag wet with the stuff was dropped behind the crossties, probably as our trespasser made a hasty exit. Mac found it. Didn't want to alarm you anymore than you already were." Peter took a moment to organize his thoughts as Kate and Reed, both worryingly stone-faced, looked on. He nodded. "Yes, Royals. I don't think it's a coincidence, Katie. He meant to do real damage this time."

She swayed in place. Reed, unencumbered by a broken leg, moved even as Peter was still trying to stand. The hors d'oeuvres tumbled to the flagstones. Reed caught Kate by the elbows and gently maneuvered her onto the bench. Peter wrapped an arm around her shoulders.

"Breathe," he ordered. "Head between your knees. In and out, slowly."

She complied, but not without a little snark. "Like the time you almost fainted when Cricket had to have her tongue sewed up?"

"Exactly like. Shut up and breathe." He looked at Reed over the top of her head. Reed stared helplessly back.

Finches rustled in the hydrangeas, scolding them. A handful broke from the shrubs and landed on a white rose bush instead. *The White Rose of York.* His mum planted the rose everywhere, because family legend said it brought good luck. Peter could hear her calling to his da now. The pig must be out of the ground. Mac and Gabriel and Teddy had made good time. His stomach rumbled. He shifted on the bench, embarrassed, but Kate only snorted.

"At least you're eating again." She raised her head. Both Peter and Reed pretended not to see the tears she dashed from her cheeks. "Mum was so sure you were going to waste away." She straightened her shoulders, addressed Reed. "My ex-husband smokes Royals. It's one of his less horrible dirty habits, domestic abuse being his worst. Mark Linden. You've probably heard his name. He was our farrier for years and is also rather well known in eventing circles."

Reed nodded slowly. They replied, "I've met him. At a dressage clinic in New York. Competent rider, though I didn't like the bit he used on his horse. It was unnecessarily punishing."

Kate's laugh was strangled. "That's Mark. Competent and unnecessarily punishing. Most people like him. I did, for too long."

Peter dragged her protectively against his side. "If Reed's met Mark, then they'll know to sound the alarm if they see him on the farm. Reed, Katie has a restraining order. If you see Linden on the property, call the cops first. Right, Katie?"

"Sure, maybe." She plucked at a thread on her skirt. "Although I still don't see how a piece of paper can protect anyone against a psychopath. I just want this to go away. I don't want to think about it, talk about it, have *nightmares* about it anymore."

"A knife is better than a piece of paper," Reed suggested, touching the one on their belt. "Also, a working knowledge of self-defense. Can you protect yourself if someone comes at you with intent to harm? Yes? No? Well. I can teach you, if you like."

Kate glanced from Peter to Reed and back again. Peter shrugged. "Wouldn't think it to look at them, but I'm beginning to think Androku could fight off an angry elephant if need be."

Reed made a show of considering. "Maybe not an angry elephant. I like elephants. But bullies I can handle. I've had plenty of practice, and it sounds like this Mark Linden problem is, how do you say it, right up my driveway."

"Alley," Kate corrected. Her shoulders relaxed. Peter thought he'd be indebted to Reed forever for the small smile on his sister's face. "Right up your alley. And, yes, please, will you show me? I think I might feel a little better if I could take back some control."

———

THERE WERE MORE white roses in vases on the picnic tables Aine had set up on the lawn. Peter eyed them as he wondered dourly about luck and whether his family had any left at all. Then Reed set a plate loaded with barbecue, and a glass of lemonade down in front of him, and the afternoon seemed immediately brighter.

"Eat up," the Russian said, joining Peter at the table. Their own plate was piled to overflowing, though Peter noticed a distinct lack of pig. The color had returned to Reed's face; they looked almost relaxed, better than they had thirty minutes earlier. Maybe there was something to Aine's belief that fresh air and birthdays were good for the soul. "I hear there'll be birthday cake and singing after the lawn bowling." They sounded amused.

"Hell. There had better not be presents. Lawn bowling is bad enough."

"Presents can be fun." Reed shrugged before tucking into a mountain of Aine's famous potato salad. Their thigh nudged against Peter's in a companionable way under the table. Then they sighed. "Tell me what to do about Mark Linden."

"Nothing. It's our problem, not yours. Just keep an eye out. If I run into that bloody bastard anywhere near my sister, I'll strangle him with my bare hands and happily go to the chair after." Peter lowered his voice so Doc Holliday and his wife, eating at the next table over, wouldn't overhear. Suppressed rage tasted like iron on his tongue.

Reed chewed slowly, studying Peter's face. Then they washed down potato salad with a gulp of Peter's lemonade. "I hope murder isn't necessary," they replied simply. "But I'll help you hide the body if it comes down to it."

Peter surprised himself by laughing out loud. Reed smirked.

Across the lawn Senior flipped burgers while Teddy and Aine looked on. Teddy waved a hand at something Peter's father said. Senior could be charming when he wanted to be. Too often Peter forgot that, forgot Senior had been something of a star in his own time, and had managed to successfully court Aine McAuley, despite her initial disdain. They loved each other still, though Peter sometimes wondered how. Age had sharpened the already hard edges of Senior's personality while at the same time his mum's spitfire temper had softened as the farm had grown.

And both of them, for many years, had been focused on Peter's successes rather than their own. He hadn't noticed then; he didn't like to realize it now.

Over by the house, Kate and Mac and Gabriel were

arguing good-naturedly over lawn bowling equipment. They'd want a game as soon as everyone's bellies were stuffed, and they'd expect Peter to join despite the crutches. On the rare occasions they were all together in the summer, the McAuley-Griffin siblings threw bowls with cutthroat competition. The smile on Kate's face looked genuine when Mac playfully tossed the jack her way. She felt safe around her family, Peter knew. And when Mark had been content to limit his malice to teenage-style mischief, Peter had thought her safe, too.

But not any longer.

"Peter?" Reed prompted, nudging him. Peter had a guilty feeling that the Russian had been chattering on while he was preoccupied. "How was it with the neurologist?" The way the Russian peeked sideways through purple lashes at Peter suggested they had an idea.

"We've decided it's time for me to retire." He'd practiced saying it into his bathroom mirror, that straw-that-broke-the-camel's-back expression on his face, because he knew once he announced he'd be saying the words several times a day for a good long time. "Not just because of the leg, although that's some of it. More that the surgeon thinks I'm about one hard knock away lasting brain trauma." He cleared away a stubborn lump in his throat. "Mum knows. I haven't told Senior yet, or the team. I thought maybe I'd get past my twenty-eighth birthday first."

"Twenty-eight!" Reed patted their heart in mock dismay. "Why, that's practically adult diapers time."

Peter surprised himself by laughing a second time. "Fuck you. I hate birthdays."

"I don't know why. I love birthdays. Maybe you've been doing them wrong." Under the table Reed's thigh brushed Peter's again, this time with intent. Reed's hand followed, warm fingers creeping along cotton toward Peter's crotch. "I could give you some pointers, yes?"

Yes, urged Peter's cock hopefully, rising to the occasion. *Definitely yes.*

"It's notoriously difficult to change my mind." Peter took a sip of lemonade to wet a mouth gone dry. He shivered in anticipation when Reed's fingers lightly brushed his rapidly swelling hardon. "But it's just occurred to me there's something behind the house I've been wanting to show you."

"Really?" Reed leaned close as their fingers walked along Peter's inseam and then back again. It was the sweetest sort of torture, designed to make him squirm. "I can't think what."

"My bedroom. Childhood bedroom, upstairs in the garage behind the house." He'd manage the stairs if it killed him.

"Oooh," Reed said, mischief in the curve of their smile. "Childhood bedroom? Kinky." They pressed their knuckles along Peter's length. Peter set down his fork and kept his eyes fixed on his plate, breathing quietly through his nose. He hadn't been this close to coming in his pants since he was a teenager on the European circuit, eagerly giving his first blow job to a smart-arsed groom behind a barn in Paris.

Under the table Reed's hand froze. Peter's side grew cold as the Russian retreated along the bench. The finches in the surrounding trees, Peter realized, were much too loud. Because the babble of party chatter had gone suddenly quiet. Even Doc Holliday was silent, which must be a terrible omen in itself.

Mortified, he glanced up and was relieved to see everyone wasn't looking his way as he'd feared. In fact, no one was looking his way. Even Reed, whose fingers had been so exquisitely busy just a moment earlier, was looking toward the house, expression frozen somewhere between glee and horror.

"Into the breach," the Russian murmured.

Peter realized what Reed meant an instant too late to make his escape. Not that he could have gotten far. Instead he groaned and watched the giggling procession as they crossed the lawn from the house. Aine and Kate and Mac and Gabriel and Senior, and behind them the knot of guests Peter knew Aine had chosen for Peter's party—staff and close friends handpicked because they were loyal to the farm and not in the habit of gossiping.

He'd been too busy trying not to come in his pants to notice when they'd left their seats and gathered on the back porch. Had Reed meant to distract him? And the silence he'd noticed was the calm before the storm, the pause before they broke out in song.

"Happy birthday to you, happy birthday to you, happy birthday dear Peter—"

Aine picked her way over the grass with extra care, holding a large prettily wrapped, lidded box against her chest. Peter remembered similar boxes from his childhood. Mac called them *prop boxes* because on television there was never time for a proper unwrapping; much easier just to lift the lid and reveal the gift. On Tulip Farm, prop boxes traditionally meant one thing.

"Oh, Mum." Peter pressed a fist against his mouth to keep from swearing. But he couldn't be angry, not when he saw the wide smile on Aine's face. "You didn't." The box quivered in her hands as if something inside had shifted, and Peter knew she had.

Mac cleared space on the table. When Aine set the box down in front of Peter, it whined piteously. Everyone, literally *every one* of the guests surrounding Peter cooed in response.

"It's been too long since we've had a dog on the farm," Aine confirmed. "I've felt the lack lately. Your birthday is just the excuse I needed."

Their last family dog, a Labrador mix named Henry, had been mostly attached to Mac, and had gone to live in the city with him years earlier. Peter had been too busy on the road to think of getting a pup, although he also had felt the lack. Not that he'd admit that to the guests now gathered expectantly around the table.

"What are you waiting for?" Senior asked while at the same time Reed nudged Peter's shoulder and demanded, "Open her up!"

Her, Peter thought, suspicions confirmed. *You were in on this, Androku?* But their eagerness was catching, and the box was quivering with alarming force, so Peter obediently lifted the lid.

So much motion for such a tiny body. He'd expected a Lab puppy, because they'd always had Labs, or maybe a Jack Russell, because Russells were a popular breed on the circuit. But the little long dog who looked up at him from the box was completely unexpected.

"A wiener dog?" He lifted her out, carefully. She was warm in his hands and surprisingly heavy. Not a puppy, he thought, but a grown adult. Still so small, not more than ten pounds of soft dapples and long snout. Her floppy ears and stubby legs seemed a second thought to her long body and whiplike, furiously wagging tail.

"Dachshund," Reed said, giving the word a decidedly German emphasis. "Very noble breed. Great hunters, fearless to a fault. Excellent choice." The 'great hunter' chose that moment to stretch up and lick Peter's face from chin to eyebrows, all the while wiggling and whining in delirious joy.

"She's a rescue," Kate explained, leaning down to stroke the dog's silky fur. "She belonged to one of Teddy's clients, poor man. Before he went into hospice Teddy promised she wouldn't let Boudica end up at the shelter."

"Boudica?" Peter asked, dodging a frankly invasive tongue. The dog had stopped whining, but she was still quivering. He clutched her gently to his chest, recalling from somewhere that he was supposed to support her long spine.

Teddy shrugged. "Don't know about the name. But she's a lovely little thing. Six years old. Trained to sit and stay and heel, which I understand is a rarity in the breed. They're stubborn. Cole worked with her a lot." She lost some of her smile but continued gamely on. "I would have kept her myself, to be honest, but she seems to prefer arrogant bastards—you and Cole would have gotten along well —and so of course Katie thought of you."

"And I knew it was an excellent idea," Aine chimed in. "Your da and I are available any time you need a dog sitter. Happy birthday, Peter Joseph. You're a fine young man. Now, let's have some of Mac's fancy cake."

———

THE CAKE, a three-layer lemon-and-cream revelation, was well worth suffering through the McAuley-Griffin birthday celebration. Not that anyone needed to know Peter was enjoying himself. Although Mac, sitting next to Peter while Reed and Kate and Teddy and Gabriel clashed over the bowls, probably suspected. He looked smug when Peter asked for a second slice.

"Sunday summer cake," Mac explained. "No one does it quite like Brooklyn." The dog pretended to sleep on Peter's lap, but Peter knew she was keeping one watchful eye pinned to the loud game playing out on the lawn. The day had slipped away without Peter noticing; the sun was sinking lower in the sky. Most of the guests had made their excuses, retreating from the heat into the air-conditioned house for dessert. Peter didn't mind. They were his parents' guests.

He'd celebrated his last birthday in Milan, in a small bar packed with teammates and rivals from all over the world. He didn't remember much of it, honestly, other than he'd gone back to the hotel drunk and in a low mood and fucked a member of the German team on the bed of a second-rate hotel all the way through until dawn. It hadn't been especially memorable and, frankly, the Brooklyn Sunday summer cake was more satisfying.

"When you moved to the city," Peter asked Mac around a forkful of bliss, while on the lawn Kate screamed like a bloodthirsty banshee "did you make many friends?"

Mac paused in peeling the label from his beer bottle. "No," he said mildly. "No time. Work keeps me busy. Besides, why would I?" He tilted the longneck at the house. "Family first, don't waste your time on lesser mortals, and all that."

"Hadn't really thought about it until lately," agreed Peter. "But my mates were mates because circumstances threw us together. Not sure they would have looked at me twice if I weren't the competition. I know I wouldn't have paid them any attention. You prefer books to warm bodies—"

"Oy!"

"—and Gabriel's never happier than holed up in his

shop doing whatever it is he does with wood. Katie's the only social animal in the family, and even she's had a bloody rough go of it."

"Mark's not Katie's fault. We all thought he was normal enough, until he wasn't."

"Exactly my point. We should have caught on sooner. But we all missed it." *Peter* should have caught on sooner.

Mac grunted sourly, set aside the longneck. "You're wrong. Linden's just good at hiding what he is. But Da and I have done some digging. Things go our way, Linden won't be a threat much longer."

Peter's plate was empty. He couldn't see his way to asking for a third piece of cake, although it was tempting. He also couldn't see his way to inquiring what exactly Mac and Senior had on Linden. He stroked Boudica instead, watching as the game on the lawn finished up with a final round of shrieks and high fives. Only the McAuley-Griffin clan could turn lawn bowls into a blood sport. Kate threw an arm over Reed's shoulder, herding the Russian back Peter's way.

"You need to teach your date a thing or two about bowling." She laughed. "Reed thinks the game is won by talent, when we all know it's threats and cheating that gets the prize."

Reed grimaced dramatically. "Now I know better. Next time I will be ready." They were rosy-cheeked from the heat and the game, sweating lightly. They winked when they noticed Peter staring.

"There was something you wanted to show me, Peter? Behind the house?" The grin they tossed his way was unrepentant.

Mac groaned loudly. Kate smirked.

"Christ Jesus, not that old line. You should know he's

been using it since he was sixteen." But she swooped Boudica off Peter's lap before he could protest, cooed as the dog immediately went to work cleaning her face. "Come on, Mac. Teddy's gone in search of more cake, and I could do with a drink myself." She bent and kissed the top of Peter's head as she and Mac left. "Happy birthday, golden boy. *Dia dhaoibh buíochas a ghabháil leat ach ní ró-luath.*"

CHAPTER FOURTEEN

Peter led Reed around back, past Senior's fancy outdoor grill—a stainless steel monstrosity mounted on flagstone—and around a pretty herb garden behind the detached garage.

"Used to be a carriage house," Peter explained as he fished a key ring out of his pocket and unlocked the door. "Mum keeps her old MINI Cooper here, and Gabriel's wood shop is in the second bay. When Mac and I got too old to share a room, I moved out here. Gets cold in the winter, but really I wasn't home enough for it to be a problem."

He waved Reed in, shut the door, fumbled for the lights. "Not as fancy as yours, I'm afraid. For one thing, no elevator, but I think I can do the stairs." He sounded grimly determined.

The garage smelled of oil and wood and rubber and not at all of horses. A classic 1960s cherry-red Austin Cooper waited on the tarmac. Reed could easily imagine Aine behind the wheel. They'd heard much about Gabriel's wood shop, and how he disappeared there for hours on end. They craned their head hoping to catch a glimpse, but Peter was already attempting a very narrow flight of stairs with only one crutch and a pained expression.

Reed hurried to catch him under one arm. "Careful."

"They're tighter than I remembered. We'll have to go up sideways. Do you mind?"

Reed remembered the hot length of Peter's cotton-clad cock beneath their fingers and didn't mind at all. "Just go carefully." If they thought they could safely lift and carry Peter up the stairs, they might have tried. "What was it she said to you, in the Irish?"

"*Dia dhaoibh buíochas a ghabháil leat ach ní ró-luath.*" Peter's pronunciation was more halting than Kate's, but that might have been because he was intent on hitching himself up the stairs, weight balanced between Reed and the crutch. "It's an old family blessing. Means something like 'God love you but not so much that he wants you by his side now.' Another birthday tradition. Irish Catholics, you know. We've got a lot of traditions."

"In Russia, on a man's birthday, we pull his ears. For good luck. And to make sure he's growing up big and strong."

Peter paused, although they were almost at the top. "You're joking."

"Oh no." Reed wiggled the fingers of one hand suggestively. "I look forward to pulling yours, Peter. For good luck."

Peter made a sound like a growl and hoisted himself up the last five steps on his own power, drawing Reed after.

It wasn't even a proper room, just a half-loft over the first floor, probably meant for hay when the garage had been a carriage house and used for storage once the garage was updated. There were still a few large Rubbermaid bins pushed up against the far wall under a shuttered window.

The bins were labeled in black Sharpie in an elegant hand: KATIE ELEMENTARY SCHOOL ART and GABRIEL ROBOTICS and MAC JOURNALS.

"Anything of mine worth keeping is in Senior's office, in case you didn't notice the excess of ribbons," Peter said, seeing Reed's interest. He rested on his crutches, catching his breath. "Like I said, not fancy. But no one ever bothered me when I was up here. Unspoken rule."

"Because you were busy fucking your teenage conquests?" Reed suggested, amused. The single piece of furniture in the room certainly suggested it. "Is that a California king? How did you ever get it up here?"

"Piece by piece and then I put it back together. The mattress was the tough part. Helped to have three strong siblings." Peter crossed to the window. He opened the shutters. Sunlight streamed into the loft, catching on dancing motes of dust. "And mostly, I was sleeping. Alone, despite what Katie says. Because trying to juggle high school and Senior's minute-by-minute training routine was exhausting. Guess that's over." He said it with a resigned shrug. "I thought I'd be crushed, once the doctor's stamp was on it and I'd made my decision. Or angry. All that single-minded drive for nothing." He blinked at Reed without seeing them. "Maybe after I talk to the team, make it official. But really all I feel is nothing."

"Well, that won't do at all, not on your birthday." Reed said quietly. They dropped onto the gigantic mattress, bouncing once to test for springs, then held out a beckoning hand. "Come here and let me pull your ear."

Peter hesitated only an instant, still caught up in his own head. Then his gaze focused on Reed, searching their eyes before dropping to their mouth. Anticipation made Reed shiver. Peter limped across the room until he stood over Reed. He let his crutch drop with a clatter to the plywood floor.

"I'm not going to fall," he said when Reed started to protest. He took Reed's hand, pulling until they stood chest to chest. And wasn't that lovely, the heat and strength of him against Reed's front, the unmistakable desire pressing against Reed's thigh. "Can I kiss you?"

"Mmmm, please." Reed slid their arms around Peter's back, under his shirt, seeking more contact. Peter was tense, his bare skin shivering under Reed's fingertips: desire restrained. Feeling it, an answering heat throbbed in Reed's groin.

Peter stared for a long minute, Lake Baikal eyes wide, lips parted. Then he dipped his head. The kiss tasted of beer and lemon icing—sweet. The golden stubble on his cheeks scraped Reed's face. Purring encouragement, Reed ran the tip of their tongue over Peter's lower lip, and Peter's mouth opened obediently. Their tongues tangled, first gently, then harder. Peter growled low in the back of his throat. His hips thrust against Reed's. He lifted his head just briefly to gasp, "Is this okay?"

"Yes." It was more than okay, it was perfect. Reed stood on their toes as if being taller would allow them a better taste of Peter's mouth.

Peter's hands found their way under Reed's blouse, stroked the small of their back, then around front again to work at the buttons. "And this?" His voice was grit and gravel against Reed's lips.

"Yes. Please. I'll tell you if it's not." To prove their point, Reed bent back just far enough to quickly undo the buttons, slithered the blouse off their shoulders, let it drop on the mattress behind them. Peter inhaled sharply. Suddenly worried, Reed glanced up at his face. What Reed saw there felt like a miracle.

"So beautiful," Peter whispered, low, and it sounded like worship. "May I?"

Reed nodded, their own fingers busy working at the waistband of Peter's joggers. Had Peter actually bothered to knot the front ties? Who did that?

Peter ran his hands along Reed's bare shoulders, kneading muscle, then brushed his calloused thumbs against Reed's nipples. Reed gasped and arched upward, wanting more than just the hint of Peter's fingertips. "Good?" Peter asked, and did it again, and Reed's legs went weak with the pleasure of it. The mattress squeaked protest as Reed sat down hard.

"So good." All Reed could think about was getting Peter's joggers down around his waist. At last the knot was free, *thank Jesus.* They tugged the cotton farther down, exposing Peter's hips and the trail of golden fur that ran from his navel to his groin. His thighs flexed in reaction, muscles shaking.

"No underwear. You arrogant, arrogant man." But Reed buried their smile against Peter's skin in the V between his thigh and his groin, inhaling deeply. They followed that delightful trail of fur lower, breathing in Peter's musky scent, nuzzling every inch of newly exposed skin.

Peter's hands landed on Reed's head, fingers tangling in Reed's hair—for balance and in obvious, groaning encouragement. Reed slipped the joggers down until they caught on Peter's cast. Peter's cock, bared at last, jutted eagerly, bumping Reed's nose.

"Big and strong, just as I suspected," Reed teased. "My turn to ask." They blew gently on Peter's slit, a promise and a tease. Peter's eyes were tightly closed, his breath coming in short bursts between parted lips. "Is this all right?"

"Jesus God and Mary. Yes, please. No, wait—" His fingers flexed on Reed's scalp, then abruptly they were gone. He fumbled in the direction of his joggers, cock bobbing. Reed couldn't help but think it was the perfect length, proud but not threatening, beautifully veined and flushed with color, already leaking. Their mouth watered. "In my pocket. I'm tested regularly, but still."

Reed was there ahead of him, freeing the condom packet from inside Peter's pocket. "Arrogant *and* optimistic."

"Careful," Peter corrected, watching Reed from beneath heavy lids. He reached down, stroked a finger down the bridge of Reed's nose, across their lips, begging entry. "I like sex. I've had a lot of it. Safely." He inhaled sharply when Reed nipped at his fingertip, then sucked hard, drawing Peter's finger in to the knuckle. "S'okay?" His eyes were closed tight again, the question little more than a gasp.

Reed backed off, laughed softly. "Yes." Ripping open the packet, they lifted their chin and kissed the planes of Peter's stomach. Peter shivered, muscles tightening beneath Reed's lips. A pang of sheer lust pulsed through Reed. Sighing in delight, they took Peter's cock in hand and deftly unrolled the condom over his length, following it with their tongue. The latex was flavored, and that was adorable. *Strawberry and sex.* Reed swallowed Peter to the root. Peter gasped, hips flexing, fingers pulling again at Reed's hair.

Reed gripped Peter's ass firmly, setting their pace. Peter groaned again but steadied, letting Reed take control. They rocked together, the mattress squeaking under Reed, slow and then faster as Peter's hips began to stutter. Reed urged

Peter on, reveling now in the feel of his powerful thrusts, his throaty gasps, the smell and taste of him, the blunt heat of him against Reed's tongue and at the back of their throat, the flex of powerful hands on the top of Reed's head.

It was hot, it was right, it was exquisite, it was like coming home.

"Reed." Peter rasped. "Christ, that feels so good. Jesus." The unconscious yank of his fingers in Reed's hair made Reed's eyes water, but in a good way. They squirmed against the mattress, squeezing Peter's ass hard in reassurance, and that was all it took. Peter broke with a shout, pumped hard once and then again, pulsing into the condom.

Perfect, Reed thought tenderly, jaw throbbing. *This man is perfect.*

Peter pulled away, collapsing sideways on the mattress next to Reed, panting. His cock gleamed on his belly, a treat in strawberry-colored latex. He pulled off the condom, tossed it aside, then reached up, easing Reed sideways across his chest. "That was incredible." Still lazy with orgasm, he kissed Reed slowly, then broke away. "I want to do something for you?"

"Oh, lovely, trust me." Reed rested their head on Peter's chest, listening to his heart race beneath his ribs. "There's nothing I love more than a good face fucking in the middle of the afternoon. Or any time of day, really. Besides, it's your birthday." But because they suspected Peter needed gentling, like a nervous weanling after a stint in the wash stall, they reached up and stroked the man's cheek. "Next time?" Reed said, making it a promise. Peter frowned, searching Reed's face, but whatever he saw there must have been answer enough because he nodded.

Afterward Reed helped Peter dress, untangling the

joggers from around his cast, hiding a sympathetic smile when Peter cursed at the difficulty.

"It's why I go commando. It's just easier," he confessed. He watched as Reed deftly did up tiny pearl buttons, settling their own clothes back into place. "A pianist would kill for your hands."

It was a pretty compliment, and it made Reed laugh. "My hands, my feet. You have very specific kinks." They helped Peter up off the bed, handed him his abandoned crutches. "No praise for my mouth?"

Peter smiled. "Your mouth has recently topped my list of favorite things." As if to prove his point, he bent his head and claimed another kiss. It was gentle and sweet, a brush of mouth across mouth, full of unexpected tenderness that made Reed sigh.

"Happy birthday, Peter Griffin."

"Thank you," Peter said against the top of Reed's head. "I can honestly say twenty-eight is one for the record books."

———

GABRIEL WAS WAITING on the back porch, Boudica in his lap. The big man and the small dog looked content to sit together and watch the finches stealing crumbs from around the abandoned picnic table. It was that time of day when the sun was the hottest even as it dropped in the sky. Reed wasn't surprised the rest of the guests had taken shelter in the house. The air outside felt too much like a warm sponge.

The dog started wiggling as soon as she saw Peter, threatening to jump free of Gabriel's lap. Gabriel set her gently on the ground. She ran immediately to Peter's side, bouncing in excitement.

"I looked up her name," Gabriel volunteered. "Teddy's client must have had a sense of humor. She seems pretty well behaved for the breed. So maybe you got off light." He quirked a smile Reed's way. "Not so sure about you, Androku. Black eye, bruised lip, and now your hair looks like it's survived a tornado. Maybe you should make a run for it while you still can."

Horrified, Reed put their hand to their head and discovered Peter's fingers had turned the morning's carefully gelled spikes into unruly, walk-of-shame curls. "Peter Griffin! Warn a person, why don't you?"

"You're gorgeous." Peter's smug tone made Reed blush. They picked up the dog to hide the color in their cheeks.

"John and his cousin and the girl's mother stopped by with a gift. They're in the kitchen talking pony club with Mum. And Ridland called the house line. Wanted to wish you a happy birthday, said you'd been avoiding his calls." Gabriel rose with a sigh, stretched his arms over his head to crack his back. "Don't keep the man on pins and needles. He needs an update. Paris isn't so far away he can wait."

Ridland, Reed realized, must be Robert Ridland, Peter's coach. And from the set expression on Peter's face, he knew better than Gabriel that he couldn't keep Ridland waiting much longer.

"Come inside, you two," Reed coaxed, changing the subject so Peter didn't have to. "It's like a swamp out here and Boudica looks thirsty."

Gabriel led the way into the house where the remainder of the birthday gathering had swarmed the kitchen island like locusts over the remnants of cake and lemonade. Senior, John, and Doc Holliday's wife—a tiny woman who by all accounts ruled her house with an iron fist—were talking politics in one corner while Mac was intently chatting up

Jolene Dotty's father. They made a handsome pair. Jolene and Aine had their heads together over something on Aine's phone screen. Neither Kate nor Teddy were in attendance. Reed hoped Kate hadn't retired early and alone to worry over her pyromaniac ex but couldn't see a polite way around to asking.

"Reed! Mr. Griffin! Is that your new dog?" Jolene made a beeline for Boudica. Aine followed, smiling fondly.

"Careful," Peter cautioned. "Remember, she doesn't know you yet. Show her your hand, let her have a sniff."

"Just like with a horse that doesn't know you, right, Mr. Griffin?" Jolene offered the back of her hand for inspection. Reed watched carefully. But Boudica remained relaxed and happy in their arms, wagging affably as she snuffed at Jolene's knuckles.

"Nicely done. Go ahead and pet her," said Peter in his team captain voice, sending a shiver down Reed's spine. Jolene looked equally affected, although Reed knew she was caught in the painful grip of teenage hero worship and not debilitating arousal.

Aine, standing behind Jolene, winked at Reed as Jolene concentrated on stroking Boudica's long piebald ears.

"Peter," she said, indicating a stack of beribboned books on the counter, "Jolene and her da brought you such a nice birthday gift. Come and see." She smiled across the room at Bule Dotty, wielding the McAuley charm. "I'm sure I don't know how they guessed about your crossword addiction."

"That's all Jo's doing." Bule pumped Peter's hand. Jolene's dad was very tall, taller than everyone else in the room. He gripped Peter's fingers like a vise. Peter supposed it helped to be big and strong when it came to raising buffalo. "She's been following you and Annie since your first World Cup. Big fan, even though jumping's not our thing. Reads everything about you two she can find, don't you, Jo?"

"I know you love crosswords, that you do them for relaxation during down time, and I thought maybe they'd keep you busy after your next surgery." Embarrassment made Jolene's eyes bright.

Suffering a pang of sympathy, Reed hastened to intervene. "I expect it'll be Mr. Griffin following Jolene's career in the near future. Your daughter's a very talented horsewoman, Bule."

"So you keep saying." He wagged his head, exasperation wrinkling his brow. "And I don't doubt it. But as I was just telling Mac here—"

"I want to jump." Jolene looked between Reed and Peter. "Not just jump. Dressage is my thing, I know that. But I want to learn how to jump, too. Pepper could do it, I know she could. And mom says she'll pay for lessons, if you'd be willing, Mr. Griffin. Once the baby arrives, just to keep me out of her hair and see if I have any *proficiency*."

Mrs. Dotty, Reed thought, must be an interesting and possibly frightening woman. Not unlike Gabriel Griffin Sr., who chose that moment to stop arguing politics and frown in their direction.

"We're a sales barn, not a lesson barn. We don't have the right kind of insurance and Peter's got zero background in teaching."

"Bule here happens to be an insurance agent when he's not wrangling buffalo," said Mac. "He and I were just discussing options. Apparently, there are quite a few young people in the area who might be interested in taking lessons, dressage and jumping. And we've got the best arena sixty miles in any direction."

"And the most talent," added Gabriel mildly. Reed caught the quick glance he sent Aine's way and wondered.

Jolene was gazing at Peter now, expression a complicated cocktail of worship and hope. Peter shook his head.

"We're a sales barn," Senior repeated before Peter could speak. "It's the family business, and a successful one at that. Why change what isn't broken? No lessons."

Jolene's face fell. Bule looked away, hiding disappointment. Reed was grateful neither of them mentioned the dressage lessons in Barn A. Kate had said she'd gotten permission for Reed to coach Jolene on-site. But it was glaringly obvious Senior had not been part of the loop.

Peter broke the silence that had fallen over the kitchen. "I'm going to take Annie a little bit of birthday cake." He scraped a few crumbs onto a paper plate, smiled at Jolene. "It's a tradition. Don't suppose you'd like to help me out? I'm afraid I'll drop the plate if I do it myself, and Annie would never forgive me."

"Yes, please, Mr. Griffin. Pepper loves sweets, too, especially granola bars. Dad, can I go?"

"Sure thing, sweetie. I'll follow you down to the barn in a few."

Jolene brightened and Reed felt a surge of affection for Peter that had nothing to do with lust. Peter hid a heart of gold beneath his arrogant exterior, though he'd never admit it.

Golden boy. Reed hid their grin in Boudica's neck. Maybe the family tease had less to do with Olympic aspirations than Peter assumed.

———

REED WOKE IN THE DARK, bewildered both by the warm weight against their back and startlingly wet swipe of a tongue across their nose.

Then Boudica began to whine and everything came rushing back—Peter's birthday party, an evening spent puttering away at barn chores while Peter hung companionably about, a dinner of cheese-and-tomato sandwiches in front of *Doctor Who* at Reed's place. Then kisses and whispers and an invitation to stay the night, and now here Reed was with Peter snoring softly in their bed and Peter's birthday present making it very clear that she needed to go out.

"Hush, now, *printsessa*." A squint at the glowing clock said it wasn't as late as Reed had first thought. Barely after eleven, which meant they'd only been asleep for just over an hour.

Quieting Boudica again, Reed shimmied back into their discarded pair of striped pajama pants. They grabbed their knife from the bedside drawer before taking a moment to admire Peter's sleeping form illuminated by the light of the moon through the open window. He was frowning slightly in his sleep, brow wrinkled. Reed soothed him with a quick kiss before taking the anxious dog downstairs to potty.

She really was well trained, Reed thought as she squatted in the grass just outside the barn. She showed no signs of wanting to gallop off after a scent, but instead kept close as Reed walked the outside perimeter of the building. Moonlight picked out the main house up the hill and the white fencing that edged each paddock. The faint scent of honeysuckle drifted on a light breeze. Boudica sniffed at a boxwood hedge while Reed admired the moon.

They heard the purr of the car engine before they saw it. Whoever was in the driver's seat had cut the lights and was moving at a snail's pace down the drive. It was the sort of trick teenagers pulled when trying to escape their parents' notice as they snuck off after bed to drink or fuck or both. Except Reed knew there were no teenagers in the main house, and they recognized the low-lying silhouette of Mac's little Mercedes. It was also the sort of trick rural car thieves pulled when they didn't want to get shot. Or it was Mark Linden back again to cause more damage.

A jolt of fury made goose bumps rise along Reed's forearms. The McAuley-Griffin family were good people who had done nothing to deserve trouble, and Reed didn't intend to look the other way while they suffered.

The car slid to a stop inside the main gates. Reed heard the sharp whispers of tense voices in muted argument. Boudica growled. Reed scooped her up and ghosted across the lawn toward the Mercedes. The damp grass was cool under their bare feet. The moonlight provided zero cover and left them painfully exposed, but Reed had never backed down from a fight in their life and they didn't plan to start now. They gripped both their knife and Peter's dog tightly, adrenaline making their heart race.

Then Boudica's growls quieted; she licked Reed's ear, relaxed again. She, like Reed, had recognized the two men sitting in the Mercedes, watching their approach through the open passenger-side window. Reassured, Reed slid the knife out of sight.

Mac climbed out of the car, shutting the car door gingerly behind him. He looked unhappy, his party clothes rumpled, an irritated tilt to his mouth.

"Androku," he said coolly. "Why are you skulking around under the moon?"

"Dog needed to piss," Reed replied. "Headed out?" It wasn't really their business, Reed supposed, now that there was no need to chase off a threat. But they couldn't help but notice the care the two brothers were taking to avoid detection.

Curiosity killed the kitten, but satisfaction brought them back.

"That's the question, isn't it." Mac scowled. "I've been arguing against, but as usual I've been wasting my breath. Gabriel here thinks family honor requires we pay Linden a midnight visit."

"Ah." Reed nodded. Gabriel's expression wasn't clear in the shadows of the car, but the way he held his shoulders spoke of barely checked tension. "I understand. Nothing quite like using the fists to speak." And Reed did understand the urge to do violence for Kate's sake, for family honor, to chase the fear away. Still. "In Russia, we call that assault."

"I'm not going to hurt the fucker," Gabriel muttered from the shadows. "Or, at least not much. Maybe bloody his nose or crack a rib. Teach the man to keep away from my sister and her property, since a court order doesn't seem to be doing the job."

"Sure, and you'll do Katie a lot of good from a jail cell," retorted Mac. "Not to mention Mum and Da, when Linden presses charges and puts it around that Tulip Farm's brewing violence." He sighed, took an e-cigarette from his pocket, lighted it. "Come now, *deartháir*. You know this is a bad idea."

"Don't use the Irish on me, you shit. TPing Sandy Branson's house after she dumped Peter at junior prom was a bad idea, too. You complained the whole way there and the whole way back then, too, but we got the job done and felt better for it."

"A bloody nose or broken ribs is not the same as

Cottonelle over a few sycamores," Mac said around his cigarette. "And Linden's monstrous temper in no way compares to Sandy Branson's fickle heart."

"Maybe." Reed could tell from the hunch in Gabriel's shoulders that he wasn't going to change his mind. "Doesn't matter. Are you coming or am I doing this on my own, McAuley?"

Mac smoked for a few more seconds in silence while Gabriel waited and Boudica dozed in Reed's arms. Then he shook his head.

"No. I don't think I am. Not this time. We're better than Linden, aren't we? We don't use our fists."

Gabriel grunted, shook his head without speaking, then rolled up the window. He must have activated the gate from inside the car because the bars split silently down the middle. Reed and Mac stood side by side, watching as the Mercedes purred away into the night. When the gate shut again, Mac stirred.

"Go back to bed, Androku. And for Chrissake, if the shit hits the fan tomorrow morning, don't let on you knew anything about it. It's a family problem, nothing to do with you."

Peter had said almost the exact same thing hours earlier. Reed nodded now like they had then, though they disagreed wholeheartedly. As far as Reed was concerned, family was more than blood, and they weren't going to look away if the McAuley-Griffin siblings were making a mess of an already ugly situation.

CHAPTER FIFTEEN

Peter made the call from Senior's office, sitting alone behind the massive old desk with only the dog to keep him company, surrounded by trophies and snapshots of the past. Ridland was kind and sympathetic, exactly as Peter knew he'd be. He didn't sound at all surprised, which meant he'd been talking to the doctors and Peter's resignation was just a formality.

"You know we've always got a place on the team for you. Public Relations would love to have you, Peter. The last five years have been our most profitable by far, and we all know that has plenty to do with how much the public loves you. Youthful good looks and charm on top of talent and all that."

Ridland didn't offer Peter a place on the coaching staff. The PR dream of youthful good looks was not a plus in an Olympic-level coach, talent be damned. And, as Senior had pointed out so bluntly, Peter had zero background in teaching.

"Just think about it," Ridland said into Peter's silence. "No rush. I know how difficult this is."

Probably he did. In his long tenure with the USET, Ridland must have seen plenty of ruined careers. Equestrian sport was dangerous, both for the rider and the horse, and there was no guarantees of success. Peter had known that hard truth since childhood, but he'd always assumed he was one of the lucky ones, untouchable.

He signed off after promising to come and watch the Games, a promise both of them knew he didn't mean to keep. His head throbbed. He swallowed down three ibuprofen, dry, and then he left the office, closing the door on gleaming silver and satin ribbons, the dog at his heels.

Aine had gone into town for groceries, and Senior was up at the stud barn, but Gabriel and Mac were waiting for Peter on the porch.

"All done?" his oldest brother asked quietly. "Bit like ripping off a Band-Aid?"

"Not at all like that," Peter replied. Still, he appreciated that they had waited to make sure he was all right. Then he took a closer look at the stubble on Gabriel's cheeks and the e-cigarette in Mac's hand, his sad slouch. Maybe they hadn't been waiting on his well-being after all.

"When did you start smoking again? Haven't we had enough trouble with cigarettes on the property? Mum will kill you."

"After the last several hours, I'm allowed." Mac frowned at Gabriel. "And Mum's not here to see."

"What's happened now?" Peter's stomach sank. He recognized the guilty expression on their faces for what it was: bad news. Gabriel's brawn and Mac's cleverness could be a dangerous combination, had been many times before they'd grown out of mischief making, although as far as Peter knew it had been almost a decade since they'd last teamed up to make some sad fuck's life sadder. "What have you two done?"

Mac protested, "Don't look at me. I sat up all night on pins and needles waiting to see my dearest treasure make it home in once piece." He blew smoke at the porch ceiling. "I mean my car, of course, and not our idiot brother."

"I told you," Gabriel retorted, "I just drove his neighborhood for a couple of hours until I cooled off. Nothing happened. I don't think Linden's even in town. The shades were pulled, and his truck and trailer were gone. Horses off property. There's an event up at Apple Knoll this weekend. He's probably rushed right out of town with his tail between his legs, coward."

Peter scrubbed a hand over his own stubble, exasperated. "And how do you know Linden's horses were off property, if you were just driving the neighborhood?" Gabriel winced, opened his mouth, shut it again. "Jesus, Gabriel. Now is not the time to be caught trespassing."

"Especially in my car," Mac pointed out mournfully. Then he straightened. "Listen. Lucky for us Linden is out of town, because Gabriel in jail is not a good look. But neither is doing nothing, when it comes to it. That man meant to cause real damage, maybe even kill some horses. He's made Katie's life a living hell. A restraining order hasn't stopped him, I doubt even extra security will slow him much. We've got to face facts. Linden's just not right in the head."

"A psychopath," Peter agreed, remembering Kate's drawn face as she'd said it.

"Not our call, unless you've got a psychiatrist's degree hanging on the wall I haven't seen. That being said, I did a little armchair detecting last night while I waited for our idiot brother to return, and I've got a plan that doesn't involve using our fists."

"And what's that?" Gabriel demanded. "Another round of useless paperwork?"

Mac secreted his cigarette away in a pocket. "Less paperwork, more legwork," he replied. "Come back inside and I'll show you."

———

"TURNS OUT LINDEN'S GOT A RECORD," Peter told Reed later. "At least two other filings, one in New Hampshire four years ago, another in Maine last July just after Kate's divorce was final. Domestic assault, the both of them. Mac's pretty sure there might be more."

"The man should be in jail." Reed narrowed their eyes at a piece of gunk on the bit they were scrubbing, used a thumbnail to scrape the dirt away, then dunked the bit into the bucket of water at their feet. "Why isn't he in jail? I thought America is all about justice for all." The last was said with a lilt of sarcasm.

They were cleaning bridles in Barn A's tack room, a daily chore that Peter had hated as a child but found soothing as an adult. He could probably strip, clean, and reassemble a bridle in his sleep. Plus, he didn't need two working legs to do it well. The tack room, while immaculate, was tiny. Peter was sitting on the captain's chair Reed had taken down from its place on the wall, Boudica at his feet. The chair and Peter's awkward cast took up most of the room's floor space. Reed was perched cross-legged on an old trunk, boots and socks kicked off for the day, bare toes wiggling occasionally as they worked.

An entry form and dressage test rested on the trunk,

marked here and there with black pen. Jolene and Pepper were ready for the first show of the season. The kid wanted Reed to watch her ride her test. Peter wanted to watch Reed watch the kid ride her test, but he sure as hell wasn't going to admit that out loud, not after he'd crushed Jolene's hopes over birthday cake. He'd done his best to put her at ease after, and she'd seemed okay when she'd finally left for home, but he'd understand if she didn't want to see his face for a while.

The small space should have been claustrophobic, but instead it was comfortable. It was nice to put in some busy-work. The scent of leather and soap was grounding. Peter felt properly useful for the first time in months. And astonishingly horny, because every time Reed scrubbed at a particularly stubborn piece of dirt, the tip of their tongue appeared between their full lips, and Peter hadn't forgotten how that mouth felt around his cock. New paint glittered on Reed's toes to match the silver on their fingernails. Peter hoped maybe Reed had added that little touch just for him.

"Peter?" Reed prompted, pausing in their cleaning, both brows raised. "Are you all right? Head bothering you again?"

"Oh. No." Peter glanced away from Reed's smug grin, gave his attention to the sponge and browband in his hands. "Um. As far as Mac can tell, Linden's not in jail because in both cases the police didn't bring charges. It's an evidence thing. Arsehole seems to have a talent for wiggling his way out of trouble." He wrung the sponge in his fist, wishing it was Linden's neck. "Mac and Da want to revisit the police reports."

"What good would that do Kate?"

"I wish I knew. Mac says he's got a plan, one that

doesn't involve Gabriel dragging Linden into the woods at gunpoint like some sort of mafia enforcer."

He said it lightly, wanting to hear Reed's laugh. Instead Reed's fingers clenched on leather. Their head came up. "What?"

"Hey. Hey, hey. I was just joking." Alarm turned Reed's expression stark, made the fading bruises on Reed's face stand out. "Just a joke," Peter promised quickly. "Gabriel's not actually like that. Hell, he insists on catch-and-release mousetraps in the grain rooms. Hey. Come here. Reed, I didn't mean to scare you."

At first, he thought Reed hadn't heard. They appeared frozen in place, unable or unwilling to move. Then all at once they dropped the bridle they'd been holding and launched themself across the small space onto Peter's lap, almost overturning the captain's chair as they pressed their face firmly against Peter's neck.

"Jesus." Peter gasped. "Androku, you're all elbows." But he brushed his palm up and down Reed's back, soothing. Reed was lighter than they looked, which made Peter scowl.

And they say I need feeding up.

"Gabriel doesn't even own a gun," he volunteered. "Dad tried to teach us all hunting when we were kids, but Mac was the only one who took to it. Should have guessed then he'd turn to law."

Reed snorted into Peter's chest. They sighed and lifted their head. "He *is* the most frightening of your siblings."

"Because of his sharp tongue?" Peter stroked his hand up and down, up and down, until finally Reed's spine relaxed.

"Because he wears Ferragamo shoes into the barn." Flustered, Reed made to stand again but Peter stopped them. "Your leg—"

"Is fine for the moment. I like the feel of you, bony elbows and all. Remember when you asked me to lunch?"

"And you ignored my texts, three times." But the distraction had worked. Reed wiggled on Peter's lap to better see his face, smiling slightly.

"How about a rain check?" Peter coaxed. "Do you like seafood? Zeke's Crab Shack in Mystic's got the best farmed and fried oysters in the state. And their baked beans aren't half bad, either. We could have some lunch, see the water, tour the city, stay the night."

"I wouldn't say no." Reed dipped their head again, nosed Peter's throat until he growled appreciation, flexed his fingers on Reed's shoulders. "Why not today? To mark the occasion?"

"The official end of my Olympic career?" Surprisingly, it hurt less to say it out loud than he'd thought. Reed's teeth on his skin were more immediate than regret. "Wish I could but I've got a five a.m. check-in at Yale New Haven tomorrow."

That made Reed lean back and away to better see Peter's face. Peter squirmed in disappointment. The alarmed expression Peter had worked so hard to chase away returned, making Reed's eyes narrow. "You didn't say your surgery was tomorrow!"

"Just did, didn't I? It's no big deal. Should be home by the end of tomorrow, just an easy hour on the table. Walk in the park, comparatively."

"Walk in the park." Reed's scowl deepened. "Is that so?"

"If I'm lucky they'll put me in a smaller cast, thank Christ. Did I mention I'm going to burn the crutches first thing? We'll have a bonfire."

"No more fires." But they sighed, relenting. "A smaller cast would be an improvement."

"And hallelujah to that. Reed?"

Reed's mouth softened, turned coy. Their pupils dilated, turning their eyes dark. Peter could see the pulse in their neck flutter. *Good.* "Peter?"

"I'd like to kiss you now."

"Ah, well. And I'd like to kiss you back."

———

PETER MEANT to take his time with it. He pressed chaste kisses on Reed's brow, on each eyelid, on that eager pulse in the hollow of Reed's throat, on the corner of Reed's mouth. Reed sighed, eyelids falling half-mast, and then groaned, before placing both hands on either side of Peter's face, pulling him close. Their mouths ground together. Reed bit at Peter's lower lip, wriggling in Peter's lap until their arse bumped his cock. Peter curled both hands on Reed's hips, urging Reed's hips forward and back, chasing friction.

"Oh." Reed pulled their mouth from Peter's, breathing heavily, still working against Peter's cockstand. "That feels so good. I should . . ." They trailed off when Peter nosed their ear, nipping at the lobe. Reed squeaked and sighed, pliant beneath Peter's mouth. "I should lock the door. Should I lock the door? And what about Boudica?"

Peter grated, "Forget the dog. She doesn't seem the sensitive sort. Just lock the door."

Reed hurried to comply, leaving Peter's lap cold, his cock bereft. Peter slid his right hand under the waistband of his pants, gripped himself lightly. He ran his thumb over the tip of his cock as he admired Reed from behind. Despite their small stature, the Russian was built like an equestrian, taut arse and impressive calf muscles shown off to their best advantage by the tight breeches Reed wore. Reed's shoulders were solid beneath their striped polo, their forearms sculpted from a lifetime of farm chores. His own, Peter knew, were much the same. But where Peter was Irish pale and freckled, towheaded and golden fuzzed, Reed was dark. Dark eyes, sun-kissed, dusky skin, hair at the roots the color of the sweet molasses Katie sometimes fed her babies as a treat, washing to light blue at the tips.

"Why, lovely," Reed purred, frozen in a half-turn away from the locked door, "look at you with your hand down your pants. How did I get so lucky?"

"I was asking myself the same thing." Peter worked his hand up and down, up and down, pleased by the way Reed stared as if hypnotized. "I bet you look like a Renaissance sculpture out of your clothes. All muscle and curves. Will you show me?"

Reed hesitated and for an instant Peter was afraid he'd asked too much. But then the Russian laughed, beautiful long fingers fumbling at the zip on their breeches in their haste.

"No one," they said, "has ever compared me to a work of art before." Their breeches were tossed onto the tack trunk, their polo on top of Boudica, who only snorted in resignation. Dressed in a pair of absurdly perfect purple briefs, they struck a pose. "Do I hold up?"

Anyone else might have missed the flicker of uncertainty behind Reed's smile. But Peter was beginning to know this person, this gorgeous sexy fucking amazing person as well as he knew himself, if not better. Meeting Reed's gaze, he edged down his joggers until his cock sprang free, the bead of moisture stretching under his thumb as he worked his way down his length to his balls. He grunted when a jolt of pleasure made him arch in the chair.

"Look. Look what you do to me."

And Reed's dry amusement sweetened to something dangerously close to tender. "Oh, Peter. Better hope that door lock holds because I'm going to take you apart until you're screaming for mercy."

———

THEY FINISHED WEDGED TOGETHER on the cold concrete floor, mostly naked atop an ancient wool cooler Reed had dug out of a tack trunk, the scent of leather and soap and sex mingling in the small space. Boudica had taken up a post by the door, back turned to the room. Peter thought he ought to apologize to the dog, once he got his breath back. He also thought maybe he should check and see if Reed was still alive because the Russian, sprawled limply across Peter's naked lap, hadn't made a sound for several blissful minutes.

At least no one had come pounding on the door. Peter hadn't been the only one begging, pleading, shouting, and cursing as he'd reached orgasm.

Yes, he definitely needed to apologize to the dog.

"Raleigh Summer I and II," he mused instead, reading off the horse show entries now scattered near his elbow. His bad leg threatened to cramp above the cast; he massaged his thigh idly. Sex on concrete had may not have been the best idea, but Peter couldn't bring himself to care. "That next month?"

Reed stirred. "Three weeks out." Grumbling, they rolled off Peter and onto their knees, wincing when muscles pulled. "I'm too old for fucking on the floor, Peter. From now on a mattress, or at least a chair."

From now on, Peter thought, and his heart bumped a little at the thought of a future spent fucking Reed Androku on a mattress or a chair.

"You weren't complaining ten minutes ago." Peter let Reed help him up, gathered the show entries before bothering with his scattered clothes. "You should enter."

"Yes." Reed tossed Peter his shirt, reached for their breeches. "That's what we're doing." They sounded bemused. "As you can see by the forms in your hand."

"Not just Jolene. You. And Annie. You should enter on Annie."

He'd never offered anyone Annie before. She was his partner, his other half on four legs, and he'd been protective of her even before the accident. A bad rider could ruin a good horse in an instant. And Annie was a very good horse.

But Reed was a very talented rider.

Who was standing motionless, breeches in hand, brows quirked. *"Prosti menya?"*

"First Level," replied Peter, warming to the idea even as he shivered in the cool tack room. "Just First Level to start, to qualify. She's out of shape, but she's a superstar, she could do it in her sleep. And you've got three weeks to work on it."

"Of course she could do it. That mare has talent in spades. But why?" Reed unfroze long enough to step into their breeches, but they didn't look away from Peter.

"Why not?" Peter retorted casually, although they both knew the offer wasn't made lightly. "You weren't wrong about her wanting to work. But what that horse really loves is *competition.*"

"Like you," Reed agreed. They popped their shirt over

their head, pointed out, "It's possible to be competitive from the ground. Have you changed your mind about coaching?"

"No." Peter reached out, tidied Reed's hair, bent for a kiss. "I thought it would make the mare happy. And you. I like to see you on her. I'd like to see you *win* on her."

"Competitive from the ground," Reed said again. They leaned in, smiled against Peter's mouth. "Thank you for the very generous offer. I'll think about it, yes?"

CHAPTER SIXTEEN

Reed thought about Peter's offer in the morning as they brushed down Angel, shedding out the mare's stubborn winter coat, and then took her for a trail ride around the farm. Angel, more than any of the other of Reed's six, was a sociable creature who enjoyed visiting every corner of her small world: the yearlings, kicking up their heels in their turnout, Katie's small group of brood mares in the east pasture and the two stallions dozing in their westside runs, and Aine's chickens free ranging in a side yard behind Barn B. She nickered pleasantly at the new security officers in their golf cart near the property gate. One of the two officers acknowledged Reed with a wave.

They continued to think about Peter's offer over lunch, a peanut butter granola bar eaten standing up while they grazed Bob in the sun. Bob was too damaged by the track to ever work hard again, but he'd make someone a pretty lawn ornament or companion horse, if Reed found a match they both could trust. Until then Bob and Reed were content in each other's company, under the sun, sharing a granola bar.

After lunch Reed checked the four cameras in Barn A.

The steadily blinking light by each watchful lens was reassuring. They took a second lap around the property, this time on the old Rhino 4x4 used for hauling hay. The yearlings were dozing in the shade of a tree, the brood mares had disappeared back into their barn, and the stallions were grazing contentedly. The hens were squawking in the side yard and the security team was down to one, a wiry young person who couldn't have been older than eighteen.

"Hello," the young person said when Reed pulled up. "It's Ben's lunch hour. He's gone to grab a couple of burgers." They promised, "No need to worry. We're keeping an eye on things."

"That obvious, is it?"

"Well. You've circled the property twice and it's barely after noon. So sure, obvious. I get it. Break-ins can be scary. But Ben and I know what we're doing."

Stay out of our way, Reed translated. "What's your name?"

"Jacob. Jacob Christie. I'm Ben's younger brother. Christie Security, family business." Pride made Jacob's chest expand.

"Thank you, Jacob." Reed said somberly, "I'm glad you're here."

The problem was, Reed admitted to themself as they sent the four-wheeler back toward Barn A, that today Peter was in the hospital, and it was easier to wonder about riding Annie at Raleigh or worry over threats to Katie and Tulip Farm than it was to think about Peter surrounded by machines and doctors. Reed avoided hospitals like the plague. Hospitals were cold and much too sterile, full of poisons meant to look like cures, and as far as Reed was concerned, bad things happened under their roof.

Reed wanted Peter home and safe with an endless supply of green tea and chicken soup at hand.

And gotu kola balm. Or an arnica and honey poultice? I need to check my supply . . .

Distracted by a mental list of after-surgery remedies, Reed almost ran over Boudica as they pulled the Rhino into Barn A. Luckily Kate had the quick reflexes born of spending time around horses and snatched the dog out of harm's way.

"Holy shit, Androku! Please don't turn Peter's birthday present into a pancake while he's in surgery." The dog and the woman glared at Reed with equally offended expressions.

Wednesdays, Reed thought sourly. They held up their hands in apology.

"She's so low to the ground." He took Boudica from Kate, stroked the dog's ears. "I'm sorry, *printsessa.* I was distracted."

Kate's frown eased. "He's out of surgery and in recovery," she said. "Everything went great. I thought you'd like to know."

The buzz of anxiety that had been tormenting Reed all morning disappeared in a burst of adrenaline. Cradling the dog in one arm, they sketched an involuntary sign of the cross with the other.

"Didn't realize you were religious," Kate said, amused. "Don't let Mum know or she'll haul you with her to church. Irish Catholic and all that." She added, "She's at the hospital now, waiting. Mac will go later, and Da. Gabe's too claustrophobic. Thought maybe you and I could go tonight and bring Peter dinner, what do you say?"

Reed considered waltzing Kate down the barn aisle but settled for a wide grin. "I'd love that."

"Good," Kate replied. "As your boss I can arrange the time off. But I want something in return."

———

REED SET their knife in Kate's hand. The yearlings, curious, gathered at the corner of the pasture where Reed and Kate stood, out of sight of the main house and away from the afternoon glare. Boudica, tied to the fence by her leash, rolled idly in the grass.

"You need a blade with a sharp stabbing point and good cutting edges. I'm comfortable with this old KA-BAR because I've used it as a hay knife since I was a child on my father's farm. You may want something different, maybe a specialty knife." Reed considered Kate's set expression. "Or a gun?"

"You don't use a gun."

"I don't like them." Too loud, and too lethal. Michael had owned a gun he kept in a lock box under his bed. It hadn't done him any good, certainly hadn't saved his life.

"Neither do I." Kate examined Reed's knife. She cleared her throat. "I'm pretty good at self-defense. Started taking classes two years ago, when . . . well. But now I think a knife might be a good idea. Just in case. And you did offer."

Just in case. In case Linden came back. In case he slipped past the Christie brothers, in case he wasn't satisfied with trying to damage buildings and frightening horses, in case he cornered Kate somewhere alone.

"Pepper spray really isn't my thing, either," she told Reed. "I know it works for many people, but sometimes it just escalates the problem." She swallowed audibly, glanced down at her feet, shoulders slumping. In that moment Reed would have cheerfully murdered Linden and danced the Barynya on his grave.

"Here." Gently, Reed showed Kate how to curl her fingers around the leather-wrapped hilt. "Like that. Fingers around the belly of the handle, thumb against pointer finger. Blade up, at an angle, see? Keep your wrist locked."

"Like this?"

"Yes, good. Remember how that feels." Reed took the knife back, returned it to its place on their belt. "Let's see what sort of self-defense you've learned. Then maybe we'll bring out the markers."

"Markers?" Kate shucked off her work shirt. Underneath she wore a plain white tank top. Her arms were muscled. They were also, Reed saw, laddered with scars from her wrist to her elbows. She lifted her chin, daring Reed to comment. Reed didn't, though they did wonder if Peter knew.

"Markers," they confirmed calmly. "There's a Sharpie or three in Annie's trunk. Washable is better, but beggars can't be bosses. That shirt needs color anyway."

"I think you mean beggars can't be choosers." Kate frowned down at her shirt. "And what do you mean, color?"

"You'll see," Reed promised. "This is a nice distraction, thank you. Much better than riding the perimeter over and over or obsessing about Raleigh. I'm going to come at you now," they warned. "Ready?"

"Uh—" Kate looked much like a deer caught in headlights.

That won't do at all, Reed thought, and then shouted with enough force to send the weanlings racing away across the pasture: "READY?!"

Kate was much better at self-defense than she'd led Reed

to believe. Like Reed, what she lacked in size she made up for in speed and strength. Using a combination of quick kicks, dodges, and hand strikes, she easily kept Reed outside of her bubble. Once she landed two fingers near Reed's right eye, and twice she stopped with her heel inches from Reed's crotch.

"You were being modest, not something I've come to expect from a McAuley-Griffin," accused Reed ten minutes in, out of breath and pleased. Kate Griffin was far from helpless. "Tae Kwon Do?"

"And kickboxing. Some Jeet Kune Do. It's a good class. And I have reason to keep up." Wisps of hair had escaped her ponytail and stuck to the perspiration on her face and neck. "You're not bad yourself."

Reed shucked off their polo. "I've had reason to keep up. Let me get the Sharpies. And then I'll lecture you on anatomy. Red or blue for your marker?"

Kate's stare flicked over Reed's worn undershirt. Just as Reed had done earlier, she kept any comments to herself. "Red," she called as Reed jogged back toward Barn A. "Like the blood of my enemies."

Thirty minutes later Kate and Reed were sprawled in the grass, sweaty and snorting with laughter, when they heard the snarl of Kate's dirt bike approaching from the direction of the main house. The yearlings scattered again. Boudica woke from her nap and jumped to attention. Kate quickly slipped her work shirt back on over her tank top—now marked all over with blue Sharpie where Reed's "knife" had connected.

Reed didn't think it was the Sharpie she was hurrying to cover up. They sat up and pulled on their polo, hiding the red marker splotches on their torso. It must have been the right decision, because Kate shot them a grateful look.

I understand keeping secrets from family, Reed thought, amusement drying up. *I'm sorry you think you need to.*

It was Senior on the Honda, red-faced in the heat but smiling. Reed had never seen Peter's father smile before. It was much more attractive than the scowl he habitually wore.

"Your mum just phoned," Senior told Kate after he'd cut the engine. "Peter's awake and grumpy with it, good lad. They'll keep him one night, but Mum says he's cleared for honest food this evening." He sounded as self-satisfied as if he'd held the scalpel himself. Reed wondered if there was any end to the man's massive ego.

Kate jumped up, threw her arms around her father. "*Buíochas le Dia.* Thank God. And didn't we tell you Peter would come out ahead? Up all night worrying about nothing, weren't you, Da?" She stepped back, cheeks flushed and violet eyes sparkling. "Reed and I will bring him burgers tonight."

To Reed's immense surprise, Senior didn't protest their inclusion. He squeezed Kate's shoulder, adding gruffly, "And one of those chocolate milkshakes he loves to sweeten the deal, Katie. Don't forget. He'll be wanting a treat, I imagine."

———

REED DRESSED for the trip to the hospital like a knight preparing for battle. The thrifted Gucci shirt in teal lace was four years out of date but deftly paired with simple tan straight-legged Levi's and Reed's going out Blundstones. The shirt's pretty lace cutouts were just whimsical enough to make Reed smile at the bathroom mirror. They added a scarlet silk square to their front pocket, fluffed their hair, grabbed their bag, and took the stairs down from the apartment two at a time.

Their herd whickered hello. Reed paused just long enough to pass out sugar cubes and nose pets before hurrying through the twilight to the main house. The air was warm, smelling of roses and summer. Fireflies flickered over the pastures. Reed's heart felt light behind their ribs.

They couldn't wait to see Peter, to make sure he ate something more nutritious than hospital food or take-out burgers, to tell him about the decision they'd finally come to in the shower.

Kate greeted Reed with a wolf whistle. "I don't know how you make it work, Androku, but you sure as shit do. Get in." She gestured at the red MINI Cooper parked in front of the house. "What's in the bag?"

"Homemade couscous salad." The inside of the classic car was beautifully maintained, just like every other thing Aine McAuley loved. "With cucumber and sweet tomatoes. Also, some herbal tea."

"Nice and healthy." Kate sounded reluctantly impressed. The MINI rumbled to life. She sent it zipping down the drive, working the stick shift with a practiced hand. "Still got to swing through The Habit, though. Promised Peter a double bacon burger, and I never break a promise." She tossed Reed a wink. "Play with the radio if you want. It's a bit of a drive."

The burgers and fries came in a greasy bag and smelled delicious. Reed tucked them away with the couscous while Kate juggled two giant chocolate shakes. The attendant standing just inside the hospital's sliding glass doors shook his head but didn't comment. He also gave Reed and Katie a thorough but discreet once-over before sending them both through a metal detector. Reed was glad they'd remembered to leave everything sharp at home.

Yale New Haven seemed a nice enough place for a hospital. Brick and glass with touches of faux stone for warmth. But it still smelled like hospital—industrial cleaner and plastic and stress. And the beeping of distant machines, the ding of elevator doors, the hushed voices combined to produce a familiar soundtrack heard in hospitals the world over.

It felt like the building air conditioning was running full blast. Reed shivered.

"Yeah, I don't much like hospitals much, either." On the main elevator, Katie pushed the button for the fourth floor. "Emergency room? In our line of work that's like a second home. But the actual hospital part? Depressing as hell. Even the maternity ward. The tiptoeing around just creeps me the fuck out."

"Bad things happen," Reed suggested, shivering again.

"Well." Kate squared her shoulders. "Not today, friend. Today it's all good because we've got warm burgers and cold couscous and Peter's in for only one night instead of weeks."

Peter was hidden away in room 402. The door was halfway open, a curtain pulled beyond it. Reed could hear Peter Capaldi's bold Scottish tones from within. Kate pushed her way past the curtain, holding the chocolate shakes up like an offering.

"Yoo-hoo, Golden Boy! I hope you're not on the loo with your pants around your ankles because I've brought sugar, carbs, and company."

"You know I'm not wearing any pants," Peter replied from beyond the curtain. "Tell me you remembered double bacon." He sounded his usual arrogant self, which gave

Reed the courage they needed to take one step into the room.

"Would I let you down in your time of need, little brother? Double bacon it is. Plus something even better. Reed, stop lurking and come in. I know you've seen him without his pants before."

Blushing, Reed slipped around the curtain. The room was larger than they'd expected, equipped with two beds, although Peter's was the only one in use. There was the usual collection of intimidating machines beeping softly beside the bed, a single uncomfortable-looking armchair in one corner, and an uninspiring view of a brick wall through a square window.

"Androku?" Peter scooted up along the hospital mattress. "Kate didn't say you were coming." His genuine smile made Reed flush. Peter beckoned. "Come and sit with me. What's in the bag?"

"Couscous and herbal tea to go with your artery clogger." They let themself be coaxed farther into the room. Peter was a much healthier picture than Reed had expected, even in a flimsy blue hospital gown and with an IV stuck into the back of his right hand. It didn't seem like he was in an any immediate danger of dying. Quite the opposite.

"Look!" he told Reed cheerfully, pointing at his left leg. "Ankle cast! Isn't that fucking amazing! No more wheelchair, no more crutches. Just one of those scooty things and then a cane. A cane's sexy, right? Do you think a cane's sexy?"

Kate snorted as she unwrapped burgers. "On the good drugs, I see."

Peter ignored her. He patted the mattress. "Sit. We can

pretend I'm eating the couscous while I wolf down the red meat."

Reed perched on the narrow hospital mattress. It was awkward, and uncomfortable, but when Peter captured their hand and brought it to his chest with a squeeze, Reed knew they wouldn't want to be anywhere else in the world.

"You look fantastic. You always look fantastic." Peter kept Reed's hand as he accepted a ginormous burger from Kate and took an equally ginormous bite. "This tastes fantastic." He groaned around a mouthful of red meat and bun. "Everything's fantastic. And that's not just the good drugs talking. Fuck. Hospital food is the worst."

"Have some fries." Kate dumped the carton on Peter's lap before settling into the armchair. "But for Chrissake don't make yourself sick or I'll be persona non grata around here."

Peter closed his eyes and took another bite, chewing more slowly. His hand was warm against Reed's colder fingers. His hair needed washing and a five o'clock shadow turned his jawline golden. The hospital gown did nothing to hide his broad shoulders or the line of his spine, which Reed appreciated.

On the TV, Peter Capaldi was saying something about squishy pears, or at least Reed thought so. Capaldi's thick accent was sometimes baffling.

Peter swallowed his food and opened his eyes.

"The good drugs make me sleepy," he confessed. "I'll probably be out like a light before Kate finishes sucking down my chocolate shake. Stay for a while anyway, will you? It's lonely here, and I've missed you."

"You haven't been gone twenty-four hours." But Reed wasn't sure they could deny that Lake Baikal stare. And besides, Peter was still clinging to Reed's hand. "I'll stay," they relented. They thought it wouldn't hurt to keep a watchful eye on Peter's nurses, just to make sure they knew what they were about. "For a little while."

Peter was drooping already. Kate stole the rest of his burger before he could drop it in the bedsheets. Reed felt a moment of irritation.

"Narcotics are dangerous and overprescribed," they told Peter.

Peter nodded somberly. "Normally I'd agree. Not today. Today I love narcotics."

"Here." Kate shoved the armchair up against the mattress, gestured at Reed. "Sit here while he naps. Peter, you need to let go of Reed's hand. That's right. Time to sleep. Do you need a lullaby with your tuck-in?"

Reed though her airy humor was misguided, especially when Peter's fingers went lax, his eyes fully closing. Reluctantly Reed shifted to the chair, which was uncomfortable and guaranteed to bruise their ass. The relief they'd first felt seeing Peter vanished. Tucked under the sterile hospital blankets, his left leg propped on a foam wedge and a line in his arm, Peter looked unusually vulnerable.

"Relax," Kate said quietly, sweeping fast food wrappers and french fries into the trash. "No bad things happening today, remember? Just hold his hand while he sleeps and before you know it, we'll all be back home at the farm."

Reed automatically sketched the shape of the cross in the air before gripping Peter's hand. The machines in the corner beeped. On the television *Doctor Who* had switched over to the BBC news. Kate left the room in search of hot water for tea.

In his sleep, Peter smiled.

CHAPTER SEVENTEEN

"Good. Move her off your leg," Peter told Reed as Annie walked briskly around Tulip Farm's outdoor arena. "Remind her who's in charge. The reins belong to you. Don't let her forget."

The outdoor arena had always been Peter's domain. Senior had put it up long ago when Peter first started training for Juniors; Gabriel kept it maintained and groomed. It was large, 100 x 300 feet. The footing, a mixture of silica and rubber, was the best money could buy.

Every spring the jumps went in until late fall, when Gabriel hauled the brightly colored stands and poles back into storage.

Every spring except this one, Peter corrected himself. Which was ridiculous, because although everyone thought of the outdoors as Peter's arena, Kate used it regularly to train young sale horses to the jumps. But it was also handy, because today Reed and Annie had the whole ring to themselves without the hassle of moving jumps.

"Nice," Peter called as Reed executed a beautifully sharp walk to canter depart. "She's warming up, relaxing.

Remember, Warmbloods take just that much longer to get their head in the game."

Peter heard Reed's loud snort of amusement from across the ring. He hid his own laugh with a cough. Annie didn't need the distraction. It was her first time back in the outdoors since Old Salem, and she was on edge, looking for jumps that weren't there. But she was sound, which was a miracle in itself, and Reed didn't seem put off by the hump in her back, which reassured Peter that his plan to pair them at Raleigh was a stroke of genius.

If only he could convince Reed of the same. Five days had passed since Peter's return from the hospital—more than enough time to bring the topic up—but he was unaccountably nervous about issuing the invitation a second time.

It's not like you're asking them to move in with you, for fuck's sake.

But somehow it felt just as intimate, if not more so.

Up near the main house a tractor started up, a rumble of diesel that gave Annie the excuse she was looking for. The hump in her back became a mountain and suddenly she was in the air, bucking and snorting, head down and ready to rip up the arena.

Boudica, startled from her nap under Peter's knee scooter, jumped up and began to bark.

"Hush up, that's not helping." Peter's heart gave a thump, but he forced himself to stand and watch as Reed calmly got Annie back under control, sending her forward at a gallop so she couldn't brace against their hands, reminding the mare that she had a job to do. Reed's quiet competency was beautiful to watch. The Russian's seat stayed glued to the saddle throughout Annie's entire airborne performance. Peter doubted Annie could have bucked Reed off even if she'd put her heart into it.

Peter's dressage saddle, built specifically for Annie, was much too deep in the seat and long in the flaps for Reed's smaller figure. Reed had a dressage saddle of their own, an Equipe Emporio. Peter called in the family saddler to make a few adjustments to the tree, and now the Emporio fit Annie like she was born to it.

As Peter watched Reed quickly bring Annie back to her paces, he thought Reed rode her as if they'd been partners for much longer than half a summer.

"Fresh as a daisy." Reed laughed as they drew up beside Peter. Annie chewed loudly on her bit in agreement. "Flatwork is boring today. She'd rather fly." They stroked her neck. "Can't say I blame her. It's a treat to ride outside." Reed paused while Annie blew, then glanced down at Peter under blue-tipped lashes. "She wants to do freestyle."

Peter's heart thumped again. He couldn't quite keep the grin from his face. "Does she?"

"Yes. If this one can't jump, she wants to dance. And, as it happens, I have a talent for musical choreography."

"Can't say I'm surprised." But Peter smiled ear to ear. "Hair metal?"

"Don't be gauche, lovely. We'll come up with something classic and spectacular, just as she deserves."

Peter very much wanted to stretch up and give Reed a kiss, but Annie was rolling a suspicious eye at the knee scooter, and they didn't need another spook. "Does that mean you've thought it over and decided to say yes?"

"Yes." Reed's fingers were nervous in Annie's mane, but their mouth was smug. "You're right. The mare has more competition in her. If you are willing to share her, even for just a little while—I think it would make her happy."

"And you?" Peter desperately wanted to hear Reed say yes. Out loud, so he could know for sure that Reed mean it. "Would it make you happy?"

"Yes, it would make me happy also." The Russian cleared their throat, cheeks flushing up under the brim of their helmet. "Very happy."

"Good." Instead of a kiss, Peter settled for squeezing Reed's ankle through their boot. "That's . . . really good. Now, take her back out. The mare can't piss off work just because she's fresh, so don't let her."

"Careful." Reed snorted as they turned Annie toward the rail. "You're beginning to sound dangerously like a coach."

———

"I DON'T UNDERSTAND why it's such a big deal," Teddy confessed as she flexed Peter's left knee. "You'd be excellent at it. I've seen the videos. Peter Griffin, USET's golden boy, giving solid advice from the sidelines with just the right amount of grim disdain."

Peter groaned, and not just because his leg throbbed under Teddy's punishing hands. "Don't you think it's time we let 'golden boy' go?"

"Christ, no," retorted Mac from where he stood frowning out the studio windows. "We've been calling you that since your lead line days. Much too late to stop now. You do realize it's never been about the medals. It's about the holier-than-thou attitude, brother dear."

Peter shot Mac a middle finger but didn't argue the point. Mac had been in an odd mood all day, showing up at the main house without warning just as Peter and Kate were finishing their morning coffee ritual, his usually

impeccable suit rumpled, his temper short. He'd immediately closeted himself in the office with Senior where they'd
stayed until it was time for Peter's PT. And then he'd shot
out of Senior's office and insisted he play Peter's chauffer,
even though everyone involved knew Kate was looking
forward to spending time with Teddy.

"Seriously, though. I bet you'd have students knocking
down your door. It could only be good for Tulip Farm,
right? You know horses, you're great at bossing people
around, and they still love you for it. What's not to like?"

Mac and Peter exchanged a glance as Teddy helped
Peter sit up and then began to unfasten the Velcro loops on
his cast.

"When Mum and Da started the farm, it was always
about training and sales, starting babies, never coaching.
Other than within the family," Peter added. "Partially, it's
an insurance issue—"

"Da can easily afford the insurance rider." Hands in his
pockets, Mac shook his head. "It was Mum's idea, you
know."

Peter had been busy watching Teddy as she examined
the scars on his calf, the newer incision on his ankle. The
flesh was still pink around the stitches, and it itched. After
months in a full cast, his leg was pale and atrophied, a long
way from sound. He might have felt sorry for himself if not
for Mac's distraction.

"What do you mean?"

"The lessons." Mac paced back and forth in front of the
windows. He was still wearing the same suit he'd arrived in,
and his dark hair, usually neatly slicked back, was beginning
to rebel around the edges. Whatever business had kept him
so long in Senior's office was distressing Peter's usually
unflappable brother.

Linden. Peter knew. *It's something to do with Linden.*

"It's Mum who wants to bring a lesson program to the farm. She put the bug in Katie's ear. And you can bet your fine arse she's working on Da. She'll have him turned around eventually, so you might as well stop pretending you don't like the idea. Mum always gets her way."

"Landscaping and now a lesson program." It wasn't impossible. Aine had always enjoyed opening her home to strangers. But hadn't they just hired security to keep the farm contained? "What's she thinking?"

"Maybe she's thinking she's given a large part of her life to her husband and adult children and would like to focus on her own dreams for a change," Teddy replied tartly. "Ms. Aine's no stranger to coaching herself, or wasn't she the first to toss you in a saddle and teach you how to stick?"

"She was." And she'd been a fixture in the stands and in the ring for most of Peter's career, bolstering his confidence on the bad days, firing up his ego when he needed to go in hot. She had a lighter touch than Senior when it came to coaching and, if Peter was honest with himself, a better eye for the distance.

And now that Peter was no longer competing, of course she was looking for another rising star to back. That stung, just a little. Still—

"Do you think she'll convince Da?"

"Mum always gets her way," Mac repeated with a shrug. "Da's probably already put in a call to our insurance agent. My bet? Mum'll have you signed up for certification before the month is out."

"Exciting." Teddy slapped Peter lightly on the back. "Coach Golden Boy has a ring to it." She handed over his cast. "Put this back on and rejoice, for I predict only another week on your knee scooter and then we can try a crutch or cane. Until then, use your weights three times a day at the minimum. God knows your gastrocnemius muscle can't do anything but improve. And I'll see you again Thursday."

"I still don't like you very much," Peter said with feeling. Every part of his body ached.

Teddy rolled her eyes. "Liar. You're a McAuley-Griffin. You think I'm the bee's knees or you would have warned me off your sister months ago."

"She has you there. The McAuley-Griffin clan looks after its own." Mac elbowed Peter. "Come on, little brother, the day's flying by and I've got better things to do than watch Teddy frown over your gastrocnemius, whatever the hell that is."

The sound of Teddy's raspberry followed them out the door. Mac led the way down the hall. Peter followed, steering the scooter carefully so as not to scrape the walls. He remembered his first time in the building, stuck in a wheelchair and Mac piloting. The industrial carpet had seemed darker that day, the windowless hallway deeply depressing. It had suited his mood perfectly.

Now he couldn't wait to get out into the fresh air and sunlight.

"What's your hurry?" Mac grumbled, barely looking up from his phone as Peter passed him by. "Be careful with that thing, these loafers are worth more than your life."

"Like you said, the morning's gone. I've got things to do. What's put you in such an ugly mood, anyway? Is it Linden?"

Mac wouldn't meet Peter's eye. "No. I mean, yes, obviously. It's always Linden." He stabbed the elevator button with his thumb. "Listen. There's something else. Something I need to show you. And you're not going to like it."

"WHAT DO YOU MEAN, you hired a PI to do a background check on Reed?" Peter scowled down at the accordion file on his lap. As soon as they were back in the car, Mac had pulled the file out from beneath the passenger seat and offered it with all the enthusiasm of a man who knew he was about to face a firing squad.

He wasn't wrong.

"We have a PI on retainer, Peter. We have had, for years. Ma had trouble with the Irish tabloids first. And then there was Katie's divorce. Comes in handy, honestly. A bit of extra help on the side, for when I can't drop everything and run after one of Da's wild hares." He sighed. "Of course I ran a background on Androku, just like I should have done on Linden before he broke Katie's heart. It's obvious you've fallen for them. Gabriel says they've been up on Annie every day in the last three weeks. That's practically a declaration of forever after."

"Piss off." Peter's fingernails left dents in the accordion file. "You're no better than *he* is. Can't ever just let anything alone."

Mac went white around the mouth, but he didn't argue. He said, "If you mean Da, then you're not wrong. He taught you 'heels down, eyes up.' He taught me family comes first. Always. And you should be glad. Because what the PI dug up on Reed Androku might save you some heartache. It's not pretty, Peter." Mac sounded regretful. "They've got some sort of connection with the Russian mob. I'm sorry."

"The Russian mob." *What the hell did that even mean?* "Jesus Christ and fuck you, McAuley." Peter exited the car awkwardly but with determination. He slammed the door shut and started limping back across the parking lot. "I don't need you managing my affairs. Get the hell out of my sight."

"Hey! What are you doing? Peter, come on. Don't be like that. How are you going to get home?"

"Teddy will give me a ride." He spoke through gritted teeth, not looking around. He didn't want to see Mac's stricken expression. Because of course Mac felt bad about interfering now that things had come up shit. No wonder he'd been in a mood all day. Unlike Senior, Mac actually cared. Not that it made things any better.

Peter thumbed up Teddy's contact on his phone. His leg throbbed angrily. "I can't look at you now. Go the fuck home." He hated that he'd left his scooter in the back of Mac's car, but even more than that he hated that he'd taken the accordion file with him, and it was tucked securely against his side as he dialed Teddy's number.

———

TEDDY DIDN'T ASK any questions. Peter appreciated her empathy. She zipped him home on her lunch break in her old Prius, radio turned up too loud for conversation. She gave the guards at the farm gate a friendly honk as she turned onto the property—"Where'd Senior get those two dorks? Craigslist?"—and booted Peter out in front of the main house where his knee scooter was waiting pointedly at the foot of the wheelchair ramp.

"Thank you," Peter said stiffly. His anger had cooled enough over the drive that now there was room for embarrassment. He was a grown man, and he'd had enough of sulking over life's curveballs.

"You're welcome. Five-star service, that's Sánchez PA.

Say hello to Ms. Aine for me." She turned the radio up again as she drove away.

He hadn't realized his mum was waiting until Teddy pointed her out. Sitting on the porch in the shade, a tall glass of lemonade in hand, her laptop closed and resting by her side, Aine watched him silently as he limped up the ramp.

Peter knew that weighted silence. It was the same absence of warmth that had greeted him at the kitchen door when as a kid he'd taken Cricket out without permission, or when as a teenager he'd stumbled home past curfew with alcohol on his breath.

"I feel like I'm fourteen again."

"No better than, maybe," she agreed, violet regard sharp. "Scaring your brother so and ignoring your doctors' orders on top of it." She nodded at the scooter, still at the bottom of the ramp. "I thought you were supposed to keep weight off your ankle for another week."

"It's fine. Good, even." That was stretching it. His ankle ached and his femur twinged as they always did after physical therapy, but the boot cast provided enough support that he made it up the ramp and into a chair without much trouble. He'd pay for it later, but he couldn't bring himself to care.

"I didn't mean to scare Mac. I also didn't want to throttle him, so it seemed best to take a break. Besides, he knew Teddy wouldn't leave me stranded. She's a good egg."

"A good egg," Aine repeated. Her expression softened. "Your granda used to say that about his horses, the fine ones, the ones he thought would go far."

"I remember."

"Teddy's been a friend to this family." She offered Peter a sip of her lemonade, sighed when he refused. "So has

Reed. I'm sorry, Peter. If your da had come to me beforehand, I would have warned him off. Reed is not Mark Linden. Only a fool would think otherwise."

"Are you calling Da a fool?" It surprised him. She wasn't usually so blunt about Senior's failings.

"He's an Englishman, isn't he?" She frowned out over the lawn, regarding her flowers like a general regarding her troops. "I love your father, but he's not perfect. None of us are. We make mistakes. But we muddle on, and we do okay, better than okay. Your da means well. He always does."

We muddle on. Peter supposed that was one way to put it. "Mac says you want to coach again."

"I miss the teaching," she confirmed. "The Pony Club days. The children, especially. You, your brothers, your sister. You're all grown up and on your way. I'd like to feel productive again."

"Mum. You hold the farm, the family, together." It saddened him that she couldn't see that.

"Exactly." She smiled at him. "Now I'd like to do something for me."

"If you can convince Da." But by now he knew it was a given. Just like Mac had said, Aine always got what she wanted.

"I suppose I'll manage. Marriage is a compromise. *Love* is a compromise." She nodded at the file in his lap. "Speaking of, what will you do with that now you have it?"

He didn't protest her assumption that he was in love with Reed. What good would it do? She'd always seen through him, known him inside and out. Better, maybe, than he knew himself.

He lifted the file. "This is shady. Without Reed's permission. It's wrong."

"Whatever the investigator dug up, Mac didn't like."

She met his gaze. "I don't like to encourage interference, *mo mhac*, but maybe you shouldn't throw it immediately into the trash. Reed isn't Linden, but that doesn't mean you should wear blinders down the track."

He'd thought about tossing the file into the living room fireplace, setting it ablaze and watching it burn. Watching temptation go up in smoke. Because he was dangerously close to opening the damn thing and reading every word. *What the hell, Reed? The Russian mob?* But—

"If there's something in Reed's past I need to know, they'll tell me."

He must have sounded more certain than he felt, because Aine relaxed, settling deeper into the swing and setting it rocking gently in the afternoon.

"Good. That's what I wanted to hear." She grabbed her laptop, patted the cushion next to her. "Now come sit next to your mum and help me with certification, aye? Registration is very complicated, and you know computers hate me. And we might as well register you while we're at it, don't you think?"

CHAPTER EIGHTEEN

"The vet says it's probably an abscess," Jolene reported. Reed could hear her despair clearly even through the speakerphone. "But what if it's not? What if it's navicular? Maybe we should do X-rays."

"It's been a bad summer for abscesses. We've had two on the farm in the last month ourselves," Reed soothed. "Have your vet call me. I know a few tricks. And don't panic, Jo. It will be fine. Peter, tell Jo not to panic."

"Don't panic, Jo," Peter called obediently. He and Gabriel were walking ahead along the west side of the property, moving carefully to keep Peter's cane from catching in the grass. The cane was plain black. He'd finally abandoned the riding gloves, which Reed had immediately noticed and kept to themself. The cane was utilitarian, even boring, but Reed loved it because it expanded Peter's world.

"Raleigh is less than one week off!" Jolene wailed. "What if she's not sound by then? This so totally sucks!" She was close to tears.

"What did I just say?" Peter demanded of the phone,

stopping. Reed made a rude face at him, but Peter ignored it.

"Don't panic. You said don't panic."

"If it's an abscess, Reed and your vet will have it blown in plenty of time for Raleigh." Peter plucked the collar of his T-shirt away from his neck. It was a muggy morning. The cotton was sweaty and wanted to stick to his skin. Reed couldn't blame it. Peter's skin, sun-kissed and freckled, was worth sticking close to. "If it's not, we'll deal with it. There's always another show, Jolene. Remember that."

Reed sneaked a glance sideways. For Peter, there would never be another show, at least seen from the saddle. But he didn't look bothered, or even as if he recognized the irony. In fact, he was smiling slightly at the phone, team captain mode in full force, radiating confidence. It looked good on him.

We'll make a coach out of you yet, lovely.

"Yes, sir." Jolene blew out a long breath, making the speaker buzz. "You're right. There's always another show. Even if I *am* trying to qualify for Nationals." The last was said in a mutter.

"Even if you're trying for Nationals, Jo. Now hang up the phone and go dig up some Epsom salts. The more you soak it, the better she'll be."

"You said 'we,'" Reed told Peter once they'd hung up the phone and slipped it back into their pocket. "'We'll deal with it.' I guess that makes it official. Well, that and the new cavaletti set up for painting in the breezeway. Coach Griffin."

Peter refused to take the bait. "The old cavaletti needed freshening up." He adjusted his grip on the cane. "Jesus, Gabriel, we could have taken the Rhino."

"Da's using it." Gabriel shortened his stride so Peter

could keep up. Barely contained worry darkened his eyes to a stormy purple. "He and Jacob Christie took it up to the house to review the tapes."

Security tapes. Because there had been another trespass overnight, which explained Gabriel's uneasy mood, Peter's fading smile, and the frisson of unease twitching along Reed's spine. Not arson this time—Reed crossed themself spontaneously—but an equally appalling act of vandalism. One that loomed large as they reached the old hay barn, spray-painted across stone in angry red.

WHORE. BITCH. SLUT.

A wave of nausea forced Reed to look away, to stare at the grass and breathe through their nose. Vandalism was bad enough, but the violence behind the graffiti was impossible to ignore.

"Some things never change," Kate said lightly from where she stood frowning up at the red letters. One of the Christie brothers—the eldest of the two, Ben, Reed remembered—hovered protectively at her shoulder. "Mark never was creative with his profanity." She sounded much too calm.

"I would have had him except for the pepper spray," Ben told Peter and Gabriel. He was built like a soldier and wore his security uniform like a second skin. Fresh scrapes and bruises covered one side of his face. The knuckles of his right hand were visibly swelling. His eyes were red and puffy, still leaking tears. "He came prepared for a fight."

Gabriel made a sound of angry sympathy. Ben brushed it off with a wave of his hand. "Leastways it wasn't a gun. And we have him on camera." He gestured at the fish-eye shining beneath one edge of the roof. "Not that it will do us much good, in the dark. Plus, his face was covered."

"Difficult to light all our outbuildings." Gabriel sighed as if he took the failure personally Probably, he did.

"Dropped a can of paint as he ran. We'll test it for fingerprints, of course. If he's in the system, something may pop."

"He's in the system," Kate said. She coughed to hide a new quiver in her voice. Peter limped across the grass and threw an arm over her shoulders, pulling her against his side. "He's in the fucking system. I was there the last time they booked him."

Ben Christie looked at her with badly disguised pity. "Don't you worry, ma'am. It's a large property. Hard for two of us to keep track of every corner, you understand? I'm thinking about bringing on a couple temps. But this is just a bit of paint, easily washed away. You stay close to the house and you'll be just fine. Sooner or later, we'll get him."

Kate laughed around a muted sniffle. "How old are you, Ben?"

He stiffened into what Reed assumed was military rest. "Just turned thirty-three."

"I'm a full two years your junior, so quit with the ma'am. And Ben?"

He tilted his head, waiting.

"This isn't 'just paint.' This is assault," she told him. "I'll keep close to the house, but you need to be careful. My ex is not a rational man. What if he *had* brought a gun?"

Ben ran a hand over the scrapes on his face. "Don't you worry. I've got his measure now. Nobody gets the jump on me twice."

"I'll go into town and get some sandpaper, some paint stripper," Gabriel volunteered. "Peter and I will get this cleaned up in no time."

"Let me snap a few pictures, walk around the site first."

Ben asked Kate, "Are you up to taking a look at the security footage? It would help if we knew for sure this was Linden's work."

"It is. This is right up his fucking alley. But, sure. Let's go take a look."

"I'll need a few minutes to finish up here. But there's no need for you to stay. Gabriel, maybe you wouldn't mind escorting your sister back up to the house? I'll join you in a few."

Reed didn't miss the way Gabriel's stark expression turned almost fond when Ben glanced his way, or the very faint blush that stained his stubbled cheeks. It was a familiar look—one Reed had come to expect from Peter in his more affectionate moments.

Interesting.

Gabriel must have caught Reed noticing. The glare he sent their way was sharp enough to draw blood, full of dislike. Reed took a surprised step backward into Peter.

"Careful," Peter murmured into their ear, steadying Reed gently. "That's my good foot you're standing on."

"Sorry." Puzzled, Reed watched Gabriel and Kate start up the hill.

"Not a problem. I'm feeling a little light-headed myself. It's an ugly display. Don't worry, we'll get it washed off."

"It's not that." Reed leaned back against Peter, grateful for the support. "Or, it is. That. But. I thought your brother liked me?"

"Gabriel? He does," Peter said, watching narrowly as Ben bagged the abandoned can of paint.

"Not anymore, I don't think. If looks could kill, I'd be bleeding out on the grass."

"I'm sure you're imagining things. Gabriel likes everyone. Or maybe it's he doesn't *not* like anyone. He really doesn't pay that much attention to other people. He's too busy with the schematics in his head." But Peter wouldn't quite meet Reed's eye.

The frisson of unease twitching along Reed's spine grew claws.

———

PETER'S HANDS were magic on Reed's bare feet, the bottle of white wine on the floor near the sofa half-finished. They were taking turns drinking straight from the bottle. Peter had complained that Reed's collection of mugs and shot glasses weren't classy enough for a Santa Barbara Chardonnay. Reed had called Peter a snob and suggested with a lewd wink that drinking from the bottle was more fun anyway. Peter had blushed and shrugged, and now they were both more than a little buzzed, tired from an afternoon spent painting over the graffiti on the barn, trying not to think about a threat splashed in red.

Peter was pretending to watch the baseball game playing silently on Reed's television. His laptop was balanced on Reed's thighs.

"Oh God." Reed groaned when Peter's fingers found just the right pressure point below the ball of their foot. "That's perfect, yes? K1."

"K what?" Peter's freckles disappeared when he blushed. For a man with a worldwide reputation in bed, he was still adorably shy about expressing his kinks.

"Kidney pressure point one." Reed let their eyes drift shut as Peter pressed harder. "Sends blood to your core. Sexy times. No, don't stop. *Puzhalsta*." They offered, "In a horse, the point is closer to the hock, in the biceps femoris."

Peter's fingers froze. He choked off a giggle, then began to laugh in earnest.

Reed opened their eyes. "What?"

"'Sexy times' and horse acupuncture in the same breath? Only you." But he gave Reed's toe an affectionate tweak.

Reed waved an airy hand. "All knowledge is good knowledge," they said. "And speaking of." They pointed at the laptop. "Only eight more online certification courses to go, lovely. Let's make that seven before bed. How do you feel about"—they squinted thoughtfully at the screen—"Equine Law and Ethics?"

"Not very optimistic." Peter abandoned Reed's feet for the wine bottle, grunting as he readjusted his cast. "Ethics and competition don't always go hand in hand, especially when it comes to the horse world."

"Which is why it's a good thing the horse world isn't losing you," Reed replied. "From what I understand, the McAuley-Griffin clan and ethics *do* go hand in hand."

"Yes, well, at the moment Linden's making me wish that weren't so." But Peter traded the Chardonnay for his laptop. "Let me see that. Mum got ninety percent on the L and E quiz," he grumbled. "And she's been holding it over my head. Which means I have to do better."

On the television a batter in a blue uniform was rounding the bases. Reed took a moment to admire their form before reluctantly climbing off the sofa. They stretched, hummed, eyed Boudica where she was asleep in a square of fading sunlight.

"The dog needs a piss and so do I. Shall we walk the perimeter and then do an early night feed?"

"Gabe's doing the five o'clock walk." Peter didn't lift his frown from the computer. "I'm scheduled for the midnight."

"Midnight's a long way away, and it's time to stretch your leg. Besides, I want to hold hands as we stroll romantically beneath the setting sun."

Peter looked up. Reed batted mauve-tinted lashes, aiming for seduction.

Peter's brows lowered. "Try that on all your rehabs, do you?"

Reed grinned, not the slightest bit repentant. "Only you, lovely, only you."

———

IN UNSPOKEN AGREEMENT they walked the perimeter all the way up the hill to the old hay barn. On the way they passed one of Ben's temps, an extremely tall person wearing an obviously brand-new *Christie Security* logo jacket. They gave Peter and Reed a salute with the heavy flashlight they carried in one hand. "Evening."

Peter acknowledged them with a brief nod before limping on. Reed flashed them a smile, grateful. They'd sleep better knowing that there was increased security on the property.

The guard flashed a crooked, gap-toothed grin in return.

"Christie better be vetting them in and out," Peter muttered once they were past. "I don't like having strangers on the property."

"I remember." Reed bumped their shoulder against Peter's, amused. "Ms. Aine is an angel, but the rest of your clan could do with lessons in hospitality."

"We're famous for our hospitality!" Peter protested. "So long as you're family. Or a paying client."

Reed opened their mouth on a suitably cutting remark, then closed it again as the old hay barn loomed on the horizon. Peter's fingers tightened on Reed's. They walked the rest of the way without speaking, then stood together in the grass, silently regarding the freshly painted exterior. Gabriel had insisted on three solid coats of paint, just to make sure the red letters didn't bleed through. Reed hoped three coats was enough.

"When Katie first brought Linden home," Peter said at last, "I thought they were the perfect match. God knows I hadn't actually spent that much time with the man. I was away too much. But he was part of our world, you know. Of our bubble. A horse person. A paying client. And he made Katie happy, at least at first. At least on the surface. Now I think I really just didn't to make the effort to look deeper. You're good at that. At looking deeper."

"Caretaking, my mother would say." Reed shrugged. "Seems to be an impossible habit to break."

"Maybe." Peter smiled faintly. "But *you* noticed. You said you had a bad feeling about Linden, from the start."

Reed let go of Peter's hand, hugged themself for comfort, sighed. They didn't like throwing accusations about, but that hadn't stopped them from standing up for Mark Linden's poor mare. It felt like a long time ago now, and it wasn't something Reed liked remembering.

"The bit," they explained. "Double-twisted wire gag with chain. Not technically eventing illegal, but only a shit would put a bit like that in a horse's mouth and then crank it tight. I told him so, but of course he just laughed and called me soft. How a person treats their animals says a lot." Reed risked a glance Peter's way. "But I didn't know the rest of it. You shouldn't blame yourself. Some people bury their secrets so deep they disappear."

"Secrets." Peter rotated his cane, drilling a shallow hole

in the turf. "I guess you'd know something about secrets." There was a question in his voice.

Reed frowned. Did he mean Kate and her hidden scars? Reed didn't think so. Did he mean Michael?

"I know secrets can sometimes be painful, or divisive," they said gently. "And sometimes they need to be kept. Me, I'm a page in an open *Vogue* magazine." They tried a flirty smile. Peter's lips curled in response, but he didn't laugh as Reed had hoped. They sighed, sobering. "Michael's secrets kept him safe. They were tricky, and they weren't mine to tell. Surely you understand that. And Linden—I reported him to the USEA for animal cruelty. As far as I know nothing came of it. If I'd realized it went as far as abuse toward his domestic partners . . ." They trailed off, uncertain. "I'd like to think I'd have done something more." It was distressing not to know for sure. "Domestic abuse situations are also tricky." Reed hated that excuse felt like failure. "I think you know by now I don't stand by and ignore suffering."

"Yes. I know that." And there was that familiar line over the bridge of Peter's nose that meant he was unhappy. Reed, glancing at the freshly painted barn, understood the feeling. They wished they could do something more to help, wished they *had* done more when they'd first realized Linden was a shit.

"Whatever you need from me, I'm here." It was the best Reed could offer. They hoped it was enough. "Also my sexy knife-fighting skills, if it comes down to it."

Peter snorted. "Thank you. Let's hope it does not come down to it." He slung an arm around Reed, looked up at the indigo sky. The stars were still hours away, but fireflies were beginning to stir in the long grass at the edge of the property. "I don't care what your mother says, I think it's my favorite thing about you."

"My knife-fighting skills? I haven't even demonstrated, to you or to her." Connecticut fireflies were different from their Russian cousins. Reed remembered delicate blue ghosts, a hint of phosphorescence in the night. Fireflies on Tulip Farm were large and flashed amber, visible even before dark.

"That you care," replied Peter gruffly. "That you don't just stand by and ignore suffering. It's good. It's unusual and very good."

"Oh," said Reed, smiling foolishly at the fireflies. *This man. This beautiful, beautiful man.* "Thank you. Most of the time, I like that best about me, too."

CHAPTER NINETEEN

The night before Raleigh, Reed gave Peter the best blow job of his life and then kicked him out of their bed.

"Nerves?" Peter repeated, as he fumbled the buttons of his jeans, still dizzy with the change in circumstances. "You don't mean it. You're the least nervy person I've met."

Reed, looking deliciously rumpled in a pair of Peter's boxers and a faded Pink Jones muscle tee, made a tsking sound.

"Everyone gets nervous first night of competition." They hopped off the raised platform and made for the expansively furnished kitchen, heading for the stove.

The horse trailer with living quarters was at least fifteen years old, but Aine tended it with the same love she extended to her Cooper, and the Featherlite had aged well. The decor might have been dated, but it was clean and elegant, the trailer sound. The drive from Tulip Farm to the Hunt Horse Complex in Raleigh had taken Peter just over eleven hours. Once he might have done it under ten, but on Teddy's orders they'd stopped often to make Peter exercise his healing leg.

"Sitting for long periods of time is not recommended at this stage of the game," she'd scolded. "Your circulatory system is still repairing itself. Let's not throw a wrench in the machine."

When Reed, who Peter knew for a fact had been regularly driving the farm truck into town, confessed they didn't *actually* have a driver's license, Peter resigned himself to a longer-than-usual haul and planned accordingly. They'd stopped here and there along I-95, for Peter to walk and Reed to check on the horses. Annie was a seasoned trailering pro, but Peter hadn't known what to expect from Pepper. He'd been impressed. The pony had loaded without complaint and tolerated the long day on the road as well as could be expected.

They'd pulled into Hunt Complex just before dinnertime, bedded down the horses in their assigned stalls. Fed and watered. Unloaded the trunks and Aine's shiny new Tulip Farm–branded tack curtains. Hooked up the trailer to water and electricity and collapsed in the living quarters with a cold beer and one of Reed's healthy salads.

After eleven hours behind the wheel, Peter would have preferred a pizza with everything, but he wasn't going to put up a fuss with sleep and possibly sex in his near future.

He got the sex—the blood still hadn't returned from his cock to his brain—but apparently sleep wasn't happening just yet.

"I know you're exhausted, lovely." Reed dug a kettle from a drawer under the sink, a new and surprising addition to the trailer. They set it on the burner, flicked on the cooktop. "I just need a half hour or so alone before bed. If you don't mind. And then we can cuddle up like two forks in a drawer and sleep." The glance they shot Peter was smug. *You just fucked my mouth with my finger up your arse, that* look said. *And left teeth marks in my shoulder when you came. Are you really going to tell me no?*

"Spoons," Peter replied. "It's called spooning."

"Of course it is." Reed shifted their attention to a collection of tea bags that had seemingly appeared from nowhere. Peter felt strangely bereft. "Go and check on Annie and Pepper," the Russian said. "Make sure they're warm enough, it's going to be a brisk night. Oh, and check Annie's wraps, make sure they're not too loose, if you wouldn't mind. Those magnetic ones can shake free." They chose a mug from a cupboard. It was the ugliest mug Peter had ever seen: a lumpy Pegasus, chipped near the tail. "I'll be waiting when you get back."

"But. What will you be doing while I'm gone?" Boudica, dozing on a fleece blanket on the couch, opened one eye at Peter's plaintive tone, then closed it again. No help from that corner, then.

Reed smiled. "Everyone has their little first-day rituals, yes? We all know about your crossword puzzles. Now, shoo. Thirty minutes, no sooner."

And just like that Peter was kicked out of his trailer and into the night. As soon as the screen door shut behind him, he wished he'd thought to grab a jacket and not just his cane. Reed was right. It was going to be a comparatively brisk one, for Raleigh. Which meant the morning would dawn bright and clear, perfect weather for a show.

No lover had ever dared remove Peter from his trailer before, but he found he wasn't the least bit angry. And not just because post orgasm endorphins were still flooding his system. It was good to be back on the circuit, even if the badge inside the pocket of the jacket he'd forgotten said *coach* instead of *competitor*, even if the arenas were set for dressage and not the more familiar show jumping.

He inhaled the crisp air, scanned the RV campground. The space was packed to bursting with trailers, fifth wheels, even a few truck campers. Lights burned behind pulled curtains, and a varied selection of quiet music tangled to make one soundtrack. Tomorrow—Saturday—night it would be much louder, full of celebration and comradery. But tonight, people were tired from hauling in, or nervous about that first ride, not quite ready to let go of preshow nerves.

Even so, Peter saw a few familiar faces as he made his way through the campground toward the site barns. They greeted him with smiles and genuine enthusiasm. He wasn't exactly the golden boy of the dressage circuit, but he was part of the larger horse community, and he was recognized. Even with his limp and his cane, or maybe because of it.

As he crossed behind the middle show ring toward Barn D, he came face to face with, of all people, Lacy Kline. She was caught up in that long-legged stride she used when she was late to nowhere, and she was almost past him before she wheeled around in surprise.

"Holy shit, is that you, Griffin? I heard you were up and about. I assumed that meant day trips to the grocery store and the physical therapist, not a jaunt down to Raleigh." But she smiled at Peter and held out a calloused hand.

"Unexpected, I know," Peter said. Lacy looked him up and down as she pumped his arm. He knew she was noting the cane and the way he tended to stand with more weight on his right leg than his left, the slight unbalance that made his hip ache at night.

"Lucky," she corrected. "You're damn lucky it was your leg and not your spine, the way the two of you went over. Did they ever catch the bastard who did it?"

"I'm sorry?" Peter arched his brows in inquiry, wondering if Lacy had started the show libations early. She had a well-known taste for small-batch bourbon, and unlike Reed, no patience for preshow rituals. "I don't know what you mean. It was an unfortunate piece of luck, that's all. An accident."

"An accident?" Lacy's smile sharpened to an angry scowl. "That was no accident, Griffin. That was sabotage. Someone was up in the stands, playing with one of those goddamn laser pointers, flashing it in the arena. Plenty of people saw, reported him after. He flashed it at me, and then he flashed it at you, at your mare. Don't you remember?"

A flash of bright angry red light, not the reflection of arena fluorescents, something painful and blinding, in Peter's eyes and in Annie's.

Peter's skull gave an angry throb. He gritted his teeth, pressed the pain back.

"I don't remember much," he confessed slowly. "But really, some kid in the stands playing with a light can't be called sabotage."

"Teenager, not a toddler. Sweatshirt, hood pulled up to hide his face. Pushed his way out of the stands like the devil was after him once you went down." She shook her head, gray eyes flinty. "Senior didn't tell you?"

"No." Of course he hadn't. Peter pinched the bridge of his nose. The last thing he needed was a migraine.

"Oh well. We all know how your dad is. Like a mother hen when it comes to his brood. Probably didn't want you worried. Besides, there's nothing saying it was directed at you, personally. The way I hear it, guy was flashing that laser all over the place, interfering with the rounds. Looking for some excitement."

"And he got it." Peter's smile felt like a grimace. Lacy slapped him gently on the shoulder.

"You know the gig. Heels down, eyes up, and never let 'em guess you've lost stride. Where you stabled? Rest of the family here?"

Peter shook his head. "Just Mum. Senior and Kate are down in Wellington. Buying trip. Gabriel's minding the farm, as usual."

"Good luck to them. I'll stop by and see you and Ms. Aine tomorrow, bring you a brew, toast your recovery."

Recovery seemed a strong word, but he wasn't going to turn down good wishes or a cold brew. Lacy might be rough as old leather, but she'd always been kind beneath the grit. "Big Barn, row twelve. You'll recognize Annie."

Lacy waved in acknowledgement, whistled as she walked down the path. Frowning, Peter watched until she disappeared into the night.

Sabotage was a word he'd been hearing too often lately. The fire, the graffiti, and now someone up in Old Salem's stands causing a disturbance. Surely Linden hadn't been up at Old Salem, flashing a laser. Besides, the man was over thirty and had a beard. No one would mistake Mark Linden for a teenager.

It had to be a coincidence.

———

THE BIG BARN was full of the peaceful sounds of preshow nighttime prep. Horses munched their hay, rattled their grain buckets, sighed, and farted in their sleep. The grooms had gone home for the day, but braiders were up and about with their stepladders and yarn belts, deftly turning mane and tail into works of art. Most had earbuds in place, but somewhere deeper in the barn a radio played. The muted strains of Pink Jones's "Lifetime Achievement" made Peter think of Reed, specifically Reed's gorgeous, talented, generous mouth.

By the time he reached Annie in row twelve, he'd shrugged off most of his worries and traded the beginnings of a headache for the beginnings of a lazy cockstand. Luckily the aisle was empty of humankind, and if Annie noticed the bulge in his jeans she was kind enough to give him a pass.

It wouldn't be the first time. Peter and Annie had been partners for the best years of his young, horny life, and he'd be lying if he pretended he'd never taken a lover in the show barn in the dead of night. Once upon a time, he'd been flying too high on success to think of consequences. Thank Christ he'd obsessively practiced safe sex, or he might be regretting more than his reputation.

"Those days are gone," he told Annie as he unlatched her stall and stepped inside. She greeted him with a low whicker, as she always did, sniffing at his face and hands in search of sugar cubes. "Time to pack up that part of our life for good, what do you think?" He ran a hand down her neck, along the Bladder Meridian, searching for tension. He'd learned the Masterson Method from one of the USET's equestrian massage therapists and had been a believer ever since. He'd even managed to impress Reed with his knowledge of Search, Response, Stay, Release, which was a plus. Peter had discovered he very much liked to impress Reed.

"I may not know colic teas or herbal poultices," he'd said, drawing on his best arrogant bastard facade, "but I'm well versed in the importance of treating my horses like athletes. And I know pressure points."

Reed had only laughed and demanded a demonstration

of Peter's massage techniques in the bedroom. Peter had acquitted himself nicely.

No, Peter thought, as he followed the Bladder Meridian with his palm over Annie's withers and along her spine, *I'm not going to miss the days of waking up with a different person in my bed every other night.* Those had been easy, breezy months full of new awakenings and unexpected delights, but he was a different person now. And not because he needed a cane to walk the distance from trailer to fairground, or because sometimes he saw spots out of the corner of his eye.

Because he couldn't imagine waking with anyone but the Russian in his bed, couldn't imagine sharing unexpected delights with anyone other than the beautiful slice of color that was Reed Androku.

But did Reed feel the same? Peter thought maybe so. But it had been weeks and despite Peter's increasingly less subtle nudges, Reed hadn't given any indication they knew the Russian mob was even a thing.

If there's something in Reed's past I need to know, they'll tell me. Easy enough to promise Aine. Less simple when he had to look at the accordion file tucked away under the socks in his underwear drawer. It was harder every day not to open the damn thing and learn Reed's secrets.

The secrets Reed was hiding from *him.*

No. That was wrong. Peter had to remind himself again and again that it wasn't personal. Reed was entitled to privacy.

It felt personal. Because Peter had never kept secrets from the ones he loved. As far as he was concerned, relationships were built on trust. Peter trusted Reed. Hell, Peter trusted Reed with *Annie.*

Why couldn't Reed return the favor?

"Chrissake." Peter buried his face in Annie's side, inhaling. The smell of horse almost always put everything right. "What am I doing? We're both adults with our fair share of baggage. And I'm acting like a moody teenager."

Annie yawned, either because Peter's heartache was boring or—more likely—because Peter's massage was releasing endorphins as intended. Peter sighed, shook his head, continued to work along her spine. By the time he'd finished her right side and moved onto her left, they were both feeling more relaxed, calm enough to face the overly chipper braider who popped her head into the stall well past 11:00 p.m.

"Oh, shoot, am I interrupting?" The braider, fresh faced, smiling, and clutching a can of Monster Energy Extra, blinked twice at Peter. "Wow, holy shit. You're Peter Griffin. Shit, I'm so sorry, I've been following you forever, I can't believe you had to drop out." The kid's bright eyes landed on Peter's cane. "It so completely sucks." Then those eyes widened, and the can of Monster shook in trembling fingers. "Wait, no way, is this . . . This is Remedy? This is Remedy! Holy *shit* I'm braiding Tulip Farm's Remedy."

Despite a pang, Peter found himself smiling. "She answers better to Annie. Braiding's not her favorite thing, but she's just had a nice massage. Should stand for you so long as you keep the hay bag full and in front of her nose."

"Oh. Good. Thanks, thank you so much. It was a pleasure meeting you, wait till I tell my sister. Hey! Could I get a selfie—"

But Peter, anticipating the question, was already limping quickly away up the aisle, the tap of his cane on concrete a counterpoint to Pink Jones's trademark bass thump.

———

WHEN PETER MADE it back to the trailer, he found Reed busy steaming the creases out of their show shirt while Dire Straits played softly on the stereo. The Russian's breeches, stock tie, and show coat were already laid out on the bed, presumably waiting their turn on the rack. Steam had turned Reed's usually impeccably cared for hair into curls; their face was washed free of makeup and beaded with moisture.

They greeted Peter with a grin, held up one finger for silence.

"Enter working trot at A. Halt, salute, proceed working trot. C: track left. H-X-F: Lengthen trot. Working trot at F. A, back down center line . . . "

Reed had surprised Peter by choosing Dire Straits for Annie's First Level freestyle. He'd expected the obvious: Pink Jones or The Rolling Stones. But Reed had insisted on an old Dire Straits medley, one they'd used at Bitsa.

For luck, they'd said. And now: "K-A-F: working trot again. F-X: leg yield left. X: circle right ten meters . . . "

"You know it by heart," Peter pointed out gently. "You've probably known it by heart since you were ten. Also, you're dripping." He reached out, gently wiped a bead of perspiration from the tip of Reed's nose. "It's bloody hot in here. Why didn't you open the windows if you were going to iron?"

"Steam," Reed corrected. "First day ritual, steaming. And of course I know the music by heart. But what if I forget?"

Their mouth crumpled into an anxious frown. Peter wanted to kiss the nerves away. Instead, he held out his hand for the steam nozzle. "Here, let me finish. Get yourself something cold to drink, you're probably losing electrolytes. And open the windows, Reed. Tell me you haven't been listening to that on loop for"—he checked his phone—"Jesus. Two hours."

"Time got away from me." Abashed, Reed watched Peter beneath lowered lashes as they gulped water from a reusable bottle wrapped in the Tulip Farm logo. "And you were supposed to be back after thirty minutes. I got caught up in the steaming, and you came back late, so let's blame you for the electrolytes."

"Let's not." Peter ordered the stereo off. He eyed the blue split-tail coat and white breeches on the bed. Immaculate, traditional. Reed, so colorful in every other part of their life, apparently preferred tradition when it came to show attire. A legacy of Bitsa, Peter assumed. "It's late. Hang those up and get into bed while I finish the shirt." He aimed a sideways look at Reed, enjoying the way his boxers showed off their strong legs. "Annie got a massage tonight. Looks to me like you'd benefit from a little Bladder Meridian work as well. And then some sleep."

Reed choked, coughed, ran the back of their hand across their mouth. "Oh. A massage, yes, please. Sleep?" The glance they returned Peter was coy. "We'll see. It's possible nerves will keep me up all night. I may need a little pregame encouragement. Coach."

Peter only snorted. Reed had been more excited on the day Peter's coaching qualifications had arrived than either of them had expected. Apparently, a certain Russian expat had a shallowly buried authority kink. *Very* shallowly buried.

"Into bed you go," Peter grated, more than willing to play along. "On your stomach, practice your breathing. I'll join you shortly."

CHAPTER TWENTY

Jolene was the perfect dressage princess in the Saturday morning warm-up ring. Her coat and breeches were spotless, her boots polished until they shone. Her hair was confined in a hairnet and tucked neatly under her helmet. Even her show gloves were clean. As a child, Reed had suffered consistently from dusty show gloves.

Pepper the Super Pony was equally well turned out, glowing healthy burnished copper, her white shocks shining. Jolene had obviously put a lot of muscle and attention into preparing for the morning's competition. Reed hadn't doubted the girl's drive to compete, but it was nice to see evidence of her devotion to the sport in the ring.

"She looks good," Peter said from Reed's side. "Confident."

"Jolene's serious about winning." Pride made Reed stand a little bit taller. It was an undeniable ego boost. Peter Griffin, ex-Olympian, complementing Reed's star pupil.

Reed's only pupil, but that hardly mattered. There would be more, now that Tulip Farm was opening up for lessons. What student wouldn't want a chance at the new

McAuley-Griffin coaching team? Peter and Aine would be in high demand.

"I meant the pony. Pepper the Super Pony is a fucking jewel. She'll score high all on her own. Look how she goes on the bit. Mum, we should see if the Dottys want to sell when Jo grows out of her. It won't be long before the kid's looking for something bigger."

"Language, Peter," Aine murmured from Reed's other side. She clutched a to-go cup of coffee, nose buried in the steam as she watched Jolene in the ring. The woman was Irish to the bone but consistently chose coffee over tea. Reed couldn't help liking her all the better for it.

To Reed, Aine said, "My son always looks first to the horse. Also, as a child he preferred to duck out on his dressage lessons, and it shows. Reed, tell me what you see?"

Because Reed planned to compete Annie for the season, they hadn't applied for the certification that would have made them a professional. Which meant Reed couldn't officially coach Jolene on the show grounds or take payment for the casual lessons given to Jolene on Tulip Farm. It didn't matter. Both Aine and Peter deferred to Reed when it came to dressage. Which Reed found incredible but also very gratifying.

"SHE'S FORGETTING TO BREATHE," Reed said, diagnosing Jolene's tight hands and even tighter shoulders with the familiarity of several months' worth of lessons. Reed's own nerves were beautifully settled after a night's worth of vigorous sex and a dollop of vodka in their coffee. "And losing control of the pony's left side."

"Breathe, Jolene," Aine called promptly. Her Dublin accent was music in the morning. Several heads turned, taking note. Yes, the students would be lining up before the day was out. "You're doing gorgeously. Pepper's happy, no buffalo. Relax and breathe."

"'Little Bunny Foo Foo,'" said Reed. "She needs to remember 'Little Bunny Foo Foo.'" Peter snorted but Aine's serene expression didn't flicker.

"'Little Bunny Foo Foo,'" Ireland's most decorated eventing star called into the ring. "Remember 'Little Bunny Foo Foo,' Jolene."

"Stop laughing." Reed nudged Peter with their elbow. "That song is perfect for keeping rhythm and lowering the heartrate."

"And look at that." Aine took a sip of coffee, swallowed. Her violet eyes were smiling beneath the brim of her Yankees baseball cap. "Like magic, her shoulders come down and chin up. Balanced again behind the pommel. Peter, you should be paying better attention instead of admiring Reed in white breeches."

Peter blushed. Reed smothered a laugh. And in the warm-up ring, Jolene remembered how to breathe.

———

IT WAS Jolene's first test of the season, which meant no one but Jolene expected perfection. And Reed had to give her credit; once inside the show ring she piloted Pepper with a confidence unusual in Children's. Even Peter looked subtly impressed, slapping Jo's boot lightly as she exited the gate.

"Congratulations," he said. "Hopefully the judge missed that little hitch between medium and collected. You smiled right through it, serene as Saint Columba. If we're lucky, he didn't notice."

"It was my fault, I saw Dad in the crowd right then, that's all. I was so excited he'd made it in time to see me go." Jolene grinned ear to ear as she swung out of the saddle. Reaching into the pocket of her breeches, she pulled out a sugar cube and fed it to Pepper. "Such a good Super Pony, the best pony." She flashed her grin at Aine. "I remembered what you said, when she stumbled. Riding is fifty percent skill, twenty-five percent luck, and—"

"Twenty-five percent acting," Peter finished. "You still using that old gem, Mum?"

"Worked with you and your sister, didn't it, *mo mhac*? It's an old gem because it's true. All of us have to be a little bit Audrey Hepburn in front of the judge. Jo and Pepper, you were wonderful." Aine gave Jolene a quick hug. "Let Peter and I take Pepper back to the barn. You and Reed can go find your da and wait for the scores to be posted. There weren't many of you in Children's, and you're down the list. It shouldn't be long."

Jolene gave Pepper a last sugar cube and a kiss on the forehead, then looked at Reed for permission. "Can we?"

"Of course. He'll want to tell you how beautiful you two were, I'm sure. Which way?"

"Over on the stands behind E. I just can't believe he got here in time!" Jolene bounced on the toes of her boots.

Before Reed could turn away, Peter bent down and awarded them a quick and wholly unexpected peck on the lips. "Don't stay away long," he said quietly. "Two o'clock will be here sooner than you think."

Two o'clock. When Reed and Annie would ride their own test, and they'd be lucky if it went half as well as Jolene's. But Peter's kiss was warm on Reed's lips and Jolene's smile brighter than the midmorning sun, and Reed was sure that nothing, not even a botched test, could ruin this first show day of the season.

Waving goodbye to Peter and Aine and Pepper the Super Pony, Reed followed Jolene clockwise around the Children's and Junior's ring, weaving through a crowd of excited parents, coaches, and competitors. There was a fuck ton of money on display in both horseflesh and fashion but Reed, who had learned early on that a secondhand saddle was usually just a good as new, or that an Hermès belt off eBay was still couture, knew better than most that looks could be deceiving. That expensive horseflesh might be half-leased for the season, those Cavallo boots borrowed.

But that drool-worthy plum Miasuki gilet? Reed thought wistfully, eyeing a beautifully dressed brunette in the crowd. *Definitely not off eBay.*

Despite attempts at diversity and equality, equestrian sport still favored the wealthy. And even clever thrifting couldn't change that. Only time and good leadership would.

"I see him!" Jolene called. "Dad, Dad! Over here!"

Reed saw Bule immediately. He stood a good head and shoulders over the rest of the crowd. If Jo took after her father, Peter was right: she'd be outgrowing Pepper sooner rather than later. How quickly did children sprout? Reed had never given it much thought before. They'd have to ask Aine. She'd had four of her own, after all, and had moved at least two from pony to horse without any apparent side effects.

Bule bent down to swoop his daughter up in a hug. As he did so he moved slightly to the side, revealing the much shorter man he'd been talking to. Shock made Reed hesitate, slowed their step like a green horse preparing to spook. But Jolene was looking back over her shoulder, calling Reed's name, and Bule was waving.

Reed covered the hitch in their stride as best they could and pinned on their best serene smile. It was the same smile they'd regularly used with Sacha Turgenev on the rare occasion Michael had brought them together. It felt strange to wear that mask again, but Reed wasn't about to let Mark Linden—standing cool as a carrot next to Bule as if he weren't an abusive shit and destroyer of property—know they had his number.

"Reed!" Bule offered his hand. Jo's papa was an enthusiastic handshaker, and also unaware of his own strength. Reed tried not to wince when those iron fingers almost crushed their own. "Wasn't she amazing? And I got it all on video. Your mom will be so pleased, Jo."

"She did beautifully," Reed agreed. They refused to look at Linden. Maybe the man would take the hint and walk away. "Hard work paying off, right? Something to celebrate!"

"We were thinking ice cream up at the pavilion," agreed Bule. "Once Jo gets Pepper washed and put up. Join us?"

"Dad!" Jo groaned. "You know Reed's showing at two, I *told* you so. They have to get Annie ready, and I bet Mr. Griffin has a lecture planned before the warm-up ring like he did for me." She rolled her eyes but couldn't quite hide her pleasure. "He had *a lot* to say."

"He's very serious about his new coaching job." Reed made themself wink at Jolene. "Check the postings on your way back to the barn. Ms. Aine is right: they should be up by now."

Bule and Jo said their goodbyes to Reed and to Linden. Reed watched father and daughter walk away, hand in hand, conscious all the while of Linden's unfriendly stare. Why was he still there? Couldn't the man take a hint?

"Androku." Apparently not. "Heard you'd made the

mistake of hooking your cart to the McAuley-Griffin luck. Novice mistake. Gone bad lately, hasn't it?"

Reed swallowed a sigh, turned on their bootheel, and looked down their nose at Linden. It was gratifying to smirk without having to crane their neck. The farrier wasn't much taller than Reed. Compact, slightly bow-kneed, hunched in the shoulders, Linden had the rosy features, unkempt beard, and bloodshot eyes of one who'd spent more time recently on a bar stool than in a saddle.

"I don't know what you're talking about." Reed let their fingers drift to the knife on their belt. "And I won't stand here and listen to you speak badly about the McAuley-Griffins."

Linden's smile was as false as Reed's. He flicked his eyes at Reed's knife, smiled wider. Passersby may have thought they were two friends stopping for a chat between rings. Reed knew better, and Linden obviously did, too. Did he realize it was Reed who'd reported him to the USEA? No. Such things were kept confidential.

"Listen." The farrier leaned in close. It took every gram of Reed's self-control not to jerk away. "I fell for their act at first, too."

"I don't know what you're talking about," Reed repeated. They were desperately glad Peter was back at the stalls. They weren't sure they would have been able to keep him from knocking Linden into the dirt, weren't sure they would have tried.

"Thought they actually meant it, when they welcomed me as part of the family." Linden said quietly, a poisonous murmur in a busy crowd. "But trust me when I say: unless you're born a McAuley-Griffin, you're nothing in their eyes. Never will be. Hell, I married into the clan and they still wouldn't give me the time of day unless I asked extra nicely.

Senior refused to hire me on as the farm farrier, can you believe it?" In a sudden change of mood, he cracked a loud, nervous laugh. A few heads turned to look. "Said I wasn't skilled enough for his horses."

"Good for Senior. Horses live and die by their feet. I wouldn't hire a man like you to look after my herd, either."

"What's that supposed to mean?" Still much too close, Linden sneered.

"You're a bad man," Reed said simply. "You shouldn't be allowed to work on animals. You shouldn't be allowed near them. You shouldn't be allowed on the show grounds. In fact—" It was Reed's turn to raise the volume, draw the attention of more onlookers. "As far as I'm concerned, you should be in jail."

Linden reared back, noticed they were becoming the center of attention, shook his head sadly. "You don't know what you're talking about. I almost feel sorry for you, Androku. Almost. Do me a favor: tell my ex-wife to stop spreading lies about me, to stop trying to ruin my business. She'd be smarter to focus on keeping her own afloat, now that the McAuley-Griffin star has fallen. Literally."

He walked off with a swagger in his step. Reed wanted to go after him, wipe the sneer off his mouth with a few cutting words and a good old knuckle sandwich.

Nothing quite like using the fists to speak.

But there were people discreetly watching and wondering. They'd already heard what Linden thought of Peter's family. Reed didn't need to muddy Tulip Farm's reputation further by starting drama in front of a crowd.

Besides, Reed wasn't that sort of person. Self-defense was one thing. Knocking Linden to the grass, even for the sake of Peter's honor, was another.

In Russia we call that assault.

Peter could take care of himself. And that was a bigger problem, Reed realized with alarm. Because if Peter found out Linden was on the grounds—

Well, Reed wasn't sure what Peter would do. But it wouldn't be good. Linden's presence at Raleigh might turn the whole weekend into a disaster, the sort of disaster that had long-term consequences for Peter and for Tulip Farm.

People were still shooting Reed subtle sideways glances. Probably because Reed was standing frozen in place, a road-block, while the crowd eddied around them. And they'd forgotten serenity.

Audrey Hepburn in front of the judges, Reed reminded themself. Pasting a smile back in place, they walked on as if they didn't have a care in the world, even as they had to unclench their fingers from around the hilt of their knife. *For Peter and for Jolene and for the rest of the McAuley-Griffins. I can be Audrey Hepburn all weekend long.*

———

REED DROPPED the boot polish in the barn aisle, watched the tin split apart on impact, watched the polishing sponge roll on the floor, picking up sawdust and bits of hay and horse shit as it went.

"Trakhni menya bokom," they cursed quietly but with feeling, scrambling after the dirtied sponge. *"I vverkh, i vniz, i nazad tozhe."*

"Doing okay?" Peter inquired from inside Annie's stall where he was applying a final misting of ShowSheen before tack-up. Reed's slot in warm-up was only fifteen minutes away. It felt like a lifetime, and also too soon. "You look a little green. Here, sit for a minute. Let me do your boots. Jo, can you start saddling Annie, please? The white PS of Sweden pad, and the Equipe Emporio."

"Sure thing!" Jolene bounced up off her tack trunk like Peter had offered her the moon. In a way, Reed supposed, he had.

"I don't need—" Reed fumbled the sponge again, threw up their hands in despair. "Maybe I do." Resigned, they sank down in Jo's place, concentrated on inhaling and exhaling. "Did Audrey Hepburn drink? Because I wouldn't say no to a shot of Stoli right about now."

"Two fingers of J&B, neat, with a cigarette." Bule sat in one of Tulip Farm's cobalt canvas captain's chairs, enjoying his own afternoon Corona. "Also suffered from depression and an eating disorder. What?" he added when Reed and Peter both turned to stare. "Wife's a big fan."

Peter finished picking debris off the sponge, crouched to take Reed's right boot in his hands. He applied polish expertly, frowning a little in concentration as he rubbed it into a shine. Reed wondered if his head was bothering him. They knew they should say something, wave him off, finish the boots themself. But it felt good to be cared for. And also they were afraid if they stood up, they might vomit.

Reed didn't *really* get preshow nerves. Rituals and superstitions to chase away that vague preshow anxiety, yes. Never before the bone-shaking, stomach-churning stage fright that many of their friends from Bitsa had endured.

But suddenly it all seemed too much. Annie. Linden. Especially Linden. Linden was the real source of the acid rising in Reed's throat. Because the more they thought about it, the more Reed was certain Peter and Linden on the same showground could only end in disaster. The show ran the whole weekend, and the fairground was not huge. Odds were good Peter and Linden would run into each other eventually.

"You're fine," Peter soothed, low and firm, interrupting Reed's spiraling panic. "You and Annie will do beautifully. She's ready. Relaxed and loose on the lunge, raring to go. She's almost as talented as Pepper the Super Pony. Olympic level, World Cup winner, etcetera etcetera. All you have to do is sit tight and smile."

"Is that the sort of pep talk you gave your team?" Reed asked, frowning. "Because it's not very inspiring."

"My team didn't get preshow nerves." Peter switched to Reed's other boot. "By the time you hit Olympic trials, you've outgrown the urge to puke at the ingate."

"Bullshit," Aine said, coming around the corner into the barn aisle. "I clearly remember Thomas McNealy casting up his breakfast all over the steward in Los Angeles, poor woman." She clapped her hands lightly. "You're up in four, Reed. Stop worrying. You're a product of Bitsa. Annie's Tulip Farm. You both could do Level Three in your sleep, and today is only First. It's supposed to be *fun*. Up you go. Peter, I'm pleased to see you remember how to polish a boot."

"Yes, Mum." Peter held out a hand, drew Reed gently to their feet. "You're a product of Bitsa, Reed Androku." He leaned down, nuzzled Reed's brow. "And you've got a fine seat."

Reed smothered a laugh. Joy chipped away at nausea. This man believed in Reed. This wonderful, wonderful man. "I'm sure you'll be watching it my entire test."

"Bet on it." Peter squeezed Reed's gloved hand as Jolene led Annie into the aisle and Aine grabbed the mare's bridle. "My eyes will be glued to your seat from A to C and back again. Ready?"

"Kiss me for luck."

Peter did, with an enthusiasm that made Reed's toes curl with pleasure in their perfectly polished boots.

"Enough!" Aine scolded, shooing Peter away. "Mount up, Androku. It's time to make your debut."

————

"YOUR SCORES WILL SUFFER if you're careless about your arena maths. The arena's precise geometry—demarcated by arena letters and quarter and centerlines—helps a ride better coordinate transitions and movements, which in turn helps improve accuracy and straightness in a horse."

At Bitsa, a young rider is taught the importance of geometry in the dressage ring before they are allowed to step into the schooling arena. Reed's Intro coach, a pale, willowy woman called Irina, had been especially preoccupied with the subject.

"The standard dressage arena is twenty meters wide by sixty meters long. It is required equipment for First Level tests and higher. The letters on the perimeter start at the opening on the centerline and move in a clockwise direction: A, K, V, E, S, H, C, M, R, B, P. By now, you should all know this already."

Reed entered at A, rode Annie down the centerline at a nice working trot, halted precisely at L, saluted the judge. Annie was warm and solid beneath them, a comfort. If she wished they were on their way to a nice gallop over fences, she didn't show it, instead waiting quietly except for an inquiring flick of an ear on Reed's next cue.

"When you have a space that is defined, it's much easier to use in a creative way. Good riding and execution are first

and foremost in any test. But when it comes to the musical freestyle, creativity will win the day."

Reed had a heartbeat to worry they hadn't been creative enough in their choice or music, their choreography. Then the announcer called, "Reed Androku riding Remedy for Tulip Farm." The first few bars of "So Far Away" began to play over the ring speakers, and nothing else in the world existed but the music in Reed's head and the horse between their legs. Joy turned the sunlight, the air, the crowd into technicolor. Time twisted all out of shape. Better than drugs, better than Stoli, better even than good sex. Somehow, they'd forgotten that nothing compared to competition.

"Okay, *printsessa*," Reed said for Annie's ears only. "Let's show them how it's done."

CHAPTER TWENTY-ONE

"Down centerline at A," Peter murmured under his breath. "Leg yield, zigzag quarter line to quarter line."

In the ring Reed and Annie worked in perfect synchronicity, the living image of a *Dressage Monthly* centerfold. Annie was buffed to a copper penny shine, every piece of white chrome spotless, perfect braids showing off her long neck. She looked fit, muscled, her topline solid. That was Reed's hard work, Reed's attention, Reed's constant reminders that the mare could come back from injury if only Peter would allow her the chance.

"X: circle right ten meters." "Telegraph Road" rattled the ring speakers. People in the audience were humming enthusiastically along. The Dire Straits medley had been a good choice, though at first Peter had worried it might be too boisterous. Peter was learning that Reed never did anything by halves.

"Keep her up in the bridle, Reed, don't let her sit on the couch," Aine said quietly by Peter's side. "That's it. Very good."

Reed in the saddle was gorgeously polished—and not

just their boots. Dressed in tails, white breeches, white gloves, hair confined beneath their helmet, the neatly tied cravat at their throat a dramatic flourish, they sat Annie like a goddamn pro, cues almost impossible to see. Horse and rider had become one animal, dancing delightedly across the ring. People in the crowd gave up restraint and began to clap in time to the music.

"Working walk, free walk, working canter left lead." And then, to Aine: "Reed's been holding out on us, I think. Talented in the schooling ring, but this is different."

This might be the most beautiful thing I've ever seen.

"You're not biased?" But his mum, eyes pinned on the ring, smiled. "Competition often brings out hidden reserves. You know that." She relented, just a little. "Perhaps Reed needs a dressage horse. Annie's very good, but on a horse trained to dressage Reed could—"

She broke off, catching the almost invisible check in Annie's stride at the same time Peter did. Not Annie's fault, as the mare executed change of lead through trot between P and S a smidge less than impeccably, but Reed's. Something had briefly distracted the Russian, something outside the ring.

"What were they looking at? Something in the crowd?" Something that had broken Reed's concentration, if only briefly. *A flash of bright angry red light, the crash after.* Remembering made Peter's fingers close convulsively on the head of his cane.

"Doesn't matter." Sensing Peter's spike of anxiety, Aine wrapped an arm around his waist. "It was nothing. Maybe the judge missed it. Open your eyes, son, they're both fine. Better than." He could hear the smile in her voice. "Working trot down centerline, halt, salute—"

"And air guitar," Peter said, opening his eyes just in time to see Reed's final dramatic flourish.

The music stopped. The crowd burst into cheers. And Peter thought seeing Reed's wide grin might be as good as winning the gold in Paris.

———

"BETTER THAN," Peter said into Reed's ear, meeting them at the ingate for a tight hug once the Russian had dismounted. His own grin made his cheeks hurt. "Better than winning Olympic gold." Had Aine gotten it all on camera? Peter hoped so. He took the reins from Reed's hands, slipped Annie sugar from his pocket. "You're art in the ring. Mum's right, you've been holding out. She's gone to wait for your score. *Discreetly,* of course, because it wouldn't do for Tulip Farm to look greedy." Lowering his voice, "And Christ Jesus, speaking of greedy, those breeches leave nothing to the imagination. I can't wait to peel them off you. Let's—"

"Peter," Reed interrupted sharply, gripping his wrist. Startled, Peter realized that Reed was no longer smiling. They didn't look celebratory at all. In fact, they'd gone slightly off-color again. Were they going to puke after the test? Did nerves work that way? Peter glanced hastily around for a trash bin. But Reed's fingers tightened on his arm, demanding his attention. "There's something I need to tell you." Then they looked over Peter's shoulder, and their gorgeous mouth went flat. "Listen, remember where we are, don't do anything you might regret. We're blocking the ingate . . ."

Annie stamped a hoof, snorted. Peter turned, adrenaline flooding his system. Because he already knew.

"Mark." And fuck but the arsehole looked full of himself, standing right there in cowboy boots and a sweat-stained wide brim, eyes red rimmed as a bloody *far darrig's* —and hell yes, why hadn't he ever noticed before? Linden fit the role of evil leprechaun nicely. What had Katie been thinking to fall for the man?

"Hello, Peter." Bold as brass Linden put his hand on Annie's neck, stroked along her mane. Peter resisted knocking it away. Reed was right, they were blocking the ingate, holding up traffic. Biting the inside of his lip because it felt viscerally wrong to turn his back again on Linden, Peter made himself lead Annie casually toward the barn.

Reed followed, drawn so tight Peter could actually feel the Russian's fury like waves of heat across the back of his neck. Linden, being a dick, came after. The crowd parted in front of them like Moses and the fucking Red Sea, congratulations cut short. And Christ Jesus, everyone but Linden could read the room.

"Fantastic ride," Katie's ex said cheerfully. "Almost perfect. Didn't realize you all were building up a dressage barn, Peter."

"We're not." The stalls seemed exceptionally far away, the crowd too close, full of people casting knowing looks their way. The horse world was too small, no one's business was sacred. Had everyone but the McAuley-Griffin clan known what a shit Linden was? Thanks to Mac's PI, Peter was beginning to believe the answer was a resounding yes.

Why hadn't anyone said anything?

But he knew the answer.

It's easier to look away and pretend than stand up and witness.

"Not what I heard. Everyone's talking about it. Tulip Farm opening up for lessons. Olympic barn and all that. Bit of a zag from Senior's 'only sales all the time' line," Linden continued, lengthening his stride to catch up with Peter. "I remember when your mom wanted to open the place up to lessons. Right after Kate and I got married, I think we were just back from our honeymoon, considering a move down to Virginia. Senior shot your mom down like the word of God." He dodged around Annie, placed himself a few feet in front of Peter, crossed his arms. Doing his best to cause a scene.

Peter's leg spasmed. The edges of the world grew hazy. Reed hissed something in Russian, reached out to soothe the confused mare.

Peter stopped, handed Reed Annie's reins silently. For a moment he couldn't find words past the rage and guilt pounding against his skull. He leaned hard on his cane to keep from falling, or maybe to keep from using it to break Linden's nose.

But he was not like Linden. He was not a violent person. And everyone who mattered—especially Reed—was watching.

"Things have changed." Peter met Linden's stare, saw the challenge in his smirk. He gripped his cane until it bit his fingers, willed his heart to stop racing. He forced calm, aware of every pricked ear and the gossip that would follow. "Obviously. Times change, and Tulip Farm won't be left behind. Yes, we're opening up to lessons. A select, very select, few spots. As we're still an Olympic-level barn."

Linden laughed, gestured at Peter's cane. "With no medals in your future."

"Don't be so sure." Peter thought his palm would have bruises if he ever managed to unclench his fist again. "With a new coaching program to supplement sales and breeding? I expect we'll need a larger display case for all the farm medals we'll be racking up. Now get the fuck out of my way before I call security and have you thrown off the property for harassment."

Linden stepped to the side. Peter walked on, chin held high, breathing through his nose. Reed didn't speak until they were almost at the barn. Peter was grateful they'd given him time to remember how to be human again.

"You're a good man, Peter Griffin," Reed said quietly. "And Linden is a very bad one. I'm afraid Kate won't be safe until he's out of her life for good.' Their brow was furrowed. They worried absently at Annie's reins, deep in thought.

A pang of fear curdled Peter's stomach. How did the Bratva handle a threat to the family? Peter wasn't sure he wanted to know. "Don't go doing anything stupid. Let Mac and his PI handle it, and the police."

"I was afraid *you* would do something stupid. It made me sick, when I first saw him in the crowd." Reed buried their chin in their snow-white cravat, ignoring Annie's impatient nuzzling, avoiding Peter's stare. "Earlier today. Much earlier, after Jo's test."

Ah.

"It was Linden, not the test, that had you green."

Reed nodded, still looking anywhere but at Peter. "I wanted to tell you. But I was afraid to spoil the day, spoil the show. I couldn't see how it would end any way other than very badly."

"I wish you had said something. You can tell me anything. I thought you understood that." Peter's own brow wrinkled. Words always came easy for everything else. Why were they suddenly so damn hard when it came to his heart and Reed? "Nothing can spoil this weekend for me, not even Linden. And Reed. I want you to feel safe with me." *I'm not your past. I want to be your future.*

Reed did look up then. Their expression softened. "I do understand. Of course I do. You make me feel safe as skyscrapers. I should have told you."

"Houses."

"Skyscrapers are also safe." Annie, limits reached, blew loudly into Reed's arm, turning a pristine coat mucky. Reed laughed, winked at Peter. "This one, it's all about the routine. I wonder where she got that? Come, you're right. Nothing will spoil today, and I want to celebrate."

―――――

"CELEBRATE" meant a late lunch in the barn aisle and drinks all around. Jo and Reed sucked down Italian sodas from the showground café to beat the heat, while Peter and Bule nursed Coronas. The afternoon humidity made everyone lethargic. The two horses—clean, dry, grained to the gills—dozed contentedly. The ring loudspeaker muttered on in the background, but Peter paid it no attention. Tulip Farm was finished for the day. Both Pepper and Annie had scored very solidly in the high seventies. Jo and Bule were visibly pleased by a good go on the card, and Reed looked happy for the first time since noon as they tucked into Aine's four-bean salad.

Peter hid a grin, watching the Russian linger over home-made brownies, adding two to their paper plate, glad that Reed's appetite had returned. Seeing Linden had been a shock all around. Peter was touched that Reed cared enough to let Kate's ex put them off their feed. But not surprised. Reed Androku was empathy on two legs, and as far as Peter was concerned, if more people were like Reed the world would be a better place.

"What are you smiling about?" Lunch plated, Reed

settled next to Peter on Annie's tack trunk, nudged him with a hip. "Planning tomorrow's successes?"

"Level One Test A for you tomorrow, I think," Peter confirmed. He snatched a corner of brownie, eluding Reed's defensive grab. "You're slumming it in the First Levels. Mum's already making noises about a Level Three horse."

Reed shook their head. Humidity and helmet hair turned their usually ruthlessly styled spikes unruly. Peter wanted to run his fingers through those wild curls, tug Reed onto his lap. He settled for stealing more brownie.

"Stop!" Reed swatted. "You've had yours already. I saw you take *three*." They sampled a square, closed their eyes in bliss. "Although I can see why you've suddenly turned to the dark side," they added around a mouthful of chocolate and sugar. "Your mum is magic in the kitchen. She puts jalapeños in her four-bean salad. Forget the coaching, she should open a restaurant."

Peter snorted. "She only cooks for friends and family. Love language, I think." And, glancing down the aisle. "Where did she go?"

"Took Boudica for a walk," Jo volunteered, glancing up from her phone. "She said goodbye, but you both were too busy cooing over Annie like she's queen of the world to notice. Ms. Aine said she wanted to see about an old friend or something."

Peter and Reed exchanged glances. "You didn't say anything?" Peter asked quietly.

"Of course I didn't." Reed scrunched up their nose. "Although I guess it was too much to hope she wouldn't find out."

"Mum always finds out," Peter said, resigned. "Eventually." He slid off the trunk. "Stay here and save me some brownies. I'll go."

"Are you sure—" Reed bounced their plate on their knee in indecision. "Maybe I should come?"

"No." Peter let his hand brush Reed's cheek, felt six inches taller when Reed leaned into his touch. "Just hold down the fort. Like I promised, I won't let anything spoil today."

He was secretly worried it would be a hard promise to keep. The McAuley-Griffin siblings all had tempers. And they didn't get that flame from their da, despite Senior's prickly exterior. No, it was the Irish in their blood that sent tempers afire, and although Aine rarely lost control, she had more than her fair share of McAuley heat.

Peter wasn't sure how much his mum knew about Linden's past. Mac and Senior would have tried to shelter her from the worst of it. But the fire in the barn, the security on the farm, the rumors Linden had spread about Kate . . . That was more than enough to turn on Mama Bear mode, and when it came to her family, Aine didn't spare the claws and teeth.

Peter limped faster, scanning the people gathered around the rings, clustered around the café, sitting six deep in the stands. No sign of either his mum or Linden. Linden hadn't been dressed to compete. He'd been dressed to work, in cowboy boots and denim to protect him from another kind of flame.

"Farriers," Peter asked a young person on a gorgeous flea-bitten gray. "Do you know where the farriers are set up?"

"Back round the show office," the young person replied. "Mr. Griffin! So good to see you—"

"Out and about, yes, thank you. I appreciate it." Peter hurried toward the show office, hoping he wasn't too late.

He heard the clang of metal on metal and the swoosh of

the forge as he approached the temporary building. The easy chatter of farrier and client, the clip-clop of hooves coming and going. No raised voices, no Irish spitting. Maybe he'd guessed wrong.

But, no. As he rounded the corner there was his mum standing still as a statue in the shadow of the office, Boudica in her arms. She might have been watching a shoeing in progress, except her gaze was fixed on a truck-size empty spot between the two remaining farriers.

Boudica turned her head and wiggled in greeting. Peter stroked her ears and then took the dog from Aine.

"Been standing here long?"

"I was too late." He'd expected heat, but her violet regard was terrifyingly cold. "Ran into Lacy in the parking lot when I was unloading lunch and she said . . ." His mum swallowed. "Well, I couldn't believe he'd dare show his face, could I? Not here, not in our territory. Not after . . . Well," she repeated. "I was too late. By the time I found out he was already gone. Jim said he just packed up and ran."

"Wasn't even here a full day," one of the farriers said around the nails in his mouth. "Lit out like he had the hounds of hell on his ass. Not surprised. Good riddance, if you ask me." The corner of his mouth ticked up as he nodded at Peter. "Heard you were about, Griffin. Nice to see you."

Up and about, yes.

"That was your doing, was it, Peter?" his mum asked, turning her back on Linden's empty spot. "You chased him away?"

He rolled his shoulders, uncomfortable. "We had words. Not enough and not the sort we should have had. We were in public. I'm sorry, Mum." He sighed, low. "And maybe I should have knocked him in the dirt, for Katie's sake, but Reed—"

"No," she gripped his elbow, fierce. "No, you were right. It's not your responsibility, Peter. It's mine, mine and Da's. We're meant to keep our children safe, and where Katie's concerned, at least, we failed."

"Mum, no." He felt a shock of sorrow, set Boudica on the ground before he dropped her.

"It keeps us both up at night. And we'll do our best to fix it, somehow. Today is not the time, or the place. Listen to me, Peter. This is not your responsibility. Stay out of it. Do you understand?"

He nodded, unable to speak out loud a promise he couldn't keep. Her expression said she knew what he was thinking, but she let it go. Instead, she nodded and linked her smaller fingers with his.

"Come now. It's a sunny day, and I want to show your Reed a very talented gelding just up for sale in the small barn. Swedish cross, and I think he'd make a lovely addition to our string."

CHAPTER TWENTY-TWO

"I've been wanting to peel those bloody breeches off you *all* weekend."

Reed paused on their way into the trailer, let the door close on their bootheels, quirked both brows. They'd recently learned the Irish leaked into Peter's American accent when he was turned on, making him sound like a cross between the devil and Rory Gallagher.

"You've told me." Reed reached behind, clicked the lock on the trailer door. Peter lounged on the trailer's long leather couch, arms spread across the back. The smile on his face was deliciously close to a leer. "And now look at you." Freshly showered, hair still damp, wearing soft cotton pajama pants and nothing more. "All scrubbed up and . . . is that champagne?"

"Dom Perignon, nicely aged." Peter's Lake Baikal eyes sparkled. "Put it away on my twenty-first birthday, for something special. Brought it along because I figured this weekend would be."

"For you or for me?" But Reed put a little sashay in their

walk as they crossed the room, felt powerful when Peter's gaze dropped immediately to their hips.

"Both, I hope." Peter licked his lips. Reed's mouth went dry. *As bad as Pavlov's dog,* they thought, and gestured to the little table by the couch. "Pour? I'm thirsty. Where's everyone else?"

"The cockblock crew, you mean?" Peter rose and popped the cork, poured golden bubbles into two flutes. "Closing out and packing up, I hope, as I'd like to be on the road before sun's up. I cried 'sore leg' and delegated." He passed Reed a flute. "Don't think Mum bought it. She offered to smuggle the dog into her hotel for the night."

"Bless her." Reed touched their glass to Peter's, took a sip. The champagne burst on their tongue, tasting of sunlight and sea spray, and very faintly of chocolate. They purred approval, looked Peter pointedly up and down, admiring wide shoulders and smooth skin and the dusting of fur around his nipples and across his pecs. "Very nice."

"Sit," Peter offered. "Sunday night, first show of the season? You must be exhausted. Shall I help you with your boots?"

Reed sank gratefully onto the couch, grinned at Peter over the top of their flute. The man knew how to ask nicely, all solicitous smiles and expensive champagne, but the unabashed erection tenting the front of his pj's was impossible to miss. Peter Griffin had a foot kink, and an ass kink, and Reed had no doubt twenty-four hours of white breeches and shiny black boots and almost zero time alone together had him on the edge.

Poor man. More than willing to play along, Reed propped their booted feet up on the low coffee table, crossed their ankles. They swallowed another mouthful of champagne, closed their eyes, came to a decision. "My spare crop's in the closet, next to the Stella McCartney fanny pack. Go and get it?"

Peter's inhale was almost a gasp. Reed opened their eyes, looked up through their lashes. "Only if you'd like, of course?"

"I—" His voice cracked. He cleared his throat. "Would you?"

"Very much, lovely. I'd like to have it in my hand while you take off my boots."

Peter finished his champagne in a gulp. Set the empty flute down with a click. Walked to the closet without saying another word, returned in record time, Reed's crop in hand. Black, leather, studded around the base of the handle with small Swarovski crystals. It was Reed's favorite.

Reed held out their hand, beckoned. Peter set the crop on Reed's palm. His eyes were wide and dark, his bare chest rising and falling in quick bursts. His skin was pale where the sun hadn't touched, sprinkled with freckles, fur glinting golden around nipples gone hard as pebbles. His erection jutted proudly beneath cotton, just begging to be freed.

Not yet.

"Good." Reed leaned forward, stroked the crop's leather tongue down Peter's cheek, along the graceful column of his throat. Peter swallowed hard, making his Adam's apple bob. Reed bit back a groan of desire, traced the crop up again until the tress touched the corner of Peter's mouth. Barely managed to keep their voice level when they said: "Now then. Take my boots off, please. While on your knees, if you don't mind."

Peter's hesitation was so slight Reed almost missed it. They held their breath, wondering if they'd gone too far. If the old rumors were true, Peter was not averse to a little light bondage. And hadn't a younger Reed brought themself off more than once imagining how Peter Griffin might look trussed up in their bed, begging for release? *Absolutely delicious.*

But now that Reed actually knew the man, saw the humanity in his kinks and quirks—well. Peter could be arrogant. And their relationship was still new, just finding its legs. Yes, they both needed a distraction from the weekend's ups and downs, but had Reed guessed incorrectly? Role playing could be immensely enjoyable but only if both parties were equally on board.

And oh Christ, they'd forgotten about Peter's leg, no wonder the poor man had faltered.

"Peter—" Reed began, ready to take it back, but there was no need to finish, because Peter was on his knees on the trailer's shag carpet, his movements careful but solid, and the look he flashed Reed was blue lightning, challenge and acceptance all at once, a look more intoxicating than the best champagne or the worst vodka.

"You'll have to help me up after," he grated through a flash of teeth, "or join me down here on the rug. Because I've been waiting two long days for this, and I plan to take my time with you."

———

PEPPER THE SUPER Pony decided to be a dick about going home.

"Well, hell," Peter said the fourth time the pony wheeled in front of the loading ramp, half rearing at the end of her lead rope. "Maybe I was unfair to the buffalo."

Reed snorted into their scarf. The sun was just coming up over the showgrounds and although Raleigh in the summer was much warmer than Connecticut, the temps had dropped enough in the night that it was almost brisk. Reed had woken cold, despite Peter's bulky warmth at their back, and being practical—and maybe too sentimental—wrapped themself in Peter's Tulip Farm barn coat and a knitted scarf in complementary colors. The scarf wasn't fashion, but it was warm and soft and comforting in the early morning hours.

"Doesn't want to go home," Reed diagnosed. "She's fallen in love with the Friesian next stall over, didn't you know? Can't say I blame her. He's a gorgeous specimen."

The gorgeous specimen in front of Reed rolled Lake Baikal eyes. "Mares. Come on, Pepper. It's just not meant to be." With the patience of a man who'd spent a good chunk of his life loading uncooperative horses, Peter led Pepper toward the horse van a fifth time, whistling tunelessly as if they had all the time in the world.

Which they didn't. Their gear was packed, the extra hay tied down on top of the van. Annie was already loaded, nosing happily at the grain in her manger. Boudica was in the truck's front seat, both paws up on the window, snout leaving marks on the glass. Jo and Bule had left for the airport an hour earlier. Aine's flight wasn't until the next day. She'd delivered Boudica and a cooler packed to bursting with snacks, kissed Peter's check, and wished them both a safe drive.

That was an hour past, and they hadn't made much headway since.

"Oh, you complete monster," Peter rumbled sweetly as Pepper wheeled halfway up the ramp, scooting backward, stumbling off rubber onto dirt. "*Is é an mhonarcha gliú duit.* And we'll use your guts on Gabriel's violin."

"No glue factory." Reed bit their lip hard to keep from laughing. "And no violin strings. You want to keep your clients, not chase them away. Even if Pepper's being a spoiled diva in front of the whole world. Would you like me to try?"

They thought Peter might refuse. And Reed wouldn't blame him. They were hardly alone on the back lot, people rushing here and there to load their own vans, pack their own trucks, get on the road in a timely manner. An ex-Olympic hopeful bested by a stubborn pony would give everyone something to talk about.

"Let's not risk injuring your leg further, yes?" Reed added quietly, reminding Peter that he had a perfectly acceptable out.

Peter, looking sleepy—after a long night of really excellent sex—and rumpled in pale blue jeans and a white Henley off the trailer floor, relented. "She likes you better anyway, I think."

"I'm more her size," Reed agreed, taking the lead rope. They threaded their fingers through Pepper's mane, murmured nonsense reassurances. Pepper rolled an eye and swished her tail, unconvinced. "It's not really the handsome Friesian, is it, pretty girl? We're tired, aren't we? It's been a long weekend. And some of us are grumpy, that's all."

"I'm not grumpy," Peter protested as Reed used the lead rope to make Pepper move her feet, wiggling the end until she backed up nicely, working it sideways until she walked a circle. "I'm in an excellent mood. Ma always says every pony has a devil inside, just waiting to show its horns."

"No horns here, right Pepper?" Reed worked Pepper toward the ramp and then away again, concentrating on her feet. A horse in motion was more willing than a horse that was not. Which Peter knew, of course. But Peter's weekend hadn't been perfect, despite the really excellent sex—and who knew the adorable man would choose *hawthorn* as his safe word?

But the confrontation with Linden had left its mark, in the dark half-moons under Peter's eyes, in the headache he'd covered with a few popped pills over breakfast, in the way he leaned a little harder on his cane when he thought no one was looking.

"There now," Reed soothed, circling the pony calmly away and then back again. "There now. Now, now." On board the van, Annie paused in her eating to nicker a welcome. In response to Reed's cooing or the pony, it didn't matter. Pepper finally decided that safety was inside the van with Annie and the familiar scents of hay and sweet mash. She followed Reed up the ramp and into her slot without protest, hooves muffled on rubber mats.

Reed clipped her into place, set the butt bar, and hopped back down the ramp. "The devil has been routed! As a reward, I get first music choice." They winked at Peter. "How do you feel about Ratt?"

"Thank Jesus." Peter hauled the ramp into place, double-checking the bolts. The grin he flashed Reed was brilliant. "Good Christ, I love you."

––––––

I LOVE YOU. Such small simple words to stop Reed's world turning. And thrown so casually in their direction, but with the weight of certainty.

The sky is blue. Dries Van Noten is God. I love you.

Even Michael had never said those three words out loud. Not that Reed had minded, not really. Reed knew the difference between love and lust. At first, with Michael, it had been all about the sex, and companionship. Later, when affection had deepened to something more, Reed had understood that Michael preferred to show his emotions in the doing of things. Passionate bouts of weekend sex followed by breakfast served to Reed in bed. Furtive, tender touches as they strolled Malaya Sadovaya Ulitsa under the moonlight. Gifts that Michael couldn't really afford: concert tickets, thrifted fashion, and once a brand-new PS of Sweden bridle.

I love you. YaA lyublyu vas. They had the same weight in any language, Reed supposed. But somehow when Peter said them, the universe paused.

Don't be so melodramatic, Androku. They glanced sideways at Peter where he sat in the driver's seat, eyes on the road, the telltale wrinkle over his nose that meant after four hours on I-95 he was sore. They would have to stop soon for a break. Maybe Reed could convince Peter to let them take a shift behind the wheel.

I love you. Probably the man had meant it like *I love brownies, I love it when you put your mouth around my cock, I love it when you scream my name in bed. I love to win.*

"Everything okay?" Peter asked, downshifting to approach a curve. The horses displayed on the small television monitor mounted below the windshield swayed with the motion. "You've been quiet since we left Raleigh."

"Just tired. The weekend's catching up." Reed threaded Boudica's ears through their fingers. Her warm weight on their lap was a comfort. "How's your leg? We could stop in Fredericksburg, get some food. I could drive after."

"You just said you're tired."

"Not too tired to drive. I'm an excellent driver."

Peter's brows rose. "Driver's license, Reed. That thing

you don't have. Excellent driver or not, I'm not taking that risk. You could end up in jail."

Reed snorted. "Excellent drivers don't get pulled over."

"I'm fine. And don't bat your lashes at me like that. I'm not going to change my mind." On the monitor Pepper coughed. Reed and Peter held their collective breath until she exhaled, sneezed, and went back to dozing. "We'll stop in Fredericksburg," Peter consented. "I'll get some coffee and walk a little. I'll be fine. Halfway home, right?"

"Halfway home," Reed agreed absently.

What if Peter *had* meant it as a declaration? Not a homemade brownies and blue ribbons sort of love. The sort of love that meant moving in together, picking out things like new sheets and cookware, combining closet space, and celebrating anniversaries year after year.

And Reed hadn't said it back.

They sneaked another peek at Peter's face. He didn't look like a man who had offered up his heart and not had that declaration returned. Tired, yes. Distracted, yes. The light through the windows gave his unshaven jaw a golden sheen. The fingers of his right hand tapped a staccato beat against the steering wheel even though they'd turned the radio off hours ago. Bored, maybe.

Not heartbroken. Not crushed. Just resigned to another few hours on the road.

"Why are you staring at me?" Peter didn't look away from the road, but the corners of his mouth curled upward.

"I'm not!" Reed protested, a little too emphatically.

"You are. And I know I haven't got anything on my face. I've checked the mirror twice."

"Just admiring your driving. Capable, very capable. But not *excellent*, I'm afraid."

Peter's smile deepened. "I told you, I'm not going to change my mind."

I love you, too, Reed almost said. Because they did, had since the day Peter showed up in Barn A with a bottle of Grey Goose and an apology. Quite possibly before that, if Reed was honest with themself. And Reed tried to be, even when it was hard work, even when it was terrifying.

Peter Griffin, I've loved you since the first time I saw you ride in London, on the spooky gray nobody else wanted to try, and you weren't afraid to tell her owners she needed a different job. Because you cared.

There was such a thing as too much honesty. What if Peter hadn't meant combining closets and celebrating an ongoing parade of anniversaries? What if Reed had got it wrong?

They felt stuck, unable to grope their way forward, unable to move back to before. Impossible to unhear those three simple—*complicated*—little words.

"Exit 126. Fredericksburg." Peter exclaimed, "Hell, yes. Look at that. There's a Waffle House. How do you feel about egg and sausage hash brown bowls?"

Turned out horror was an excellent distraction from matters of the heart. "Peter." Reed grimaced in disgust as Peter took the off-ramp. "Hash brown bowls? Really?" Definitely a heart attack waiting to happen.

"Best coffee off the interstate." Peter winked. "Besides, Boudica wants bacon."

"Boudica does?" Reed rolled their eyes. "At least promise you'll get a side of fruit. So I won't sit up all night worrying about your arteries."

The sun sets in the west. Pink Jones's "Absolute" was robbed of a Grammy.

I love you, too.

CHAPTER TWENTY-THREE

By the time they turned off the back road onto Tulip Farm, Peter was desperate for a hot shower, two TUMS washed down with cold beer, and a night in front of the BBC. The drive home, while not quite a disaster, had also not been without its difficulties.

The egg and sausage hash brown bowls, an absolute treat in Fredericksburg, had necessitated a surprise toilet stop in Arlington and then again just outside Baltimore. To Peter's embarrassment, the Waffle House favorite knocked his previously ironclad digestive system for a complete loop. Boudica probably appreciated the extra breaks, but Peter did not. Not the forced delay or the disgusting rest stop toilets.

Maybe he should have listened to Teddy's suggestion to add probiotics to his diet. She'd warned him that half a year of on-again, off-again antibiotics would do a number on his gut, but he hadn't had any trouble, so he'd refused to listen.

"You've been eating Ms. Aine's homecooked meals," Reed pointed out after Baltimore. "The Waffle House is definitely not homecooked." They'd wrinkled their nose but had resisted any "I told you so"s for which Peter was grateful.

His head was broken, his leg damaged, and now his gut was getting in on the party. He didn't need any more reminders that life had changed, thank you very much.

A heatwave muffled the entire Northeast, making the sky gray and the air outside the truck sticky. Thank God the truck's air conditioning held. There was traffic outside New York, and their steady drive dragged to a snail's pace. Luckily by that point Peter's stomach had stopped rebelling, and he was fairly certain he wasn't in any further danger of shitting his pants. Pepper and Annie were quiet although no longer sleeping. And Reed, curled up in the passenger seat, seemed content to watch the stop and go as it ebbed and flowed outside their window.

They'd been unusually silent throughout the drive. Tired, Peter assumed at first. But Reed had napped between Baltimore and Edison. Awake again, they'd seemed peaceful enough but still very quiet. Peter missed their chatter, their cheerful flirting, the way they hummed under their breath when the radio was on and when the radio was off.

Reed had assured Peter they were just fine, and because Peter couldn't think of anything—other than the Waffle House menu—that would have soured the Russian's mood, he decided to believe them. Besides, you couldn't ask your lover "Are you sure you're okay?" more than once every three hours without looking like a complete arsehole.

So he was relieved when Ben Christie waved them through the gate, grateful when Annie and Pepper came off the trailer and into their stalls like champs. Pepper would stay the night in Barn A and be ready for pickup the next day. While Reed fussed over their herd, making sure everyone was still happy and healthy, Peter unhooked the trailer in its place on the west side of the property. The drive back took him past the old hay barn. He was relieved to see the new paint was untouched, free of graffiti. Remembering Linden's malice made him grit his teeth. Despite Aine's admonishment, Peter knew there was no way he could look the other way and pretend Linden wasn't an infected thorn working deeper into the McAuley-Griffin family's side.

He'd seen the bone-deep hatred in the other man's eyes. Whatever imaginary grievance Linden had worked up in his head, he wasn't about to let Katie get away unpunished.

"We'll just see about that, won't we, you evil bastard?"

In the passenger seat Boudica looked Peter's way and whined, wagging uncertainly. He soothed her with a gentle stroke along the spine.

Reed was waiting when Peter pulled up behind Barn A, a small duffel hooked over their shoulder, a bottle of Stoli in hand. Peter's scowl softened. Gabriel, in a surprisingly perceptive mood, had offered to take the room over the garage for the night, which meant Peter and Reed had the main house to themselves and Peter meant to make the most of it, from the ginormous rain shower in his parent's master to the California king in the second-floor guest room. Reed had offered to make a simple soup on Aine's fancy stove— "Chicken and vegetables for your poor abused stomach."— and Peter was looking forward to watching the Russian work in the kitchen.

"Everyone's happy," Reed announced, nudging Boudica over as they climbed into the car. The dachshund hopped into Peter's lap, her tail thumping against his chest. "Sent John home. I'll do night check later."

"Sure?" Peter was relieved to see Reed looked more

themself, hands and face animated, dark eyes bright. "I know you're wiped—"

"It's fine." Reed squeezed Peter's thigh. "I'll worry otherwise. Now, let's get this play on the road. I can't wait to try Ms. Aine's AGA stove. You're sure she won't mind?"

"Show. It's 'get this show on the road.' And of course Mum won't mind. She's talking about finding you a horse, for Chrissake, and she pays more attention to your horse sense than mine." Peter thought he should be jealous, but instead he felt a thrill of pride. "You're practically part of the family."

"Do you think so?" Reed leaned toward Peter as the truck rumbled up the hill. They gnawed on their very plush lower lip, and for a minute Peter forgot to keep his eyes on the drive. "I mean, is that how you feel also, Peter? Because I want you to know that these last months . . . You and I . . . I want you to know . . ." They glanced away again, up and out the windshield at the evening shadows cloaking the main house. Then they stiffened, "I thought you said Gabriel was expecting us."

"What?" It took Peter a moment to catch up. He'd been entirely focused on Reed's mouth and the words coming out of it. Words that somehow made his palms go slick and his heart pound like he was about to enter the ring for the world's most important qualifier.

Brow wrinkled, Reed pointed up the driveway. "I've never seen it shut up like that before. I thought you said your brother knew we were back tonight."

Halfway up the drive, Peter put his foot on the brake, let the truck slow. He blinked up at McAuley-Griffin house, and now the nervous pounding behind his ribs tipped over from expectation to dismay.

His family never left the property unattended. It was

part of having a farm, of having very expensive animals in their care. When it came to horses, things could go from good to very bad in a matter of minutes. Senior insisted on having at least one family member on the farm at all times, which meant for as long as Peter could remember they'd never vacationed together, but that was okay, because everyone understood the family business came first.

It also meant that the main house always looked lived in. Never shuttered as it was now, shades drawn tight, windows dark, not a single light on to welcome Peter and Reed home. A shiver ghosted along his spine as they coasted slowly to a stop in front of the porch. He shut off the truck.

"Something's wrong." The porch light was off in spite of the sinking sun, the sidelights on either side of the door black rectangles. "We never close up the house, not like that. Gabriel knew we were coming." He thumbed through the contacts on his phone, passed it to Reed. "That's Christie. Call him."

"But—" Reed gripped Peter's wrist. "What are you going to do? You can't just walk in there, not if something's wrong."

"Gabriel might be hurt." Peter refused to let the fear lurking somewhere around his knees rise to the surface. He reached for rage instead. "It's got to be Linden. I don't know how he got on the property this time, but it has to stop." Gently he disentangled himself from Reed's hold. "Don't look like that. I can handle Linden. And I'm not going to sit here and wait, not if Gabriel needs me."

"Handle Linden? With what?" Reed whispered fiercely. "Your cane?"

"If I need to. Call Christie. Then call the police. And for fuck's sake, stay in the truck."

"Peter!" Reed's hiss edged into a nervous squeak, but

Peter was already out on the driveway, closing the driver's side door as quietly as possible, limping up the steps to the front door. He clenched his cane tightly, grateful of the weight in his hand.

The porch light wasn't switched off as he'd first thought. It was smashed, pieces of glass crunching under Peter's shoes, the broken filament hanging from the socket. The hair on the back of Peter's neck rose, goose bumps broke in a wave down his arms. If they'd arrived home even just an hour later, it would have been too dark to see the overturned flowerpots near Aine's swing, or the dark stain on the welcome mat.

"Is that blood?"

"I told you to stay in the car." Peter couldn't pull his eyes from the stain.

"Nobody tells me to do anything." Reed retorted quietly. "Besides, one of us knows how to use a deadly weapon, and it's not you." They added, "Christie's on his way up. He'll be here in seconds. Peter, just wait. Please."

"Are you carrying the dog? You're carrying the fucking dog."

"It's a thousand degrees. I'm not leaving her in the truck." But Reed set Boudica down, looped the end of her leash around a porch rail, hushed her with a murmur.

"The door's left open." Just a crack. Peter hadn't noticed at first. The broken glass had taken up all his attention, and the blood.

"Peter Griffin!" Reed's whisper cracked when Peter toed the door open and slipped through. Curses hissed in Russian followed him through.

The foyer was silent except for the muted tick of the McAuley carriage clock Aine kept on the side table next to a collection of antique Waterford knickknacks and a small black-and-white photo of her father standing in front of a bar in Dublin.

The knickknacks were undisturbed, as was the spray of flowers in a large crystal vase displayed prominently on a round table in the middle of the room. Behind the table a flight of stairs swooped toward the second floor, shrouded in gloom.

Too dark and too quiet. And where were his mum's two cats, the wedge-faced Siamese who always came to great Peter at the door?

A shadow moved on Peter's right. Reed, knife in hand.

"Light," Reed suggested. Peter knew he should try a third time to send the Russian back outside, but it would only be a waste of time. Reed obviously wasn't going to listen. Besides which, there was only one person in the foyer who had combat training, and Reed was right, it certainly wasn't Peter.

He flicked a switch. Nothing happened. His mum's beautiful Art Deco table lamps and the chandelier above the staircase stayed dark.

"Cut the bloody line. Just like last time." Another shiver ghosted across his shoulders. Linden was a bully, and a coward. In Peter's experience the man tended to act first and think later. The graffiti, the vandalism, sure. That felt like Linden. But cutting the electricity—to the house, to the security cameras in Barn A—that was the sort of cold, calculated move that took forethought.

And shouldn't Christie have shown by now? Peter knew it only took a handful of minutes to zip the Rhino from the front gate to the house.

Standing in the dark, Reed breathing steadily at his side, Peter wondered if he'd made a very bad mistake.

A thump came from overhead, and a crash that sounded like a shit ton of glass breaking, and then a strangled shout.

"Gabriel!" Mistake or not, Peter was up the stairs as quickly as his leg allowed. Reed passed him on the last five steps, hesitating at the top before vanishing through the shadows toward the master suite. "Reed!" Gripping his cane like a lifeline, Peter raced after.

Aine and Senior's bedroom suite was all pretty antiques and modern art surrounding a gigantic four-poster bed. Two large windows looked out over the back garden. Opposite the windows floating shelves climbed up the far wall. Last time Peter had seen those shelves they'd been loaded with trophies. Trophies from his mum and da's career: cut glass bowls, sterling trophies, and crystal statues arranged in aesthetically pleasing groups across reclaimed barnwood. Gabriel had made the shelves in high school woodworking class.

Now Gabriel lay on the floor underneath them in a mess of scattered boards and broken glass. Unlike those at the front of the house, the bedroom windows weren't shuttered, and in the evening light through the panes Peter could see the bloody gash on his older brother's head, more blood down the front of his shirt, on his Carhartt jeans, and staining his parents' white Berber carpet. His eyes were closed, his body limp.

"Gabriel!"

"Nope, don't move." The man standing over Gabriel with a gun in his hand was not Mark Linden. This man was tall, with long dark hair falling in a ponytail down his back. He sounded like New York but wore a Red Sox hoodie over his jeans. He tilted his head slightly in Reed and Peter's direction, flicked his glance between them to Gabriel and back again. "Another step and your big friend here gets a bullet in the head. Which would be a shame. He fights like a bull, and it's not personal with him, you know?"

"Not personal?" Peter sounded much calmer than he felt. The adrenaline pumping through his system was a low buzz. Everything was very clear, very bright. Time slowed to a crawl. That was fine. He knew how to use his body's fight or flight instinct to win. "Then what are you doing in our fucking house? Who are you?"

The man had a pretty smile. He used it on Peter, then looked at Reed. The gun in his hand never wavered. Yes, definitely a professional. A hit man? And yes, it looked like Peter had made a bad mistake.

"Waiting for Androku. Only Big Guy here showed up first, surprised me downstairs. We had a little chase." The man's gaze roved the room again. "Suppose there's a gun up here under the bed, or something. There always is." He nudged Gabriel with the toe of his tennis shoe. Gabriel groaned softly but didn't move. "He's not dead. Just winged a little."

Winged a little. Peter swayed forward, planning murder, but Reed caught his sleeve.

"Security is coming," Reed said, vowels clipped. "And also the police."

"We've met before," the man said as if Reed hadn't spoken at all. "Do you remember?"

"Yes. Down by the babies. You were pretending to work construction."

"Fuck that. I *was* working construction. I'm a man of many talents." He shrugged. "Almost did you there, but, you know, cameras. Funny, isn't it? All this brand-new fancy security and no one thought to do the house. Stupid, stupid. So." He shrugged again. "Guess I'll have to do you here." Time lurched forward again and the man moved, much more quickly than Peter thought possible, across the room in three quick steps, gun pointing at Reed's head. "Sacha sends his love, you perverted little freak."

The man might have been astonishingly fast, but Peter was faster by far, made powerful by the resignation on Reed's face, the wide-eyed acceptance, the tiny sigh escaping their mouth, the phrase *little freak*.

He heard a low growl and thought it was coming from his own throat, animal rage and terror slipping free, because how dare anyone threaten *Reed*. Peter brought his cane up just as the gun went off, a hard slice up and sideways.

He missed. His balance was off, his body changed, and he wasn't yet used to new limitations. The cane arced too high, and the force of his swing sent him tipping. Peter twisted, trying to stay on his feet, staggered a painful step, and his ankle went out from underneath him. He hit the carpet, stunned. Someone screamed.

Reed.

Ignoring the warning throb in his ankle, he scrambled to his hands and knees. There was new blood on the white carpet, a scarlet splash near his right hand. It felt like his heart stopped behind his ribs. *Fuck.*

"Reed!" Clutching one bedpost, he levered himself upright, turned. Froze.

His heart restarted. He had to blink away dizziness, not 100 percent sure what he was seeing.

"It's fine, Peter." Reed replied firmly, still standing just inside the doorway, blood-stained knife in hand. They seemed somehow taller than Peter remembered, and colder. Not someone Peter would ever want to piss off. "I told you I was very good. Now you see, yes? Also, *he* was not as good as he pretended. Cheap Bratva hire, I think." Their sigh was a scrape of regret. "But, maybe you should grab the dog?"

The growling hadn't stopped. The vicious snarl wasn't coming from Peter's throat, but from Boudica's. The little dog had attached herself to the hitman's ankle and was worrying at his boot, teeth bared, eyes wide. The hitman, up on his elbows, watched her stupidly. One hand was pressed hard against his ribs as he tried to staunch the blood leaking between his fingers.

"Boudica!" Peter snapped, wondering if somehow he'd bumped his head again in the fall. Hadn't he left the dog securely tied on the porch? "Boudi, come!" The dog, in a rage, ignored him. "Come! Boudica, come!"

"I let her free. She was like to choke herself on the leash, she was straining so hard. And then it was between my feet and up the stairs. Brave little thing."

Peter turned his head and understood that the hitman was staying down and still despite the shark on his ankle because Ben Christie stood in the doorway, Glock pointed at the intruder. His face was very grim.

"Sorry I was late. Someone disabled the Rhino. Sugar in the gas tank, I think. Reed, take the cuffs off my belt and use them. Peter, sit down before you fall down. And get your dog under control. The cops are three minutes out." His mouth thinned to a sneer as he regarded the hit man over his gun. "Mafia. I should have guessed. If you're lucky you won't bleed out before they arrive."

———

POLICE SWARMED THE PROPERTY, cordoning off the main house with yellow caution tape, going barn to barn with flashlights and pistols, frightening the horses. Gabriel —muzzy and confused but standing on his own power—was taken to the hospital in one ambulance, the hit man away in another. Reed left the property in the back of a police cruiser despite Peter's furious protests. The Russian gave Peter a kiss on the cheek before they left.

"It will be okay, *lyubimiy*. Get your ankle looked at, give the dog a biscuit, and go to bed."

Peter wanted to shout. Reed was a hero, Reed had saved their lives, Reed did not belong in the back of a police cruiser, personality reduced to muted acceptance. Peter looked to Christie for help, but he was busy in a huddle with a police detective, and he looked, if possible, more defeated than Reed.

The cops had already called Senior. Senior had probably called Mac, who likely had phoned the family lawyer. Boudica was locked in Barn A's tack room, consoled with a blanket and a biscuit. Peter's ankle was tingling, but he could stand, so he waved away offers of medical help and called his own backup.

"Hello? Teddy? Sorry, I know it's short notice. I need your help."

CHAPTER TWENTY-FOUR

"About damn time. I was beginning to think we'd need the fancy family lawyer after all."

Reed wasn't sure what to expect when they stepped out of the New Haven Police Department and into the night, but it wasn't Peter Griffin waiting to great them, looking equal parts furious and concerned. Arms crossed, brows furrowed, dangerous scowl. It was a good look, one Reed wished they were allowed more time to appreciate.

Regret, exhaustion, and the shock of muggy air after hours in an air-conditioned office made them almost miss a step on the brick walkway. Peter's steadying arm around their waist was undeserved, but Reed leaned into it anyway.

"You're here. I didn't think you would be. How is Gabriel? They wouldn't tell me. Only that I hadn't committed murder." Sacha's hired gun would recover. Reed hadn't quite decided how they felt about that.

"Of course I'm here." Grit and gravel over tightly controlled emotion. Poor Peter. Reed wished they could soothe away his anxiety, kiss away his temper. But Reed had lost that privilege the moment Sacha's thug set foot on the McAuley-Griffin property.

No, before that. *Stop fooling yourself.* Reed had never really earned the privilege of Peter's affections, because Reed had never really told Peter the truth. Of who they had been, of who they were.

"Gabriel's fine," Peter continued. "A couple of broken ribs, lump on the back of his head." He steered Reed not into the parking lot as they expected, but around the large brick building to a patch of grass and trees. "They're holding him overnight for observation, but he's got a harder head than the rest of us. He'll be fine. Mac's keeping him company."

There was picnic table on the grass illuminated by a badly flickering streetlight. The table was crooked, metal frame slightly bent. It looked like it had seen too many lunch breaks.

It was also draped in a red-and-white checked plastic tablecloth and covered with white take-out bags. Reed blinked stupidly at the logo on the bags, then at Peter.

"Is that?"

"Zeke's Crab Shack." Peter shepherded Reed the rest of the way to the table. Reed absently assessed Peter's sound-ness—it seemed second nature by now—and decided that the leg probably needed ice and rest, but not yet a trip to the emergency room. "Fried oysters, crab cakes, lobster salad. I promised you a date not so long ago. Bit late, but thank Christ for Uber Eats." He indicated the bench, took a seat across the table. Reed missed his touch immediately, so much so that they had to blink back weary tears. Would Peter ever embrace them again, once he knew about the Bratva?

"It's almost ten o'clock at night."

"Zeke's is good any time of day. Besides, you must be starving. Like I said, I was beginning to think we'd need a lawyer to spring you."

"Self-defense. There will be more questions later, I imagine." About Reed's visa, employment, and living arrangements. And maybe they would need to find an immigration lawyer, but for now, Reed *was* starving. They were watching their life go to shit in real time, and still somehow the thought of food made saliva flood their mouth in anticipation. But the body knew what it needed, and the last time Reed had eaten was at the Waffle House, and one small vegetarian omelet just couldn't carry anyone far.

They slumped onto the bench, watched as Peter unloaded Zeke's Crab Shack onto paper plates.

"Katie wants to see you first thing in the morning. So let's get some food into you and then get you back to the farm for some sleep."

"To fire me." Reed stared down at the mug of steaming liquid Peter slid across the table. "Is that tea? Hot tea?"

"Not iced coffee, sorry. Chamomile. Mum says it's good for the nerves, and for sleep." Peter finished loading Reed's plate. "Katie doesn't want to fire you. She wants to see you're okay for herself. Yesterday was a bloody nightmare." He glanced down and away, and on the tablecloth his hands fisted together. "You were almost killed."

"Probably he wouldn't have stopped with me. Witnesses." Reed took a hesitant sip of tea, picked up a plastic fork, set it down again. "Sacha doesn't like to leave witnesses."

"Sacha. Michael's father. OPG big man, in Saint Petersburg." Peter was looking at Reed again, and his expression was glacial. Reed's stomach rumbled loudly, in dismay or starvation. Peter sighed.

"Eat, please. Unless they fed you something from the vending machine, you haven't had anything since the road. I'll wait."

It was difficult to eat under Peter's stare. But the food was good. Better than good. Before Reed realized, they'd finished the mountain of food on their plate. The fog in their head began to clear. Peter was right. Once they'd had a few hours of sleep, they'd be able to at least pretend everything would be okay.

They straightened their shoulders, lifted their chin, met Peter's stare without wobbling.

"You know, then. About Sacha. The Bratva."

Peter nodded, tapped an accordion file on the table by his elbow. "I had to read about it. In here. Apparently, the mess with Linden has turned Mac to paranoid. He and Gabriel have been using the family PI rather liberally."

Reed knew it shouldn't hurt, shouldn't feel like a punch to the ribs. "That's why Gabriel has decided he doesn't like me."

"He likes you just fine. It's the Russian mafia he has a problem with. For good reason, obviously."

That hurt, too, and this time the punch was to the heart. Reed wrapped their fingers around the mug of tea. "Yes." That was obvious. But Reed had a more pressing question that needed an answer. "How long have you known?"

"What's in this bloody file? For approximately four hours," Peter replied evenly. "I've had it for quite a while, shoved in a drawer. I was hoping you'd tell me about it yourself, Reed. Eventually. But I don't think you would have. So, yeah. Now I've read it. Several times."

Reed opened their mouth on *I'm sorry*, then closed it again.

"It's not my fault," they said instead. They lifted their

chin. "It's not my fault Sacha is a very bad man who can think of nothing but revenge. It's not my fault Michael was his son. It's not my fault there are monsters in the world. That Gabriel was attacked, the barn set afire . . ." They faltered. "It's not my fault Michael died."

The expression that crossed Peter's face was one that Reed had never seen before. His mouth set into a flat, white line. His jaw bunched. His blue eyes narrowed to cold slits. He seemed, without rising from the bench, to grow three inches taller.

The legendary McAuley temper in action. If Reed had been anyone else, if *Peter* had been anyone else, Reed would be reaching for their knife.

Which they didn't have. Because the police had taken it in as evidence.

"Of course it's not your fault." A low, tightly controlled snarl. "Why would you even think that?"

"Everyone thinks so. Everyone *thought* so. Michael's parents. *My* parents. Many of our friends." To keep their hands from trembling, Reed sipped tea. It was strong, and too hot in the muggy weather, not as good as iced coffee. But it was also proof that Peter still cared. "I was too out, too blue, not cautious enough. Too proud, too brave, too color-ful. And then, when I left him for America . . ." They snuck a glance at Peter, couldn't help admiring the muscles bunching in his jaw. *Get a grip, Androku. Now is not the time.* They cleared the boulder-size lump in their throat. "Then I was too driven, too selfish, cruel to leave Michael behind when maybe he needed me to keep him on track." They tried a small smile. "Caretaker tendencies are a bitch."

"It isn't your fault. Reed. None of it is your fault. Blame Michael's death on those human monsters you mentioned.

And this." Peter thumped knuckles on the accordion file. "This bloody mafia thing. Also not your fault. I only wish you'd let me help you."

"I don't know what you could have done. I've always handled the hard things by myself. I'm not sure I know another way. But," they relented, "I should have told you. I almost did, after the fire in Barn A."

Peter limped around the table, settled heavily on the bench beside Reed. Reed was reminded of Peter's birthday party, and another picnic table, the comforting press of Peter's thigh against their own. And somehow Peter was still offering up that comfort—in food, in tea, in an embrace beneath a flickering streetlight.

"Mac brought me the file." He looked and sounded stiff, though the McAuley blaze was fading. "Warned me you had a past I should look into. Like we should have done with Linden. But you aren't Linden. So I put the fucking thing in a drawer and waited, hoped, eventually you'd tell me yourself."

Reed turned the mug in their hands. "I persuaded myself that maybe it *was* Linden, that I didn't have to worry. I let you and Kate convince me. And Linden made it easy to believe, also. The graffiti, and at the horse show. Well. It was easy to hope. Things were very nice. My herd is happy. Your family is kind. And you, Peter Griffin . . ." They snorted without humor. "I guess I just didn't want to run again, didn't want it to end. But because I didn't say anything, it almost did. And you and Gabriel . . ." They choked off, set the mug down on the table, pressed their palms to their eyes, trying to hold back tears.

"Not your fault," Peter repeated. He twisted sideways on the bench, pulled Reed almost into his lap. "Not your fault. And you're not alone with it anymore, Reed. You have me, for as long as you need me, and my mildly fucked up but yes, very kind family. Hush now." He soothed one hand down Reed's spine. Just that gentle caress made the tears run like the Selenga River to Lake Baikal, dramatic and unstoppable. "Okay, okay. That's fine. Have a nice good cry. Tears are fine." He sounded a little damp himself, and Reed would have laughed at the two having a sob over Zeke's if they could only remember how to stop crying. "I'm here. You're okay. It's not your fault. I'm here, you don't have to handle the hard things by yourself anymore."

———

PETER HAD bits of hay in his hair because he'd been tossing morning feed while Reed slept. He pressed "End" on his phone as he slipped into the room, tossed it onto the bedside table. Reed stretched on the mattress until their spine gave a satisfying pop, then squinted at the alarm clock. Eight in the morning already and they'd slept right through the night, pressed against Peter, soothed by the beat of his heart in Reed's ear.

"Good morning, lovely." They scooted up onto their elbow to better appreciate the view. Besides the pieces of hay in his hair, Peter looked deliciously rumpled in loose lounge pants and one of Reed's old concert T-shirts that was just a little too tight across his chest. Reed decided then and there that they'd have to share clothes more often. "Everything okay downstairs?"

"Everybody's happy, munching away at breakfast." Peter smiled faintly as he sat on the edge of Reed's bed. "That was Katie on the phone. I talked her out of an early morning confab, but she does still want to talk to you. To both of us, actually. Something about Jacob Christie and the sugar in Ben's Rhino. I think the kid might be in trouble." He rubbed absently at his left thigh, brow creasing. "But I convinced her to wait until a more reasonable hour. And Mac's agreed to meet later this evening, once Gabriel's home. I want to get our lawyer involved with your visa. Just in case immigration has anything to say about self-defense." The furrows over his nose deepened. "Da says it's possible Sacha might try to get you deported. Because you stabbed the arsehole he sent to shoot you."

Reed was astounded. "You've been talking to Senior about my visa?" The very idea was almost more alarming than Sacha's manipulations.

"Of course I have." Peter flopped over on his back next to Reed, careful to keep his muck boots off the quilt. "Da can be a bloody prick, but he's also a *wily* bloody prick, and he won't let you get deported for saving Gabriel's life."

That seemed a roundabout way to look at things, considering the hit man was only in the main house because of Reed.

"I won't object to his help," they said slowly. "His or Mac's. If help is needed." Reed hesitated, then—*in for a penny, in for a ruble*—turned on their side until their nose brushed Peter's cheek. "I love you, too."

Peter stilled. He blinked once, blond lashes briefly obscuring Lake Baikal eyes. He turned his head, and now they were nose to nose. Peter's mouth curled into a smirk.

"Do you?" Using that low rasp that made Reed's toes curl. "I'm glad."

"You look like the cat that got the cheese." Far too smug for his own good. Reed slipped their hands under that too-tight T-shirt, prodded with long fingers. "I wasn't sure you meant it when you told me so because there were no flowers or champagne involved, only a stubborn pony and a long drive ahead." They prodded again, scratching a little until Peter sighed and shivered.

"Is that why you were so quiet on the drive home? I meant it. Didn't realize you needed a production. Actually, I sort of thought you knew already." He captured Reed's punishing hands, cupped them against his pecs. "I don't know if I understand how to do romance, to tell you the truth, but what about this: I got tested, last time I was in hospital. Full STI panel. Not that I was worried. I'm always careful. But . . ." Pink rose beneath his freckles. "Well, you know my rep and it's not completely exaggerated. I wanted to make sure. Because from now on it's just you and me. If— if you'll have me, that is. I know I'm not quite the catch I once was, but I rather like who I'm becoming. More and more every day, but especially when I'm with you."

"So do I." Heart full to bursting, and dangerously close to tears again, Reed squirmed lower on the mattress, pressed their mouth against Peter's chin, then against his throat, nipping lightly. Peter smelled of barn, and clean sweat, and beneath that the musky perfume of desire. He wasn't the same man Reed had worshipped as a teenager, the golden boy centerfold Reed had wanked to in secret. He was real, complicated, perfectly imperfect, and he was so much better than young Reed could have imagined.

"Take off your boots," Reed said into Peter's throat, teeth against his Adam's apple, "so I can take off your pants."

———

NAKED IN THE morning light through the bedroom windows, Reed worked themself open with lube and three fingers, enjoying the lazy stretch and burn, gaze on Peter's cock. It was heavy and engorged, already leaking as Peter carefully unrolled a condom from tip to root. Peter might have tested clean, and Reed didn't doubt they would, too, but sexual safety was something Reed never second-guessed, and so strawberry-flavored latex would have to do for now.

Not that Reed minded. They'd have Peter any way they could, for as long as they could, and sing hallelujah for the pleasure of it.

"Are you sure?" Peter loomed over Reed where they were stretched on the quilt, knees spread. "This way, are you sure?" The muscles on his arms were knotted, his jaw tight, his eyes a little wild. Desire held in check by bare fingernails.

Reed knew the feeling.

But Peter's voice was gentle, and Reed knew if they said "no, not like this, I've changed my mind," Peter would listen.

"Yes. This way." Nerves made Reed's voice squeak, but that was fine. They were the good sort of nerves. Anticipation, appreciation, lust. "Please. Now. But with romance, Peter Griffin. Tell me you love me while you fuck me into the mattress."

Peter made a sound between a laugh and a sob and lined himself up between Reed's thighs. Reed knew it would hurt a little. Maybe a lot, at first. It had been a long time, after all. Since Michael. And even then, with Michael, this was not always a position Reed preferred.

This morning, it felt right. Even more right when Peter

said between gritted teeth, "I love you. Tell me if you want me to stop and I will."

"I know." Reed spread their legs wider, tilted their hips, looked down between them to watch as Peter pushed carefully in. "Ah! No." They gasped. "No, yes. Don't stop."

"You're beautiful. Look at you. So gorgeous."

Reed groaned at the feel of him, a breaching, a filling, a promise of pleasure after pain. Biting their lip hard, they peeked up between their lashes and watched Peter watching them. Peter's face was a study. Consternation, desire, worship wrapped together like a Christmas present.

"Oh, Christ. You feel so good. Reed. Is this okay?"

"Yes." It was, finally, more than okay, the burn turning into a pleasant buzz, and then something deeper as Reed's body accommodated Peter's size and then began to celebrate. "Yes. It's *good*, Peter. You can move now." *Please.*

Peter laughed again, bent and kissed Reed on the nose, brushed a hand down Reed's chest, twisting a nipple until Reed bucked in pleasure. Peter skimmed his hand lower, teasing.

"Peter!" Pleasure so quickly edged to desperation. "That, there. Do that again. Say it again."

"I love you," Peter murmured as if in agreement, and then he began to move in earnest. Slow, controlled thrusts until Reed scolded him to *hurry, hurry, yes, there again,* moy Bog! and sunk their teeth hard into Peter's shoulder in case he wasn't listening.

"I love you." Peter gasped, hips stuttering, and Reed knew he was close. They reached down and worked themself quickly, knuckles brushing Peter's balls, and came with a cry, muscles clenching violently, eyes closing helplessly in blissful release.

Peter shouted, went still, and then tumbled after, his release a warm rush that made Reed quiver and sigh. "Thank you," he murmured into Reed's ear, cuddling close, already turning sleepy and sated—and Reed didn't mind. Reed didn't mind at all.

EPILOGUE

The black Trakehner was young but talented, with delicate bones, four white socks, and a wide white blaze down her nose. She was on the delicate-looking side for her breed, but she complimented Reed's small stature perfectly.

"Mum still knows how to make a match," Katie said, watching as Reed and Aine and the mare stood together in the outdoor arena, heads together. Ears pricked, eyes soft, it looked like the mare was in on whatever conversation Reed and Aine were having, but Peter knew she was probably just begging for the sugar cubes Reed had in their pocket.

"Mum's superpower," Mac agreed, glancing up from his phone to watch. He seemed glued to the thing recently, even more than usual, and only deflected with vulgar comments when any of the family suggested he take a break. "Remember when she plucked up Cricket from a backyard auction and you were all sure that pony wouldn't amount to anything?"

"Best pony in the world." Gabriel scratched absently on the stitches over his right brow. "Somehow she worked for all four of us. And Mum knew from the start."

They stood for a minute in silence, afternoon heat beating down on their shoulders, all four McAuley-Griffin siblings content to watch Reed and Aine and the new mare. Then Kate sighed, and straightened against the arena fence. She tossed a steely look Mac's way.

"All right, *dearthàir mòr*. Let's get it over with. I've got babies to worm. You called this briefing, stop stalling."

"Darling, you know I never stall." Despite the muggy weather, Mac managed to look fresh as a daisy in dark slacks and a gray silk button-down. "I was just allowing Peter a moment to enjoy Reed's arse in those frankly delightful breeches. Does Reed purposefully buy them just a smidge too small, do you think?"

"Fuck you," Peter said without heat while Gabriel snorted. "And keep your eyes to yourself. Spit it out, McAuley. You called, we came."

Gabriel added, "Can't help notice Da wasn't invited."

"No." Mac's dark brows drew into a V between his eyes. "I think we can all agree that maybe it's time for us to handle this on our own. We don't need Da flying off the handle. Subtlety has never been his thing. And we've got Tulip Farm's new rep as a lesson barn to consider."

"By 'handle this' you mean Mark." Katie shoved her hands in the pockets of her jeans, rocked back and forth on her heels. "Well, spit it out. You promised you'd stop keeping me in the dark. I don't need you running interference, any of you."

Mac held up a hand, the one that wasn't gripping his phone. "And I keep a promise, little bird." Kate softened at the childhood nickname, nodded once, but didn't look away. "Three items on the agenda today," Mac went on. "First, security. We've agreed to keep Ben Christie's firm on so long as young Jacob's not on roster. Kid's feeling bad enough he left the Rhino unattended while he went to take a piss. I understand Ben's reassigned him to a smaller job."

"Wouldn't want to be on Ben Christie's bad side," murmured Gabriel with some sympathy. "Jacob won't forget his mistake any time soon, I think."

"No doubt." Mac didn't sound sympathetic at all. "Let's just remember his mistake put those six stitches in your admittedly hard head. Speaking of thugs"—he nodded at Peter—"I did as you asked and had Ace, the family PI, look into Sacha Turgenev. Could be this last mess was the man's final hurrah. Sacha's old. He doesn't have the reach he once did, and his bank accounts are running on empty. The ones Ace could find, anyway. It's possible Reed's safe."

Relief made Peter exhale slowly. He hadn't realized he'd been holding his breath since opening Reed's file—and after the ambush at the big house, jumping at every shadow. Reed seemed mostly unaffected, but Peter knew he'd never forget how close he'd come to losing the Russian.

"And it's possible Reed's not," he said now. "We're not relaxing security until we're certain."

"Didn't I just say that?" Mac sighed. "Calm down, golden boy. It's red alert all the way for Tulip Farm. Speaking of." He tilted his head at Kate.

"Get on with it." She scrubbed her hand through her hair. It was shorter, chin-length, bouncier than Peter remembered. Teddy's doing, she'd said. A fresh haircut to lighten the mood.

Mac met her stare with his own. "Nothing new re: Linden, not exactly. He's laying low. But Ace has managed to get a lead on the kid at Devon. You know"—now he speared Peter with their mother's violet gaze—"the one with the laser pointer. First name Arthur, last name Spinner.

Turns out he used to groom for Linden on the fall circuit, a few years back."

"You've got to be kidding me." Fury flushed Kate's complexion bright red. "You're fucking kidding me."

Mac rolled his shoulders. "Ace is still looking into it. But seems like."

"What kind of name is Ace?" Gabriel rumbled when Peter couldn't bring himself to speak past the constriction in his throat, and the silence had lasted a little too long. "Are you sure you and Da haven't hired us a pet detective?"

Now Mac was flushing up, and that was interesting, but Peter was still stuck on Linden and the laser pointer, and gave his brother's reaction no more than a passing thought.

"I believe Ace is short for Alexander," Mac said coolly, cheeks pink. "And he's quite good at his job."

Gabriel drawled, "Is he?" Then he waved a hand. "Fine. Have him follow up. Maybe we'll get lucky. Hell. We deserve a break. Katie, you okay?"

"Just fine." Kate was staring back into the arena, watching as Reed sent the young mare in a circle on the lunge. "My ex might have ruined Peter's Olympic career. But I'm just fine. Peter." She nudged his shoulder with hers, and her voice cracked when she said, "I'm sorry."

Peter wondered why all the best people in his life felt the need to apologize for things that weren't their fault. He gripped his cane, used it to work a divot from the grass while he watched Reed laughing with Aine in the arena. He couldn't find it in himself to regret the lost promise of gold or glory, not when he'd found something so much more precious in return.

"If it was Linden behind my accident, then that's on him, not you, Katie. Never on you." He looked at each of the McAuley-Griffin siblings in turn, letting them see the determination on his face. "Mac's right. No more looking the other way, making excuses because he used to be part of the family. It's time we get this handled."

END

The Tulip Farm Series will continue with

Absolute.

Coming Summer of 2022

ABOUT THE AUTHOR

Sarah Remy / Alex Hall is a nonbinary, animal-loving, proud gamer geek. Their work can be found in a variety of cool places, including HarperVoyager, EDGE, NineStar Press, and SkullGate Media.

ALSO BY ALEX HALL

Beastly Manor

Earnest Ink

Midas Touch

As Sarah Remy

Stonehill Downs

The Bone Cave

Across the Long Sea

The Exiled King

ANTHOLOGIES

Fairly Twisted Tales for a Horribly Ever After

Achten Tan: Land of Dust and Bone

Under New Suns

MIDAS TOUCH

Balancing on the precarious breeze, Frankie Porter lifted her arms and flattened her palms, stretching her fingers until they ached. Her arms were sleek from the humid Virginia air, her muscles buoyant. The wind lifted briefly, warm gusts flattening her hair to her scalp. Above her head and below her feet, leaves rustled. Frankie could smell the perfume of the river and hear the muffled gurgle of the water.

She tensed, straining upward, face lifted to the freedom of the sky. Her shoulders quivered, and her bare toes scraped crumbling mortar, clinging.

"Francis!"

Her lips parted and she tasted the air. Another gust wrapped around her body. She rocked, her heart singing. When she opened her eyes, she would be far above the clouds.

"Frankie Ross! You get down from there!"

Frankie swallowed a sigh. She kept her eyes clamped shut, firmly ignoring the splashing and shouts down below.

Something fluttered past her cheek, and she thought she felt tiny wings. A bird, or a butterfly. She smiled.

Another flutter of air and then a sting and a wet slap. Frankie's eyes flew open. Not a butterfly or a bird—a clod of moss, perfectly aimed. Scowling, she wiped the grit from her cheek.

"Come down, or I'll throw another!"

Still rubbing her throbbing cheek, Frankie peered between her toes. A good twenty feet below College Creek swirled, green and brown and almost as deep as its mother, the James River. Trees from the opposite bank hung over the rush. Leaves and vines brushed at the water's surface. The woods surrounding the creek were old and deeply shadowed.

A skiff floated in a small square of sunlight. From high in the air, the little boat looked bright and clean, but Frankie knew better. The paint on the hull was cracked and peeling. A hole in the stern was patched with a bit of scavenged plywood. The skiff might be usable, but it sure wasn't pretty.

The owner of the little boat stood upright and unsteady between the oars. She looked as though she might tumble into the creek at any moment. Frankie hoped she would.

"Are you coming down?"

Frankie let her arms drop. She settled back onto her heels. A chunk of old brick fell from beneath her feet, tumbled into the water. It broke the current with a splash.

"Go home, Gwen."

Even from her perch between sky and water, Frankie could see the other girl's sullen scowl. "No way. Come on down. I've brought you a birthday present."

A birthday present. Today was June 10, and Frankie had finally turned sixteen. Still one year behind Gwen

Cook, who thought she knew everything—and maybe she did, but Frankie would never admit it. She preferred cataloging Gwen's faults, and there were many. For instance, when Gwen wasn't being brave and funny and quick with words, she was moody, crass, stubborn, and as bossy as a mama hen.

She was also afraid of heights, which meant that Frankie was safe on the edge of the decaying boathouse because Gwen wouldn't dare climb up and bring her down.

A birthday present. Frankie set her fists on her hips and craned her neck, trying to see what Gwen might have in her boat. She could tell her friend was in a temper. She supposed Gwen's father was on a bender again, which meant Gwen would spend all afternoon and evening on the creek, hiding.

"What kind of birthday present?" She hadn't expected any gifts to mark the day. Her mom had baked a plain poppy-seed cake, when what Frankie had really wanted was the frilly pink buttercream from the local bakery.

"There's no such thing as a perfect day," her mom had scolded when Frankie burst into tears over the homemade cake. "Not even on your birthday. So stop your sniffling, and be grateful for what you have."

Frankie understood now that there had been no money for something as frivolous as pink buttercream and that perfect days were as rare as unicorns.

"Come down and see!"

She could tell from Gwen's satisfied tone that she thought she'd won. Gwen knew that curiosity was Frankie's Achilles' heel.

Frankie rocked in place, considering. Her long hair spiraled on the wind and plastered her brow. Humidity stuck her cutoff jeans to her legs. Her tattered T-shirt clung in itchy spots to her skin. If she couldn't fly, she thought, she might as well swim.

She heard a swoosh and a plop as Gwen anchored the skiff. Bent at the knees for balance, Gwen waited, peering up. In the scattered sunlight she looked sun browned and gangly, all knees and elbows and a nose that was too big in her face. Gwen's hair was as black as a crow's wing, smooth and shiny where it fell almost to her shoulders. Her eyes were as muddy green as the creek, her temper as unpredictable as the currents below.

Frankie didn't mind Gwen's temper because it was mostly just for show. Besides, Gwen was Frankie's best friend, had been for years and would be forever—even though lately their friendship had been changing into something different.

Suspicious, Frankie frowned. "You're not thinking of kisses, are you?"

In the last month Gwen had taken a definite liking to Frankie's mouth. Frankie didn't mind the fumbling kisses. They were sweet and shy in a way Gwen normally was not. Frankie had only been kissed twice before in her life: once by Ralph MacGuillivray, whose father fished on a boat on the Chesapeake, and once by Mr. White, the man who picked up their garbage every other Thursday. She supposed she needed as much practice at the game as anyone, and Gwen's kisses usually made Frankie's toes curl up in pleasure.

But today she didn't feel like kissing.

"I might be," Gwen confessed. The wind took her voice, thinned it. "But not as your present. It's the real thing. In a box, wrapped with a ribbon." To prove it, she held up her hand. A small square box—all tied up with a pretty yellow ribbon—rested on her palm.

Frankie was suitably impressed. Gwen's family was as poor as her own, so a present, even a small one, was an unasked-for surprise of the best kind. And Frankie hadn't had a real birthday present since she'd turned twelve and Ma had scraped together enough money to order a peach-colored swimsuit from the Lands' End catalog.

"Francis!" Gwen shouted. "Stop dawdling and come down!"

The sun ducked behind a high cloud, and the breeze turned cool. Goose bumps rose on Frankie's arms. She shivered.

Curiosity killed the cat, Frankie knew. But no matter where she stuck her nose, Frankie Ross always managed to land on her feet.

"Well?" Gwen coaxed.

"Coming!" Frankie said, deciding. She turned, intending to climb down the side of the boathouse as she always did—barefoot and monkey-like, fingers and toes wormed into splitting bricks. Then she paused, struck by something as hard to catch as the breeze. She glanced back over her shoulder.

College Creek looked very far away down below, swirling around the curve of the bank. She could hear the faint slosh of the water against Gwen's boat, see the shift of light and shadow across her face.

Frankie turned back and stood again on the edge of the sagging roof. Mortar cracked and fell, raining down in a rattle and splash.

"What are you doing?" Gwen yelled.

She stretched up on her toes and lifted her arms over her head. The breeze stung her eyes.

"Frankie?" She sounded afraid. Gwen Cook, seventeen years old and frightened of heights. Frankie laughed.

Today was June 10, and Frankie Ross had gained another year. The sun was warm, school was out, and her best friend had brought her a birthday present in a box with a ribbon. Maybe the day would be perfect after all.

Frankie arched her back and spread her fingers. A perfect day to fly.

"Frankie!"

She jumped.

The boathouse had barely changed in twelve years. The creek ran quite a bit deeper and wider. Brown water had swallowed up much of the far bank and licked in pools about the base of the boathouse itself. Frankie had to shove back kudzu and sumac as she walked. The soles of her boots sank inches into mud. Tiny pink-and-white wildflowers grew up between the trees, and here and there she spotted a drooping hedge bright with red berries.

She made her way cautiously through the undergrowth until she could touch the old building. Standing against the foundation, she cocked her head and squinted up along brick walls. The boathouse seemed as sturdy as she remembered. Two stories high and crumbling on the outside, it was ruler straight and strong except for the roof, which still sagged but hadn't given in to the elements and fallen.

"Used to be, they knew how to build to last." Frankie patted the warm brick.

The structure didn't tower the way it had in her childhood, but she supposed it wouldn't. She had grown—her bones had lengthened into adulthood. She'd managed to top five feet, barely. At sixteen, she'd feared she would be stuck forever just above four.

Frankie hesitated, glancing up into the sky. The trees had

grown tall, and she could see less of the sun than she remembered. The place was definitely cooler, definitely shadier; but on a warm summer afternoon, shade wasn't such a bad thing.

She leaned against the boathouse and untied her boots. Stripping off her shoes and socks, she stood barefoot in the mud, regarding the brick walls. Twelve years gone and she was no longer a child. Could she do it?

Of course she could. Was it wise?

Probably not.

But her fingers and toes found the old cracks easily, and before she knew it, she was halfway up the wall. The brick brushed her khaki shorts, leaving brown stains. A branch streaked her white shirt with sap. Frankie didn't notice. At the top she hoisted herself over the edge of the roof and onto the shingles. She sat very still, holding her breath, waiting to see if the roof would protest. The shingles held, even when she rose to her feet and tiptoed across the top of the boathouse to her old perch.

She looked up and around first, admiring the oak and the dogwood and the ash with their green-as-grass leaves. She sucked in the fragrance of the creek as she brushed her bangs from her eyes. Then she took a deeper breath and looked down.

James Creek glittered below, cut into geometric shapes by dim sunlight. Shadows gathered at the edges of the water and then spread away along the bank. From where she stood, the water looked deep and inviting.

The breeze whispered and the trees moved in the wind. Something shone metallic on the far shore. Frankie shaded her eyes, squinting. Then she knew: Gwen's skiff, abandoned in the long grasses—overturned, belly to the sky. She guessed the little boat was no longer watertight. The plywood plug had certainly rotted away over the years. Probably the old oars, too.

She wondered, fleetingly, if she should rescue the old boat. Find the time to repair it, replug the hole, and repaint the skin. Maybe dig up a pair of used oars at the discount sports shop. She and Chris could sail the thing along the creek on lazy afternoons. She knew Chris would enjoy the adventure, and it had been a very long time since Frankie had dipped her toe in any creek water.

Frankie sighed and dismissed the idea. It wouldn't be stealing—not really. The skiff had obviously been forgotten for over a decade. But it wouldn't exactly be right, either.

Maybe if she skimped a bit, let the household repairs go another month, maybe then she could save enough to buy Chris a little boat.

Maybe.

Hands on her hips, Frankie turned and looked up the slope behind the boathouse. Through the trees she could just make out the Cook mansion. A two-story brick American colonial, the building had been in severe disrepair when cancer finally sent Edward to rest. Frankie had spent a good two years and much of the old man's legacy in restoring the place.

She'd repaved the long driveway and refitted the peaked roof. She'd put down new hardwood floor and rehabbed the antique bathroom fittings and replaced the dangerous wiring. Gutted the plumbing and updated the kitchen. There had been just enough money left over to landscape the wide yard and rebuild the old gazebo, where a teenaged Gwen had hidden her stash of beer and cigarettes.

Frankie had turned the house into a beauty, a gem. It had taken hard work and every spare moment, but she managed. And when at last she'd put the house on the market, it sold in less than a month, in spite of the admittedly inflated asking price.

She still couldn't quite believe her luck.

Thanks to Edward, she now had a start on Chris's college fund, and if they continued to count every penny, her Ivy League dreams were that much closer to reality.

Thanks to Edward *and* to the house's new owner, who would be arriving within the hour. Frankie glanced at her watch. She should be excited, even ecstatic. She'd taken Edward's gift and tripled it—but in the process, she'd also learned to love the house. She had put her heart and soul into its rebirth, and she was suddenly reluctant to let it go.

Silly, she scolded herself. *Don't be sentimental.*

Frankie put her hand to her shorts, testing the right pocket, making sure the house keys were still safely zipped against her thigh. She had one last repair to make, one screw to turn. Then she would trade the keys for a nice hefty check and let the mansion go.

Sucking in a resigned breath, she padded back across the boathouse roof and scrambled down the brick. Her feet were irreparably muddy. She grimaced as she pulled her socks and shoes over filthy toes.

Struggling back up the bank, through tree and hedge and vine, Frankie left the burble of College Creek behind. She stopped once to pick a handful of wild flowers. The purple flowers smelled sweet, like honeysuckle. She stuck the bunch behind her ear as she broke free of the woods. She cleaned her muddy boots on grass before she stepped onto the newly paved drive.

She straightened her shoulders as she walked slowly uphill to Edward's house. Her chin lifted. She was proud of her work.

The mansion sparkled in the sunlight, smooth red brick

shining as though oiled. The trim was traditional cream, but she'd painted the front door a deep green. The windows were beveled glass between crosshatched frames—very expensive and very beautiful. Four chimney stacks sprouted from the roof. The detached garage sported two wide doors and a living space above.

A new brass mailbox stood on a pedestal by the front door, and on the stoop Frankie had placed a pot of happy pansies. The entire impression was charming and cheerful.

She'd left her telescopic ladder on the drive in front of the garage, along with her bucket of nails, her toolbox, and an iron weather vane. The weather vane was handcrafted, a replica of one that adorned the Wren Building at the nearby College of William and Mary. Frankie wanted to have it in place before her client arrived.

She set the ladder up against the garage and secured it with ropes and weights. Then she hefted the weather vane over her shoulder and stuck a screwdriver into her pocket. She climbed the ladder carefully, afraid of scraping the recently shingled roof.

Frankie had chosen the exact place for her weather vane: at the very peak of the roof, just between the garage doors. She bent her knees, balancing against the slope, and walked steadily along the roof to the spot. Setting the weather vane in place, she began securing the iron base to the peak.

Eyes fixed on her hands and tools, Frankie worked automatically, ignoring the world around her. She didn't feel the sweat that trickled between her shoulder blades, and she didn't notice time as it passed.

She'd just positioned the last screw when the rumble of a distant motor broke her concentration. A car growled up the long drive. It could only be her client—nobody without business came so far along the creek. She frowned at her watch and saw that she'd lost time in her work.

She spun the screw one last time before she straightened. Then she grabbed her tools and walked to the edge of the roof. Wind cooled the damp on her brow. In the garden below, pink tulips danced, nodding as if in welcome.

The car slowed, rounding the last curve before the house. A sports car, European. Frankie should have guessed. Any person who would spend $2.5 million on a house, sight unseen, would drive a flashy car.

The car gunned before it pulled to a precise stop in front of the garage. A shiny black door sprang open, and the driver unfolded herself. Hair black as a crow's wing, cut in a blunt bob, a little too short for the latest fashion. Lennon-style sunglasses balanced on a sharp nose, blue lenses reflecting light. A neat pantsuit the color of the morning sky, and shoes with heels that had to be at least four inches.

As Frankie watched, the woman squatted in the driveway before the left front tire, apparently examining the treads.

She ran a careful hand over the black rubber, searching. After a moment, apparently satisfied, she rose again and turned her attention to the house.

Rounding the hood of the car, she skirted the garage, stopping twice to touch the brick before pausing to stare down at a bed of daffodils and tulips. Finally, she turned away from the flowers and looked up at the front porch. Then she froze, head tilted.

Frankie held her breath. She'd hoped the woman couldn't see her past the edge of the roof. She could. She took two easy steps back, turned, and looked right at her.

Her mouth—deliciously full and painted a subtle pink—quirked as she examined Frankie with the same consideration she'd given the garden. She stuck one hand into the pocket of her slacks, jingling change or keys, and used the other to pull away her shades.

She had wide green eyes, clear and dark as the creek. Her cheekbones were as sharp as her nose; a dimple softened the planes of her face. Her smile turned from surprised to self-mocking, and Frankie found herself grinning in return.

"Why, Francis," she said in a husky Virginian drawl, "you still trying to grow wings?"

Shock turned Frankie's knees to Jell-O. She teetered, the shingles suddenly slippery beneath the muddy soles of her boots.

———

From two stories below, Gwen watched Frankie sway. In a flash she was a teenager again, frozen in place, watching her best friend fall from the boathouse, heart pounding as Frankie crashed into the creek. She'd gone under twice before Gwen had managed to grab her arm and pull her from the water. Then she'd slumped so still in the bottom of the boat, so limp and lifeless, Gwen had been sure she was dead.

She'd only been concussed and half-drowned, but it meant the end of their summers together, the end of Gwen's youth.

"Don't you dare fall on me again, Francis!" she called up at the woman posed on the roof of her new home. "My heart might not survive the shock."

But Frankie had already righted herself. Gwen's breath caught as she squatted at the very lip of the roof.

"Gwen?"

"Who else?" Gwen wished she wouldn't stand so near the edge.

"But I thought . . ." Frankie trailed off and began again. "What are you doing here?"

"It's my house," Gwen said mildly. "I've come to have a peek." She replaced her sunglasses to hide her eyes and stuck both hands into her pockets to keep them from trembling. Frankie had driven Gwen mad that final summer, climbing everything in sight: trees, buildings, bridges. Always trying to reach the clouds.

"Come down from there, Francis."

"All right. Sure. Just let me get my things." She disappeared from view. Gwen could hear her scrambling about on the shingles. "Okay, be right down. Don't go anywhere."

And where would I go? Gwen thought, regarding the garage through narrowed eyes. *Come all this way just to do a runner at the last moment?* It was tempting.

A ladder stood slanted against the bricks. As Gwen watched, slim brown legs appeared over the lip of the shingle, and then Frankie slithered into view. She dropped two stories, barely touching the ladder rungs, and hit the ground with a smile.

Gwen studied her through her blue lenses as she crossed the drive. She was still small. Tiny but mighty, they'd said as children, and that hadn't changed. Her long hair was gathered back from her face in a messy ponytail. Gwen recognized the look in her wide dark eyes: determined good humor.

Frankie held out a delicate, grimy hand. "Gwen Cook! Imagine that. I thought you were somewhere west. Seattle?"

"Seattle," Gwen said. She took Frankie's hand with a practiced smile. She remembered those same sturdy hands, cool and wet against her skin as they wrestled together in the creek.

That last summer their water battles had started over possession of Gwen's little boat and ended in a bout of heavy breathing, overactive teenage hormones boiling. Gwen had dreamed nightly of Frankie's body and their kisses. Their mostly innocent encounters had been sweetness and freedom when Gwen had spent all of that summer trapped in the dark.

Gwen realized she was staring at Frankie's mouth. Embarrassed, she released her hand. "I've taken some time off. Come back to revisit my roots, see the old place."

Frankie frowned. "Gwen, I'm so sorry, but the house is off the market. In fact, it just sold—"

"To me." Gwen made a show of studying the manicured yard and pointed bricks. "And I'm pleasantly surprised. It hardly looks like the same place."

Frankie frowned. "But I thought—I mean, a Mr. Windsor from the Pinnacle Group—"

"My personal assistant. I'm Pinnacle. And I like to do business quietly when I can." She waved a hand. "The money's cleared, I assume."

"Yes." Frankie's assessing stare made Gwen want to twitch. She held herself still. No need for Frankie to know Gwen had been fighting an anxious snakes' nest behind her ribs all the way down from DC. Apparently, Frankie couldn't read Gwen like she used to, because she only shrugged. "Well, would you like a tour?"

"That won't be necessary." She wasn't sure she was ready yet to step through the front door. Seeing Frankie again was more of an emotional shock than she'd expected. More than a decade spent trying to escape James Creek, but Frankie's warm smile made Gwen feel like she'd never left.

"Let me at least show you the fuses. You'll need to know where they are." Without waiting for an answer, Frankie climbed the front steps, glanced over her shoulder. "The locks are funny. You have to jiggle a little. I kept Edward's old door handles; just cleaned them up some. Historically accurate and all that."

Gwen eyed the gleaming lockset. The handles were certainly much shinier than she remembered. "Remarkable."

Frankie opened the front door and stepped over the threshold. Gwen followed. The interior was cool and smelled of beeswax and lemon. During Gwen's childhood the walls had stunk of booze and sweat and fear.

"I refinished the entry floors," continued Frankie. "They're good hardwood. A few of the boards needed replacing, and the banisters."

Gwen trailed Frankie through the entryway. She remembered the spacious rooms and the high, wide fire-places—of course she did. She didn't remember the large windows or the color of the afternoon across the wood floors. The old man had kept the shades drawn and shag carpets over the wood.

Frankie led Gwen down a bright hallway and into a shining kitchen. While Gwen stood blinking, she opened a small cupboard.

"Fuses are in here. Box used to be just bare on the wall, but of course you know that. I had the shelving built around to hide it."

Gwen fought unwelcome appreciation. "Jesus. The counters are new, and the appliances. And did you cut a new window here?"

Frankie flushed, nodding. Gwen watched the pink creep into her cheeks. She'd always been an easy blusher, had hated that tell. Gwen wondered if she still smelled of spring and wildflowers.

"It must have taken quite a bit of time and money to fix this place up," Gwen said after a pause, turning in place to see every corner of the kitchen. "Last I recall, it was a rat trap."

"You're not wrong. But the place has good bones. And I've made the money back five times over, thanks to the sale. Thanks to you, I guess." She grinned, but it faded quickly. "I didn't realize you were so attached. Maybe . . . I suppose you were surprised it wasn't part of your inheritance."

"My inheritance? What, nightmares and a healthy dose of undiagnosed PTSD?" Gwen regretted the words as soon as they were said. They felt like a confession, and she wasn't in the habit of confessing anything to anyone anymore. "I didn't expect to get the house. I figured it was going to pay off the old man's debts. So, yes, I was surprised when I heard he'd left it to you. Guess I shouldn't have been. We both know about my father and his women."

Fuck. That hadn't come out at all the way she meant. But before Gwen could backpedal, Frankie's palm flashed up and out. She had a solid right arm—the slap stung. Gwen rocked back on her heels. She supposed she deserved it.

No, wait. She *didn't* deserve it. She'd spent years in therapy before she understood no one deserved to be hit.

"Please don't do that again." She rubbed her throbbing cheek. "I only meant . . . he formed attachments. We both know that." Usually the old man's attachments had been of the sexual variety, but not always. Sometimes the bastard had just wanted a caretaker to supply the booze and clean the toilets.

"You don't know what you're talking about," Frankie replied coldly. Her gorgeous mouth was a straight line of anger and embarrassment. "You've been away for a long time, Gwen. People change."

Not Edward. But Gwen nodded. "You're right. And really, it's none of my business. It's good to see you again, Frankie, but let's just get this done. Keys?"

They clattered across the countertop, metal on stone. "I'm sorry I hit you," Frankie said stiffly. Her cheeks burned bright red. "I don't usually . . . I mean, I never . . . But it felt like you were calling me one of your father's girlfriends. *Me*, Gwen. Of all people. 'Two halves of a whole,' remember? You're supposed to know better. Fuck you for not."

Gwen winced. Frankie was already across the kitchen and down the hall. Gwen chased after, heels clicking on refinished hardwood.

"Francis."

"Enjoy the house, Gwen. Have fun revisiting your roots." She marched outside, slammed the front door at her back. Leaving Gwen alone in the old man's house, alone with the ghosts of her past.

———

Rain fell in sheets. Water pounded cracked walls, turning the already-stifling basement air as humid as a hot shower. Gwen leaned her elbows against the sill of the single window and peered up and out at the world beyond her father's kingdom. In the summer cloudbursts came like clockwork. This shower was right on schedule: five o'clock, by Gwen's battered Timex—almost suppertime.

In a moment, she would climb the wood plank stairs up from the basement to the kitchen and scrounge up something edible. The old man was probably already snarling with hunger.

If he hadn't already passed out in front of the boob tube, beer can slipping from lax fingers, adding another stain to the mildewing shag carpet.

In a moment, Gwen would go up. In a moment. For now, it was soothing to watch the rain fall gray across the creek woods. Wildflowers nodded their heads against the onslaught, and birds fluttered under dripping shrubs. Down below, the creek would be swollen, the air cooler. It was a perfect evening for a swim or a sail.

Gwen guessed Frankie was probably already down on the bank, absurd and eager in a bathing suit two sizes too small. She wondered how long she would wait. Maybe, if Edward was out before the TV, Gwen would steal a snack and sneak down to the water.

Thunder rolled overhead—not the natural rumble of the storm, but the rumble of heavy feet on old floorboards. Then the rattle of glass as the fridge door was thrown open and slammed shut again.

"Gwen!"

No time for a swim, then. Maybe she would escape after dark, sail the creek by moonlight. Maybe the old man would forget to lock her in.

"Gwen, dammit! Get your ass up here!" The rain was slowing up, but the thunder overhead grew closer. "Have you got a joint down there?"

His cowboy boots hammered to a stop at the top of the basement steps.

"No, Dad! Coming!" Gwen moved away from the window. Edward rarely descended into the depths of the house, but it wouldn't do to give him reason.

"What're you doing down there?" The old man's voice was slurred and pitiful. "Lookin' at those dyke girlie magazines?"

Gwen felt rage and shame creep up the back of her neck.

"No, Dad." Slowly, she started up the steps.

"You know your mother wouldn't approve." Edward's whine deepened dangerously. "You lookin' to chase her away again? You with your drugs and magazines. You think I don't know? You think she don't know? Come up and apologize to your mother, girl."

Gwen stood very still on the warped wood. She gazed up into the square of kitchen light, regarding her father's shadow uneasily. If there was a woman up there in Edward's territory, she wasn't Gwen's mother. One of the old man's meth-head girlfriends, maybe, or a college girl who hadn't learned any better.

Gwen's stomach turned. She swallowed hard to keep the sour taste down.

"Gwen!" Edward roared,

DEC 17 2021

NO LONGER PROPERTY OF
THE QUEENS LIBRARY.
SALE OF THIS ITEM
SUPPORTED THE LIBRARY.

CPSIA information can be obtained
at www.ICGtesting.com
Printed in the USA
LVHW021517221021
701206LV00020B/2128